After it Happened

Book 9: Home

Devon C Ford

PRESS

Published by Vulpine Press in the United Kingdom in 2020
Cover by Claire Wood

ISBN: 978-1-83919-034-6

www.vulpine-press.com

For Cora

Impatient to meet us, you arrived way too early.
For almost four months we sat next to your cot in hospital, worried ourselves stupid over every surgery, until we finally brought you home.
You're always perfect to us; our newest member of the writing team.

PART ONE

STEVE

PROLOGUE

The radio set, once so old and out of place but now representing the pinnacle of their technological capabilities, crackled and buzzed through the earphones of the woman sat in front of it. Her face registered such concentration that her consciousness appeared to have vacated her body as all of her being was focussed on interpreting the sounds coming to her.

Anne Kershaw turned around in her chair and translated the final message.

"Got to go now," she said, "have baby to feed. Stay Safe. D."

Steve smiled, giving her his own farewell to send before leaving the small, dingy office that had been sequestered for use as a radio room. His limp was still pronounced, and parts of his body still ached from the exertion of their coup despite the weeks that had passed since.

He needed to sleep. Needed to eat. Needed a shower.

"I need a holiday," he grumbled out loud to himself as he reached the sunlight outside and closed his eyes briefly to let it soak in.

"What's that, boss?" an eager young voice asked, startling him slightly so that he had to recover himself before he answered.

"Nothing," he told the young man who he would have referred to as a boy in the world so recently gone, "just moaning. And you don't need to call me that, you know?"

"Okay, boss." The boy smiled, adjusting the belt holding his trousers up. It was either too large or the weight of the pouch pulled it down with gravity to threaten to expose his skinny backside to the world with every other step.

"Walk with me, George," Steve said, setting off towards the main body of their camp which was alive with activity. Activity, he mused, and a lot more hope than it had seen before. "Perimeter?" he asked.

"All clear."

"Any activity to report from the guards with the farming parties?" Steve enquired.

"None."

"Any joy with more fuel stores?"

"Reg and his lot aren't back yet," George said with a frown. "Due back this morning but they might've been delayed. It's like that sometimes, stuff just happens."

Steve stifled an exasperated sigh. He liked the kid, but he seemed to lack the ability to have any kind of internal monologue.

"Yeah," the boy said, having thought about it a little more, "they're only a few hours overdue so they probably found something interesting."

"Probably," Steve answered, keeping his annoyance in check because he knew it was unfounded. "Come find me when they get back and I'll go see them."

Steve took a stroll back towards the main building still standing in their little settlement that had once represented oppression and power by force. It had been repurposed as Richards' military headquarters, and after the fall of his regime Steve had found himself summarily elected as the leader of their people.

He was a natural leader, a former Royal Air Force helicopter pilot, but the similarities between him and Richards started and ended at the fact that they had both been commissioned officers in Her Majesty's armed forces.

Steve was a calm, methodical, empathetic and capable man focussed only on the survival and happiness of the people he was responsible for, whereas Richards had envisioned a dictatorship which he ruled over with supreme authority.

He tried to plead with them that he was old; old before his time at least as the injuries from the helicopter crash he barely survived should have killed him. He tried to reason with them that there were better people among them capable of leadership, and all of them would be more suitable candidates for the task of running their group. He outright told them that he didn't ask for the job, but when it was put to him that he had the job anyway because he was the one, the central point, the fulcrum of the movement to overthrow their captors and free them, he had to admit that he did put his name in the hat by those actions alone.

It had taken over a week for the air of excitement and violence to die down after their hostile takeover. It took even longer for the blood to wash away from the stone steps of the headquarters building he climbed then, glancing involuntarily down at the spot where Richards had died and seeing where the porous stone had soaked up the man's lifeblood to leave a permanent reminder. Steve took that reminder as a lesson in what happened to insane people who tried to control the will of others, whereas other people saw it as something more positive and ultimately less ominous.

Just as he had tried and failed to refuse the job of leadership, he had tried to refuse the trappings that came with it. It wasn't that he didn't want a private room with a double bed he shared most nights. It wasn't because he didn't enjoy having an ornately decorated office older than he was to sit in and perform the duties of a leader, but he tried to refuse them all the same because that office and that private room had belonged to Richards.

He wasn't the same, he told himself often. Lizzie had assured him of that fact, knowing what the brooding man was thinking every time his mood darkened at some reminder of his predecessor. Every day he tried to prove the differences between him and Richards to everyone else, as well as to himself.

Making contact with Dan and the others, hearing of their struggles and losses on their long and meandering journey south, had been the single biggest uplifting experience he had felt since he first got the working helicopter off the ground so many months and a lifetime before. That brief period of elation until the fuel had run out, coupled with the lack of aircraft maintenance that had damn near killed him, paled into insignificance just knowing that they were safe. That they still lived, with the sad, odd exception, and that his little Nikita was still kicking arse and taking names.

He missed them, and more than once he had imagined himself just landing the helicopter on the Dorset coast and joining Mitch and Adam on the adventure instead of turning back to go through everything that came after. He spent nights awake thinking that if he had, then Jack might still be alive. He tortured himself with all of those what ifs so much that he had blurted them all out to Lizzie one night, letting the calm, stoic woman hear his fears and soothe him with empathetic logic.

She felt the pangs of guilt for not joining them too, she told him. She'd considered how different things would have or could have been if she'd just upped and gone with them, admitting that her fear of the unknown and of the potential for the endless discomfort of travel were the main reasons she didn't join them.

She also admitted that a big deciding factor in why she didn't go was because Steve chose not to. That made him feel even worse for his selfish and wistful thoughts of abandoning them all to run off on the adventure, but he kept that to himself after Lizzie had spoken.

He doubled down on his focus of leading a lot of people from imprisoned despair back into a thriving, enjoyable life as a co-operative society; just like the model they lived by back at the prison.

There were farming parties going out every morning and coming back every night. There were guard rotations and rosters to be organised and delegated, and finding trustworthy, intelligent people who were interested enough to undertake the tasks was a constant source of annoyance. Finding people to take on more responsibility would have been easier if they lived with a currency system, but in a world where everyone was cared for by the whole equally, he found that many of those willing to take on more stress were unsuited to the jobs because they were looking for the next job up the chain to be easier than the one they already had.

There were parties going out to pick clean every conceivable item from the rest of the world, much like they had done at the prison, but when they numbered over three hundred even the biggest hauls vanished in startlingly quick time.

Every minute of the day was spent putting out the metaphorical fires that people brought to him, and each time he dispensed the logical, common-sense answer to whatever problem they threw at him, he felt either like a fraud or else just pissed off that nobody would take the initiative for themselves.

He followed the old model just like they had created when he had willingly stayed in the old prison and taken a position of responsibility based on his previous experience. He spoke to the different people who had taken on the jobs like farming and scavenging. Like storing the food and items recovered from the outside world.

He spoke with them to find out who was who, and when he had gauged it as best he could he invited those people to take on a leadership role. He had men and women in charge of guards, in charge of exploration and scavenging parties. He had people in charge of medical services, stores, citizens representatives…

He had all of these things, but when the world simply refused to give him a break, he realised that what he needed most of all was a deluxe model Dan with optional Ash.

SLIM PICKINGS

Reg, who once admitted that it wasn't his name but a moniker awarded to him in jest that simply stuck, was starting to panic that he was overdue to return home. He hadn't been with their new leader before they met at Richards' camp; in fact, they hadn't even met that he knew of until after Richards managed to get himself killed for being a bastard.

Reg had technically been one of Richards' guards, although he preferred to be outside of the stifling rigidity of the town walls in the open air, and roved around under the banner of exploration as he was adept at finding things they needed.

In the world before he had been a logistics manager for a haulage firm, and when the shit first hit the fan, he had known what things were likely to be transported from where, proving himself to be an unexpected wealth of resources in the form of that previously uninteresting knowledge. What they had been before was a subject that seemed to start every conversation nowadays, as though a person was only worth what they knew or what they could do, but he guessed that was just how life was.

Finding a stash of canned goods and enough trucks with diesel still in their tanks to make it worth staying and draining as much as possible had put them hours overdue but that wasn't the source of his unease. He couldn't say exactly why he felt uneasy, only that he had a tickling sense of discomfort at the back of his mind similar to the feeling he got when he suspected someone was watching him.

He was no military man by any stretch of the imagination but he was sensible, and he was careful never to take unnecessary risks and leave himself and his people exposed. He put guards with guns up in high places whenever he stopped his scavenging convoy and he kept a kind of managerial overview so that he knew what was happening everywhere as others performed the tasks he gave them. He had people siphoning fuel into the tanker truck they used, which Steve had smiled at because apparently it reminded him of one his group used to have.

The air around them was filled with the loud noise the small generator powering the pump made as the collection hose was moved from fuel tank to fuel tank to suck up all of the precious, oily fluid they relied on for as long as it was still viable. They were careful, after ruining a handful of vehicles, not to draw up the jelly-like substance that settled to the bottom of the fuel which clogged every fuel filter in seconds.

The additives and biocides used to make the diesel viable was running out, and unless anyone could figure out how to refine crude oil they were staring down the barrel of the remaining days of transport courtesy of fossil fuel.

Reg fell into his thoughts for a moment, contemplating what would happen when it finally ran out or degraded too far and they had to start using horses which others were sent out to look for. They were already using them for some of the agricultural work as only a few people knew how to work the massive machines to plough and seed the ground.

He scoffed lightly to himself at the thought. The term *agricultural* was usually used to describe things that were rough and rudimentary. Simple and almost derisive. The truth was that those machines represented some of the most cutting-edge technology the human race had achieved, and he recalled a conversation with the old guy who knew about these things and told him about satellite-controlled seeders that mapped the field to within half an inch of accuracy from space and ran on a kind of autopilot, only requiring a human to press the start and stop buttons.

Those days were gone, obviously, as the satellites needed constant adjustments to keep them working, and as all of those people – so far as he knew – were long gone then so was that technology.

"Did you hear me?" a voice asked behind him, bringing him back to the present.

"Sorry," Reg said as he turned to see one of his collection crew, "what?"

"I said there's people here," the man told him.

"Friendly?" Reg asked, not wanting another conflict mainly because the inevitable run-ins with others played hell with his schedule.

"Don't know, but they've got guns."

"*We've* got guns, lad," Reg said tiredly, wondering why he had to explain that finding a shotgun in a house in the country or else taking a weapon from a dead police officer's body was just a fact of life. In his opinion, going around unarmed and trusting in the inherent kindness of human nature was little more than outright stupidity.

The young man shrugged at him as though he didn't care much for the fact; he only felt like he should report the matter to the man in charge, otherwise he'd have to consider a solution to a potential problem all by himself.

Reg sighed. "Are they coming towards us?"

"No, just watching."

"Then we watch them right back," the older man explained as he glanced at his watch to worry over their timeline once more. "If they want to come and talk then we talk. If they don't, then we leave them

9

be. We've got enough mouths to feed as it is; no sense in looking for more if they're doing fine by themselves."

The man who had reported the information backed away without answering. His opinion differed to Reg's but he didn't feel strongly enough to argue.

Reg was of the opinion that other people had the job of going out and talking to survivors, whereas his job was to take out convoys of empty trucks and bring them back full. He didn't much care for digging potatoes out of the ground and he had no burning desire to extend his feeling of power or manhood by strutting up and down a perimeter wall holding a gun in endless boredom. This was his job, and the news that there were people watching them made no difference to him unless they interfered with his operation.

He walked the short distance to where the little generator thrummed angrily to suck the fuel from the big tanks of the trucks sitting terminally stationary on long-dead tyres and called out loudly to ask how long they needed. The man operating the pump looked up and cupped a hand over his ear. Reg lifted his hands and tapped his right index finger on his left wrist where his watch was, and the man glanced at the tanker before turning back to him and holding up all of the digits of his free hand.

Five minutes, Reg thought, *standard answer of a man who doesn't have a clue how long the job will take.* He didn't doubt that if he returned in five minutes the answer to the same question would remain unchanged.

He hated inaccuracy. He'd always hated it and when his drivers got caught up behind motorway pile-ups or delayed through roadworks and had to stop driving to meet the legal requirements on their time behind the wheel, it threw him into a flurry of reorganisation that he cursed but secretly enjoyed.

It wasn't just that one load that would be delayed, but the return load he'd organised to maximise potential because an empty truck on the road represented a wasted opportunity and a further waste of fuel and driving time. He'd have to organise new drivers, change routes as well as collection and drop-off times. At least he didn't have to factor in the crossing to the continent any longer, and that in itself represented a massive reduction in his stress levels.

Of course, there was the fact that almost everyone he knew had died, and that the world no longer turned on the process of profit and earnings and that none of the services he relied on to keep him warm and fed existed any longer, but he dismissed all of those things because there was quite literally nothing he could do about it.

Reg chewed his lower lip as he thought, the scratchy hair of his beard grown out of a lack of need to shave for appearances sake tickling his lips. Deciding that the little luck he possessed shouldn't be stretched too far in case he needed it in the near future, he opted to call it a day.

As he signalled a cutting gesture across his neck with the flattened fingers of his right hand, Reg felt the ambience of the world change as the generator was cut to plunge them into an echoing silence. That silence sounded ominous, even if he couldn't say why, and he called out for his people to pack it up, heading for the cab of the lead truck while making a whirling helicopter blade motion above his head.

It was time to go, he knew. The trip was a successful one; they had brought back more food and fuel than the expedition had cost them by a factor of ten. To stay out in the dark for a few more gallons of diesel and some tinned peaches wasn't worth the risk.

11

Three people, two men and a woman, watched the small convoy roll out of the rest area and head east on one of the few remaining major A-roads not to have fallen into utter disrepair. Smaller cars would have struggled with some of the larger potholes, grounding out and damaging vital components on their vulnerable undersides, but the ground clearance and torque of the bigger trucks rendered them more of an inconvenience than a danger so long as they didn't drive too fast.

"They look well provisioned," one of the men said.

"They're not nomads, either," the other said. The woman said nothing. She stood stock still and tried to ignore the itching in her armpits or the soreness of her thighs that no longer rubbed together as she walked due to the weight she had lost. Her skin felt raw and she wondered how the men in her party didn't feel the same discomfort at not being clean every day. That was one thing she still couldn't cope with – the lack of cleaning facilities – and she availed herself of every opportunity to wash and shave the parts of her body that she didn't enjoy growing hair from. She knew that any such routine would only last for a few days before the discomfort and the itching returned, but she enjoyed those few days more than she enjoyed eating.

"Come on," she said, ignoring their obvious observations, "let's go down and see what they were taking."

The three people walked down the slope to the overgrown weeds climbing the solid metal fence that kept the service station secure from the rest of the surrounding countryside. Behind them, taking their silent cue, others rose from the grass and from behind trees without instruction to follow.

FROM THE ASHES

Steve sat back in his chair, a gorgeous thing made of dark wood and oxblood-red leather that was more comfortable than it had a right to be given its old-fashioned look, and rolled his head around to loosen up the stiffness in his neck.

He had spoken briefly to Reg, finding him late that night consuming a dish of cold food and seeming not to care one bit as though the meal was just the diesel to his personal engine. He had apologised for interrupting him eating and said he'd wait but the grizzled old trucker waved him to sit down. Wordlessly Reg slid a piece of paper to Steve which contained the best estimate of the fuel and food and other items they'd recovered, along with another set of figures showing what that haul cost in spent resources. The man was thorough, Steve gave him that, and he rapidly calculated the net gain after deducting the costs of gathering those resources mentally.

They were still very much in the green, and Steve thanked Reg for a good job.

"There's more," Reg said as he picked at his teeth with a grubby fingernail. Steve hid any reaction and kept his face neutral before asking him to explain. Reg pulled a battered road map of the area from the bench beside him and scanned it for a second before dropping it on the table and tapping a meaty, blunt fingertip onto a spot ringed with what looked like blue ballpoint pen that had run out as the marks were made. Deep scores ringed an area without ink filling the microscopic trench in the tough paper and Steve looked at it, finding nothing of significance. He raised his eyes back to Reg in silent question.

"People," he said. "Armed people according to one of my convoy guards. We left fuel and resources there because I didn't want to be heading back during darkness."

"How many?" Steve asked.

"Only a few," Reg told him, "like I said that's according to one of my guards. I didn't see them myself." The answer was designed to stop the inevitable questions that the military types liked to bombard normal people with.

What guns did they have? Were they using any communications? How were they dressed? Did they seem organised and was there someone obviously in charge? What did *that* person look like? How did their body language seem to you? Their posture? Their vehicles?

Reg didn't know any of that, and even if he'd seen them up close, he didn't feel qualified to answer those questions with any kind of authority, so he avoided the subject in case his answers gave the wrong impression.

Steve thanked him and pocketed the slip of paper, intending to hand it to the people in their stores department before it found its way onto the end of week reports that passed across his desk. The inward flow of stores, both food and equipment, was good. They were beginning to thrive after the brief period of chaos brought about by the change of management, and the feeling in their settlement was totally different from the way it had been before.

Gone was the oppression and imprisonment, and more than one group came to the headquarters building seeking an audience with Steve to ask permission to leave and head back to places where they had previously lived in peace.

To be asked for his permission for people he considered free to leave the camp had shocked him, and he stammered out the explanation that nobody needed his permission to leave. He didn't keep anyone there who didn't want to stay, and in the first two weeks after he had taken up the mantle of leadership he had granted a good portion of their stores, vehicles and weapons to people who were heading to their respective homes. Every time he did that he felt the sharp stab of memory from the times when Dan had faced such questions, and each time made Steve yearn to turn back time.

Others had tried to advise him against the course of action, citing the effect on their stores and their reduced numbers making them a potential target for other groups. Steve stuck to his principles, reminding those who objected that they wanted him to be in charge and his decision was that if anyone wanted to leave then they could. The implied risk that he would renounce the job was enough to silence the critics.

He'd considered packing up and heading back to the prison, had even discussed it with Lizzie to see if she supported the idea, but finding that she didn't want to leave just solidified it for him. He couldn't leave, and the more he thought about heading back to their former home the more he found the terrifying recurring dreams of the crash returning to him. He imagined himself driving down the tree-lined road towards the ornate building and feeling happiness, a sense of belonging, but his imagination took a glance to the left of that drive and took in the wreckage of the Merlin helicopter that had been his last ride off the ground, and he knew he couldn't face those reminders.

A crash that severe would have ended his military career for the injuries alone, not even taking into account the effect of the trauma on his mind.

He couldn't sit in the chair that Dan had occupied with the grumbling dog at his feet, brooding into a glass of scotch as he mused the stresses of his position. Steve was more like him now than ever before; being forced to the front of the line of decision makers even though it wasn't his primary wish in life. He couldn't go back and be a ranger. Couldn't face the graves of the people they had lost or deal with the echoes left behind.

Like it or not, this was the hand life had dealt him now and as much as he wanted things to go back to how they were before, he knew they never could.

The real irony, he thought, was the fact that the reason their group split in the first place was an irrelevance given that they now knew what caused the problems of reproducing. Dan didn't have to take Marie away, didn't have to fracture their group, their family, in the quest to save their baby.

It was reassuring – no, it felt *good* – to know that they were happy in the south of France, living in safety behind high, old walls and thriving off the bounty of the sea. The comfort of that knowledge didn't make it any easier, didn't make up for the sense of loss at not having him and the others, most of all Leah, with them now, but Dan had told him to do his best and stick to his guns and that was what he tried to do every day.

Anyone who wished to leave could go, and they would go appropriately provisioned and equipped. They were always welcome to come back at any time, for trade or otherwise, and those who felt comfortable enough to do so gave the precise locations of their homes and extended an invitation for anyone from the former labour camp to visit.

That was how the survivors of mainland Britain, of the world, would rebuild; through co-operation and friendship.

From the ashes of their former lives, he thought, they would rise again.

THE WANDERER

Jan woke with the dawn shining through the windows of his sparsely equipped van. It was a unique creation – raised suspension and chunky tyres as though the long-forgotten former owner had anticipated the needs of a man living alone in an empty world.

It had a bed, plenty of storage space, a water dispenser and even a small cooking hob running on bottled gas that was secured underneath in a cabinet. It had everything except curtains thick enough to block out even the lightest ray of sunlight which was why Jan was awake shortly after dawn each day.

He didn't mind that; despite not being much of a morning person, the familiar comfort of his routine started early each day. He got up, made his small bed and tucked the covers down tight under the mattress, stretched and poured himself a large cup of water which he chugged down in one go. Picking up the gun, taken on Steve's insistence, he tucked it in the back of his waistband to return it to the cab where it could be reached easily from the driving position.

His body responded to the water almost immediately, forcing him to climb out between the front seats and step down onto dew-covered grass not yet warmed by the rising sun. He walked a few paces away to issue a steaming jet of liquid onto the overgrown bushes at the side of the road he was travelling.

Finishing up with a shake and an involuntary shudder with the accompanying noise people often made during that activity, he climbed back inside to put on his day clothes and replace the loose set he wore for the night times spent inside his mobile home.

Emerging back into the growing sunlight after a few minutes holding a tin mug that steamed gently, Jan sipped his morning brew and consulted the map he had been working his way through systematically.

He was about eighty miles, as the crow flies, from what had been the camp and was now becoming the thriving town, but those eighty straight miles equated to almost five hundred spent criss-crossing the landscape going from village to town to village in a methodical search.

He wasn't scavenging, no more than he needed to which wasn't much, but he was looking to gather a resource that was infinitely more important than canned peaches or batteries.

He was looking for people.

Steve had been surprised when his former nurse asked for a leave of absence. The man who had given him pain medication and cleaned him up from the cold sweat brought on by his nightmares, only to force him to engage in physical therapy to recover some of the strength he had lost after ditching his helicopter into a field, admitted that he had a few issues being in the camp in the aftermath of their rebellion.

As much as his smiling face portrayed an image of calm collection, inside he was falling apart at times after the stress and the guilt of the role he played in the downfall of Richards and his cronies.

Everywhere he went in the settlement he saw constant reminders. It was the suspicious and frightened looks that Kev gave him or the looks of admiration he received for his fighting prowess. It was the slack-faced glare of hatred he got from the wheelchair-bound of the brothers whenever the broken-bodied man was wheeled into the sunlight to watch the human traffic flow past his biological prison.

All of these things were too difficult for Jan to bear so soon afterwards, which led him to ask if he could be of use outside of the settlement.

Acting as an emissary of sorts suited him, because it allowed for an autonomous decision-making lifestyle and total freedom. Some days he drove for long periods, covering ground and bypassing places simply because he liked the name of the village or town he had seen on the map and wanted to visit there. Other days were spent consolidating, washing his few clothes or helping himself to others from the dust-covered racks of the long-abandoned shops. He collected fuel, which was lasting much longer than many had predicted and he found it was no great difficulty to siphon diesel to replace the stores he used driving, although his sedate pace behind the wheel meant that he went through much less of the precious resource than he had expected.

His journey had taken him all over the rich, mostly flat landscape and the summer sun filled his body with an energy he never felt during the cold winters. He guessed that was something to do with growing up in a hot country but he saw no sense in lamenting his position; it was what it was, and he saw no sense in complaining about things he couldn't control.

After eating a breakfast of canned fruit and brushing his teeth outside to spit a jet of foamy fluid into the overgrown grass he climbed back inside to start the engine. He wound down the driver's window with a single click of the button beside him and set off with his destination already set. He'd reached a spot a few miles out the previous evening, but not wanting to roll into somewhere new after dark he'd parked up and eaten before getting his head down for the night and facing the day fresh with a full quota of sunlight behind him.

The small town, little more than a village really, was both unique in its makeup and yet so familiar, so standardised in that new world that it could've been anywhere. Buildings sprouted greenery from places no self-respecting owner would have tolerated, and roadways and pavements had been reclaimed by the plant life through every crack and gap. That abundance of greenery, that reclamation by mother nature, sometimes seemed foreboding and brooding but other times it left him feeling pleased and at peace with the world. He was no hippy by any stretch of the imagination, but he liked to see the earth sneak back a little of what humanity had stolen.

That daydream about the encroaching plant life took a couple of seconds away from his concentration and he shook himself back into the danger of reality once more. He saw no obvious signs of human activity; no barricades or signs warned any traveller that the town was occupied, but neither did he see the total absence of life that he witnessed in other places.

It was almost impossible to explain, but he felt that the town wasn't entirely abandoned. Small, subtle clues tickled his consciousness without fully forming into individual thoughts, like the fact that a tall weed growing from a crack in the tarmac was bent over in a way that couldn't have been done by even a strong wind. The faint trace of wood smoke in the air, not from a burning fire but perhaps from one in the last day like the hint of a distant barbecue in the earliest days of summer. All of these things made his senses tingle with alertness and anticipation and made him glance up to the storage section above his sun visor where the gun was nestled ready for use if he needed it.

A view opened up out of the passenger window which made him take his foot off the throttle quickly. Rolling to a gentle stop to keep the noise low, he selected reverse and inched backwards until the line of sight opened up once more to show his eyes what his brain had alerted him to.

Crops.

Tended, neat rows of plants not overgrown by any tall weeds and with carefully preserved furrows of dirt that were undoubtedly manmade and unmistakably recent. The presence of crops told him two things: there were people here or at least nearby, and they were surviving well without living off canned food nearing its use-by date. That meant that these people, whoever they were, were organised and educated.

Jan stopped his van, slipping it out of gear and letting the engine idle as he waited. He'd encountered a few people on his travels and experience had taught him to be cautious as the population, what was left of it, was inclined towards being jumpy when it came to strangers.

He knew why; in the early days after it happened those that were left seemed to fall either side of the line when it came to enjoying looting and feeling guilty over it. Those who had enjoyed it, he felt, were inclined towards more hostile actions when it came to other people and their hoarded supplies, seeing those not ready to be violent as weaker than themselves. Human nature, that's all it was, and survival of the fittest meant being more cruel than others.

That was one way of looking at it. He preferred the mentality of working together, of helping each other and finding ways that each person's skills from their previous life could be best employed for the benefit of everyone. It was communism after a fashion, only that purist ideal wasn't always tainted by the vicious and the power hungry. In his opinion the theory worked, but the application of human nature to it was too strong of a corrupting force.

His patience paid off as a face appeared around the corner of a building in the middle distance. He watched, waiting until they made a decision, until his patience began to wear thin and he flipped the control on the steering column to flash the van's headlights once to signal that he had seen them. The face disappeared, ducking back out of sight and prompting a sigh of disappointment from his lips as his chest deflated to slump his posture slightly.

Sometimes it was easy, other times it wasn't. He hoped this wasn't going to be one of the latter. People were cagey about strangers, understandably, but in the past he had always tried to present himself as peaceful and unthreatening. Being a trained nurse helped, as everywhere he went there were people in need of medical care that they couldn't find. Although he was a powerfully built man capable of unseemly violence when the situation dictated, he was a kind person at heart who just wanted to help others. That was his thing – seeing gratitude and fixing people like mechanics fixed engines.

He waited a few more minutes until he decided that staying put was achieving nothing. He was dipping the clutch with his left foot and slipping the gear stick into first when a man emerged around the same building where the face had been. Jan stopped, keeping the van in gear just in case as he felt his heart rate elevate in response to the gun the man was carrying. Even from that distance Jan could tell a hunting shotgun when he saw it, and the next three people to emerge from the gap in the buildings were similarly armed. He forced himself to be calm, knowing that the carrying of weapons was a fact of life now and not allowing himself to be threatened by it until he knew their intentions. His eyes flicked upwards to where the grip of the pistol was visible just above his head to the front, feeling reassured in the knowledge that he could raise his hands as a sign of surrender and draw it quickly. Unlike their weapons, he didn't need to reload after two shots and had more than enough bullets to take down all of them so long as they were all close enough and didn't encircle him. Still, the weapon was a last resort as he would just leave if they didn't want him there. It was up to them if they wanted to try and stop him.

His naivety in that thought showed his lack of military experience, as he knew they were there now and if they didn't want him to leave and potentially bring others back then there was little he could do to dissuade them without resorting to the animalistic need for violence.

As they neared him they spread out, not one of them standing beside another which would make any engagement difficult with his solitary handgun. Taking measured breaths to combat the influx of adrenaline to his body, he kept his hands visible on top of the steering wheel and smiled out of the window, straight down the raised barrel of the nearest shotgun.

LISTS, LISTS AND MORE LISTS

Steve took off the reading glasses he had taken to wearing after he spent more time doing paperwork than anything else. Running the camp was less of a leadership matter and more of a management role.

He longed to be back behind the wheel exploring the country; back behind the controls of a helicopter would be even better but the chances of the former were slim and the latter was an impossibility. He didn't get the time to get away from administrative duties most days, even when he did others insisted on accompanying him as though he was some kind of high-value target. Even if they'd found a helicopter in working order and had enough precious aviation fuel to run it, his injuries left him physically incapable of lifting the violent machine off the deck. If he had longer to think, if he had more than a few moments each day to be left alone to his own dark thoughts, the history of the past year would likely leave him in a deep depression for all that he had been through and all that he had lost.

His list of tasks – of problems – that day had landed on his desk by the time he'd finished eating his breakfast of thick toast and eggs which were cooked up in massive amounts each morning. The constant noise of the chickens housed at the rear of the cookhouse combined with the smell they generated had an adverse effect on his appetite sometimes, but that morning he woke with a ravenous hunger and a need to stack up on energy ready for the day's long headache.

Parts were required for farm machinery, and given that the growing of food over summer was their highest priority to survive the next winter he had to prioritise a collection team – he'd abandoned the use of the term scavenging as he felt they'd progressed further than that – to seek out the parts. That meant diverting a team from the collection of fuel, food and water which were still plentiful…if an experienced person knew where to look. It also meant taking away one of their mechanics assigned to keeping their small fleet of vehicles alive and well so that the correct parts were brought back, and that, he knew, would have a knock-on effect on something in a week or two.

There was a large farm identified by one of his scouts about forty miles inland which would require their heavier vehicles to travel to in order to bring back enough in one convoy to make the trip cost-effective. In terms of work hours and fuel expended, that was.

He also had a nagging doubt in the back of his mind about the report from Reg. He'd spoken to the man and found his attitude almost dismissive at the time, but he knew now with hindsight that the apathy he sensed was more of a discomfort with all things surrounding conflict.

He sat forwards again, restored the glasses to sit on the bridge of his nose and picked up the piece of paper holding the scant details about the sighting of armed people watching one of their collection operations. That nagging doubt wouldn't go away, which led him to call out to his assistant in the outer office.

"Sophie?" he said loudly in a tone that he hoped wouldn't sound like an impolite summons. Sophie, late teens with a mop of dark curly hair looking as fantastic as it always did as it fell over her light brown skin, poked her head around the door and beamed a bright smile at him.

"Yes, boss?" she said, the smile disarming him quicker than Dan could have on his best day.

"Who has the duty team today?" he asked, meaning to find out who was rostered to be in charge of their meagre defence force.

"That would be Iain."

"Great, can you send a runner for him, please?" Sophie bobbed her head in a small nod and disappeared from view to find one of the few children kept around headquarters for running messages to different people. In the absence of decent communications and full-time schooling it was a good way to keep the half-feral kids gainfully employed and out of the chicken pens. He removed the glasses again and rubbed at his eyes. He considered calling Sophie back in to ask her for a coffee but felt uncomfortable with having anyone wait on him, so he stood to fetch it himself. He wasn't entirely sure what he was going to do when he spoke to Iain, a former soldier who'd ended up doing something with car finance when the event hit. Steve had listened when he explained it but was lost after a short while as the world wasn't one he existed in. He'd never had a car on finance, never seen the need to buy something brand new just to pay more in tax to the government, instead electing to purchase for cash and picking cars that were young enough to be reliable but old enough to be cheap.

Cars were never his passion; he preferred to be in the air.

He smiled at Sophie as they wordlessly crossed paths in the corridor, his cheeks flushing imperceptibly, and he recalled Lizzie's words about him having a young and glamorous assistant. He'd laughed off her half-joking objections, knowing that there was an edge of seriousness lying beneath the surface, assuring her that he had no interest in becoming Richards in that sense. The mention of their former dictator and the young man he had kept close for his own egotistical wants led his train of thought to the death of that young man after he had followed Steve's orders.

He fetched his coffee, heating the metal kettle on the hob kept warm all day by a small stove before pouring a cup and splashing a distinctly unmeasured amount of instant coffee into it and stirring. He'd taken to having his coffee black and without sugar, just as Dan had his, for the simple ease of it being the only drink order nobody could mess up. Nobody but him, apparently, as his face screwed up after the first sip of the too-strong liquid took all the taste out of his mouth and made his brain itch. He shook his cheeks as if to recover and reasoned that he probably needed a septuple espresso with the mountain of work he had to get through.

Regaining his chair he scanned over the other reports awaiting his attention and requiring decisions: requests for medical supplies, a second memo from one of the team leaders asking for more weaponry after he had ignored the first thinking that food and warmth had been more of a priority over the remains of the previous winter. A knock at the door snapped his head up for him to see Iain standing in the doorway. Half a head shorter than Steve and bald-headed, he wore a look of what appeared to be resting malice until a smile of greeting transformed him to his true character of a man eager to see happiness in others.

"You wanted to see me?"

"Yes," Steve said gesturing to the chair opposite him, "please."

Iain took the chair, propped the British military rifle against the side of it and adjusted himself for comfort. Steve was about to offer the man a coffee, deciding it was best not to make it himself given the massacre of his last attempt, when Sophie reappeared bearing a cup. Iain smiled warmly and thanked her as he took the mug with both hands like it was a precious artefact. That was one of the reasons Sophie was perfect for the job: she had anticipated a need long before

Steve had. He wished he could step down and propose her as their leader.

"What'cha need?" Iain asked, blowing the top of his drink to cool it as his intelligent eyes regarded their top man. Steve liked that. Straight to the point. Without giving an explanation he slid the brief report from Reg across the desk and leaned back to take another swallow of his coffee, grimacing as he'd forgotten it was strong enough to rouse his ancestors. The other man's eyes switched from left to right before snapping back, like he was watching a one-sided tennis match or keeping up with the progress of an old typewriter. When he'd finished his eyes went back up and skimmed it again to be thorough. Dropping the paper, he looked up at Steve.

"You want me and my lot to check it out," he said. A statement, not a question. Steve nodded slowly.

"Probably just another group," Iain offered. "Didn't want to come close because of our numbers?"

"Possible," Steve admitted, "but I'd rather make contact and be certain. Standard offer – join us, trade with us, welcome here et cetera, et cetera…"

"Roger," Iain said, taking another sip and letting the bliss of caffeine smooth his wrinkled brow briefly. "We're on perimeter duty until tonight. Happy if we go tomorrow?"

Steve considered it for a moment, then decided that if his Spidey senses were tingling enough to summon the man then it shouldn't wait another day.

"You good to go today if I send the relief force to cover your duties?"

Iain regarded the man, asking himself the question of why he didn't just send the relief force and choosing to believe that it was a matter in Steve's faith in him. He took a large swallow of the drink which filled his cheeks and left his lips wet. Wiping the back of one hand over his mouth he stood, stifled a burp behind the same hand and stooped to pick up his rifle.

"Reg in or out today?" he asked as he slung the weapon over his shoulder.

"In. Still sorting out the unloading of the haul. It was dark when they got back yesterday."

"I'll run him down for some more gen and routes," he said, using the British army terminology for intelligence. Steve nodded his thanks as Iain left, trusting him to assemble his team and equip themselves properly. Steve leaned back, taking a third sip of his coffee and finally giving up on it as undrinkable. Hunching over the desk to get back to the reports he was disturbed by another knock at the door. Looking up into Sophie's face he saw slight concern and asked what was wrong.

"Runner just came in from the main accommodation," she said, pulling a face as though she was smelling something unpleasant, "the drains from the toilet blocks are overflowing…"

Steve sighed. Without any heavy rainfall the previous day that could only mean that the drains were blocked and the whole settlement would smell like sewerage for a few days until the blocked section was located and the obstruction pried free by the people who used to be paid well for doing the jobs others didn't want to.

"Thank you," he said tiredly, looking on another list for the name he needed to solve this latest problem.

LOVE THY NEIGHBOUR

"Out of the van," the man holding the wavering shotgun said in a voice that lacked the confidence the weapon deserved.

"Okay, man," Jan said gently, "just stay calm." He spoke but made no attempts to get out of the cab.

"Now!" the man yelled, waving the business end of the shotgun around like it was a stick.

"Are you going to rob me?" Jan asked. "Is that how it is?" The shotgun barrel lowered as the face behind it registered confusion.

"Rob you…? No, we, err…"

"Because if you're going to do that, I can tell you now I'll be very unhappy," Jan said, disappointment heavy in his tone.

"Look," another voice called out from in front of the van, "we're not like that. We just don't want you to rob *us*!" Jan looked between shotgun man and the woman who had spoken and back again.

"*Me* rob *you*?" he asked. "How the bloody hell am I going to do that on my own?"

"Just making sure, friend," the woman said, her interest in his accent taking over the conversation. "You're not from around here, are you?"

"What gave me away?" Jan said with a wide smile. She smiled back, although only with a fraction of his own gesture.

"Call it my heightened sense of awareness," she said in mild amusement. "Now, have you got any weapons?"

Jan saw no sense in lying. "Yes, but I wasn't planning on using them. I haven't needed to before, and I don't feel like today is my day to start, you know?"

"I do know," she answered as she lowered her gun and stepped towards the open window of his cab without signalling for any of the others holding guns to relax. "It's like this," she explained, "we've been doing just fine until recently when people have started taking our shit. Are you here to take our shit?"

"I'm here," Jan said slowly and carefully, "looking for other decent people who are like my own. I'm not here for trouble; God knows I've seen more than enough for one lifetime."

She seemed to hesitate, narrowing her eyes at him as he returned her fixed gaze. She thought, weighed him up, and let out a breath he didn't realise she was holding.

"Lock your van up and leave it here," she told him. "Nobody will mess with it; you have my word."

"Where are we going?" Jan asked, not making any move to get out or switch off the engine.

"To talk, like civilised people," she told him flatly, as though there was still a healthy suspicion that he might represent a threat to them.

Their little village had been called North Creake, and none of them saw any point in changing it. They had no defensive walls, and existed in what was effectively a small collection of buildings surrounded by flat farmland where two minor roads met at a staggered crossroads. Neither of the roads gave Jan the impression that they saw much traffic back when the world still turned, and what seemed to pass for the focal point of the settlement was an old white-painted pub on one corner of the junction.

He was led directly to it, seeing more than a few frightened faces peering from the edges of buildings and from inside windows of the small houses. Stooping under the low lintel of the front door his eyes blinked to adjust to the sudden gloom inside. It was one of those buildings built so long ago that no architect seemed to consider how natural light could get inside. In the darkness, with a fire roaring in the large hearth and a beer in his hand, Jan was sure it would feel cosy, but in the daytime it felt somehow incomplete.

"Coffee?" she asked, propping her shotgun against the bar and taking a seat on a leather-topped stool that creaked as she rested her weight on it.

"You have real milk?" Jan asked hopefully.

"We do."

"Then I'll have a coffee, thanks."

She nodded her chin up to someone on the other side of the bar and Jan watched as a young man eyed him sullenly as he walked off, maintaining the eye contact and bumping into another stool, ruining his attempt at looking tough. Jan bit back the laugh out of good manners and turned back to the woman who was giving off the very clear impression that she was in charge.

Deciding to keep things cordial, the South African gestured at a vacant seat well out of reach of her shotgun and asked with raised eyebrows if he could sit. She nodded, and he made a show of taking the weight off his feet in spite of it being still early in the morning. He leaned back a little trying to give the air of a man unconcerned with the hostility shown towards him before thinking that perhaps that was the wrong way to be in case that made him look like one of the people who had been stealing from them.

"Where are you from?" she asked.

"Originally or more recently?" he asked back, not thinking that she was making small talk.

"Originally."

"Cape Town," he said, "or just outside of it really."

"Hmm," she responded, not giving away any real emotional response to his answer as though it was just to satisfy her curiosity. "Never been. What's it like there?"

"Well it *was* pretty rough in places. I imagine it's changed a little now…"

Before she could answer or ask another innocuous question the door of the pub banged open and a man strode in. He stopped in the middle of the bar area and looked around at the faces there, resting finally on Jan's and not softening one bit to his smile.

"I'm Ray," he said gruffly, his voice sounding a little breathless which made Jan think he'd been moving fast to get back there. "I'm in charge around here."

Jan replied with his own name, standing to offer to shake the man's hand and looking him hard in the face as he evidently considered ignoring his offer. He shook it briefly, giving one sharp squeeze as though it pained him to press flesh with a man he wasn't sure was his enemy or not.

"Why are you here, Jan?" Ray asked getting straight to the point.

"I'm travelling around, seeing if anyone needs medical help, and looking for friends," he said, adding a shrug to the last words as though it was an insufficient explanation.

"You don't live in that van all the time, I'm guessing," Ray said, "so where are you from?"

"Originally or recently?" he asked again, echoing his conversation from only seconds before the man's arrival.

"I mean now."

34

"We have a camp," Jan told them, "quite a large settlement...more of a town really. It's a long story how we got here, but I'm guessing you aren't looking for a history lesson."

"Humour me," Ray said as he perched on a stool. Jan sighed, turning the gesture into an exaggerated breath in before he spoke.

"Our camp was a kind of amalgamation of lots of smaller camps which someone decided to drag together in one place. Not very many of us liked the idea and it was pretty much a prison camp run by this crazy bastard who ended up getting killed by his own people in a small revolution we organised last year." He sat back wearing a small smile and letting the barrage of concise information sink in.

When no follow-up questions came his way he asked one of his own. "Now, do you want to tell me what's got you so jumpy?"

Ray exchanged a look with the woman who answered him with a shrug. With a tired sigh of his own, he sat back and rubbed both hands over his face to play a scratchy symphony on his beard.

"We've started suffering small raids," he began. "Nothing big to begin with, just a little food here and there, but recently we've lost large parts of growing crops which messes us up a little for next year, you know?"

Jan nodded. He knew what the man meant.

"So we started putting guards out at night, still thinking it was one of our own, you know?" He sighed again. "We've had three people injured and one killed in the two weeks."

"What are you going to do about it?" Jan asked.

"Do?" the woman asked in a tone that sounded angry but Jan guessed was borne more of frustration and fear. "What can we *do*? We don't have any soldiers and we don't know who's attacking us."

The problem was a simple, yet insurmountable one. Insurmountable at least for decent, normal people who didn't think defensively.

Jan thought more about that, guessing that they didn't think defensively because none of them would ever act *offensively*.

He knew what he'd do, but he also knew he possessed a streak of violence, or at least the skill to do violent things, that made him at least partly *not* normal. Instead of turning the conversation towards that darkness he fell back on his more socially acceptable skill set.

"Your injured people, where are they?"

Wordlessly Ray stood, gesturing with a tired wave of one hand for him to follow. Jan stood and went with him, taking note of the exit into a side street and gaining his bearings back towards his van should he need to move in a hurry, which was more of a habit than an anticipated need.

A nondescript door in a small, off-white cottage set back from the road was opened and instantly he recoiled at the smell of infected, rotting flesh. Lifting his left sleeve to his face he ducked under the doorway and immediately triaged the three injured people.

One was unconscious with a large bruise over her right eye which was swollen shut. Another lay face down, crying softly with large areas of their back and legs covered in dressings peppered with small, red dots of blood.

One, the source of the terrible smell, had been stabbed in the stomach, the colour drawn almost entirely from their face. Jan ducked low to look under the table they lay on, hoping – bizarrely – to see a pool of blood there. When he saw none he stood again, mumbling under his breath as his suspicion of internal bleeding had been confirmed.

He shouldered his way past the two people tending to the man, snatching two latex gloves from a half empty box beside him.

"When?" he asked in a clipped, efficient tone.

"Last night some time," Ray said. "We didn't find him until dawn."

Jan peeled back the sodden dressing over the wound, seeing the black blood well up from the wide puncture wound which bubbled to release another foul wave of stink.

"The stab wound punctured the intestine," he said as he tapped at the rock-hard stomach of the man. "And the internal bleeding is bad. I'm sorry, but he won't last long."

His words seemed to only confirm Ray's suspicions, and the face of grim realisation told Jan that these people weren't in any way equipped to deal with either the injuries or the violence.

They needed help.

"I assume you don't have a doctor? Or a vet?"

Ray shook his head. Jan sighed as he stepped back and removed his gloves. He knew that the man likely wouldn't survive the journey back to the town but he saw no other way that he had even a chance of surviving.

Between a rock and a hard place, he thought to himself. *Where I seem to live my life…*

IMPOSTERS

Iain made good ground, opting to travel with just six of his team for ease of economy. The area marked out by Reg was simple enough to find given that it was on a major road. The only thing that slowed their progress was the fact that they could never travel more than five hundred yards without having to swerve around an obstruction or a jagged dip in the road that could see them all walking back if their driver lost concentration for even a few seconds.

Another downside of their ponderous slalom driving was the propensity towards motion sickness, especially for those sat sideways in the uncomfortable seats in the rear. When the journey ended and Iain called a stop half a mile short of the place Reg had seen the people, the unlucky passengers in the back spilled out on unsteady legs as they adjusted to being static.

"Spread out," Iain said as he pulled his weapon sling over his head and settled it over his equipment. "Two stay with the vehicle and keep an eye on us; we'll wave you up when we've checked it out."

He led four of them with him as he moved slowly forwards. He walked in the open, not through any kind of death wish or arrogance but to show that he was intending to be seen if anyone was watching. The others with him moved in pairs to either side of the road keeping mostly out of the open if they could; he reasoned that if he was the one defending the position and he saw all of them approaching tactically then he'd be less inclined to believe they weren't there with bad intentions.

Stopping at the road entrance to the place where fresh tyre tracks through the crusted dirt hadn't faded, he fought the urge to give hand signals to his team because, well, because he thought it might make him look like a dickhead. He scanned to his right where two sets of eyes watched him, nodding once in the direction he wanted them to go before turning to his other side and repeating it.

He stood his ground in the open and watched as the two pairs looped the area to check it out. That he was stood still wasn't to mean that he was idle; he visually searched the area, cutting his field of view up into small sections and looking at each part for anything that caught his interest. As he did so, he imagined a printer running from side to side as words appeared on a page and if he listened hard enough he could even hear his mind making the faint sounds to accompany it.

When his people walked back towards him from behind the small, single storey building with all the body language of people who had relaxed, he stifled a sigh at the resources he was forced to work with. He'd been trained by the army in his teens, and even if the weaponry and the tactics had evolved over the years since he left to join the rat race, the instincts he'd had drilled into him had remained. These kids had grown up engaging in full-scale games console war from the safety and comfort of their own bedrooms and seeing as none of them had ever been on the receiving end of incoming fire, he doubted the abilities of a single one of them to hold up should the time come when they were.

"Nothing," one of them said confidently.

"Nobody here at all," another added in support.

"Call up the motor," Iain told one of them, watching as both speakers jogged off to get in direct sight of their vehicle and wave at the driver to come to them.

From almost half a mile away Iain heard the clattering of the engine as it approached, knowing from long experience that even though it sounded tired it would go on like that for years so long as it was regularly topped up with oil and fluids.

Giving his instructions for the vehicle to be turned around and pointed in the direction of their exit, he took one pair of his team with him to search the building, moving methodically around the left side of the interior after the heavy doors had been pried open.

He looked over the dusty remnants of the service station, almost able to imagine how it had been in the days before everything shut down for good. He knew better than most people how the real lifeblood of the economy was the trucks which transported all of the consumable goods people wanted and needed all over the country each night. As most people were tucked up safely in their own homes and beds each evening, they rarely spared a thought for the lorry driver bringing the steaks a couple of hundred miles from the chilled distribution centres to the shops where they were sifted through and picked up by the end consumers.

He physically shook his head to clear the boring thoughts of logistics from his mind, seeing the section where all of the gambling machines were tucked away, chuckling at the weak barrier warning travellers that they had to be over eighteen to enter that area.

"Why," he asked his two companions in a low voice, "did these companies think that everyone who stopped here wanted to buy an overpriced sandwich and chuck twenty quid into a gambler?"

A noise that usually accompanied a shrug answered him, along with another question.

"More to the point," the other one whispered unnecessarily, "why is there always one trap with the toilet seat missing? I mean, for fuck sake, who pinches a bog seat from a service station? Who walks in and thinks to themselves, 'You know what? I like that. We need a new one for the downstairs shitter!'"

Iain snorted an involuntary noise of humour at the observation, having experienced the odd phenomenon more than once in his own life before *and* after the change. He elected not to check the toilets on account of more memories of how they smelled back in the day, instead looking around him at all the other tell-tale signs that he'd expect to see if people were, or had been, there.

He saw no footprints in the dust. No clean sections where a moving body had brushed the grime off a surface by passing close by. No evidence that the space had been adapted in any way to accommodate someone camping out there.

Deciding that the service station was a bust, he straightened fully and turned to lead the way out, gesturing up to his left at the obligatory one of two choices for premium coffee that these places seemed to grow like weeds.

"Regular Americano, anyone?" he asked.

"Can I get a mocha?" one of his people asked, joining in on the poor joke. "With a double shot of vanilla, please."

Iain turned sufficiently to give him a look of annoyed disdain.

"Mocha with a double shot of vanilla?" he sneered in a mocking voice. "Is that what you used to drink, back when your whole generation self-identified as part red squirrel or a gender-neutral organic deckchair or whatever?"

"Actually," the other said, feeling just as sensitive to offending people as Iain clearly did, "we had one of those in my class in college. He decided that he wanted to b—"

"Yeah, I don't care," Iain interrupted, "and before one of you calls me a Boomer I swear I'll dick-punch y—"

He never finished his sentence, because the glass doors they'd originally walked through burst inwards in an eruption of noise and shards of glass moving at deadly velocities which, had they been five feet further ahead, would've impaled all of them to varying degrees with the lethal projectiles.

"You!" shouted an accented voice which none of them could hear clearly over the ringing of their temporarily deafened ears. "In the building. Come on outsides."

Iain moved his head to get both of the others to look at him in turn, forcing them to make eye contact to prove to him that where were okay. Both nodded that they were fine. Iain stood, taking cover behind the sturdy concrete pillar beside the entrance and called outside.

"Who's there?" he asked, as though this particular big bad wolf would leave without attempting to blow his house down.

"My names is not important," the voice shouted back. "You must come out here." The voice sounded somehow...*wrong*. Wrong for the situation, at least, Iain thought. It sounded too young to be shooting at them and issuing demands like that.

"I'm not bloody coming out if you're shooting, am I?" Iain yelled, stalling for time to think and gather more information.

"This is just, how you say, knocking on the doors?" the voice called back with a cruel chuckle. The way he formed the words and the accent made it undeniably clear that the language wasn't his primary one, and Iain had worked with enough foreign truck drivers over the last fifteen years to tie the inflection down to Slovakia or Hungary. Still, that was a guess, but the chuckle told Iain more about the speaker than his words or accent did, and he didn't like what he'd surmised one little bit; this man was cruel and violent and he enjoyed it.

42

"What about my people?" he asked, meaning the four others with their vehicle.

"Do not worry about them, they are keeping my friends company."

Iain opened his mouth to answer but another weapon report silenced him. The gunshot, distant and sharper than the up-close boom of the shotgun he'd guessed had blown out all of the glass next to him, echoed away before the voice spoke again. He risked a peek around the thick pillar to see four of them arrayed across the entrance steps, all wearing camouflage military uniform and equipment and carrying military rifles just the same as his own, with the addition of one of them holding a black shotgun that was most definitely not a civilian design. He decided on a different approach.

"Are you British Army?" he asked, allowing his voice to sound hopeful. He was carrying the same rifle as they were, but given that he didn't know if he could count on his two untested people in their first firefight he was already outgunned by seventy-five percent.

"Yes, mate," the voice answered with about as much believability as a second-hand Rolex with two l's. "Come outsides."

"Who are you with?" The question, so simply phrased, would elicit only one kind of response from a serving soldier.

"Just me and a few others," he answered, failing the obvious test.

"What regiment?" Iain yelled, stalling for time and wanting a second assurance that they weren't the real deal even though he was already past one hundred percent sure.

"We're with the, err, parachutes battalion," the voice answered. Sniggers of stifled laughter were quickly hushed and Iain's mind was made up. Already convinced that they weren't friendly, and now incensed that they were pretending to be part of the army he still held in high regard on a cellular level, Iain gave his answer.

43

"Give us a second," he called out trying to sound relieved, turning to lock eyes with the two terrified young men cowering behind him and pointing desperately, gesturing for them to run towards the rear of the building as fast as they could.

Instead of stepping out into the dull sunlight to be shredded by the bullets he expected to be coming his way any second, he stood and switched the grip on his SA80-A2 so that his left hand held the trigger grip instead of his right. Committing a cardinal sin on any range anywhere in the civilised world, he pointed the weapon out of cover and fired on fully automatic blindly, emptying the magazine and only reloading it after he'd run in the direction his two team mates did, finding them waiting in terrified uncertainty by a fire door with faded red paint flaking off it. Surprising them, Iain didn't stop and leapt into the air as he ran towards them, connecting the sole of his right boot with the locking bar to burst open the door and let in a wash of grey light. Slowed marginally by the impact, Iain's boots hit the ground outside the wide door and his gun came up to sweep a panicked one-eighty from left to right. Seeing the area clear of immediate threats, he hissed for the others to follow him and forced his way through the tall weeds as he sucked in precious air to put as much distance between himself and the building as he could.

He heard the sounds of the other two following, both heaving air into their chests just as he did, and after what he gauged to be a hundred paces he turned a sharp right and slowed, ducking down to lower his profile.

His age and lack of regular exercise nagged at him, took over control of his chest muscles and tortured him, forcing his eyes to close as his body fought to regain the expended energy.

In spite of his superior age, Iain regained his senses sooner than the others and crawled low through the overgrown foliage to try and see anything.

He hadn't realised how much ground he'd covered and didn't recall running uphill, but gently parting the stalks of two large thistles with the barrel of his rifle he saw the distant sight of their vehicle from his higher elevation, and his four men on their knees with their hands above their heads.

One man in army uniform, wearing what Iain could now see was the insignia of a sergeant, along with a recognition patch he couldn't place, was pacing behind them. His mouth moved as though he was asking them all a question; his body language showed annoyance that nobody had told him the answer. Iain knew instinctively that this was the one he had been talking to only a minute or so before, and studying him through the scope showed that he was barely more than a boy.

The boy shrugged, held the barrel of his rifle against the back of a kneeling man's head, and pulled the trigger.

Iain flinched, gasping and biting down on the anger that threatened to bring tears with it. The boy, his face speckled with bright red patterns, asked the question again before repeating the execution on another man. A low growl began in Iain's throat as the barrel was placed against the back of the third man's head, and the fourth man broke.

He didn't talk, instead he scrambled to his feet and tried to run. A blast from the black shotgun tore open his back before he'd made it ten paces away, making him fling his arms upwards as he fell with as little grace as was humanly possible to bounce off the concrete and skid to a repulsive, gnarled final rest.

The last surviving man talked. It was clear from his gestures and rapidly moving lips that he was pleading with them, promising to tell them everything he knew in payment for his life.

"Don't blame you, kid," Iain said to himself. "Plenty of dead heroes in the world." He meant it. He saw no super-human pride in saying nothing and ending up dead for no reason.

Watching with disgust as their last surviving teammate was dragged and bundled into the rear of their vehicle, Iain let out a sigh at the thought of such a long walk back as they watched their ride pull away in the distance.

"We're going back for them, right?" one of his survivors asked. "We can't just leave them there…"

"You want to live?" Iain asked. "The bastards have left people hidden there, expecting us to do exactly that. Come on" – he shuffled backwards and rose to a crouch to point in the direction of home – "we've got a bloody long walk ahead."

MULTIPLE PROBLEMS

This was just one of the things that Steve disliked about leadership: the issue of delegation. He knew it had to be done and he was forcing himself to learn, but in the first few months after taking the position as leader he still yearned to be out doing something instead of sending others to do it because he said so.

He had been faced with two problems almost simultaneously and wanted to solve both of them by grabbing a rifle and vest, jumping behind the wheel and heading out to bring justice to the wild world outside their walls like some middle-aged Batman with a gimpy leg. Perhaps he could blare Ride of the Valkyries on the stereo as he did.

Jan had returned late in the day, walking directly up to Steve as he ate and bending to whisper in his ear to make Steve abandon his dinner and fast-walk away with the man. As he was listening to his story, checking it out on the map adorning one wall of his office as he followed the described route, his eyes flickered left and right between where his finger was and the red push pin indicating where Iain had taken a team to recce the sighting of others.

The pin dropped, two and two were added up, and the lightbulb of angry fear illuminated in his mind.

"Shit," he cursed, turning away to shout for someone to run a message for him. The summoned runner didn't need to leave the office, because he'd apparently not long heard from the main gates and had thought to ask if everyone had come back.

"Definitely no Iain?" Steve confirmed.

"Definitely," the runner confirmed. Steve nodded his dismissal and turned back to Jan.

"That doesn't necessarily mean the two are linked," he reasoned to his former nurse, who shrugged before he answered.

"What does your gut say?"

Steve thought about it, consulting said gut for a few beats before he answered honestly. "My gut says a hostile group is pushing into our area from the north east, where we have vulnerable neighbours we didn't know about, and I'm currently missing a recce team sent to investigate a sighting of armed strangers. You do the maths."

Jan shrugged again, as though he wasn't so much an active participant in the conversation but more of Steve's spirit guide helping him realise the answers to his own questions.

Steve sat and corrected himself with logical fact instead of alarmist suppositions.

"Iain and his team might be holed up for the night, obviously," he reasoned as much to himself as to Jan. "And they'd be well beyond CB range. I think we need to wait until tomorrow when they *should* come back before I pull the trigger on anything."

"And in the meantime?" Jan asked gently, as though it was a prompt. Steve called the runner back in to issue orders for the perimeter to go on lockdown and for the standby team, as they were called when they were far from any kind of real military reactionary force, to be armed and ready to move instead of sleeping.

"We'll go see your new friends tomorrow," Steve told him. "Work it out from there."

A knock at the door made them turn to see the familiar slim, tall figure of Alice. She was wiping her bloody hands on a cloth, betraying that she hadn't even washed her hands in her haste to bring them the news, and told them both what had happened with a slow, sad shake of her head.

"It's okay," Steve said, his words sounding hollow even to himself. "Jan said there was little chance he'd survive the journey, so I knew you all did everything you could have."

⁓

Morning came without incident, and feeling far from rested as he'd seen every hour on the clock throughout the night, Steve dressed in the clothing he'd reserved for just this eventuality.

He'd elected to step away from what had been their customary black since taking up the supposedly more comfortable role of leadership. He knew that he would have to delegate such things like defending their town and escorting the collection teams to others, but in the back of his mind he always yearned for the freedom that being a ranger had afforded him.

That freedom, he now fully understood, was a freedom from responsibility to and for others.

Leaving Lizzie in charge of the camp for the day with strict instructions that nobody should venture out of sight of their lightly fortified town, he rode with Jan in his van with two other vehicles, appropriately equipped to handle the lack of smooth roads, following.

The occupants of those vehicles were volunteers taken from each shift of guards in equal numbers so that no one place or team would be left noticeably short. But even that consideration had annoyed Steve; he had to think for everyone and reject volunteers based on the equality of numbers. Winding down the window to let some cool air wash over his face, he allowed himself to empty his mind as much as was safe as he left some of the stress of adjustment behind.

He didn't know when he'd drifted off to sleep, but when he woke he had no time to chide himself because what had woken him was a thump on the arm from Jan who was reaching above his sun visor to retrieve a gun. Steve looked from him to the road ahead, seeing a small pillar of black smoke rising in the middle distance.

"Them?" Steve asked, hearing the affirmative grunt from his driver as he checked his weapon in anticipation of using it. Unlike most of his guards who used the standard British military rifle, Steve had sifted through the personal armoury of his much-hated predecessor and located the American carbine he'd previously possessed. He'd had no cause to even take it from the cupboard in his office where it lived, but the reassurance of the grip in his hand at that moment seemed to connect him to something as though he was tapping into the power he used to feel comfortable with.

"Pull up short," he instructed Jan who was wearing such a look of angry resolve that Steve worried he was just going to drive straight into the village and look for a fist fight. He pointed to the only other building between their small convoy and the distant fire as he reached for the speaker mic of the radio set.

"Two jump out here," he instructed as the van began to slow. "Whoever has the long-distance rifle and one to watch their back." His orders were acknowledged and he pushed down the irrelevant wish that he was dropping Lexi or Mitch or Leah there to cover him and Dan. There was something that felt so empty to go into conflict without them that left him almost hindered by anxiety.

Setting off again and picking up as much speed as was safe, the van slowed again on Steve's instruction a few hundred paces from the closest buildings of the village and he led the way by spilling out of his door and limping fast away from it. Vehicles attract fire, that was the mantra he'd drilled into Leah on Dan's insistence, and he knew it to be true from his own tastes of warfare.

With hushed shouts or orders he moved his team in two parallel, leapfrogging lines either side of the road towards the buildings. Moving along the sides of the buildings with weapons up and ready, Steve peered into a cobbled courtyard area with people surrounding the source of the fire as though it was some kind of ceremony.

Before he could figure it out, a shriek of petrified alarm rang out.

Eyes shot towards the screamer, followed the line of her accusatory finger, and looked straight at Steve – a stranger in their home holding a gun.

Three things happened at once.

Steve dropped the gun to hang on the sling and showed both palms just as two people fired panicked shots in his direction. Steve, seeing the threat just in time to save himself from any debilitating injury, ducked back behind the wall issuing a hiss of pain and clutching at the blood welling between his fingers where they gripped his forearm.

Jan began shouting in a voice loud enough to cut over the panic and yells of alarm, identifying himself and calling out the name of the only person he knew there.

"Ray! Ray!" he bawled. "Don't shoot!"

Hush descended inside the small village, allowing the sound of the scream from behind them to carry all the way back to the lonely building where they had left a sniper. Turning towards the sound of the scream, Jan immediately threw himself towards the man on his back clawing and grabbing at the bloody ruin of his calf muscle where one of the panicked shotgun blasts had torn away a chunk of flesh and fabric.

Steve, lips pressed tightly together in pain, watched as the man deftly but unsympathetically staunched the bleeding with a tightly applied tourniquet and set about cleaning and dressing it where the man had fallen.

"I'm sorry," a voice said behind Steve. I'm so sorr— *oh my god, are you okay?*" she added, seeing the blood dripping from between his whitened fingers.

"Nothing vital hit," Steve hissed, hoping he was right. Without removing his sleeve and looking at it, especially with the adrenaline numbing his pain receptors, he had no real way to tell if it was worse than he sensed it was. "We thought you were in trouble," he gasped. "The fire?"

"Our friend," the woman began, swallowing hard as her eyes glazed momentarily. "One of the injured people died not long after Jan left yesterday. She wanted to be cremated…"

"So you did it in broad bloody daylight?" Steve hissed, the pain throbbing up his arm making him speak more harshly than he intended. "What did you think was going to happen, sending up a signal like that visible for miles?"

She didn't answer, realising their mistake and having no justification for their collective naivety.

Steve turned away, walking towards Jan who was covered in blood up to both elbows. "How is he?"

"He'll be fine," Jan answered gruffly as the man he treated whimpered and cried. "Wasn't as bad as it looked; he's just being a pussy."

"Get him inside," Steve ordered two of his people. "We need to get him cleaned up so we can get out of here." He turned to find himself face to face with an unsmiling man wearing a look somewhere between hostile and guilty.

"We didn't mean…" he began, not quite sure what he wanted to say.

"No," Steve answered. "I'm sure you didn't. Why didn't you have anyone watching the roads?"

"We don't…"

"No, which is why your people are getting hurt and your resources are being stolen. We came to help because Jan asked me to, but I don't see why we should bother if you can't even help yourselves." Steve still spoke angrily, which he recognised was partly due to the handful of shotgun pellets peppering the scarred flesh of his forearm and partly due to his annoyance at these people who didn't seem to understand the first thing about survival.

"We post guards at night," the man protested, straightening himself. "Which is when they come."

They mostly come at night, an impression in the back of his mind taunted him in Neil's voice. *Mostly.*

Steve shook his head to dismiss the man's flawed logic, demanding that they show him where Jan could work to repair the damage done.

Half a mile away, in the only other building visible to the village, a young man and his three companions woke to the sound of the door being kicked open and the noise of boots running upstairs.

He held a finger to his lips to keep the others quiet and rose as he unsheathed a long blade – the bayonet to his stolen rifle – and crept out of the door to follow the sounds of the invasion.

He'd hidden their newly acquired vehicle miles away, taking only one of his people he trusted to join the others who had been sent to test the defences of the small settlement, after having used that same blade to wring every last answer he could from the only surviving member of the enemy patrol he'd captured.

Those answers had intrigued him enough to consider going back and convincing their leader to move all of their people further south and take over what these others had built.

He listened to the descriptions of how life had been in their camp, finding that he much preferred the description of how it had been before the revolution and change of leadership, and incorrectly assumed that they were weakened by this.

"Goran," one of the others hissed. "Where are you going?" The young man named Goran stopped, turning to issue a smile of utter cruelty, before answering simply with a wink.

SPREAD THIN

Steve sat, his left hand gripping the edge of the table so tightly that he lifted it every time Jan dug into the flesh of his other arm with the tweezers to remove the tiny balls of lead.

He was up to eight, with two more to pick out after the current target of his rummaging, taking the total to eleven pieces of shot he'd collected with his arm. Where three of them had hit his arm on the thick scar courtesy of a knife fight in a hospital very far away that he didn't want to remember, they'd penetrated much less of his body and were curiously less painful to remove. Whereas the deeper ones into the undamaged flesh where the nerves were fully intact hurt like a…

"Ffffffucking *bastard*," he hissed, spittle falling from his mouth to leave a string of it over his chin. Jan paused, carefully watching the man he had nursed back from a drug-fogged near-death only too recently.

"You want something for the pain?" he asked his patient quietly, seeing the flash of conflict behind his eyes when his body wanted to say yes but his mind stamped its foot and told him no. Not after the last time. Never again.

He shook his head, again holding his breath and gripping the table hard as a signal for Jan to start digging again.

Twenty minutes later, and after having to cut Steve to remove the penultimate projectile, they re-emerged into the weak sunlight to find a subdued gaggle of people not quite waiting for them, and also not quite succeeding in looking like they were minding their own business all that much.

"We'll be leaving then," Steve announced, recognising two of the faces as the ones who'd identified themselves as leaders.

"Wait," the man asked. "We're sorry, the people who shot at you have had their guns taken away an—"

"You *what?*" Steve asked, unable to keep the criticism from his voice. "You've punished the only people who did the right thing. Well done. *You* fucked up by not posting sentries – day *and* night – watching your approaches. At least they reacted well, so you should give them back…" He waved his good arm dismissively at them, giving up on dispensing good sense and worrying that he was becoming a little too accustomed to issuing orders everywhere he went. These people weren't under his protection, and he certainly didn't owe them anything.

Something else nagged at him, cutting through the pain clouding his logic, and he paused before storming out. If these people, as foolish and unprepared as they were, had a pest control problem then that could impact on him and his people who, in the grand scheme of things, were only a hop, skip and a jump from the undefended crossroads.

He turned to face Jan, seeing in his expression the same realisation, and let out a sigh of exasperation. Glancing back to the man and the woman who seemed to be doing the talking for them all, he relented.

"Who do you have with any kind of training?"

They exchanged a glance, fear or guilt passing between them; Steve couldn't be sure.

"We had Manjit," the woman began uncertainly. "She was a policeman. Woman. She was the one who suggested we put guards out at night…"

"Great," Steve said, glad that at least one of them had a modicum of self-preservation. "Can we have a chat with Manjit?"

They exchanged the same look again, only with more intensity this time. Then it dawned on Steve.

"Except it was Manjit's cremation we just interrupted, wasn't it?"

The man nodded sadly.

"And you have nobody else?"

The man, Ray, shrugged with a definite negative connotation. Steve actually hung his head for a few seconds, the pain killing his self-control with every cruel throb through his forearm. "Right, four of mine will stay. I expect they'll be looked after," he added as though his expectation was most definitely that his people would be well cared for. "Two will work the night shift and two the day; they'll need volunteers from your own people to fill the gaps, but you'll need to follow their instructions until we come up with a more permanent solution."

"How permanent?" the woman asked.

"Permanent as in you either relocate to us, or we deal with the problem and some of our people move here and fortify the village," Steve answered. He saw their faces change as though the concept of becoming a militarised zone was abhorrent to them, and he wondered just how much the world had taken a swing at them over the last year or so.

"Have you not had anything like this happen before?" he asked, shooting a look at Jan as though he wanted confirmation that he wasn't losing his mind. He couldn't comprehend, not with everything that he'd personally experienced since *it* happened, that a group of people living so exposed and out in the open could have bypassed all of the cruelty and suffering that afflicted every other group he'd ever met.

As if to underline how ignorant they were of the dangers the world posed, Ray offered another shrug.

Steve bit back the words he knew threatened to pour out of his mouth, cursing the injury for lowering the standards of his manners, and let out another sigh instead.

"The world isn't…" he said, waving his uninjured arm vaguely at the daylight outside. "It isn't like this everywhere. People steal, they hurt others and they take what others have found and made. I can't believe you've escaped all of that…"

"We've had *some* problems," the woman said, as though some-how trying to show they weren't entirely blessed. "We had to kick a few people out not long after…well, not long after people started to find their way here."

Steve considered that, realising very few major roads cut through what was effectively a large swathe of eastern England serving what would have been a fairly large population, the village was actually a natural place for survivors to congregate.

"Kick them out?" he asked, his brain catching up with her words.

"Yeah, they weren't very nice. *He* wasn't, anyway."

"He?"

"Just some boy. One of the migrant worker's kids. He had a cou-ple of friends and they didn't want to work, wanted to drink instead, so we…" It was her turn to shrug. "We sent them away. Told them they weren't welcome here any longer."

"Do you have any idea who could be doing this? Could it be the kid?" Steve asked.

"He was just a kid," Ray said dismissively, uncomprehendingly. "A teenager. Besides, Manjit said something before she lost consciousness."

Steve stared at the man, waiting for the grand reveal.

"Well?" he blurted out.

"Oh," Ray said with a start, clearly not firing on all cylinders after the recent stresses. "She said it was the army who attacked them."

Steve took a long, pensive breath and held it as he thought. He said nothing further on the matter, turning to give his orders for four volunteers to stay. Jan caught his elbow before he left, leaning in to mutter into his ear and say that he would hang around and to see if Steve didn't mind finding another ride home. Steve nodded, unhappy to lose Jan but understanding why he preferred to keep his own company nowadays.

Pausing at the building on the outskirts of the town, Steve's driver slowed to a stop and honked the horn twice to recall the two men left there before driving off towards home.

Steve said very little on the way back, not that he would've had any lengthy conversation if it had been him and Jan occupying the front seats of a different vehicle, but something about the man wanting to stay behind left him feeling a little lonely.

It wasn't the first time he'd felt that – indeed he felt it pretty often, usually when he was surrounded by other people which was counter-intuitive – and he thought more about whether he should admit that he suffered from any one of a dozen reasons to have depression, or anxiety, or suffering effects from any one of the traumas he'd experienced recently.

A stab of pain from the most recent of those traumas shot up his arm and brought him back to the present with an uncomfortable jolt. Hissing a sharp intake of breath through his teeth he shot a baleful look at the driver responsible for the nasty bump in the road, seeing the look of apologetic fear on his young face and instantly feeling like an arse.

Fearing a barrage of abuse for hitting the pothole the driver cowered, waiting for the words to leave Steve's mouth. He surprised the man by saying nothing, leaning back in his seat and readjusting the carbine for the short barrel to rest on the sill of the open window.

"Base, Base," he said into the CB radio when they neared home. "Base from Steve, over."

He'd toyed with the concept of rotating callsigns but had quickly abandoned the idea because it would just add to the long list of things he had to do for other people.

"Steve, Base. Go on," came the voice of the woman who seemed to live in the dimly lit room their radios occupied.

"On the way back, Anne," he said, imagining the small smile she'd be wearing that someone knew her by just four words. "Any word from Iain's team yet?"

Anne wasn't smiling, because she'd been waiting for Steve to come back into range, trying the set intermittently until she got him. As he wasn't reporting any major malfunction or requesting assistance, she hit him with another problem.

"Yes–yes," she said, her usual clipped, professional radio tone edged with more than a little apprehension. "Standby."

Steve waited for whatever transmission was coming next, puzzled at the irregularity of it as his brain hadn't caught up sufficiently to recognise that something was definitely wrong. Iain's voice cut through the cab of the vehicle as it burst from the speaker.

"Steve," he gasped, sounding as though he was out of breath, "we were attacked. Lost four men."

60

His report was as short as his words were simple, but the gravity of what he said wasn't diminished at all by the brevity.

They hadn't been attacked for weeks, *months*, and even when there had been conflict it had been small-scale and was invariably the panicked discharge of a shotgun used either to serve as a warning or without enough knowledge, skill or intent to cause injury. Now they'd lost four people.

Four. People.

He chewed over the words in his mind for long enough to cause the others inside his truck hearing the news to doubt he knew what to say, but he snapped the mic back up to his face and pressed the button without a single detectable shake of his hand.

"Understood," he said. "Back in fifteen. Out."

THE NATURE OF HUMAN CRUELTY

Goran, cursing silently because he had been denied the thrill of killing someone, watched from the shadows as the two careless people abandoned the position without even noticing that it was occupied.

He hadn't used the rifle, as much as he wanted to because it was new to him, but he still relished the feel of a blade pushing into flesh; the way it resisted the point of the weapon until the hard steel won the battle and punctured the soft tissue. He liked that feeling. It aroused something deep inside him. He liked the look in a person's eyes when the realisation of what was happening, along with the pain, dawned on them.

Watching from a grimy window as the two ignorant men climbed back inside their vehicle, Goran decided to head in the direction they left very soon and see what delights their home held.

But first, he was going to pay a visit to the place that had exiled him so long ago.

"We go," he said to his two companions. "Tonight."

They said nothing. They didn't relish the enjoyment of cruelty as their leader did.

He'd been their leader for months after he'd simply walked into their community one day and invited himself to stay. Their group weren't exactly farmers, and they'd made a living by scavenging and setting up a toll where a major river route to the sea crossed over the biggest road in their area. Goran started undermining the leader after a day by questioning his instructions and forcing him to explain his strategies in front of others.

Their leader took Goran out one night alone, and when the young man returned in the morning alone, saying only that the other man wouldn't be back, their group fell under his rule. Many had left, simply melting away in the night to find somewhere else to be, and the onset of winter saw none of them return.

The fact that they both took orders from a teenager wasn't an issue for either because they both lived in fear of him and what he would do to them if he was disobeyed.

They'd seen it happen. When one of their own, a man noticeably bigger than Goran, had challenged him over a decision he'd cut the potential usurper over and over again, slicing and jabbing him with the point of his knife repeatedly even when his pleading and crying and screaming had ended. There was almost no blood left in his body by the time he was carried outside and dumped at the side of the road.

When their existence had become monotonous, he'd kept their interest by leading them further afield to explore new areas. One of those areas was an abandoned Royal Air Force base which yielded weapons and uniforms that made their preferred ruse of representing the authorities much simpler. He trusted only one other person, one of the only women to stay with them, to lead his gang and when she had brought back the news of an armed and organised convoy systematically raiding supply stores he couldn't resist returning to his old life for a look.

He found the fools happily farming and enjoying village life – the life they never allowed his father or any of their friends to become a part of – and the lure of hurting them was simply too great.

He'd taken time away from haunting the village by night and using the bayonet for his new gun, obsessively sharpened at every opportunity, to wreak terror on the weak people who had shunned him.

He decided to have one more night of fun before the people who had left their soldiers behind would be back with more, and if his guess was correct and these people were the ones who were missing four of their own and a vehicle then they would be doubly angry.

The simplicity of it appealed to Goran who, born in a poverty-stricken region of post-conflict Serbia, found himself as a young boy living in the UK where his father worked long hours in seasonal agriculture. As much as he wanted to be accepted by society, by the other children in his school, by everyone in the world, his differences marked him out as a person to be avoided.

He thought those differences were his heritage and his accent, or the fact that his family was poor, when in truth it was something people sensed about him on a more instinctive level.

He was cruel. He was sadistic. The other children who were allowed to play with him when they weren't in school wouldn't join in with him throwing stones at animals. The only two friends he had left wanted nothing to do with him after he'd bought his first knife at a weekend market and began his obsession with cutting things.

Waiting until it was fully dark, Goran slipped from the building and began walking slowly, crouching low to the ground, through the drainage ditch running either side of the pocked road leading in a straight line to the village.

Two hundred paces or so from the edge of the village he froze, dropping down and listening to the thuds of bodies on dry, packed earth as his followers did the same. He lowered his eyes as the torch beam swept from his left to right and back again pushing further out away from the buildings until, he guessed, the power of the beam was too weak to make anything out.

He waited, flat on his stomach, until the person with the torch moved on before resuming his slow assault and was again thankful for the camouflage clothing he'd taken from the base. He sneered in derision at the fools left to guard the place from him, thinking that if they were stupid enough to use lights then the night's work would be much simpler.

The first man standing guard made hunting him simple because he smoked a pungent, hand-rolled cigarette that acted like a beacon for his senses. He left his two companions at the entrance to the cluster of buildings and crept forwards alone; his imagination ran riot with the few video games he'd played before the power went off. He imagined himself as a super-assassin, enhanced with special skills which the regular guards didn't possess, breaking into a secret facility.

At only nineteen he still held some tendencies towards the youthful, imaginative play of children, only his enjoyment came from mixing that imagination with savage reality.

He crept up behind the man, barely breathing as he approached with stealth worthy of the character from the game he imagined himself to be. Unsheathing the bayonet inch by inch, almost daring the man to hear the whisper of steel on leather and turn like it was movie scene, he rose behind him with the gun still on his back and the knife gripped tightly in his right hand.

Not wanting to waste the opportunity of seeing a person's face change when they experienced true fear, he breathed gently on the exposed skin at the back of his neck.

The man froze, his skin tightening in response to the unexpected stimulus. Spinning to face the direction of the sensation his eyes went wide as the blade crunched between the ribs on his left side and drove upwards. Goran clamped a hand over his victim's mouth and hugged his tensed body in close as the sucking sound muffled by his fingers told him he'd successfully punctured the man's chest cavity. Leaning his face in until their noses squashed together, the stabbed guard began to jerk and spasm as his last view of the world was Goran's smiling eyes.

He withdrew the blade, leaning down to the body he had lowered to sit on the ground and wipe it clean on the man's clothes. He didn't strip him of his weapons because he had no need to. Instead he controlled his excited breathing and withdrew to the shadows to watch and wait.

"Greg?" a voice called softly in the darkness. Goran began to tense his muscles slowly to wake up his body which he had allowed to go into a kind of post-adrenaline rest. "Greg, for fuck sake, where are you?"

The man came into sight in the inky night, stooping to retrieve the still-burning cigarette which his friend hadn't had the chance to finish. The attack came fast and savage from the deeper shadows the second his foot hit the outstretched boot of his dead companion. Just as the gasp escaped his mouth, Goran leapt forward to begin a frenzied attack as he drove the knife into the man five times, each time aiming to injure and not kill him quickly like he had the other man.

Six, seven, eight times he jabbed the upward-sweeping point of the bayonet into the man who jerked and yelped with every strike. He tried to backpedal and get away, but his attacker moved towards him with every stab so that he couldn't gain any distance from his unseen assailant.

Fatigued from the frenzy, Goran stopped and stood to watch as the jerking, panicked movements of the man continued for a few seconds until his body caught up and figured out it was no longer being attacked. When that realisation travelled from mind to body, the man's legs gave out on him without warning to drop him flat on his back.

Goran stepped forwards, kneeling down with his left knee to crush the flesh and nerves of the man's left arm and followed up with the right knee on the other side to add to the pain as he crushed the two limbs. Panting and feeling his body overheating inside his warm clothes, Goran leaned down again and slapped his left palm hard onto the man's head, pinning it to the cold concrete as he slowly brought the blade in his right hand into direct view in front of his eyes.

He saw the fear, loving the response with every part of his body and feeling that electric pulse of being alive that only another person's realisation of death would bring. He shushed him almost tenderly as he twirled the bayonet back and forth to fully demonstrate to his victim what would end his life.

Crooning a reassuring whisper in his native language, Goran gently rested the blade against the man's throat and smiled at his desperate pleas before his face contorted into a grimace of rage and effort and he shoved his weight down on the weapon to saw at the tough tubes inside the soft flesh of the throat.

Panting from the effort and sheeted with a spray of arterial blood, he stood and whistled softly to bring his other two men forwards.

ABOUT TURN

Steve walked straight into his office, finding Iain there with two others. Lizzie was with them, as was Alice who was packing up a small medical kit after treating a few minor cuts with clean dressings. Seeing Steve's bandaged arm seeping dark blood through the white dressing, she sighed and opened her kit back up again.

Steve sat at his desk and smiled his thanks at Alice who started to unwrap his forearm to go to work.

"Who did this?" she asked with a tut.

"Jan," Steve answered, hoping that she meant the hatchet-job of a dressing and not the original gunshot.

"You're sure he got it all out?" she asked. Steve glanced up at Lizzie who was fixing him with a reproving look.

"He got it all out," Steve confirmed, adding to Lizzie, "it's nothing, honestly. Just an accident."

"An accident with a shotgun?" she asked, recognising the injury pattern just as quickly as her protégé had. Steve shook his head to explain that he didn't have the time to explain and turned to Iain.

"You okay?" he asked simply, inviting the man to fill him in on the details.

"Been a long day and night," he said by way of excusing their appearance. "Ended up finding a cycle shop and getting back here that way. It was either that or Shanks' Pony."

Steve smiled, unable to not find Iain's chosen terminology for walking amusing even given the circumstances. He thought that Iain and Neil would've got along like a house on fire.

"Got there, checked it out, found nothing," Iain explained. "We" – he gestured at the other two survivors of his patrol – "went inside and the other four left with the vehicle must've been snuck up on. The bastards tried to get us to come out like they were friendly; pretended to be army but the uniform wasn't right."

"Wasn't right how?"

"I only saw it for a second," Iain said, "and it's been a while, you know?" Steve understood, and his patient nod said so. "The recognition flash wasn't one I knew. It was like the French flag, only with a thin white stripe down the middle instead."

Steve's face flickered recognition and Iain saw it. "DPM?" he asked, using the acronym to describe what normal people would call camouflage.

Iain nodded.

"RAF, mate," Steve said, watching the penny drop behind Iain's eyes. Iain opened his mouth to speak but flinched as Steve leapt up from the chair and swore loudly. Alice had just finished sticking down the fresh gauze over his wounds and avoided his rising shoulder expertly.

"What…?" Ian tried, cautious of the usually calm man who was flying into a panicked rage.

"Fucking hell," Steve roared. Two armed guards ran into the office, stopping in their tracks as Steve picked up his weapon and gear and paced for the door, shouting orders for every available guard not currently on the perimeter to get ready to move out in a hurry.

"About fucking turn," Steve snapped, sounding every bit the officer he used to be.

Iain caught up with him in spite of being exhausted and having aches in places he didn't much want to think about after his desperate cycle back to their home.

Steve sensed Iain beside him without turning and filled in the gaps for him. "The fuckers who attacked the village where I just left Jan and four of our people were wearing military uniform," he said. "Tell me, after months of *no* fucking problems at all, that that's a coincidence."

Iain couldn't. He'd come to precisely the same conclusion that Steve had just done and grabbed a passing guard from his team, still keeping pace with Steve.

"Get all of our off-duty together and get ready to roll," he told her, waving away whatever question she was going to ask or inane problem she was going to lay at his feet. His gesture said it all; no time to explain, just get it done.

Steve didn't even flinch at the blood seeping through the brand-new, clean bandages – didn't even feel the sting of those damaged muscles as he gripped the interior handle above the passenger-side window of the Land Rover and hauled himself inside.

He looked at his watch, calculating that it had taken them close to two hours to get back in the last of the daylight and knowing that the return journey in the gathering dark would take longer.

He just hoped they'd be there in time to stop something bad happening.

LIGHT SLEEPER

Jan woke. He didn't know why he woke but as he was an incredibly light sleeper, he didn't have that sinking feeling of panic that deep sleepers – the people of whom he was permanently jealous – would experience.

That wasn't to say that he didn't have a concern growing in the pit of his stomach, because something about the *feel* of the night made him uneasy. He was, and he was the first to admit it, a very superstitious man. He believed in ghosts and spirits and aliens, not that he ever openly discussed it with anyone in case they smiled and nodded and spread the word that he was insane, and he constantly saw animals in his peripheral vision that weren't actually there.

None of these glimpses of a different realm or time or whatever they were ever frightened him, but sometimes he got a curious sensation that was similar to a chill wind, only in his feelings and not on his skin.

He had that cold chill now, and he lay still on his back with only his open eyes as an indication that he was conscious, listening and extending his senses into the night outside the partly open window of the van.

He'd refused, politely, the offer of company and a bed inside one of the houses. He preferred to keep his own company even among the people he knew and counted as friends, so there was little chance of him voluntarily electing to stay with strangers.

He heard nothing, but that wasn't to say there was nothing to hear.

The usual sounds of the night, insects and animals, were absent. They remained absent for over a minute as he lay there and listened, which told him that something was definitely wrong. That could be something as simple as a predator moving through the area near his van which was parked on the edge of the village, or it could be infinitely more sinister.

A whistle, low and totally alien to the night-time countryside in this part of the world, told him that the something which he wasn't happy with had a manmade origin.

Sitting up to throw off the covers, he swung his feet sideways and slipped them straight into his boots which he speed-laced, and then stood to retrieve his shirt before opening the sliding door and stepping out into the cool night air.

Still holding his T-shirt, he walked towards the buildings and listened to the night diverting his direction to intercept the sound of a person running from his right.

He timed it perfectly, stepping out into their path and relying on surprise to disarm whoever it was if they had a weapon. The running person yelped in fright and half collided with him to trip and sprawl on the rough ground.

"You okay, man?" Jan said, convinced that they weren't one of the guards posted from the village and still not entirely convinced that they posed an immediate danger to him.

He was proven wrong by the young man's response, as he scrambled to his feet and fought with the sling of a military rifle in a blind panic to point it at him.

Jan, fighting clinically as he always did with a calmness and a controlled aggression, stepped close to put himself inside the reach of the barrel and render the long gun useless. He grabbed it, rotating the top of the weapon towards him and simultaneously twisting it outwards to trap any finger inside a trigger guard painfully and prevent them from firing the gun.

The man realised the fight for gun was lost and quickly managed to slip his finger from the trigger guard, by little more than pure luck, to reach into his waistband and grasp the handle of a knife.

Jan experienced a sudden and total sense of humour failure as all of his good will towards others evaporated. His right hand let go of the rifle and gripped the knife hand hard, pushing the weapon back down into the sheath to prevent the dangerous bit from making an appearance. Applying the concept of connecting the closest body weapon to the closest body target, he snapped his head forwards without telegraphing it with an exaggerated wind-up as most amateurs did when they unleashed their first headbutt.

This wasn't Jan's first, and he knew better than most the truth behind the adage that 'nobody wins with a headbutt', but he knew well enough the effects it would have on them individually and he was almost entirely certain that he'd emerge victorious in their brief conflict.

With a sound like a hammer hitting hard wood, the smaller man's knees instantly forgot how to keep his body weight upright and collapsed him to the ground with little more than what would be a minor concussion. Jan could've broken his nose easily with the same move, could even have broken his arms or his legs or his spine with a follow-up, but he was a healer at heart and he never chose to inflict damage unless it was necessary.

He knew his recent experiences had a lot to do with that, and his odd juxtaposition of being both a nurse and a man skilled at brutal violence was emphasised in his thoughts since their rebellion against Richards, but he was still satisfied with the outcome.

He took two long, deep breaths to clear his head which swam with the impact, but as he was expecting it the effects of the shock were nullified, unlike the recipient who was enjoying a deeper sleep than Jan had experienced for many months.

Perhaps it was the adrenaline of the confrontation, or the ringing in his ears from the delivery of the savage blow, but Jan didn't hear the second man approaching him from behind. He didn't even know anyone else was there until the metal butt of the rifle cracked into the back of his head to pitch him forwards and wrench his neck first backwards before it snapped violently forwards as he fell. It might've been a compound effect of the rifle butt adding to the stun he'd given his own brain, but he was out cold by the time he fell on top of the first man. His floppy neck couldn't control the descent of his skull and it cracked the unconscious man's nose loudly when he fell on him.

~

Jan woke with a start, gasping for air as though he'd been dreaming of a room filling with water. Any hope he had for gathering intelligence on his attackers before they realised he'd come around was lost, and he blinked open his eyes to see two men looking at him with cold, murderous expressions.

Leaning slightly to his left, he saw a third man in the low moonlight, and Jan nodded groggily in his direction as he spoke.

"You need to put him on his side," he said, the words thick and slow in his mouth as though the rest of his body hadn't fully woken up yet. "He'll drown in his own blood if you don't," he added, taking in the dark liquid running from a ruined nose which he was certain he hadn't done.

The two men looked at one another before the shorter one muttered something in a language Jan didn't understand. He took a laboured breath and opened his mouth to speak again, stopping as the tip of a large knife pressed into the skin under his chin. He tensed, noticing that his hands were bound behind his back and wondering why he hadn't figured that out before.

"You hurt my friend," the one with the knife whispered acidly, accented English riding on a wave of bad breath and the metallic tinge of fresh blood which covered his face and hands. The silence that followed seemed to invite an answer, but the knife stayed firmly in place which kept Jan's mouth resolutely closed.

He looked directly into the eyes over the blade, seeing someone he sensed was more than a little detached from reality.

"You are big guy, yes?" he whispered again, wild eyes flickering down to take in the slab of meat that was Jan's bare chest. "You *think* you are big guy, but I wondering if you are bigger than my knife?" Again, Jan said nothing, even when the knife was withdrawn so fast that he didn't know if he'd been cut.

"You can come with us," he said quietly, sheathing the blade. "I want to be taking my time with you."

"Goran," the other man hissed, "look!"

"*Govno yedno*!" Goran, the one with the knife, spat. Jan sensed he was unhappy and didn't want to hazard any guesses at what the words meant. He turned and grabbed Jan by his upper arm to drag him to his feet. Jan didn't actively resist but didn't exactly comply, resulting in the knife making a reappearance at his throat as the bastard actually bared his teeth at him.

"Get up, you piece of shit," he snarled. Jan fought the urge to smile as the sounds of alarm and other shouts filled the air. He went with them; Goran pushed him ahead and the other man dragged the loser of the hardest head contest by the hands with no regard for any neck injury he probably had.

Goran pointed the tip of his knife at Jan's face, bringing his own close enough to strike if it wouldn't have meant impaling himself on the blade.

"You run that way," Goran told him, jerking his head towards the greying horizon over miles of nothing. "I give you head start, then I come for you. No guns, just this." Jan's face did nothing as the knife was twirled in front of his eyes. It showed no reaction to the words and Goran misunderstood that he hadn't comprehended the instructions.

"You hear me? You run, I chase you down."

Jan stared him out, taking in every detail of the boy's face and deciding that he was fine with breaking his own rules on hurting people in this particular case.

In fact, if he got the chance, he'd probably enjoy it.

THE HUNT

Jan stumbled over the ground which looked flat from the road but was in truth littered with the hard troughs caused by years of agricultural treatment. It was hardly fair, given that his hands were still bound behind his back, but he was confident enough in using his legs that he could do enough damage to them should they catch up to him. His main concern, and one which the bastards had already anticipated, was that he needed to get to the village and raise the alarm.

He was too far away from the buildings to shout for help, and yelling would only bring his two hunters down on his head faster than was healthy. He was on his own, he was shirtless and denied the use of his hands, so it was time to fight smart.

He took off as fast as he could, heading directly away in a straight line and gambling everything on there being another drainage ditch at the border of the field.

He heard noises to his left, directly between his position and the village, and he knew that his escape route was being cut off to force him into the wide-open spaces of the countryside.

He found the ditch. If he'd been unlucky and had fallen differently he could have broken his neck or turned an ankle to maim himself, but he felt oddly lucky to have only slammed the side of his skull into the hard-packed dirt instead. It was deep, but not deep enough to stand in so that he could run at a crouch. If he'd managed to get his hands free he could crawl, but the bonds were tight and his strength was failing fast.

He stopped, sucking in big breaths to try and fill his body with oxygen and hope that it returned some of the senses he'd lost by being knocked unconscious briefly. He began to move, walking as fast as he could on his knees in the only direction available to him.

Moving like that sapped his strength quicker than he had anticipated, and on one of the breaks he was forced to take to draw in more air he heard sounds over his own rasping breaths.

Slowly, carefully, he forced his body into a crouch in the ditch. If he had to, he knew he'd go down trying to bite the bastard's nose off, but the ever-present fear of losing his life to a blade drove him to a state of readiness where the violence he could visit on someone else was almost unspeakable.

He waited, sensing the approach of a body moving just as carefully as he had as the only hiding place in a square mile was searched. He half expected them to be stupid enough to use a light, but it seemed like they wanted to immerse themselves in the game fully, having no additional advantage over their prey other than the use of their hands, clothing, and weapons.

Jan couldn't help but follow his wandering mind, imagining how many others they had hunted through the dark and killed. How many others had crouched in wet ditches, listening to the sound of approaching footsteps, terrified.

He also wondered if any of their victims had ever fought back like he had – like he *would* – and he readied himself to leap up and sweep a leg out of the ditch to bring the bastard down where he could use his head, his teeth, could wrap his thighs around their neck and wrench it sideways with all the force he could muster.

It wasn't like he hadn't done it before. Wasn't like he'd never broken another man's neck and felt the sickening pop as the muscles offered far more resistance than anything on screen had ever accurately represented. He almost laughed, half delirious with exhaustion and fear, at the mental image of someone sneaking up behind an unsuspecting guard and simply twisting their head with no more force than taking the lid off a jar of peanut butter, only for them to fall down dead.

But the movies he loved, as inaccurate as they were, only served to distract from real life. Nothing ever made had showed how brutal people could be to one another.

The footsteps got closer, and Jan reared up to leap from the ditch and throw a knee into the darker shape with no mind to accuracy, relying instead on pure savagery to achieve a result.

The knee connected, only without the devastating results he had hoped for. The man had taken the blow, only it had connected with something hard, maybe the man's hip, Jan thought, and served only to knock him down instead of debilitating him like a shot to the abdomen or the soft part of the thigh would achieve.

He stamped his foot down again and again, trying to maintain his momentum and deal the man a bad enough blow that he could knock him out or kill him and find his knife to free his hands. He still didn't know if he was fighting Goran or the other piece of shit until a sharp crack on the back of his skull staggered him forwards. Without the use of his hands, he fell hard and cracked his face on a piece of rock half buried in the dirt, and before he could regain his feet he felt the cold edge of steel against his throat.

"Too easy," Goran crooned in Jan's ear, his hot breath feeling like it would infect him, forcing Jan to screw his face up to avoid it.

"You're too weak to take me on with my hands free," he tried. He hoped to goad him into a rematch with his hands untied so he could turn on them and do as much damage as he could before their blades found his body. He realised then that he didn't expect to get out of the situation alive, but he sure as hell wanted to go out having evened the score.

"I take you home," Goran said. "I think I will enjoy this again, yes?"

They dragged him back towards the road, walking parallel to the ditch until they located the third member of their group who was still sleeping off the effects of losing the hardest skull competition.

Jan walked with them, racking his brain for a way to escape before he was taken as a prize to be toyed with until they killed him. He'd been the entertainment too many times before, although that had been a means to an end, but he felt his anger rising at being kept like a fighting dog.

The two men hissed warnings at each other before he realised he might escape that fate after all.

Jan saw the cause for their concern as the road in the distance was brightly lit with a string of approaching headlights. He didn't know how Steve knew, at least he hoped with every part of his body that it was Steve, but the arrival of the cavalry couldn't have come at a better time.

Jan was pushed down into the drainage ditch and told not to make a sound or he'd be killed. He said nothing, falling on his back and trapping his bound hands underneath him. Exhausted, shirtless and handless, most people would be disarmed and frightened, but Jan possessed a cold, methodical sense of such pure pragmatism that he simply rerouted the usual thought patterns and found another way to achieve what he wanted.

He stayed still and silent as the vehicles made their slow progress towards them on the arrow-straight road, not shifting position or moving at all in case his plan was given away by a subtle movement or gesture.

When the lead car was close enough to be clearly heard, when the glare of the lights threatened to penetrate the darkness of the ditch, he drew up both feet in a display of flexibility that nobody would expect of a man his size and age, pressed both boot soles into the back of the nearest man and shoved with all of his might.

Jan, when he made a rare appearance in the gym back at the camp, was something of a local legend in more ways than one. His name was written on a board next to the metal frame where people did heavy squats, and the number beside his name represented about the same weight as three adults. So when he shoved he sent the man sailing into the air with perfect timing so that he had no chance to regain his feet and avoid the brutal metal bumper of the lead vehicle before it smashed into his skull and killed him instantly. His lifeless body was thrown clear of the vehicle only for it to be crushed and dragged underneath the second one following close behind.

ROAD TRAFFIC COLLISION

"What the *fuck* was that?" Steve yelled, banging his own head off the doorframe as the driver screamed in fear and anguish at having hit something. He'd stood hard on the brakes to slew the truck to a stop, luckily not inviting a pile-up behind them.

Steve was out before they'd come to a complete rest; his gun was up and legs crouched as he limped fast to their front, giving himself enough reactionary space from anything that might still be there by stepping outwards and around like he was clearing a building. He took his left hand away from the forward grip and covered his mouth, stepping close to shine the torch light attached to his barrel onto the bumper and decipher the deconstructed puzzle of bone and hair among the splatter of blood and that bizarre, unidentifiable jelly that made up so much of a human body's insides.

He wanted to throw up but resisted it, tracking back instead to where the former pedestrian had come from. Shouts from further back in their stalled convoy made him break into an awkward run as his damaged leg slowed him at any speed even if he'd regained his strength and fitness.

He arrived at a melee of torch beams and shouts as he laid eyes on a topless Jan with his hands bound behind his back. He was yelling, nodding with his head into the darkness behind him until Steve finally made out his words.

"He went that way! Get that bloody light out of my eyes!"

"Who?" he called to his friend. "Who went that way?"

"The fucker who's been killing people, that's who!"

"Ten men, five-metre intervals in a straight line. Go now."

"I've got it," Iain's voice said from beside him, immediately taking over to organise the hunt in the darkness for their adversary. Steve dropped down into the ditch beside Jan, thumb flicking the safety of his weapon and letting it drop on the sling to spin the man by both shoulders and draw a short, straight-bladed knife to cut the bright blue, plasticky twine cutting into his wrists. Jan rubbed both wrists and bent forwards, letting out a huge sigh of exasperated relief.

"You okay?" Steve asked, knowing the question was a stupid one but hoping the sentiment wasn't lost.

"Yeah," Jan answered, feeling that his answer was just as stupid as the question but answering it automatically, before taking a breath and feeling his lower lip quiver. It was an involuntary reaction to the situation, which surprised him because he'd felt so calm throughout the brief ordeal, and he allowed himself a moment to take stock.

He was alive, even after a brush with being otherwise. That was okay. That didn't bother him. What bothered him was how out of control he'd been in that situation, and how much he'd had to trust in fate to decide what became of him.

"I just need a minute," he said as he set off walking back towards the village. "Go catch that bastard."

Steve tried.

He deployed almost all of his people, including one or two dogs who'd tagged along, but at that moment he'd trade them all for just one man and the ashy-grey mutt who rarely left his side.

But they were a continent away, and the south of France may as well have been the moon right then for all the good that distance did him.

83

The hunters returned having searched for an hour reporting no sign of the one who ran, which left Steve with precisely two lines of enquiry.

One was quite literally a line, only he was a line of blood and gore with undetermined body parts adorning the swathe of unpleasantness. That wasn't to say that Steve could discern nothing from the enforced road traffic collision victim, as the uniform smock he wore identified itself as having once belonged to a member of his old gang. The rifle, a standard British forces one, was discarded at the side of the road with a bent barrel and heavily damaged furniture, but he noted that the magazine had been removed so guessed these people still had some scavenging sense even if they couldn't find a piece of Lego with a bare foot.

His other line of enquiry was still sleeping off the Glaswegian kiss Jan had administered some time ago. He hoped the man wouldn't be suffering from too severe a concussion as to wipe his memory of the things he wanted to know.

Images of Dan came back to him again as he retold the story – with much less violence and brutality than had actually happened – of inviting Ash to join him in questioning a suspect. He smiled as he walked towards the village from where their vehicles were stopped on the approach road from the south, missing his friend as one of the few men who didn't need to exaggerate a story to make it fun, but often had to omit certain truths to make it fit for public consumption.

"He's awake," a voice said from his left as he entered the sprawl of buildings. "And Jan wants to help you."

Steve looked at Iain, wondering when the man had slept in the last three days because he genuinely looked awful. His words sunk in and his footsteps slowed as it computed. Nodding his thanks and considering telling him to go and find somewhere to rest, he decided the advice would simply be ignored so he walked away to the house where their injured attacker was being detained.

"Let me go!" squawked the man in an incredibly nasal tone the second Steve entered the room. He was tied to the long table used as a treatment bed – the same table where Steve had very recently had a handful of buckshot pulled out of his arm – and he bucked at the restraints, stopping only to promise to kill anyone he made eye contact with.

Before Steve could do or say anything, a hand rested on his shoulder as Jan walked in behind him. He edged his way past, stopping in sight of the man. He froze, staring cold death at Jan over his shattered nose and blood-streaked face. For a second Steve thought he was going to try and lash out at Jan, but instead he pulled his head back and made a hacking noise which filled the imagination with bloody mucus flying across the room.

Jan saw it coming and was faster. Stepping close he used the fingers and thumb of his right hand to dig deep under the man's left collar bone, eliciting a high-pitched howl of agony as the nerve cluster was crushed. Steve's chin twitched in that very British of gestures that conveyed someone either having a fair point, or else just to show a mild appreciation for something.

"First off," Jan said, "I didn't break your fucking nose, okay? Secondly, my friend wants to ask you some questions. You answer them, you don't fuck him around, and that way I won't have to snap this." He gave the man's collar bone another painful squeeze before letting go just to underline his point, staying in range of any foolish counterattack he might've been foolish enough to attempt. He made no move other than to shudder in pain on the table, so Jan gave Steve a nod and he stepped aside.

"How many of you were here?" he asked, getting straight to the point and speaking in a low voice to convey his control over the situation.

"Three."

"Who is the one who ran away?"

The man smiled, knowing that one of his group escaped. The smile faded as he understood the words and asked who else they had captured.

"Nobody else got caught," Jan put in helpfully. "The other one fell under a moving car. My friend means Goran. Tell us about Goran."

"Goran is a *bad* person," he said, suddenly wanting to be helpful now that he knew one of them was dead already.

"I'm astutely aware of that fact," Steve said, recalling the image of the two dead men with brutal knife wounds telling a story of an attacker with a taste for it. "Tell me something I don't know about him."

"He's a kid, really, but he took over our group and nobody challenges him. He's...he's *nasty*, and ever since we found the guns and uniforms at the army base he's been branching out to extend our territory."

Steve took two slow steps to the pile of bloodstained camouflage material and inspected the insignia.

"Why is it," he asked nobody in particular, "that whenever anyone sees this material, they automatically think army?" He turned to the man still strapped down and educated him. "Does the fact that it says Royal Air Force on here not tell you anything?" The question went unanswered as rhetoric. "Anyway, where's your base?"

"I don't know."

Steve sighed as Jan pushed himself off the counter he was leaning on and flexed his fingers. Oddly, Steve was disappointed that they didn't crack like they would if they were in a movie.

"Let's just assume that I've asked you a dozen times and threatened you and then Jan here promises to break a couple of your fingers and you still say you don't know, shall we?" He nodded to Jan who wrapped a strong hand very deliberately around a wrist, then followed suit with the pinky finger.

They hadn't rehearsed that, but it worked perfectly. Jan sucked in a breath ready for the effort of snapping the finger, which he could do with barely any effort at all, but it was all part of the act and the prisoner started to shriek.

"Map! Get me a map and I'll show you!"

"It just so happens…" Steve said, pulling out a map from his thigh pocket. He spread it on the man's chest and held it up a little as his eyes roamed over it.

"It would help if I knew on here where we are," he said. With a tut of annoyance Steve looked at the map for all of five seconds and jabbed a finger at the staggered crossroads.

"Okay, go up," the man instructed. Steve did. "Left…no, *my* left."

Steve slapped him around the back of the head. "Your left is the same as my left, dickhead. You mean right?"

He did. As he was still complying and giving them directions the door banged open and the man from the village stood there, chest rising and falling in either anger or exertion and a shotgun held across his body. He said nothing, simply rested the weapon down and leaned against a worktop in silence.

The directions resumed until he declared that was where their camp was.

"Good boy," Steve said, taking the map away. "How many there?"

"Depends."

"Depends on what?"

"On how many's out."

Steve applied a hand to a tired forehead and rubbed it slowly.

"This little piggy?" Jan asked him, providing a gentle reminder of the threat of broken fingers while also fully prepared to actually dislocate the man's joints. After all, he could relocate them and strap him up afterwards leaving no lasting damage so he was fine with it from a moral standpoint.

"God, grant me the serenity," Steve complained to himself.

"There's about twenty or twenty-five when everyone's home," their prisoner blurted out.

"That's better," Steve said. Before he could ask anything further a shout from outside caught his attention and he walked out to see what was going on.

"It's the last of the search party," Iain told him from his position leaning against a wall with a lit cigarette between his lips. "They drove the surrounding roads and didn't see anything. He's long gone I reckon."

"Well, we know where the bugger hangs his hat now," Steve said, "so we can pay *him* a visit in the night and see how he likes it." He didn't truly believe in his bloodthirsty sentiment as much as it sounded like he did, and even if he did they didn't have the necessary people to conduct such a mission as he counted any combat experience gained through video games to be a hindrance and not a valid item to put on a resumé.

The door behind them banged and the man from the village walked off fast. Steve made for the door and walked in to find Jan already there with his head flat on the man's chest. His eyes met Steve's and he offered a brief shake of his head as he stood, picking up a dirty cushion with a fresh bloodstain in the centre of it where the life had been suffocated out of the bound man.

The death didn't really bother either of them as the prisoner had been a murderer, or had at least been complicit in the murders as part of a joint venture, and it solved the difficult question they hadn't asked themselves yet as to what they should do with him.

"You want to round up the village people?" Steve asked, stifling a laugh at his weak and unintentional joke just as Jan chuckled. "Ask them what they want to do? If they want to come back and join us then we can send some people home to bring bigger trucks back. Anyone who wants to stay here needs to know the likely consequences, so if they don't come it's down to them and we won't be able to send help." Jan nodded and left.

Steve used his good leg to propel himself up to sit his backside on the worktop where he reached out for the uniform and ran his thumb over the recognition flash he'd seen so many times. Knowing that a nearby RAF base had been plundered when he'd lacked the time and resources to get to it yet irked him; like the feeling after being burgled when you knew someone had been in your home and it left you on edge for weeks.

It was an irrelevance now anyway. He'd have another fifty or so mouths to feed after today. Another fifty or so beds to find. Another fifty or so people to go through the induction process and see Lizzie and the other nurses for a check-up. Another fifty people needing to find work, to bring him more problems and complaints. Another fifty people to protect, even if that meant against their own stupidity or ignorance sometimes.

Another fifty lives, he mused with satisfaction, that he'd saved from a bastard who didn't treat people well; just like the first one he'd killed since it all changed and he'd found himself pointing a rifle at a huge monster of a man near the Bristol docks so long ago.

RATS NEST

The intel had been solid, not that Steve suspected to have been given deliberate misinformation because the man who told them had fully believed he'd live. It had taken him three days to find and scout the area, opting to spend the days watching from what Iain had lovingly called their OP, and moving by night when he was sure that the people living in the camp by the road bridge spanning the wide river were either so comfortable or so arrogant that they didn't guard themselves.

They moved in late on the third night, creeping slowly forwards so that when the dawn broke, they simply walked in and rounded up the sleeping occupants amid shouts and pointed weapons. Being woken up at dawn with guns pointed in your face and having three people yelling at you was still as effective as it had been when such actions required lawful authority or a warrant from the courts.

Steve was one of the few people to face any kind of resistance, and when the bullets flew through the thin wooden door to splinter great chunks of the frame away he had responded proportionately by flanking the building and firing through the window. When the gunfire stopped and the remnants of the door was kicked in, they found two people – a man and a woman – dead inside still holding their guns and totally unaware of any threat other than from their front.

The prisoners were lined up, all expecting a firing squad, and inspected by a large man with a bruised face.

Jan recognised Goran by his reaction, as he was the only person to have laid eyes on him. Instead of the fearful, pleading look he would have expected to see, he found only acidic malice in the boy's face.

Teenager or not, Jan decided to judge him according to his actions and treat him like an adult. He formally identified him with a brutal uppercut to the solar plexus before stepping back and raising his right knee to meet the downward movement of Goran's face.

A crunch echoed out over the dawn as the nose skewed sideways and popped to release a wash of hot blood. Gasping, sobbing not in weakness but from an inability to breathe properly, Goran lay on his side and convulsed until the pain began to subside. Slowly, with obvious difficulty, he forced himself back to his feet where he fixed Jan with his wet eyes set hard over his now twisted nose and smiled.

"You would have made good fun to hunt again," he said thickly through his swollen features.

"I would have killed you," Jan said simply like he was stating fact and not bragging at all. "And that would have pissed me off."

He walked away, done with the boy. He went to sit in one of the vehicles that they'd brought up after securing the camp, which was already being systematically burnt down by their people setting fires with accelerants in all of the buildings.

Steve stepped forwards as he went, speaking up for all twelve of the survivors to hear him.

"I'm not in the habit of executing people," he said. "But if any of you step foot in this area again you can consider yourselves dead men." He scanned their expressions as he spoke, seeing mixed reactions ranging from relief to amused confusion. He'd thought long and hard over what to do with them, hoping that they would fight back when they took the camp so that they could be killed legitimately to make things easier, but executing a prisoner was something he could neither live with nor condone.

"Where are we supposed to go?" a voice asked.

"Anywhere," Steve told them, "just not near here. Not ever again." He knew he couldn't leave them in the area because they'd settled dangerously close to the route between their town and The Wash on the coast where trade caravans moved weekly most of the year round.

"My advice is to go directly west, and don't stop for a few days at least. That way we shouldn't come up against each other ever again."

"And what if we want to stay around here?" one of them asked in a tone of voice that suggested he was trying to be funny.

"Then I'll kill you," Steve told him. The man had no smart answer for that. Iain walked up behind Steve and cleared his throat softly, leaning in to mutter in his ear.

"You, err, you sure about letting them *all* go?" he asked.

"Speak your mind," Steve answered in a low voice, not in the mood for guessing games.

"The one who captured Jan," he answered. "The one who executed four of mine. The sicko. I say we do him."

Steve opened his mouth to answer but stopped. Killing someone in a fight was one thing, but he just couldn't bring himself to murder another person. He felt it was one of the things that made him, made *them*, different. Banishment was the only way, he was sure of it.

One of his soldiers walked down the line of men and women, taking a polaroid of each of their faces and handing it to another armed guard following until all of their faces were as captured as their bodies were.

"We have your faces," Steve told them, "and we'll distribute them to every settlement, every village and every town in the surrounding hundred miles. Like I said, my advice is to go west and never come back this way. And one other thing," he said, ad-libbing. "Take off the uniforms."

Hesitant faces looked left and right, sparking his anger.

"I said take them off, now! You didn't earn them so you don't wear them." He stepped forwards to reach out and tear the patch from the arm of the nearest man, daring him to retaliate. The man cast his eyes down and said nothing, quailing in fear under the on-slaught of Steve's righteous anger.

A shout of alarm at the other end of the line made him step back out of arm's reach and look up in time to see one of their prisoners land a second punch on one of his people before sprinting with eve-rything he had to get away.

He didn't get far as one of his people emerged from between two burning buildings and looked left and right to assess the situation before bringing his rifle into his shoulder and firing a single shot.

The runner arched his back in mid-sprint, seeming to be mim-icking a free faller for a heartbeat before his broken body slammed into the road and skid lifelessly to a stop.

Now certain of the consequences, all thoughts of resistance fled the prisoners and they all shuffled away to the one vehicle they'd been left with.

Watching them drive away he gave orders for Iain.

"Follow them until you've used a third of your fuel," he said, "then come home. If they stop, or if they try to turn around, I trust you to know what to do."

Iain nodded, turning away to follow them and hoping that they were stupid enough to give him the opportunity to cut them all down.

SEVEN YEARS
LATER

REVENGE

The years since the day when Jan had launched someone under the wheels of his Land Rover had been suspiciously kind to Steve and his people.

He'd hung up his gun some time before, allowing younger and more enthusiastic men and women to enjoy the hardships of sleeping outside overnight and surviving on a few hours' rest before covering enough miles to put an average person on their exhausted back for an entire day.

He had, in spite of calling two elections, remained in charge of their group which had swelled to become a thriving town full of commerce, production and bartering with other settlements.

He had transitioned from the leader of a military coup to become town mayor. Eager to reintroduce as much democracy as possible now that society was reasserting itself with more rules than they had people, he had developed a system not too dissimilar to their original departmental council of elders which had been the brainchild of a highly efficient former teacher...when she hadn't been at the sherry that was.

His new council was more of a parliament in a way, only instead of constituencies being represented by an elected official, their areas of industry chose a spokesperson to act on their behalf. This way, after developing more than a few people into the roles because of their ability to hear a problem, understand the nature of it and make a decision, Steve was left to deal with the more important matters.

With additional people came additional responsibilities, but by the time Steve had understood that those additional responsibilities could be devolved to the additional people he'd all but cracked the idea of their new way of life.

Iain, now one of his trusted close advisers, ran and organised the military matters which included a recruitment and training section which used the collective experiences of all the former servicemen and women they had to create their own version of a boot camp.

One of the men who had been through that new training and graduated with glowing reports had been his first runner, who back then had been a jug-eared, overly eager boy but was now a tall, solid young man with a keen intellect and a strong sense of watchfulness. George, after a couple of years protecting the walls and gate, had been promoted to work on the protection teams who still escorted people away from their home to retrieve the things they needed. Those things were almost always machinery parts nowadays as they had been growing and raising all of their own food for over half a decade; so much so that they over-produced certain things that grew easily in their rich, flat farmland such as maize, and traded it with the nearest large settlement which existed in the same era of peace by the coast.

As the risk of banditry lessened with time, their military forces took on more of a security role, morphing into a kind of militia who kept the public safe and were generally afforded the same respect as police in their old lives had been when they acted with the consent of the people. That said, occasionally the law had to be enforced when strong words of good sense were ignored – most often through the excess intake of alcohol – and in those times, to quote an old friend of Steve's, 'Some dickhead got their skull slapped.'

With his well-trained force of paramilitaries who, at least for the majority of them inside the town limits, went without firearms as they simply weren't needed, Steve's people enjoyed enough peace to believe that nothing bad would happen to them and that they could rebuild their lives and the lives of the many children who ran around.

It was, Steve often marvelled, life as normal. There still weren't any communications networks but the grid was re-established on a small scale and they had limited electricity and hot water courtesy of the sun and some relatively simple plumbing and wiring. He constantly kicked himself for never having installed it at home years ago, but then he remembered that he'd barely *been* at home all those years. Instead he was working away playing taxi to oil rigs or on a base somewhere in the world. Thoughts of back before always darkened his mood and it took something good or at least something distracting to snap him out of the funk.

A knock at the open door of his office was accompanied by the words, "Knock, knock," which did nothing to brighten his mood and quite simply pissed him off.

"Your knuckles already did that," he said. "I'm not so old that I need subtitles."

"Sorry, boss," George said as he walked in and waited to be invited to sit. Steve forgave him instantly having never been able to be annoyed at the boy – the man, he corrected himself – for longer than a few seconds. Technically, George was a captain in the protection force, as it had been called without his consultation, but to call the boy captain and for him to call him something equally contrite like, *Mr Mayor*, would just be too much.

"*Siddown*, George," he said.

On hearing that Steve had company his faithful assistant Sophie poked her own head around the doorframe and repeated the, "Knock, knock," intentionally to goad her grumpy employer.

"Not you as well," Steve groaned, mostly to himself.

"Tea?" she asked, knowing the answer would be yes and not needing to ask either of them how they took it. She disappeared from view again, followed by the rest of her unruly hair, leaving both men wearing a smile as a direct result of her infectious happiness and striking looks which had only been enhanced by the years since Steve had first met her. George's smile was broader and lasted longer, but Steve thought that was understandable given that the two of them were a couple now.

"Are you nights or days?" Steve asked to start the conversation, seeing if George had just come from his bed or whether he would be heading there very soon. It was impossible to tell if he'd been awake all night given his youthful energy, but Steve honestly couldn't call it either way.

"Days," he said, still smiling. Steve fell down a guilty rabbit hole of imagination as to where the young man had been a couple of hours ago and snapped himself out of it before his thoughts turned inappropriate.

"Much on?"

"Not really," George answered. "No reports from night shift. Three groups out today, all with a small escort, and a convoy should be due in from The Wash sometime later." Steve nodded along with him. It was business as usual, and the news on the incoming convoy made his stomach growl for fresh cod and plaice. When combined with their plentiful harvest of potatoes, he felt that today's take on the original British dish of fish 'n' chips was unrivalled.

"Anything else?"

"Some trouble among the locals," George told him with a frown. "Seems we had some backlash from the scrap last week and a couple of people have taken it upon themselves to seek a little extra retribution."

"Hmm," Steve answered thoughtfully. The previous week had seen a fight break out in one of the places where the local home brew was sold, and the two respective groups didn't seem to want to let it go. "Assign patrols to the area of the pubs until it dies down," he instructed.

"Already done."

Sophie reappeared with two mugs and handed one first to George before walking to the desk and placing Steve's on the coaster beside his right hand. She smiled at him as she retreated, catching George's eye as she went and doing something Steve couldn't see to make the young man blush. He tried to cover his boyish embarrassment and excitement with a sip of his drink which was too hot.

"No biscuits?" Steve asked hopefully towards Sophie's back, knowing that she would have some of the locally made shortbread stashed somewhere.

"Orders from Lizzie," she answered without breaking step. "Sorry."

Steve muttered to himself and looked down – seeing that part of his body resting against his desk when the rest of him was sat back made the point for him. With a sigh he looked up again to dismiss George and get on with the mundane tasks of the day.

"Go take your tea and drink it with her if there's nothing else," Steve told him, seeing the young face light up at the dismissal. "She's better to look at than I am."

"No argument there, boss."

"Cheeky shit," Steve shot back, leaning over his scattering of paperwork and guessing he'd be finished by the afternoon and would be able to take a walk.

Life was good. It was hard work sometimes but, on the whole, it was easier than it had been for much of his life *after*, and he had to admit that he was happy and comfortable.

~

The convoy didn't arrive from their neighbours that day, nor did either of their two small groups who had ventured away from town for various reasons. The late arrival of the convoy was nothing to cause concern. A group often elected to stay out overnight either at another small settlement or else just camped on the road, but for three expected arrivals not to show on the same day sent that cold feeling down Steve's spine that was all too familiar.

He'd ordered a relief force to be added to the night shift patrols, ensuring that all of his people were armed, and was still awake in the darkness as the dawn began to glow in the distance and the alarm was raised.

He was out of bed and dressing before the panicked hammering started at his door and the look of wide-eyed horror on the young soldier's face told him that whatever had happened was bad.

He was wrong.

What had happened was worse than anything he'd seen yet. It was worse than slaves being kept in terrible conditions, worse than foul-smelling creatures hunting people through the dark corridors of a hospital, worse than the terror brought by an invasion into their home.

The dawn revealed crudely made crosses only a few hundred paces from their gates, and many of them had either fallen over in the soft earth where they were buried or else had skewed away from being vertical. If the angles were wrong then the message wasn't lost, because each of the crosses held a person suspended above the ground.

Steve snatched a weapon from the nearest guard and limped fast for the gate not even calling for anyone to come with him. They did anyway, and the journey of his half-run, half-limp over the tended cropland seemed to take forever, with each step giving him more sensory input to the display ahead.

A sob, soft and weak. Mumbled words repeated over and over in pain like a slowly dying man was praying. All of these things came to him as he moved as fast as he could towards them regardless of the danger.

He reached the first one, tipped forwards as the base hadn't been buried deeply enough in the ploughed earth, to find a woman hanging limply from the rough wood. Her hair was lank and fell over her face, but the blood and swollen flesh at her hands told Steve what ordeal she had suffered well enough; the large nail had been driven through her flesh for appearance sake, as rope held her torso to the main beam and prevented her from falling to the dirt.

"Help me," Steve gasped as he fought against the combined weight of woman and cross to lay it down so she could be cut free. As the weight of her body put pressure on the nails she cried out, releasing a fresh gout of blood when the swollen flesh was agitated.

"Send someone to fetch tools to get these out," he snapped at the nearest guard.

"What tools do they need?"

"Just tell them to bring tools," Steve snapped harshly, not having the capacity to think for everyone else. "And medics. All of them."

The cry of pain had told him that she was still alive, so he moved on to the next. Three of them had died – through a combination of injuries or positional asphyxia he couldn't say – but the fifth person he reached was still fixed firmly to the upright wood and the only movement was their lips as they muttered repeatedly.

"Hang on," Steve reassured him, pausing as he saw the disgusting mess that the heavy deck screw had made when it was driven through both of the man's bare feet. "Can I get some help over here?" he barked. Two others joined and helped push the simple frame so that it began to lean back, prompting shouts for more hands to lower it safely.

As he lay on his back, hands and feet still fixed to the wood, Steve noticed with utter repulsion and angry horror that two more brutal screws had been driven through the man's shoulders to keep him in place. His lips still flapped as he muttered something weakly over and over. Steve put his ear close to the man's face.

"Goran," he whispered, his eyes fluttering and vacant. "Goran, Goran, Gora—"

Steve froze, hearing only the soft hiss of the man's final breath in its slow release.

PART TWO
DAN

GRUMPY GRAMPS

Marie lay on her back in their bed. He could tell from her breathing that she'd crossed the divide from asleep to awake and remained still so that his bladder didn't start screaming at him to get up and face the chilly air to deal with it.

She sniffed, suspiciously at first then faster until she made a gagging noise and clamped a hand over her nose and mouth.

"Oh my god, is that you?"

Dan stifled a laugh, covering his inability to lie to her by addressing the other occupant of the room.

"Jesus, Ash. No more raw chicken for you." Ash grumbled, not at the threat of less tasty food but at being unwillingly made complicit in his fiction. He jumped up on the bed, mistaking the blame for an invitation while forgetting that he was an eighty-pound landshark as he seemed to think of himself as a puppy in perpetuity.

The noises of pain that his ballistic arrival brought provided the background noise for both of them spilling from the bed. Dan made it to the bathroom first but a manipulative look of sorrow from Marie was enough to put her at the front of the line. Ash took full advantage of the now vacant warm bed and lay on his back to twist and grumble until the perfect position was achieved. His bubble of bliss was disallowed as soon as Marie re-emerged and told him to get down.

He grumbled again, and Dan noticed how his movements were slower nowadays, like his joints were as stiff as Dan's were. They were both ageing warriors in their own right, but both still felt mentally ready to do their part even if their bodies were beginning to betray them.

"Has Seb come in yet?" she asked him.

Dan had heard their son get up and try to close his creaking door opposite their own over an hour before, and knew he'd be in the kitchen stuffing his face with warm, fresh bread and croissants long before they found their way to the dining hall.

"He's already gone down, I think," Dan told her.

She began tidying her appearance and putting on the warmer clothes they'd need to roam the breezy stone castle they lived in as Dan dressed in his usual black, even if a lot of it was either getting a little tight around him or turning more to grey, much like the remainder of his hair, he thought, feeling sorry for himself.

"I told him to come in to us if he wakes up early," she complained without any real force behind her words.

"True, but we don't feed him sweet stuff first thing in the morning, do we?"

She made a noise in response that he didn't know how to interpret, even after all the time they'd been together, so he decided to say nothing else and remain on the safe side.

"Come on," he said unnecessarily to Ash who was waiting by the door for the human part of the duo, before adding more words to the dog so that Marie could hear them. "Let's swing by and get your daughter, shall we?"

Marie grunted at him again as she pulled a face and held her hair up on the back of her head, looking in the mirror hung on their wall. "Tell her I'll be there in a bit," she said, meaning Leah and not her dog, Nemesis.

Dan had been doing that for a few weeks now, and exercising both dogs in the morning due to Leah's condition. He preferred to say it that way: her *condition*. To admit that she was pregnant made him face the illogical desire to hang Lucien in the air by a couple of things he guessed were precious to the young man. She seemed to follow some kind of pregnancy guide book and had started suffering bouts of debilitating morning sickness before she even started to show but, being Leah and needing to be different, the 'morning' part of the affliction seemed to extend well into the evening until it was pretty much a twenty-four-seven thing.

He knocked on her, on *their* door he corrected himself, and cracked it open enough for a dog to escape but not far enough to see anything inside.

"I've got Nem," he called inside, earning a strangled groan of acknowledgment that echoed with the just the right resonance to let him know she had her head in a bowl.

The dogs fast-walked along as the younger and much leaner dog slobbered at Ash's face as they sped up perpetually until both hit the next doorway as one and tried to occupy the same space at once, forcing Nemesis to give way to her sire's superior bulk or be squashed into the doorframe.

Dan groaned involuntarily as he took the steps; his joints issued cracks in sequence until his whole body was loosened up ready for the day. The dogs knew the way just as well as he did, and they stretched their legs to crank up to a full run and race one another when they hit the wet sand below the tide mark on the beach.

Dan leaned his back against a large rock, leaning to one side so he wasn't pressing the worn grip of a Walther too painfully into his kidneys, and retrieved a battered tin and a disposable lighter to touch flame to one of the recent batch he'd bought in trade from Andorra on their last visit escorting a delivery of salted fish.

Inhaling deeply only to lose the moment to a sudden cough that got away from him, he tried again and watched as Ash tried to balance on three legs while lifting the fourth impossibly high in the air to water a very specific patch of absolutely nothing. Nem, being the helpful offspring that she was, bumped into him as her own nose was glued to the sand searching for the perfect spot to make a deposit.

He smiled, seeing the relationship between the dogs not too dissimilar to his own with Leah; he was just trying to go about his business and she was being annoying.

Wandering back with thoughts of fried eggs, baked fish and fresh bread sliced thickly just how he liked it, he found his path blocked by Neil who stood in his way, balled fists on his hips.

"See 'im off, Ash," Dan goaded his dog, knowing the instruction would never be taken literally when the target was his oldest friend in the whole world. As if to prove the point, Ash bounded towards Neil with his tail wagging and none of the bowel-loosening attitude as if the attack was real. Nem, not entirely in on the joke, ran alongside Ash as if nagging him to tell her what game they were playing.

Neil played along, waiting until the last minute before bending down and allowing the savage attack to adorn his patchy white goatee with liberal amounts of dog drool.

Ending the gratuitous brutality, Dan called his dog back and greeted Neil kindly. "Have you lost weight?"

"Piss off," Neil shot back, switching into an over-the-top American accent. "You're hardly the lean, mean fighting machine you were when we first met."

Dan looked down, not that he didn't know what he was going to see but it was a reflex like looking at your watch. He'd put on some weight, granted, and he'd slowed down along with suffering from the long-term effects of so many injuries, but he was still in pretty good shape for a man in his early forties with high mileage and a poor service history.

Neil, on the other hand, had fully embraced what he claimed to be his well-earned retirement.

"It's true, Neil," Dan admitted with a sigh. "You're literally *twice* the man I am…"

Neil squinted his eyes at him, making Dan suspect he was going to be treated to a quote he either would or wouldn't get, and more than likely wouldn't allow Neil to know he found funny.

"We all set?" Dan asked his friend. Neil hesitated before inflating his chest and replying.

"Solid *shmaybe*."

"Meaning?"

"Meaning we're all set. All you need to do now is be granted clearance."

"Leave that to me. I do what I want, when I want," he said, trying to sound cool and in control. It might've worked had Neil never met Marie before, and the timing of Leah having a bun in the oven complicated matters further. Dan walked back towards the main house, as they called it, even though it was more of a medieval stone castle, and prepared to drop the bombshell.

~

"Say that again?" Marie asked quietly. Dan knew she'd heard him. The only things she *always* heard him say were the things that would get him in trouble anyway. He recognised her words for what they truly were: a dare. It was like when she said something was 'fine', or that he 'should do whatever he wants'.

A vision of Admiral Ackbar leapt into his mind, crying out to him that it was a trap.

"It's not going to be for long," he promised. "You know I've been meaning to go for ages now, only with Leah…with how she is…I don't want to go after that and there'll be loads to do and—"

"So you want to take yourself away on a jolly when Leah isn't in any kind of fit state to fight, leaving us down *two* leaders?"

"When you put it like that it's always going to sound ba—"

"And how the hell are you going to drive a boat all the way back there? You remember the last time you went on a boat? Actually, you remember the time before that as well? Not to mention almost killing everyone just crossing the Channel…"

"Well, technically none of those were my fau—"

"Don't forget you aren't as young as you used to be," she threw in, finally succeeding in getting the bite she'd been fishing for.

"You're almost the same age as me," he said. Her eyebrows went up, which in his mind was the same as hearing the soft click of a land mine activating, telling him he'd stepped on dangerous ground.

"Look, I'm just saying that it's now or probably never. We can be back before the baby's born, an—"

"We?" she enquired, her eyes flickering to her peripheral vision and her right hand snapping out with a click of her fingers to fix their son to the spot where she'd seen him attempting to sneak out along the wall. The pointed finger rotated and morphed into a beckoning digit which seemed to reel him in like he'd been hooked. Still not breaking eye contact with the boy's father, the beckoning finger changed again to indicate her intention that he should sit.

Dan cleared his throat and saw his own look of feeling chided reflected in the boy's eyes. "Neil can handle the boat and any mechanica—"

"Oh, so now it's you and *Neil* going? Just admit it, you want a lads' trip."

"Jimmy as well, but it's not like that," Dan assured her, sticking to his guns and standing up for himself a little more. She leaned back and fixed him with a look as the couple stared it out for a few seconds.

They both knew the inevitability of the conversation, but neither of them would ever give up on having their say. Marie knew he'd go anyway, even if they parted on bad terms because she knew him well enough to know that he'd already promised to go. Dan knew that she'd be unhappy with him going because she'd been nagging him for years to hang up his guns and retire; to stay at home and do something that held no more danger than an office job.

As much as she didn't want him to go, she recognised that he needed to and, if she was honest, she guessed that he was right when he said that it was now or never.

"Fine," she said, giving in sooner than expected and earning a very suspicious glower from Dan. "Even if I'm obviously the last person to know about this, but she's due in four and a half months so you're back here in two." The way she said it left zero wiggle room for any answer other than agreement, and it helped that he actually agreed with the timeline.

"Seems sensible," he said.

"I mean it," Marie warned him with a mischievous smile, "you get back here before you're a grandpa or I swear to god I'll geld you with a plastic spork. Now," she said, turning to their son and allowing no response to her promise to Dan, "what time did you get up and start eating pastries in the kitchen?"

Sebastian opened his mouth to answer, his eyes on his father as though pleading for support, but Marie cut him off.

"And before you answer, just remember that I already know the truth." The truth, such as it was, was evident in the flaky crumbs of what she suspected was a freshly baked croissant still on his clothing and chin.

Sebastian deflated, admitting everything as he folded like a piece of paper. Dan felt for the boy, hoping that he never decided on a life of crime as his career would be ridiculously short.

Dan snuck away as soon as he could without drawing attention to the fact that he wanted to be somewhere else, taking the spiral stairs to the tower their reclusive scholar occupied and rarely left. Neil, melting from the shadows of one of the many nooks the castle provided, fell in behind him and ahead of Ash as though the three of them were trying to act casual and pretend they weren't all headed to the same place.

Knocking and entering the room a second after, Dan nodded to the two men hunched over the old radio set.

"Anything?" Dan asked without preamble.

"Our friend Jason in America has been in touch," Victor, their resident scholar, answered.

"Anything from Steve?" Dan asked, dismissing the other information as he had other priorities.

"Nothing," Victor said with a shake of his head. No news was good news in most cases, but not hearing from their friends after their last message which had been kept under heavy wraps gave them all a deep sense of unease.

Marie didn't know everything, Dan thought, because if she did then there was no way on earth she'd want any of them to go back.

To go home.

LADS' TRIP

Although the cryptic messages about Steve's people coming under attack was the primary reason for the journey, Dan couldn't help but experience the thrill of being on the road again. He'd always been an adventurer at heart, and even back when their group had been small, he'd always felt the need to be out exploring rather than digging up potatoes or standing guard.

He hadn't broken the news to Ash yet, expecting the dog to suffer and grumble as he did every time he was forced onto a boat, but the concept and logistics of journeying over land was simply unachievable in the timeframe he had.

Since the vast ship obscuring their southern view had disappeared a few months before, and since the bruises from the severe beating Dan had taken at the hands of the pirate had faded, the feeling inside the walls of Sanctuary had returned to one of peace and happiness. They were expecting a tight winter given that they'd fallen behind on stocking up with the plentiful fish the hot weather brought to their reach in the coastal waters, but even that wasn't enough to dampen the spirits of his own people.

Although the massive tanker and the bruises were gone, the memory of what they had been through – of having their home attacked and invaded – had left a scar on Dan's memory to add to the many others which formed his decision-making processes. Along with the memory, the aches and pains from his most recent injuries remained so that each morning he crunched and cracked worse than he did before.

"It's not the year on the plate," he'd often say to Leah, "but the mileage on the clock you need to look at."

Well, his mileage was pretty high, and if he was honest with himself he'd skipped more than a few scheduled services if the analogy was to be taken fully. He was still suffering from the beating he'd been forced to endure on the bridge of the tanker while Leah did her thing, and he was struggling to admit even to himself that he was past his best.

Marie, of course, was still going on at him to hang up the vest but he knew he'd be himself until he died.

He thought about the others coming with him. Mitch had seemed torn, opting to stay and keep their township safe to be close to his wife, Alita, and their baby girl. Dan didn't blame him or hold his change of nature against him in any way.

Jimmy, despite appearing settled for the years since they'd arrived, seemed to have been going through a phase for the last two years.

He'd tried his hand at fishing, at the production lines dealing with their hauls, and at the water sterilisation plants Neil had set up so long ago. He'd run the supply wagons to and from the farms, The Orchards and had even gone on a few of the longer trips back and forth from their allied enclave in Andorra. He'd spent a few weeks at the farms fixing their various technical issues, but his sense of wandering made him feel more and more temporary everywhere he went.

As soon as word of Dan taking a boat back to visit Steve and the others who had survived from their old home reached his ears, he pretty much packed his bag and asked for a seat.

"It'd be nice to see Kev again," Jimmy said. "See how he's getting along. Maggie and Cedric, too. And the others, obviously."

Dan smiled at him, feeling the pang of memory from a time where they had been happier, even if that happiness was a temporary reprieve through naivety. He agreed, instantly, but he also had to trust him with the additional information that the others not joining them wouldn't have.

"Listen, mate," Dan said softly, "I need you to know *all* the facts before you come with us. This isn't strictly a social call, if you follow me…"

Jimmy's eyebrows went up, waiting for more intel.

"Steve's people reported that they were attacked a couple of weeks ago," he explained. "Since then we've heard nothing."

"So what? You're going in as a one-man-band to save the world?"

"It's not like that," Dan said again, feeling annoyed that so many people made assumptions about what his responses were. They were mostly correct, which was why it annoyed him so much.

"We're going to see what's going on," he explained carefully. "And after that we can decide what – if anything – needs to be done."

Jimmy had agreed to keep his secret, insisting that he was coming anyway, regardless of the risk. If anything, it hardened his resolve to go.

Neil's cheerful greeting pulled him from his reverie as he swung his pack off his shoulder.

"Alright, dickhead?"

"Morning," Dan answered, not rising to the bait and not taking any offense from the man who dreamed of ways to push people's buttons purely for the entertainment value. He looked down to his left where Ash fixed him with a suspicious look bordering on accusatory. Seeing as how he'd just dropped his bag over the railings of a boat, the suspicion was understandable.

"Sorry boy," he said, earning a warbling grumble from the dog in response. "It's got to be done. No other way, I'm afraid." And there wasn't, not anymore. There was every likelihood that there would still be serviceable aircraft hidden away which could be nursed back into life, but trusting an old diesel truck to run on degraded fuel was a very different prospect to trusting a small plane. Similarly, carrying enough fuel to make the journey by car would be too difficult to manage so they went back to the way they first escaped their island home and planned to go by sea.

Both of them had rather vivid memories of their journey to France in the first place, and their inexperience at the controls of a boat was, without doubt, the cause for the risk they were all in back then. That risk was negated by the recruitment of a third accomplice.

"You are late, my friend," Mateo announced in his booming voice, still heavily accented in Spanish no matter how long he had been speaking English. Tall and muscled like the stereotypical image of a hardened sailor back in the time before ships had anything but the power of the elements to propel them, the dark skin around his eyes seemed permanently crinkled as though he'd spent a lifetime squinting at the sun.

"Sorry," Dan said weakly. In truth he'd taken longer than expected to say goodbye to his wife and son, and that was before he'd even found Leah to speak to her and the bump that stretched the skin of her belly. He'd been hit with a wave of fear when saying goodbye; he believed for a moment that he was too old to be travelling so far from home and even considered abandoning the trip in favour of a form of semi-retirement.

"It is no matter," Mateo told him, reaching down to scratch under Ash's chin. The dog lifted his head to allow it, seeming more to permit the man to touch him as opposed to enjoying it. "He will have the tide for one more hour to help us."

"It's ready?" Neil asked. "The boat?"

"It is ready," Mateo answered, sounding solemn and dolorous as he always did. As permanently unimpressed as the Spanish fisherman seemed, he would never deny Dan anything since the day he and others had risked their lives to bring back the man's younger brother who had been taken prisoner by men attacking their friends in Andorra. Leah had escaped that attempt, and together they had made every one of the bastards sorry.

The boat they were talking about was the one they'd actually be using to travel, not the fishing boat they were about to board. Their boat was another yacht found on a private pier years before and recovered to Sanctuary. It was only half as grand and big as the one they'd liberated from the Dorset coast years before. It had been taken out of the docks and into deeper water where Mateo had tested it for seaworthiness. Since then it had been anchored just beyond the sea wall waiting for them.

"All the supplies loaded?" Dan asked, stepping back in anticipation of heading off his dog who was already beginning to backpedal away from the evil moving floor he knew he didn't want to walk on.

"Food, water and fuel," Mateo answered.

"And the, er, *other* supplies?" Dan added, raising his eyebrows at Neil knowingly.

"Already loaded," he said quietly. Anyone who knew Neil knew that something was up because he never gave a quiet, simple answer when he could quote a film or do some other impression. Dan nodded, not wanting to ask more when there were other people around.

Any of those could carry word back to Marie that their journey was something more than a friendly reunion.

Dan reached down to stroke Ash, tricking him and slipping a lead around the dog's neck which immediately started the struggle for the dog to escape being forced onto a boat. Between him and Neil amid a significant amount of snarling and threatening snaps of the dog's big teeth, it took over a minute to fight Ash over the railing where he immediately tried to break free and return to dry land. Neil managed to get him behind the door of the small cabin on the deck and shut it, muttering something in between gasps for breath that Dan probably wouldn't have understood the reference to if he'd heard it.

He was sweating at the effort too, feeling out of shape. Glancing at Neil trying to recover made him feel better about his physical condition, and recognising the cruelty in that didn't bother him one bit.

Throwing his bag against a plastic tub lashed to the railings he settled himself into a comfortable standing spot and turned back to face the docks at the call of his name.

Mitch, the only other person to know the true reason for their trip, stood holding something in his left hand that still looked odd on him. Since he and Alita had finally managed to have a little girl, the tough Scot had softened in so many ways. Unless his home or his family was threatened, that was, then he became capable of worse savagery than Dan had previously known but understood on a cellular level. The two of them had felt awkward around one another for a few weeks after they'd come to blows borne of stress and an excess of adrenaline, but neither of them were the type to hold a grudge against a friend for something so small as a punch-up.

Dan watched as he tenderly kissed the mostly bald head of the pink and white bundle before turning to hand her over to Alita. The baby's mother took her carefully, settling her in the crook of her right arm as she reached her left hand around the back of Mitch's head to pull him towards her.

Normally such a quiet, timid woman, Alita had evolved like so many of them had.

Leah had become a strong, capable fighter who was brave and charismatic. Neil had put on more weight and enjoyed running what passed for the town's first brewery. Alita had been transformed by motherhood, on top of the traumatic experience of defending her baby against an attacker, and had found a strength that she projected everywhere she went. She was still a quiet person, but behind that mask of meekness was a woman every bit as fierce and protective as the soldier she had married.

Dan turned away, giving them their moment just as he had enjoyed his own in private, but inside he was awash with joy and relief that Mitch had agreed to come along after all.

He'd been undecided for the last week since Dan had first decided he was going and began the campaign to wear Marie down into agreeing. Neil had willingly dropped everything and been prepared to leave the same afternoon, and Dan marvelled at how he never actually did anything fully for himself; he relied on one of the many people to follow him around and learn to do the things he did. Leaving the delicate task of managing the wooden casks of light ale and the noxiously strong cider made from the fruit of the apple orchards nearby in the hands of an understudy, Neil expressed his opinion that they needed another gun they could trust.

"Mitch won't want to go," Dan had told him. "Not with the baby."

And he didn't, not at first, but the evident eleventh-hour change of heart filled Dan with an immense feeling of relief.

"I put your toys on the big boat yesterday," Neil said, shooting a wry smile at Dan who he'd kept in the dark about Mitch joining them.

"And more supplies?" Dan asked, logic and logistics taking over.

"And more supplies," Neil promised. Dan met Mitch's gaze as the soldier climbed aboard and offered him his hand. Mitch took it, squeezing with his own as he smiled at Dan.

"Back on the road again," he said.

"Like a reunion tour," Neil said as he leaned back against the rail to extend his large belly in their direction. "You know, like we were in a band in the early nineties or something. Hey, wouldn't it be funny if a group set up shop in an old Butlins resort?"

Dan and Mitch ignored him, recognising his turbo-talking and bad jokes as a cover for his excitement and trepidation, as the boat's engine barked and revved.

"Knock, knock," Neil blurted out after a chuckle that told Dan he already found himself hilarious.

"Who's there?" he replied reluctantly, knowing he'd likely regret playing along.

"Maia."

"Maia who?"

"Maia *hee*, maia *haa,* maia *HA-haa.*"

Dan did well to hide the embarrassed laugh that threatened to escape his mouth and turned to give Mitch a withering look, recognising the same suppressed laughter in his expression. Neil, evidently satisfied with himself, walked off still humming the rest of the tune.

Mateo was steering the boat from the controls on deck, as using the comfortable captain's seat inside the cabin would mean releasing the dog who had his face pressed up to the glass fixing his owner with a death stare.

It took them only a few minutes to reach the yacht. Dan looked up at it and thought it was less than half the size of the one they'd all packed into so long ago, but given that it was only going to be five men and a dog they hardly needed the extra rooms.

As the engine idled and they bobbed alongside the bigger vessel in its shadow, Dan picked up the life jacket he'd brought for a specific purpose and let Ash out on deck.

The response was immediate, and he felt bad at his involuntary laugh at the dog's expense. Ash tumbled from the small cabin and weaved left and right like he was escaping an unstable structure. Dan caught him before he meandered too close to the side of the boat and knelt to lift his front paws in turn and zip the vest up along his back being careful not to catch the thick fur. In addition to the moving deck that destabilised the unfortunate animal, Ash now had to contend with being forced to wear clothing.

"For your own good, mate," Dan said, standing and using the straps on the vest to haul him up. Ash had never been a small dog, but feeling as out of shape as Dan did and trying to lift over a third of his own body weight as it thrashed and struggled against him made him far heavier than he was. With Neil's help from the deck of their ride, Ash was pulled aboard and the others followed. Mateo, the last man aboard, turned and spoke in slow Spanish to the French-speaking man on the deck of the fishing boat before dropping his own bag inside and climbing up to what Neil still called the flight deck to start the engines and pull up the anchor.

PLAIN SAILING

Ash, true to form, bolted for the lower decks as soon as he was onboard, catching his life jacket on every doorway as he yelped and skittered his way to find somewhere dark and enclosed to vomit in peace.

Dan, heaving his own bag off the deck as the wind began to pick up, lifted Mateo's pack and carried it down the narrow stairs to the lower deck to drop it on one of the bunks. Other rooms, or cabins as people insisted on calling a room when it was on a boat, had been given over to storing their gear and the additional fuel their journey would require.

He opened one door, seeing a sight laid out on one of the beds that made his body tingle with a mixture of excitement and appreciation. He picked up his own gun, as individual as it was courtesy of the additions he'd made, checking it and resting it back down to lift the old plate-carrying vest he'd worn so many times.

He hadn't worn it since the day he'd piloted a small boat out into the deep water near their home and given himself up to the people – if they could even be called that – who had besieged their coastline.

It felt heavier than he remembered, as he went through the natural routine of filling his lungs with air to give the measure of how tight it needed to be, sucking in his gut at the same time as all the Velcro fasteners found their perfect fit. Settling the spare, loaded magazines for his carbine into the pouches, he added one to the weapon which he clipped to the sling attached to the vest. The gun

125

from his hip went into the holster on the chest after he added the fat suppressor to the end of the barrel. He popped the clasp on the sheath attached to the left shoulder strap and pulled the knife from it before replacing and securing it.

Finally, and with a degree of reverence which others would have found bizarre to watch, he lifted the short, fat shotgun from where it sat and carefully loaded it with heavy shot before reversing it and slotting it into the elasticated holder sewn to the back of his vest.

Dressed for war, and feeling a little more like the person he recognised himself to be, he went back outside onto the deck where he pulled a tin from his leg pocket and struggled to strike a flame in the breeze of the open water. He was forced back inside the main cabin to light the smoke before stepping smartly outside and letting out the cloud from his mouth and nostrils.

"Not even past the end of the road and he's already changed into a mini-skirt," Neil quipped, raising his voice over the rush of air as they sailed into the wind.

"Well," Dan shot back, playing along, "*you're* not going out dressed like *that*, missy."

Neil looked down at his T-shirt, loose trousers and comfortable shoes.

"Fair point," he admitted, walking past Dan to go and change. Dan saw Mitch at the aft rail, staring back at their home as it grew smaller and became obscured by the shoreline.

Eventually, he knew, Sanctuary would disappear into the rocky cliffs that made it such an easy place to defend, and the only unnatural blemish on the landscape would be the straight edges of their sky fort overlooking their home. He decided to leave Mitch to his own thoughts, knowing that he wouldn't be there if he didn't want to be.

"Dressed to impress," Mitch announced softly as he approached. Dan hadn't seen him leave the railing, hadn't seen him turn his back on their home and take a breath to transform himself into the person he'd been before his life had grown comfortable there.

"Yeah," Dan answered, not sure how else to respond. "They'll be fine, mate," he said, making the statement so close to a question that he needed to clear his throat and repeat it more firmly. "They'll be fine."

"Oh, I know they will," Mitch told him. "We've trained a good bunch, and there's more than one person there capable of keeping it all on the rails when we're away."

Dan's mind ran through the lists of people assigned to ensure the safety and security of Sanctuary remained intact and unmolested in their absence, and he was sure of the man left in charge.

He had better be, he told himself, given that the man was his son-in-law now.

"All your stuff's down below," Dan told him, meaning his personal weapon which he assumed Neil had smuggled onboard. Mitch nodded his thanks or his understanding, Dan couldn't tell which, and walked inside.

Looking down at the rolled cigarette between this forefinger and thumb, Dan was annoyed to see that half of it had burned down to leave a curled tube of ash attached to it. He shook it away, lifting it to his mouth to take a long, final draw on it before flicking it away over the side. He climbed the ladder to the flight deck, careful not to knock the suppressor against the metal rungs, and joined Mateo.

"We make Barcelona later today," he said after glancing over his shoulder to see who it was climbing the ladder. He showed no reaction to Dan being in his full gear; it was a sight he'd seen plenty of

times before and had even played taxi to some of their more dangerous activities earlier that year.

"Valencia the morning after if we are having lucky. In two days
is your Gibraltar. Another two and we will be passing by the coast of
Galicia."

Dan thought he made hundreds of miles hugging the south coast
of mainland Europe sound easy. To him, a man who had spent his
life in coastal waters, it was.

To Dan, well, he nearly got everyone killed crossing the Channel
in summer.

"And after that?"

"After that we cross into deeper water for a day, then we find
France."

"Then we head into the Channel and get to the east coast," Dan
finished, sounding less certain than Mateo had done.

"Yes, then we follow our noses for the smell…"

Dan responded to the weak jab at the country of his birth with
all the aloof condescension he could learn from both Leah and Marie
combined by pointedly ignoring it. Mateo smirked, daring Dan to
bite back, but Dan decided that a few days spent at the controls with
Neil for company would be all the payback he would need.

"And we're good for fuel?" Dan asked, for about the tenth time
since Mateo had first mapped out their route.

"So long as your friend has fuel for us at the places, then yes. We
keep the speed only as fast as we need to, okay?"

Dan nodded. He'd had the long explanation from Neil which
he'd switched off part of his hearing to when it became overly technical just for the sake of it. Long story short, Mateo had tested their
yacht up the coast towards Marseille and back to find the optimum
cruising speed with fuel economy in mind. Dan had to agree that it

was better to turn up a day or two after they technically could have arrived if they made sure they didn't have to worry about a refuelling stop along the way. That didn't qualify as a plan in his mind, and would likely result in him making it back to Sanctuary on a rusty pedal bike in time for Leah's baby's first birthday.

Dan lapsed into silence, treating himself to another of his cigarettes and begrudgingly offering one to Mateo who he had seen smoking a pipe on occasion. He thought as he smoked, wondering if he should get a pipe too as it was far easier than rolling his own. He abandoned the thought as he wouldn't be able to get used to not having it between his fingers, and wasn't exactly in short supply of them.

Neil called out as he climbed the ladder, this time putting on an appallingly extravagant and, Dan had to admit, mildly racist stereotypical French accent.

"Permission to come on deck?" he drawled sleazily.

He didn't turn, but part of him expected the man to appear dressed as a mime wearing a beret with a string of onions around his neck and holding a stick of French bread like a firearm.

He didn't, luckily, although Dan couldn't quite shake the mental image. Dan did however have to stifle a smile, as Neil had obviously neglected to update his sizing in the tactical gear. His growing belly, a thing Neil was quick to show people he was proud of, strained at the black shirt he wore and threatened to expose a flash of pasty white skin at the midriff. The trousers were a little snug in the seat – something he was obviously conscious of as he tugged and fussed at the affected area in discomfort – and when combined with the weapons and vest Dan couldn't contain himself any longer. He cracked, laughing at the sight of his friend.

"What?" Neil challenged him with narrowing eyes. "Come on, get it off your chest." He leaned back, inviting Dan to give him his best with beckoning hands.

"We...we need to give you a callsign..." He sobbed through laughter he was still trying to hold back. He was sure it wasn't the wind in his face, but tears began to leak from his eyes with the effort of keeping it all inside.

"Wait, wait," he gasped, "I've got one..." He doubled over with laughter just as Mitch joined them and almost fell off the ladder as he fought the urge to point as he laughed.

"Meal..." he gasped, snorting involuntarily which made them all laugh harder. "Meal Team Six!" he wailed, clutching at his side.

"No, wait," Mitch squeaked. "How about *Ham*bo?"

Dan squealed, catching Neil's blank expression and knowing that he would crack eventually.

"Spets—" Dan stopped, cutting himself off with a hacking cough that he fought to control. When he could speak again his voice was hoarse. "Spet*snacks*!"

Mitch let out a roaring belly laugh in response and almost lost his footing a second time.

"Alright," Neil said. "You've had your fun." He tried to squeeze past them to descend the ladder and get changed, retaining his dignity as both Dan and Mitch still laughed when they got out of his way. Neil made everything infinitely worse when he swung his leg out first to spin and face the correct way for the ladder, filling the tiny silence with the pitch-perfect *kkkkrtch* of ripping material.

They were still laughing intermittently over an hour later. One would chuckle, either dreaming up another comment to deploy when the time came or simply recalling the incident, then the other would catch the hilarity like an infection and it would spread uncontrollably until both were collapsed in fits of laughter again.

Neil tutted loudly at them, decrying them as children whenever he passed their sniggering to bring Mateo food and drinks.

By late afternoon they had passed by Barcelona. Dan stared north over the railing on the aft deck, seeing nothing but a distant sprawl of dead and decaying buildings. He thought for a moment about how bad things would've been in the early days with so many people packed into the big cities. How any survivor would likely go out of their minds surrounded by so many dead.

His mind turned back to that time, and how they'd somehow all made a conscious decision never to go anywhere near the city. He knew it was the right call, especially given as the one time they got close to it they'd been attacked by a pack of dogs. He shivered at the memory, his back convulsing as the shudder ran down his spine.

"Cold?" Mitch asked from behind him, staggering towards the rail as an unexpected swell of water forced the deck to wobble. Reaching the railing he clamped his left hand on to it and tried to steady his right hand to bring the mug to his lips. He slurped loudly, adding a satisfied *aaah*, and turned to Dan wearing a light brown moustache of froth over his salt-and-pepper beard.

"Where'd you find hot chocolate?" Dan demanded jealously.

"In the kitchen. Great big tub of the stuff."

"Galley," Dan corrected him for no real reason. "And it must be out of date by now."

"Only by a year," Mitch countered evenly, as if the standards of whether something so rare was spoiled or not existed on a sliding scale instead of something absolute. "And so long as you break up the lumpy bits you'd never know."

Dan pulled a face that said he wasn't entirely convinced, but knew he'd probably try it anyway.

"We should be stopping in about three hours, Mateo reckons," he said to change the subject. "Stretch our legs and see if Ash has forgiven me yet."

He hadn't.

The precautionary vest had been removed somehow, and converted from a buoyant life saving device into a collection of small pieces of foam and red material. The spiteful destruction had been entirely expected, only Dan had no idea how he'd eaten his way out of it.

They'd anticipated Ash's dive for the lower decks as soon as he was onboard, and shut off all the rooms barring a bathroom which was an entire wet room and could be hosed down with the shower along with the occupant if the need arose.

Apart from one patch of drying vomit on his left flank, Ash was remarkably devoid of mess and bounded up the stairs before allowing Dan to help him down to the lower section of deck where he jumped into the water without a second's hesitation to swim the short distance to the shore from the mooring they were occupying.

Mateo had done well to find a private mooring large enough to accommodate them while being far removed from anything resembling civilisation. All around them, as they stood in alert readiness while Ash did his thing, they could sense the total absence of human presence in everything. The smells, the sounds, all were purely natural with none of the interference that people brought with them as they changed every environment to suit their comfort and needs.

Getting Ash back on the boat was far less simple than getting him off and simultaneously washing him, but it was achieved in time for them to head back out and reach the safety of deeper water as the sun was setting.

THE NIGHT SHIFT

Mateo had relocated to the interior equivalent of the flight deck after a break, and planned to continue their journey overnight at slower speeds. He argued against their protestations that he needed to rest, showing about as much ability to relinquish control of anything as Dan did.

The gentle progress of the night passed Dan by as he slipped off his vest and weapons, unlacing his boots and unbuckling the belt of his trousers before slumping down on one of the long couches in the main cabin. He never quite saw the point in going to bed like he was on dry land; it was like stripping off to sleep in a sleeping bag in the back of a car – something he'd done plenty of times – and he simply didn't waste time.

Neil had taken himself to bed, still complaining under his breath at how kind his friends had been to him about the clothing he'd forgotten to check still fit, leaving Mitch asleep in a corner somewhere and Jimmy still below where he'd been for most of the journey.

He was one of those people who had to lie down in the dark to be able to cope with the effect a moving body of water had on him, so when Dan was awoken by him running past to burst through the door onto the aft deck he slipped his feet into his boots and fastened his trousers before stepping outside.

The chill of the night air moving without any landscape to shape it and trap warmth made his skin prickle and tighten immediately,

134

making him consider for a moment going back inside for a jacket. He didn't, telling himself that he should endure a little discomfort early on in the journey as training. He reached instinctively into his leg pocket and patted it when he found it empty, tutting at himself as he remembered his tin of cigarettes was in the custom pouch on his vest.

"Have one of mine," Jimmy said, holding on to the railings for stability. In the low light Dan could see how pale he looked as his hand reached into his pocket to bring out a tin similar to Dan's with matches inside. He took the tin, cupping his hands and hunching over as he lit two and offered Jimmy one of his own. He grunted, shaking his head so Dan snubbed one out, made sure it was extinguished properly before putting it back in the tin.

"You doing okay?"

Jimmy grunted again, this time with a more affirmative inflection, before arching his back and expelling the contents of his stomach over the side. Dan waited patiently, saying nothing and blowing his smoke away from Jimmy in case the smell triggered another bout. Spitting to clear his mouth Jimmy stood, still clutching the railing, and looked directly at Dan.

"Yeah, actually," he said, sounding surprised. "Better for that," he added, gesturing at the darkness where he'd made a deposit. He took back his tin and lit one using a windproof lighter taken from his pocket Dan hadn't seen before. Jimmy noticed his interest and offered it to him.

"It's like a tiny little flamethrower," he said. "Pretty snazzy, eh?"

Dan was indeed impressed, and handed it back wishing he had one of his own. The two men stayed on deck enjoying a companionable silence for a while before Jimmy declared he was going to get some sleep if he could. Dan went to take more water to Ash who was

135

sleeping soundly, then went back up via the galley to make two cups of the out-of-date hot chocolate and carried them to the small internal bridge. He found Mateo reclined in the captain's chair with his feet on the instrument panel. He cleared his throat, hoping that their driver wasn't entirely asleep at the wheel.

"I am awake," Mateo answered the noise. "And the boat is set to the *automático*."

"Autopilot?" Dan asked. His understanding of French was good, even if his pronunciation was still set to the level of a Brit abroad. His Spanish was less so, even when the obvious words weren't jumping out at him, but Mateo's form of Spanish was so regional that Dan wasn't the only one struggling. He was Catalan, he said, as though that explained everything.

"Yes," Mateo told him. "We go in the straight line away from land so there is no danger. This will show me if we approach anything," he finished, tapping a lazy finger against a screen.

"Radar?" Dan guessed. "Expecting many other boats?"

Mateo shrugged. "It is possible, yes?"

"I suppose so," Dan allowed, lowering himself into another seat to find the leather cool and supportive. "We going to find somewhere to stop first thing?"

Mateo nodded slowly. As tough as he was, he knew he couldn't survive on no sleep. A few hours' rest would be enough for him, he promised.

"We have enough time," he assured their driver. "We can stop off for longer."

"I know this," Mateo answered. "But I would rather go fast and rest at the end." Dan accepted that, trusting him not to push it so far that he endangered their journey. He'd made it clear when he offered to get them there that he'd be staying on the boat to wait for them

136

to return, promising to defend their valuable asset and save them from having to find another way to get home.

Robbery, even though the world's population had decreased, was still a risk that had risen.

"At dawn, we will find somewhere to stop. There is too much of houses in places, so you should take the *bote de remos*," he said, miming the backward stroke of oars.

"I'm good with that," Dan said. He was, as usual, unphased by the sea's movement that so many land-based mammals found unnatural. "Just let me know if you need anything," he added, standing and draining the gritty sludge at the bottom of his cup to slurp in the processed sugar like it was an old-fashioned drug they no longer manufactured.

He found the others sitting at the round table in the main cabin, none of them seemingly able to sleep. Mitch had transformed, so much in that he had opened his eyes and sat upright where he'd recently been slouched and unconscious.

A deck of cards had appeared, dog-eared and stained from so many nights spent replacing anything with a screen and a connection. He'd personally re-lived a lot of his youth in the downtime he'd learned to enjoy, and taught himself how to play two new versions of solitaire on top of the few solo card games he knew.

Poker had become a thing, with one night a week seeing a table hosted in the town somewhere. Neil had obviously been at the heart of that as his beverages were in high demand for such activities. They'd tried to keep it from Dan when a game had got out of hand over an allegation of cheating, but the ruckus of a fist fight twenty yards from the spot on the ramparts he was walking along could hardly be missed and the resulting punishments spread the word far and wide.

"Thirteen-card gin rummy?" Jimmy offered him as he walked in.

"Why the fuck not?" Dan responded casually, unfastening one side of his vest to extricate himself of the entire rig, guns included, before flopping down into a seat and catching a glass that was slid over the polished wood towards him. It only held a small measure, what Neil would call a 'tactical' serving, and Dan's eyes responded to the fumes from the fierce apple brandy by watering as he lifted it to his mouth to take a sip. The cards were dealt and the four friends arranged their hands in silence before Jimmy, the dealer, looked at Dan expectantly as he was seated immediately to his left.

"We'd better have a conversation about what we might find when we get there," Dan said, dropping down the three of hearts from his hand of fourteen cards to begin the game.

"*If* we get there," Mitch said, his voice straining a little as he reached forwards to snatch up the card Dan had just laid. His look of glee rendered him unsuited to poker as he laid down a trio of threes to begin the point scoring. "Although it's not Captain Birdseye at the wheel this time, is it."

"Bollocks to you too, mate," Neil responded, ignoring Mitch's card and picking from the remainder of the deck. "I got us to the right side of the Channel, didn't I?"

"Eventually," Jimmy answered in a mumble, also lifting the top card from the deck before dropping the ten of diamonds and treating Dan to a look devoid of all emotion.

"Well we don't want any mishaps this time," Dan said as he pulled a face and pondered the ten even, though he never had any intention of lifting it. "I don't fancy an E&E from Normandy all the way back." He picked from the deck and put the card into his hand before taking it back out as though he'd kept it and turned to regard Mitch.

The Scotsman frowned, shuffling his cards around to pick up from the deck.

"A walk that far?" he said, unable to disguise the smirk on his face that told them he could barely contain the joke he was planning. "That's SAS in the Gulf War kind of distance. That's Bravo Two Zero…or…or…*Burger* Two Zero!" He burst out laughing pointing at Neil who did his best to appear bored with the taunts already even though Dan would bet good money on him having thought up better ones than Mitch had.

Dan jumped onboard anyway, throwing one off his own list in as it was on-trend.

"Yeah, actually mate you do look like one of them Bravo Two Zero blokes."

"Really?" Neil asked, still in a bored tone like he knew where it was going.

"Yeah, that Andy McRib guy…"

Mitch squealed like a set of rusted brakes as he erupted with laughter. Even Neil laughed until he managed to control himself and force the annoyed expression back onto his face.

"I'm spotting a theme," he said nonchalantly. "Still your turn, nobber," he told Mitch.

By the time the cards had got back around to Dan the laughter had died off save for the occasional snigger which threatened to catch as it had earlier.

Dan kept the five sevens in his hand, not laying them down the second he got them as he knew Mitch would, dropping another low value card to feed his eager friend scraps.

"Seriously though," he said, "we have no idea what we could be walking in to."

"So we treat it like everything else," Neil said simply, adding a shrug to appear more casual and not betray the fact that he'd lost a significant amount of sleep through worry. He'd also lost some weight, but he knew his audience well enough not to mention that. "We sneak in, see what's what, plan and deal accordingly."

Dan nodded sagely, letting the silence fill another three rounds and watching as the others laid down trios and short straights of various cards, arranging his own deck surreptitiously as he constantly gauged the right time to start making it rain. He kept back the cards he would be able to add to the displayed cards of the others, counting himself down to two to find a home for. He knew it was a gamble to play like that, but if he wasn't running the risk of losing money then he always opted to play big.

Unbeknown to him, Neil knew him well enough to recognise that was his strategy after the third round and kept a close eye on him for any sign that he was about to drop a couple of hundred points and end the hand. The game continued on in silence; none of them needed to fill the empty air with idle chatter.

"Funny you mention the Gulf, actually," Dan said, rearranging his cards and beginning to lay them on the table amid huffs and sounds of annoyance at what he had been holding. "Wasn't that Operation *Dessert* Storm?"

He stood, barely containing the smile that wanted to break out on his face as he was so pleased with his comedic timing. Dropping his last card face down on the deck as though it was a microphone, he picked up his vest and slipped back into it before heading back out on deck.

GUIDED TOUR

"That, my friend, is Galicia. It was a kingdom for many generations," Mateo said as he gestured to the coastline with the tip of his pipe.

"Portugal?" Dan asked, confused as to the geography.

"It borders Portugal," Mateo answered. "But is *españa*. Is like Catalan in some ways; they are their own peoples."

Dan grunted in answer. The days spent onboard had sapped all of them of their excitement and energy, and their few short forays to dry land had brought more anxiety than Dan expected.

Ever since their first stop at the abandoned pier, they had been forced to unstrap the small dinghy from the lower aft deck and row themselves ashore. Dan had learned the lesson and only put Ash in a life-vest for the boat journeys, and was glad he had as the dog had bailed out on every occasion as soon as he judged the lure of dry land to be within reach.

Each time the dog swam alongside their boat, shooting Dan looks of mixed annoyance and desperation as he grew heavier when his thick coat took on enough water to add significant weight to him. He shed that weight as soon as he hit land, showering anyone and anything inside a ten-metre radius and not giving the slightest hint of a shit about it.

Dan's anxiety at securing a new, unfamiliar place returned with reinforcements every time, and each time the fear intensified as though his anxiety's friends brought beer and pizza with them.

He recognised it for what it was: unfamiliarity with the responses of his body to the adrenaline. He'd only been out of action for a few short months, but he knew that the long periods of peace his people had enjoyed since the battle for their town had left him mentally soft as well as physically.

He still possessed the skills and the mindset, but it was as though the edge of his personal blade had dulled. Knowing this with all the self-awareness of a man highly critical of himself, he worked them all hard to secure their landing areas fast and slick.

Jimmy, being the opposite of warrior-minded on a cellular level, operated the oars as he trusted those more comfortable with their guns to do the necessary work. He carried a Glock with spare magazines and had a shotgun resting beside his feet, but the working parts of those weapons were simplistic when compared to Dan's short rifle with what looked to him like a lot of black gadgets stuck to it and a complicated sequence of movements required to make it work. Those movements, he knew from first-hand experience, Dan could do when concussed and exhausted but it just wasn't for him. His compromise, when the time came, was that he carried the shotgun when they went to places where they might need another gun. Dan watched him as he handled it, seeing the grim reluctance and the subtle way he wiped his palms on his clothing.

"Relax, mate," Dan told him. Jimmy looked up into his eyes and Dan could almost see the reflection of his memories. He'd killed someone with a similar weapon once. It was the desperate action of a man prepared to give his own life in the protection of others, and he would most certainly have paid that price had Leah not gunned down all of the man's accomplices.

Jimmy smiled back at him, passing off the feelings he got every time he picked up a gun as nothing.

Sitting on a low wall near a shallow bay in a part of what was Spain-but-not-Spain-bordering-Portugal, Dan tried to relax and force his hands to stop quivering. He was suffering, as many of them were, at the hands of peace.

Peacetime gave him too many hours to relive the things he'd seen; too long to consider the things he'd done; too long to torture his mind into finding a different way he could have done all of it until the faces of people no longer with them forced themselves into his mind and wouldn't go away.

He went over and over the incidents of his life, and the ones that bothered him the most were the ones from *before*, as if he could even change the things he'd done a week or a year ago.

In his existence before he'd taken one particular life, even if that fatal shot was honestly taken but horribly wrong in hindsight, he hadn't suffered with those memories. He'd shot at others in confusing engagements in war time and had probably killed more than one, but he'd only once in his *before* life seen someone die at his hands.

Hindsight wasn't something he could afford to entertain, as the bias it gave him always forced criticism like an avalanche of guilt and judgement.

Since then he'd killed more people than he could count. He huffed a dark chuckle at himself for even thinking that, as though it was so casually callous that he would hate to hear anyone say it of him. He'd tried, a few times in his tortured hours without television to blanche his brain, to recall the lives he'd taken since he'd proclaimed himself chief good guy and decided to protect the strays he so desperately tried to collect around him as though it validated his existence.

It was like the characters in books he'd read or movies he'd watched so closely stacking up the actual body count. He'd find such

143

a ridiculously high figure at the end that the character, if they were real, would probably never sleep again unless they were a pure sociopath.

He lost count well into double figures of the lives he'd taken, and the vast majority of those had been faceless nothings to him with only a few exceptions. Some of the killings held no remorse for him at all, but lots haunted him as his mind wormed the thought that they were just like his own people trying to survive in their own way.

How many Lexis, how many Joes and Pauls and Neils had he killed just because they were in his way? Who decided that his way was right? What made *him* right and the others wrong?

He wasn't *right*, he told himself in a growling voice in his head, he was *left*. If he hadn't been the one left alive when he had met those people, then he knew that other people – *his* people – wouldn't be. No amount of logic pushed those doubts aside, and he'd spent more than one night unable to take himself to bed beside Marie and in the same room as their baby boy because he felt too much of a darkness to his presence. It was as though he could infect their souls with the stink of death that followed him.

A branch cracked under the weight of a boot and Dan rose, spinning to bring the carbine up and sink down into a firing position startling Ash.

"Fuck sake, mate," Neil said, one hand on his chest and eyes wide with shock. Dan stood, the safety catch clicking back to safe as the carbine rested against his body.

"Sorry," he muttered. "I was daydreaming." Ash grumbled at him, as though the dog was either asking if he was okay, or possibly enquiring as to what the actual fuck he was playing at.

Or to ask for food, Dan couldn't be certain.

Realising that it couldn't have been anyone they didn't know because his dog was still the best early warning system on the planet, he felt doubly stupid for overreacting. Neil recognised the edginess in Dan for what it was and sat beside him with a groan of his bulk lowering and the effort it took to do so in a controlled manner.

"You need a little time to get your head back into this, don't you?"

"That obvious?" Dan asked.

"Not to everyone," Neil answered honestly. "But you need to know you aren't the only one sitting on a splinter, if you know what I mean."

"Is this the bit where you give me a pep talk?"

Neil's lip curled up in a grimace as he adopted a voice that wasn't a bad Snipes impression, from what Dan could recall, given that it had been years since he'd watched a screen.

"You better wake up," he snarled. "The world you live in is just a sugar-coated topping; there is another world beneath it, and if you want to survive that world you need to learn to pul—"

"I get it," Dan said, not unkindly but also not wanting the full film quoted to him. He stood, patting the man on the shoulder when a signature rumble issued from Ash's throat. Dan's gun was back up and ready to fire in a second; the safety was off and his right forefinger extended along the side of the trigger guard as naturally as breathing.

The growl undulated and paused as the dog sucked in a quick breath before the noise intensified and changed pitch. A glance down at Ash told Dan that the dog had turned his head to face a new direction, which good sense told him he had to take as multiple threats from different directions. Experience told him that ignoring the warning was a quick way to get dead.

145

"Back to the boat," he called out loudly. "Jimmy? Mitch? Sound off."

"Huh?" Jimmy yelled back, popping his head up from a dense bush further down the bay.

"Cut the cigar, Jimmy," Neil warned. "Something's up." Muttered curses answered the instruction as Jimmy scrambled to get himself together. Mitch arrived from their left, gun up ready because theirs were, but with a look of confusion on his face.

"What's up?" he asked, eyes scanning the overgrown landscape ahead until movement caught his eye. A scratching noise accompanied the blur, and was the same as the sound Ash's claws made on the deck of the boat.

The streak of sable brown fur morphed out of the higher ground as Dan realised they were looking at a wolf, easily the same size as Ash, standing on what had once been a car before nature decided to use it as an oversized plant pot, looking down at them with hungry interest.

Ash responded with a ripping snarl and a series of short, aggressive stamps with both front paws that would scare off just about anyone or anything. The wolf regarded them with interest still, canting its head to one side at the dog's display as though it found it...*cute*.

"Time to leave," Dan said, reaching down to take a firm hold on the vest his dog still wore. Ash probably believed that his owner was saving the other dogs from him, and if the two could talk then Dan would probably agree that was right, just to save from disappointing his four-legged friend.

"No argument from me," Mitch said. "Bastard thing's the size of a small cow." More movement flickered at the periphery, promising that the worryingly confident pack leader had more backup on hand than they did.

Jimmy was in the boat ready, pushing off from the sand and wading into the water up to his knees before falling over the side and getting control of the oars. They joined him, Dan dropping his gun to unceremoniously haul his dog up into their unpowered getaway vehicle, before they made slow progress away from the beach.

Twenty paces away, the rest of the pack showed themselves. All Ash's size or close enough, it made no difference. Dan counted twelve and shuddered at another close call his sidekick had averted.

"Where's that big Russian bugger when we need him, eh?" Mitch asked, feeling instantly like a piece of shit because their once-famous wolf killer had given his life defending them against another pack of hunters.

"You're a good boy," Dan said in a shameless baby voice as he gripped the dog with both hands by the fur on the side of his face. Ash's long tongue shot out to slap Dan in the face as punishment for getting close enough, but his owner didn't care in spite of the smell of his breath. "*Oozagoodboy?*" he asked again in the same voice rising an octave. Ash knew it was him, clearly, and couldn't understand why he was being asked such an obvious question.

"Yeah," Neil added, reaching over to hand something small and edible to the dog who hoovered it too fast to see, like it was their stash and the cops were watching. "You're a good boy."

That evening, as the sun set far over and behind their left side, Dan's hands shook again as he smoked alone on deck. He had run through the scenario again, cursing himself for staying too long. For not being alert. For not doing a recce further inland.

All of these scrapes with a potentially violent end were avoidable, but the only way anyone could know that was to view the with the bias of hindsight. It was a crippling thing to do, to second-guess every decision and action you've ever taken, but Dan's memories treated him to a whistle-stop tour of every bad thing he'd ever done and every mistake he'd ever made until he felt very undeserving of the people around him.

Dan spent the night tossing and turning on top of the narrow cot he'd tried to sleep on as these thoughts tumbled over in his mind like it was set on spin. For all of them it was spent heading north east from the tip of Spain and back into the waters they had already travelled in the nautical version of the stupid leading the blind so many years prior.

Dan watched the distant land to their left after they'd turned east into the English Channel, seeing his first glimpse of home since he'd been much younger – in terms of mileage – and had felt far more certain of himself than he did right then.

"Ah, good ole blighty," Neil crowed, returning to his go-to wing commander impersonation.

"Seven years," Dan said incredulously. "Seems stupid it's been so long, doesn't it?"

"Always a reason to put things off, isn't there?"

"Yeah, like family; all it takes to get everyone in the same place is a wedding."

"Or a funeral," Neil answered, saying the words Dan had left unspoken for a reason.

True to form, as soon as they came into sight of the south coast of England, the heavens opened and the rain welcomed them back.

KUMBAYA

They took their time, travelling east and hugging the south coast of England until the familiar white chalk cliffs came into sight late in the day. They seemed to glow in the low light of dusk, standing out from the bleak, empty coastline like a beacon.

The only beacons Dan knew about on the shoreline were lighthouses, and they were designed to keep people away. He couldn't shake his dark mood. He'd been falling deeper and deeper into his current funk from the moment they left home, and while it was a return to his old self in a way, he didn't like the feeling of living under the stress of permanent threat.

It was like living a life on the run from the authorities – never staying in one place for long and never relaxing as though he expected the front door to come off the hinges at any moment.

Looking out towards the coast, Mateo called down to him. Dan didn't hear what he said, but he followed the direction of his outstretched hand and saw the small bay Mateo had spied. Dan held up an upturned thumb, poking his head back inside to call the others.

"Fancy a night al fresco, do we?" Neil asked when he joined Dan and saw what was on offer. He looked at the sky, seeing a scarcity of clouds that experience taught him would mean a chilly if dry night. Skills like that had returned to him

"A night on dry land?" Mitch put in. "Sold!"

Mateo joined them, shutting down their boat's engines and taking an oar as the five men and a dog crammed into the small boat.

Mateo stepped onto shore first, turning to haul the boat up onto the sand and shale as Dan and Mitch fanned out left and right to secure the abandoned stretch of beach more out of habit than necessity. Ash, on wobbly legs, tried to flank Dan but struggled to keep up as he grew accustomed to the ground beneath his paws not moving too much.

"Tide's on the way out I reckon," Neil said as he helped to haul the boat up onto the beach.

"Is true," Mateo added, confirming his guess. "We will be dry to stay higher than here," he said, giving Dan a moment's pause as he translated the translation in his head.

Neil began arranging driftwood into a crude circle and digging into his pack for something no doubt weird and wonderful. Dan ran a brush through Ash's coat as he rested his backside on a cold rock. The dog grumbled at him in between panting whenever the brush teased a patch of fur that didn't want to give way, making Dan reassure him and be more gentle.

"You'll need a proper bath soon," he purred at his friend, "none of this sea water dip."

"What's that?" Neil asked, mistaking Dan's half-heard words for conversation.

"I said you'll need a proper bath soon," Dan told him, leaving out the fact that he'd been talking to Ash. Neil paused, sniffed at an armpit and made a face of uneasy assessment before shrugging and continuing with his task. That task was lighting a fire, and with the damp wood littering the beach all along the tide line there was no shortage of material…if he could get it to light.

For Neil, obviously, that was no problem. He dug a small pit in the gritty sand and lined the edge with stones the size of his fist before producing a tightly rolled ball of steel wire wool. Dan didn't look impressed by the trick as he'd seen and done it more times than he could count, but Neil performed his chore as though he was under the scrutiny of unforgiving talent show judges and added a typical Neil level of flamboyance to it.

He used his knife to shave a dryish piece of driftwood into splinters before producing an old rectangular nine-volt battery from a plastic bag and dabbing the open connectors onto the wool in various places. The fire took straight away, rippling over the steel wool and smouldering the edges of the wood splinters. A gust of wind flared it briefly before it died down, and Mitch offered his opinion.

"That won't catch like that. You'll need a—"

He stopped speaking and stepped back as the whole thing erupted into a sudden tower of flame that billowed upwards.

Eyes turned to see Neil with a can of lighter fluid, holding it with both hands in front of his crotch and whistling as he squirted the fire again with a side to side motion of his hips.

The onlookers were giving eye rolls and smiles in equal proportions, but regardless the fire caught and more wood was added until the flames were steady and the damp wood crackled and split in the heat.

"Keep it small though," Dan warned.

"Oh, Mister GrumpyPants," Neil chided him in a baby voice before dropping the impression. "You see any way onto this beach without falling fifty feet?"

"No, but that's not the point," Dan lectured back.

"Live a little," Neil told him. "*We're* the most frightening thing around here I'd wager."

Dan grunted as if to concede that he had at least part of a point but had made it badly as usual.

If Dan had reverted to the sullen, watchful form of himself then Neil had gone the other way and returned to the extroverted character who was the group's self-appointed morale officer. As if to prove a point, he produced a rustling plastic packet from his bag and made excited noises as he showed the others his stash.

"How far out of date are those?" Dan asked with a laugh as Neil tossed him the packet and searched for anything long enough to use as a roasting prong.

"Cham-allow gé-ant," Dan said, sounding out the French words to describe the oversized balls of sticky sugar. He turned over the packet and squinted at the small numbers printed on the plastic. "And less than a year out of date. Nice find!"

"Argh," Neil answered, doing his best Captain Barbosa, "the best before date's more what you'd call *guidelines* than actual rules…"

"Well this is nice," Jimmy said. "All we need now is for someone to whip out a guitar and start the songs."

As Dan suspected, the oversized marshmallows which had technically expired eight months prior were sticky and more hassle than they were worth in terms of calorie intake, but the process had lightened their collective mood. They ate, they drank from bottles of water until Neil passed around a large metal flask of something fiery that warmed their stomachs like Dan imagined an unstable chemical reaction would, and they laid out their roll mats to settle down after much removal of larger lumps of stone.

Forming a rough hexagon around the fire that now radiated pieces of wood like the spokes of a wheel, Ash spun three times before settling down on the mat laid out for him between the fire and Dan's sleeping spot.

"Never actually thought I'd make it back here," Jimmy said wistfully, lying on his back with his hands behind his head, staring up at the stars.

Mateo huffed in annoyance at the remark.

"I didn't mean your driving," Jimmy chuckled. "I meant…you know…I never thought there'd *be* a home to come back to."

Dan sucked in a breath and held it before letting it out through his nose. He shifted a hand down to his vest to retrieve his tin and lighter. The vest was devoid of the attached weapons bar the pistol, and kept on mainly for warmth and ease of access so that he didn't lose the precious means to feed his only real vice.

He blew a thin stream of smoke upwards, seeing the future in the small cloud as he could tell from the tone of Jimmy's voice how the trip would likely end for him.

The conversation died off as the fire burned down to leave the glowing chunks of charcoal keeping them warm as they slept.

Dawn brought with it the incessant screech of seagulls and a light, stinging rain that dropped Dan's mood instantly.

He could handle wet, he could handle cold and he could handle hungry but when any two of those things ganged up on him he suffered an immediate sense of humour failure. Making a noise he'd probably describe as chuntering as he policed up his gear, he sent Ash off after a small sub-committee of noisy birds that had landed nearby to start pressing in on their turf.

"Get'm!" Dan said, seeing Ash excitedly run a few steps towards the mob before turning to check that he was actually allowed as he spent most of his existence being told no when it came to chasing animals. Dan repeated his order, muttering darkly at the fleeing birds as they scattered from the lumbering dog who jumped and snapped at the tail feather of one, coming a lot closer than any of them expected…most of all Ash.

"Fucking shite hawks," Neil exclaimed disgustedly, drawing his knife to use the straight edge and scrape the white glob of oil deposit from the strap of his pack.

"Give that one a rifle," Mitch joked. "It's got a good aim!"

"It did get the biggest target here," Jimmy added quietly, prompting another round of laughs at Neil's expense.

"You keep laughing," Neil warned them. "When you need me to come rescue you like usual, I doubt you'll be taking the piss as much…"

THE WASH

Dan steadied himself against the large table in the main cabin with the others all sheltering from the rain. Mateo had returned to the internal bridge, forced from his preferred perch with the wind in his face by the miserable British weather.

The only one of them not to have complained about the rain was Mitch, but given that he was Scottish he goaded them all about what *real* rain was like.

The biggest surprise was Ash who, when they'd climbed back aboard the lower aft deck and secured the boat, hadn't bolted for the lower deck and instead helped himself to the comfortable long couch beside Neil who surreptitiously fed him something from a pocket.

Dan's focus was on the map which he was going over for the tenth time before taking it to Mateo and discussing the final leg of their seaward journey.

Folding it up and straightening, pausing as his lower back reminded him he'd hunched over for too long, he took himself and his map to the bridge with the most British of irrelevant commentaries.

"Right then," he said, for no real reason other than to announce he was about to do something not worthy of description, and earning the attention of Ash who shot upright to watch him leave, waiting for the order to follow.

They'd rounded the lower east corner of England, and Mateo muttered as he mentally calculated whether to head north-north-east into deeper water or to hug the coast.

"We may not make to land by the dark," he said, making Dan do that momentary pause as he rearranged the words as though he was talking to Yoda and not a Spanish fisherman. "It is you to choose?"

Dan shrugged. A night onboard was no hardship and, given their close call with the wildlife days before and the general feeling of crippling unease every time they stepped onto land in an unknown area, he'd prefer it from a tactical standpoint.

"Overnight on the water gets us to The Wash when?" he asked. To assist demonstrating his point he dropped a grubby fingertip onto their destination deep inside the sheltered bay on England's hip.

"By midday tomorrow." Mateo shrugged, making Dan guess he was leaving out a few 'what ifs'.

"That'll do me," Dan said, leaving to go and start the conversation about who was going to lose whatever bet he could come up with and cook their dinner.

The night, although unsettled enough to force Ash back into a state of seasickness, was uneventful. Dan couldn't shake a feeling of unease which seemed to have followed him back from their last trip ashore. He stayed on deck searching the darkening shoreline for lights or any other sign of life that he knew he'd treat as hostile until such time as they proved themselves otherwise, but was eventually forced inside by a combination of cold and a lack of cigarettes. He checked on Ash and crashed on the nearest bed to his snoring dog, waking a few hours later as a lurch of movement told him that something was different.

He rushed upstairs to find it was simply a shift in wind and current as they'd headed into the sheltered coastal waters.

"One hours," Mateo called down to him. He looked up to see the Spaniard wrapped in a thick winter coat that made him seem far bigger than his already gorilla-like stature.

Dan mumbled his thanks for the information, ducking back inside in search of caffeine which he was presented with as soon as he neared the galley. Neil thrust a cup in his direction, finding it filled with his personal brand of cocaine.

Strong, black coffee in one hand and a lit cigarette in the other from his fourth tin since setting off, he tucked the smoke between his lips and rested the cup down as he unzipped and watered their wake, taking care and balancing his need not to tip overboard against sprinkling his own clothing.

Resuming his nicotine and caffeine breakfast, he completed the trifecta with a few over-the-counter strength ibuprofen tablets reckoning that the three substances constituted a high percentage of his body some days.

As the details of the coast came in and out of focus through the intermittent mist, the large opening of a wide tributary revealed itself. The description of it, given sparsely through Morse code, made it obvious it was their destination while simultaneously failing to do it justice. This was the place called The Wash, he was sure of it, and that meant that they would see a seaside town just inside that tributary.

Instead of finding that, Dan's heart sank as his bile rose when two small boats started heading their way fast. Recent memories of skiffs filled with brutal pirates threatened to snap his fraught nerves.

"Mitch, Neil!" he yelled, tossing his coffee and leaning into the rail to bring the carbine up into his shoulder. Hissing a curse at himself he took his eye away from the optic and snapped the zoom portion of it into place before looking again, this time seeing the nearest boat containing two men huddled down against the stinging spray. He saw no weapons but that didn't fill him with any confidence they weren't unfriendly.

"I see them," Mitch called out from the upper deck. Dan glanced up to him, feeling reassured that the forty-mil grenade launcher slung under his barrel was pointed at them.

"One to port," Neil cried out, punctuating his warning with the obvious sound of a charging handle snapping back into place and chambering a round.

Dan didn't want to get into a firefight boat to boat – he'd been in that situation only too recently – but his nerves were ready to snap and the release of a fight would be just what he needed.

"Jimmy, get Ash below please?" Jimmy didn't answer him directly, just made a fuss of Ash and raised his voice in volume and pitch to encourage the dog to follow him. Dan put his eye back to the scope, taking a few annoying moments to locate the approaching boat bobbing in the swell.

The man in the front half was standing and waving his arms in the most unthreatening way. He cupped his hands around his mouth to yell but the words didn't reach Dan's ears at that distance.

"Guns up," he told his small force. "But yellow card rules," he said, telling them in the most succinct way they would all understand not to fire unless fired upon first, referencing the British army's rules of engagement.

"Friendly!" the distant voice yelled over the sound of three boat engines. "Friendly!"

Dan lowered his gun, holding up one hand in greeting but secure in the knowledge that Mitch could obliterate them in a second if they made a move. That was what came of working so closely with the same people for years; he knew Mitch's finger was on the forward trigger ready to send the boat down in a fireball.

"Who are you?" Dan shouted as they got close.

"My name's Luke," he shouted back. Dan took in every detail about him in a flash and assessed it all.

Male, early twenties, tall and lean with a shaved head that spoke of a do-it-yourself look. He was clearly accustomed to the chilly seaside life as he wore only a thin waterproof over trousers and boots. He was unarmed and bore no resemblance to any kind of soldier; not in his clothing, manner or bearing. Temporarily assigning him the label of being a civilian non-combatant – it still helped to put people in those brackets – he shouted back. The small boat slowed and turned to swing alongside them.

"Dan," he said. "Why the welcome committee?"

Luke's eyes lit up with a relief that threatened to bring tears to his face.

"Dan? Like, *Steve's* Dan?"

Dan had the sudden and irrelevant thought that he was Marie's Dan if he was anyone's, but the words stuck in his throat where they belonged.

"You know Steve?" he asked.

"Know him? Yeah! He…he said to keep an eye out for you in case you came."

"He's here?"

"He was," Luke answered, his expression turning again to one of fearful apprehension. "He told us to seal up the town and not let anyone in. There's been some trouble."

A thought hit Dan and his relaxed grip on the weapon tightened slightly.

"Describe Steve to me," he instructed the man. Luke seemed confused but answered anyway.

"Tallish, thin. Limps badly after a helicopter crash. Has a big scar on his forearm which he said he got at the same time as yours." A smile crept onto his face as Dan played ball and asked the next question.

"How did you recognise me?"

"He…" Luke hesitated in case he caused offence. "He said to look for an older version of PTSD Action Man with a stripe down his face."

DRY LAND

The Wash was basically a small fishing port which had been fortified, as so many small settlements had been.

Luke spoke fast, like he was nervous and excited at the same time, rapidly explaining that he'd been a kid when it all happened and was one of only two people there who had survived. The other was his uncle, who had spent the next months helping him get over what had happened as they went up and down the coast looking for other people. The two had become a few, and by the first winter there were over fifty people surviving on what the coastal waters could provide, which given the sudden decrease in people, turned out to be a plentiful bounty.

The town had been reformed, and by their third summer they'd made contact with other groups in the area. Some of them had joined The Wash, swelling their town so much that they had to extend and build, and others were happy to remain further inland.

The Wash became a major focal point for trade, and Luke led one of a few fishing fleets which fed more than themselves, and the fish was exchanged for vegetables as humanity began to re-establish itself into community.

"Uncle Dave," Luke said. "This is Dan, the one Ste—"

"Pleased to meet you, mate!" Uncle Dave said, beaming a genuine smile at Dan as he took his hand and pumped it rigorously. His smile was so warm, so sincere, that Dan found himself wishing that the man, who could only have been a handful of years older than him, was his uncle too. He was also a very tall man and lean, but the strength in his grip reminded Dan that overt bulk was in no way an indicator of power.

"Likewise," Dan mumbled, feeling some of his social awkwardness creep back in and force out a small portion of the foreboding anxiety from his active brain space. "Luke said Steve warned you to be on the lookout for us?"

"Yeah…yeah…" Dave said, eyes glazing as though he was replaying a memory in real time and unaware that he was making others wait for him. "He said you might be by some time. Said a lot, actually…"

"Like…?" Dan prompted, feeling like he should be annoyed with the man's vagueness but unable to bring himself to feel that way.

"What? Oh, yeah, he said we should shut the gates and not let anyone in or out unless we were sure we knew all of them."

"Did he say why?" Dan asked, drawing out the last word and worrying that he might come across as impatient.

"Yeah, some bad types about, you know? Come across any yourself?"

"Not recently," Dan said stiffly, leaving out the fact that he'd killed most 'bad types' he'd encountered over the years, and some days he wondered which category he fell into.

"Well there's enough about now," Dave told him, gesturing them inside a building and stopping when Ash tottered forwards on uncertain legs as he shot furtive glances at all the new people he wasn't sure about just yet. They were either food givers or people to be bitten, and he hadn't been told which yet so he stayed by Dan's side.

"Hello puppy!" Dave exclaimed, bending down stiffly and reaching out to the dog.

"I wouldn't," Dan warned, "he's not a pe—" He stopped, seeing his dog make a total fool of him as Ash slunk towards the kindly man and flopped onto his side with his tongue falling out of his mouth like a goon. Dave fussed the dog for a few moments, crooning baby noises at him until Dan snapped his fingers.

"Oi. Enough of that," he muttered to Ash, who at least had the decency to look embarrassed for a heartbeat.

"Drinks," Dave declared, making a statement and not asking a question as he led them inside. No mention was made of them still wearing their weapons, and Dan looked around to see that none of the people gathered were overtly armed. Dave saw his glances and proved that he possessed a more shrewd mind than his manner suggested.

"We've got guns," he said, "more since Steve gave us some and the people to show us how they worked. They're either on the gates where they're needed or locked away."

"Not much use locked away," Dan muttered, wishing he could take back the words as he was criticising how another person ran their own enclave. Dave took no offence and shrugged the comment away.

"More dangerous to me in my hands than locked away," he said, still wearing the same wide smile to show he felt no disrespect at Dan's words. "Never shot one and wouldn't know where to start!"

Dan respected his honesty and allowed himself to be swept along to where Dave started pouring hot water into mugs himself instead of asking someone else to do it for him. He liked the man instantly, and knew that Steve would have had the same impression of him.

"So," Dan said, "you've had trouble?"

"How do you take it?" Dave asked, holding up a battered tin of instant coffee and a stained teaspoon.

"Black, no sugar," Dan answered on autopilot.

Dave nodded and turned to the others, getting the differing responses from Mitch and Jimmy. Neil, being awkward, asked if they had any Earl Grey, which backfired on him because it turned out they had.

"Yes, well *we* haven't, had trouble that is, not as such, but we haven't had our trade people come back for two weeks which hasn't happened before. Some people want to go looking for them, but when Steve turned up with some of his boys and girls he said not to go out or let anyone in and he'd look for them."

"And when was that?" Neil asked.

"Nine days ago."

"Ten," corrected Luke.

"Can you show us a map?" Dan asked him, sipping the drink and finding it at the perfect temperature to take a large gulp to supercharge his brain power.

Dave did.

He took them to a room with short-range maritime radio sets and maps of the coastal region as well as the inland area which was adorned with pins and notes. The soldier in Dan cringed, looking at the treasure trove of actionable intelligence on offer if anyone ever took the town by force.

"This is us," Dave said as he tapped a finger at the large inlet where their fresh water ran into the sea. "This is Sue's place," he said indicating an area roughly fifteen or twenty miles directly inland on the river. "She does fruit and veg and eggs. Steve was heading there after he left here."

"And this one?" Dan asked, pointing at another marked area to the west.

"That's Steve's lot," Dave said. "Big convoy moved in years ago and a few months later they had some fireworks." He chuckled as if recalling Steve's account of the bloody coup he led. "*Change in management*, Steve called it." Dave shrugged and smiled as if to say that such things weren't his concern, but Dan had already got the measure of him and knew that he knew and cared more than he let on. He pointed to another place beside the wide river.

"Can't go much further than here," he said as he pointed to a spot between the two settlements where a road intersected the snaking blue line depicting the watercourse. "Big, low bridge there stopping anything tall, mind you the draught isn't deep enough to take anything like your footballer's yacht."

"Ha," Mitch laughed, "you should've seen our old one."

"Why? What happened to it?"

"Twice the size," Neil bragged. "A Sunseeker. We blew it up in Belgium because someone wanted to take it."

Dave stared at him for a moment before the smile widened and kept on going until he started to chuckle again and shake his head.

"Steve said you lot were batshit," he chortled. "He was right."

Dan smiled, sipped his coffee which was bitter and metallic and, he guessed, as past it's sell-by date as their French marshmallows had been. He'd drunk worse, he told himself, even *before*.

"Like I said," Dave went on. "Your boat won't go down there, but we can lend you one of ours. We'll have to keep yours as a security deposit, obviously…"

"You'll have a job," Neil said with evident amusement. "There's a big Spaniard on board and he isn't known for sharing."

"I was joking, obviously," Dave said, sounding a little disappointed in Neil. "Your mate's welcome to stay here or out on the

165

boat if he prefers. Just let him know he's welcome here. We'll bring out some stuff for him if he wants to stay, it's up to him."

Dan nodded his thanks, silently indicating that he would pass on the offer.

"You want to rest up the night first?" Dave offered.

"Something tells me we need to get moving," Dan said quietly, giving voice to the ominous feeling he had in his stomach. "I don't have a great feeling about what's going on."

"Me neither," Dave muttered, as he made a show of adjusting his chair so he could lean closer to Dan's ear.

PAYING THE PRICE

True to his word, Dave's people produced a wide, low-hulled boat with a tiny outboard motor clamped to the stern. It was little more than a wide skip according to Dan, who was careful to be well beyond earshot before making the comment, but Neil told him not to be ungrateful.

Mateo had stayed onboard their boat in the protected waters of the bay, electing to keep to himself for as long as he needed to until they returned. They hadn't discussed what he should do if they didn't, mostly because Dan couldn't bring himself to consider the implications to all those people he'd be leaving behind.

Carrying only a single pack each with the kit they'd need the four men were overloaded as it was, and still Mitch complained that he hadn't brought enough with him.

"What else do you need?" Neil asked him from his position at the tiller, eyes wide at the size of what he still called his Bergen, which he lay over at the prow of their tin tub using it as a firing position. Mitch's shoulders shrugged once before he gave his answer in a low voice.

"Explosives," he said, as though the simple wish list was a normal thing. Dan said nothing. That was partly because he agreed with Mitch and partly because he'd hated explosives even before a detonation had gone off in his face and atomised a man he'd once called a friend.

Ash, freed from the rolling motion of the sea, had regained most of his normal attitude despite still being on the water and sat beside Dan scanning the overgrown edges of the river.

Their watery road was wide and calm, but the encroaching trees and greenery hanging low over both banks narrowed their route to the very centre of the river a few times and twice they had to carefully steer around partly submerged obstacles. One of these was a car, slowly rusting away to nothing.

"How the hell did a car get in here?" Jimmy asked.

"Same way that did, probably," Dan answered, pointing into the water at the unmistakable shape of a shopping trolley shimmering just below the murky surface.

"Some people just don't need their pound coin back," Neil intoned in an upper-class voice dripping with disdain for the classes. "If you could all afford to shop at Waitrose, I'm sure you'd understand."

"I shopped in Waitrose once," Dan said absent-mindedly. "Same stuff as the regular shops just with fancy packaging."

"And double the price," Jimmy added.

"It's all about not rubbing shoulders with the riff-raff," Neil carried on in the same voice, making Dan conjure the image of a woman in her early fifties with enough cash in her bank account to think she was born twenty years later than she was.

"Speaking as a member of said riff-raff," Dan answered, "you can stick your quid where the su—"

"Heads up," Mitch snapped from the prow, silencing their fun. Dan crouched, weapon swinging up to face their front and scanning the right-side bank.

"What you got?"

"Trees ahead cut back from a mooring," he said.

"This'll be Sue's place then," Neil said as he cut the weak throttle and coasted their skip onwards.

"Steer us in," Dan told him. "Mitch on me, you two stay on the boat with guns up. Watch the opposite bank too."

As soon as their boat glided silently to bump against the wooden jetty Dan rose and stepped onto the damp wood, almost slipping but regaining his composure as Ash hopped lithely to his side. Neil threw a short loop of old rope around the raised pole and hauled on it to arrest their drift so Mitch could climb out. He stood behind Dan and slapped him twice on the shoulder before both men set off towards the buildings nestled in the tree line.

Dan went forwards with Ash pressed into his left calf muscle waiting for an instruction, his legs bent slightly and his carbine pointing everywhere his eyes looked. Although it had only been a few months since he'd moved like that, his body nagged at him for the effort it was exerting. He ignored it, pressing forwards until the slippery jetty reached concrete steps leading upwards.

Dan went up, knowing that Mitch would be waiting at the foot of the steps covering him, and he stepped slower, so he didn't trip over Ash as he went.

He waited at the top, stepping left to clear the stairs and kneeling to provide cover and rest his legs for a few seconds. Mitch joined him, stepping to the right with his larger, longer weapon raised and scanning.

"On me," Dan whispered. "Moving."

He went left, meaning to circle the settlement if indeed it was one, but he was sure that people still lived there otherwise the phenomenon of self-trimming trees would need to be explained or else he wouldn't sleep.

His other senses came into play and he detected the smell of wet charcoal as though a fire had been put out by the rain. That wasn't a smell he'd have recognised instantly in his *before* life, but now that an open fire was, for many people, their only source of clean water, heat and cooking it was more common.

He glanced down at Ash, seeing the dog's look of concentration fixed ahead where his far superior sense of smell would have picked something up long before the humans did.

He stopped, not needing to use a hand signal as Mitch was one of the most experienced people at this kind of work still alive, and jerked his head forwards with eye contact from Ash. The dog went, body low and nose hoovering the wet ground like he was following an invisible length of string. Dan didn't panic when he went out of sight but carried on slowly stepping around the left side of the buildings until another smell hit him.

It was a greenhouse. A smell that brought back an image of the gardens at their old home after the warm interior contents had been freshly watered.

A few more steps revealed a partially obscured sign telling him that the place they were circling had been a garden centre and coffee shop back in the world. That made sense, he thought, if Sue and her people were producing vegetables then this was likely the best place around to be doing it.

A single low bark from Ash sounded ahead. Dan kept his nerve and followed cautiously, knowing that the dog wouldn't have made a sound unless he'd detected something which he'd been trained to label as a threat he shouldn't attempt to nullify; that usually meant a knife or other weapon, which Dan would always look to counter with high-velocity ammunition in multiples unless the person holding it gave up.

"Stay back," a wavering voice cried out from the shadowed side of the main building. Dan couldn't see them but he froze anyway, figuring that they probably saw him.

"We're not here to hurt anyone," he said gently. "Dave sent us down from The Wash to check on you. We're friends of Steve's."

"Prove it!" the voice demanded, hint of tearful desperation in the words.

"How can I?" he asked back, lowering his weapon into a ready position from the firing position and standing taller; to an untrained onlooker it would appear that he'd come out of fighting mode entirely when he'd simply taken it down a single notch, and that scale slid upwards fast when he needed it to.

"I…I don't know…"

"We're not going to hurt anyone," Dan said, chiding himself for knowing his words weren't entirely accurate as he was more than prepared to hurt anyone who wasn't playing by the rules. "What happened here?"

"You know what happened," the voice spat back, tears choking the words this time. "You're with *them*, aren't you?"

"Listen, I don't know who *they* are. Like I said, we've come from The Wash an—"

"Yeah, you said. You dropped Dave's and Steve's names to make it sound like you know us. But here's the thing – we don't know *you.*"

Ash growled and backpedalled two paces towards Dan as noises from the trees to their left sounded. Dan wasn't concerned about that, as any attempt to flank him would be met with an angry ball of teeth, fur and muscle as well as Mitch who, he knew from their long hours spent working together, was already outflanking the flanking manoeuvre.

"Enough of this," Dan said. "We're not here to cause trouble. We're looking for Steve."

Silence answered him, as though the chosen negotiator didn't have a plan past accusing him of being an arsehole and hoping he'd simply admit it.

"Steve…Steve hasn't been here for three days," the voice answered.

"Where did he go?"

"They crossed the river," was all the answer he got, as though it would mean something to him. "And they haven't come back."

"So why are you so frightened?" Dan asked, wanting to move the blind conversation along. "Sack that," he said as he stepped forwards, "I'm coming out and I'd appreciate not being shot at."

He did, stepping into the open area which bore faded white lines painted beneath the wet leaves under his boots. As the front entrance of the compound came into view, he saw the burned remnants of two lengths of wood nailed together at right angles. His mind jumped to any feasible conclusion as to why they'd be burning crosses there, but the people he saw – red rings around their eyes and muddy shovels in their hands – told him what conclusion to jump to.

He was looking at two people, two civilian non-combatants, who had been digging graves.

His reaction gave him away as being innocent of the crimes and unaware of the horrors that had been visited on these people. He called Ash to his side and dropped his weapon on its sling to walk forwards and demand to know what had happened.

"They came two nights ago," a woman said as she stepped into sight from the building. She was stocky with thick arms, but a face that bore wide eyes over pronounced cheekbones lent her an appearance of being strong and kind.

"Two of ours had gone missing and we were worried about them, but we thought they'd run away to The Wash or somewhere else. We woke up to find them…" Her head sagged, and she took long, controlled breaths. Dan guessed the tears she was fighting back had less to do with fear and sadness than they did at an angry, impotent rage at the bastards who had done it. He could tell from the shape of the burned beams and the horrified look of shock on the faces of everyone he saw that their people had been crucified and burned.

"The screams," the woman said, unable to finish the sentence.

Crucified and burned alive, Dan noted. He was already looking forward to catching up with the new people in town and educating them.

"And Steve?" Dan asked. "Where did he go?"

"Over the river," she said just as unhelpfully as the last time he'd heard the words. "They've set up a roadblock at the bridge."

"Who has, Steve?"

"No, *them.*"

"Oh. In that case that's where we're heading," he told her. "Can you get your people to The Wash?"

She nodded, seemingly already having given that instruction as people were gathering and holding belongings in preparation of a long walk.

"I'd offer you our boat, only…"

"Only you need it," she finished for him.

"What's the fastest way to get to Steve's place?" he asked. The look she gave him spoke volumes.

"The bridge. Tell me one thing?" Dan asked her, changing the subject. "Why did they do this to your people?"

She shrugged, pulling a face that seemed to dismiss the cruellest darkness of human nature as though it was an inevitability.

"Because we wouldn't let them in to take what we have," she said. "So this was the price we paid."

THE BALROG

Neil whistled as he chugged his little boat downriver, rounding a bend and straightening up. Jimmy sat at the prow, happily smoking a cigarette as though he didn't have a care in the world, and between them was a large mound of things covered with an old, threadbare tarpaulin.

They approached the bridge with its low lattice work of interlocking steel beams spanning the river in an area suspiciously devoid of foliage. Neil stopped whistling and cut the engine to drift towards it as though his happy day was suddenly interrupted by the appearance of the obstacle. Before he could assess whether their boat would slide underneath unhindered, a challenge rang out from ahead of them.

"Hello," the voice called, carrying no sense of greeting at all. The single word was tinged with such malice, such cruel anticipation of what the speaker expected to follow, that Neil blanched.

"Err, 'ello?" he answered.

Jimmy sat up, looking around startled for the source of their interruption. Three men appeared at the edge of the bridge; all were armed, bearded, and wearing a semblance of military uniform which made them appear like some partisan paramilitary force with no legitimacy whatsoever.

"What's in the boat?" the man in the centre asked. His question was asked innocently enough, even sounded friendly and conversational in a way, but the tension ramped up like he'd dropped two gears ready for an overtake on a risky road.

Neil, playing his part like it was the audition of his life as he always did, glanced nervously at the covered mound and visibly swallowed.

"What?" he asked, stalling for time until they were closer.

"I said, you fat fuck, what's in the boat?"

"No need for name calling," Neil responded peevishly, sounding hurt by the insult and probably not faking it too much. He stared up at the man who stared right back at him wearing an expectant look. Neil huffed a sigh and waved a hand at his haul.

"It's our stuff, what's it got to do with you? Where's Leonardo?" he asked, making up a name on the spot and, being Neil, coming up with something outrageously uncommon.

The man shifted uneasily like he wanted to change the subject, telling Neil that the trio facing them down had replaced the people he suspected had been there with more peaceful intent.

"Leonardo's gone somewhere else," came the uncertain reply as the speaker gathered a little confidence and continued, "this is a toll bridge now, so you'll need to show me what's in the boat."

"Yeah," laughed another one of them like a moron, "he went with Donatello to see Splinter."

"Toll bridge?" Neil exploded, ignoring the joke he was secretly impressed by, huffing and looking left and right as though searching for a non-existent audience to share in his incredulity. "Since when? I think I need to speak to your supervisor." He folded his arms and sat back in the small boat, just floating slowly back the way he'd come from. In the few seconds it took for all three of them to process his words and start laughing, Neil contemplated his missed calling in life and wished he'd had the opportunity to become the great actor he knew he was deep down.

He'd seen enough disgruntled housewives tapping their foot waiting for the duty manager half their age to arrive and deal with their obnoxious complaints to break into that character with ease. His body language exuded the sentiment that he wasn't going any-where until he spoke to someone more senior.

As if sensing that, the speaker of the bridge crew decided to skip the middleman of entertainment and move directly to the conclu-sion. He raised his rifle at Neil, waiting for the look of shock to de-scend on him, and when it didn't happen, he switched his aim to the thinner man sitting very quietly in the boat and started counting.

"One," he barked, sounding for all the world as if he was having a standoff with a toddler who was refusing to get in the car because they didn't want to be wearing shoes.

"Two!"

"Thr—"

"*Okay!*" Neil yelled, arms unfolding and flapping at him as though his nerve broke. It hadn't, he'd just wasted as much time as he could for the other pieces of their game to fall into place. "You want to see what's in the boat? Fine. Here!" He leaned over, grasped one corner of the battered plastic sheet, and whipped it hard to one side.

~

Before the bend in the river Dan pointed out an accessible patch of riverbank where he could scramble ashore before using his free hand to haul the dog after him. Ash, despite the assist, dipped his entire back end in the cold water and dragged himself past Dan to shake violently before he could take cover.

Dan, his face dripping with dirty river water, didn't utter a word as he was in full stalking mode, crouching beside the riverbank as Mitch was deposited on the far bank. The two men made eye contact and exchanged a nod, going to work as Neil counted down the twenty minutes they'd agreed on.

Dan moved slowly, cautious not to disturb the overgrown bushes and create noise and movement to betray his approach. Ash skulked behind him, crouching low to the ground as he always did when he recognised it was time to work, and after a few minutes he located a meandering animal track created by something tall enough that meant moving was twice as fast and twice as easy.

He trusted Mitch to make his own way, and if anything, he knew that the former infantryman was probably more experienced and adept at this kind of warfare than he had been.

Twenty minutes was a short time to cover even a small distance stealthily when every branch or thorn could snag on his clothing and equipment to give him away. If the people he guessed were watching the road and the river from the bridge that should be just up ahead of them saw him approaching, then the whole plan was shot to shit before it even began.

He settled into place ten full strides from the edge of the foliage where the road intersected the water at a right angle. Dan could make out the unnatural straight edges of the bridge through the trees, and when he settled down to breathe and lower his heartrate, he began to hear noises to indicate the position was occupied.

A series of tiny, muted clicks came from behind him, muffled by the dog's closed mouth as Ash issued the most silent warning he could manage. Dan reached his left hand back slowly to touch his big muzzle and reassure him that he knew there were people there, and he waited for the show to start.

Raised voices came from ahead and to his right where the bridge spanned the river, and he heard the tone of Neil's responses which brought a smile to his face at how much his friend enjoyed a good charade. He wiped the smirk away and set his expression back to one of ruthless resolve as the consequences of their game were very real to all of them.

He could make out three shapes on the bridge, and while he couldn't see them clearly, he could tell from the way they stood and held themselves that they were carrying weapons. He couldn't say for certain, but it was better to err on the side of caution and assume they were armed.

The reason he didn't want to engage them as a complete unit from the boat was simple and twofold; the river wasn't easy to run through and find cover, and he doubted all of the bridge's defenders would walk into a single killing ground to make his life any easier.

He crept forwards until he was at the threshold of wild bushes and pitted roadway, glancing right to where the verbal exchange was happening. Looking forwards he saw the only building nearby that wasn't overgrown and obviously disused, so he timed his movement for when Neil raised his voice to answer the first shout and slipped low over the road to take cover beside the open door and listen.

He heard nothing from inside so risked a glance, seeing and smelling an arrayed mess of sleeping bags and other detritus left behind by undisciplined people on guard duty.

He did a full circuit of the small building to be certain, and just as Ash growled to warn him of an approaching sound or smell a man rounded the corner and stopped face to face with him.

The two men froze.

Ash crouched, paused ready for the short leap and savage takedown should he be given the word. Dan's weapon was up in his shoulder and pointed directly at the man's face, and in turn the surprised sentry was staring into the fat end of the carbine's suppressor. His eyes stayed wide as his body reacted without consulting his brain first. He sucked in a gasp of breath as his lips began to form the start of the word he never uttered because Dan stabbed the end of his weapon straight outwards to jab it cruelly into the man's windpipe.

Both hands went to his throat, his face went instantly red and his eyes bulged impossibly large. Unable to make a sound other than the wet, rasping noise brought on by the spasming muscles in his neck, his legs gave out and he dropped to his knees still clutching his throat, making it easy for Dan to lower the gun and cup his left hand against the man's right ear.

Slamming his skull into the side of the wall with a muffled crack the man slumped backwards like a drunk and stayed down. Dan whipped the gun back up and scanned quickly, taking forced breaths in and out through pursed lips as he fought to control his pulse so he could react more cognitively to anything else that decided to jump out on him.

No more threats appeared. Nobody reacted to the small noises the silent and brutal takedown had made. Ash sniffed at the unconscious man, glancing up at Dan before cocking his leg and squeezing out a sprinkle onto their victim's right sleeve.

If he hadn't been under such intense stress Dan would've burst out laughing at Ash's unsportsmanlike conduct. He satisfied himself with a disapproving look and a slow, disappointed shake of his head which the dog totally ignored.

"Fine," Neil's voice roared from the direction of the bridge. "Here!"

Dan waited, creeping to the edge of the building to peer around and finding himself with line of sight on two of the ambushers.

"There was four of them," the one in the middle of the bridge said. "They said there was fucking *four* of them and a dog!" He raised his gun, pointing it down at the river which sealed his fate. Dan squeezed off four rounds into his back, his shots climbing higher as he went with the recoil. He didn't know if the man was wearing any kind of body armour but at that range the ballistic impacts of the five-five-six rounds drilling into him were sufficient to throw off his aim at the very least.

He went down, strings cut, and Dan lined up on the other man in his sight trusting that Mitch would have the third one covered.

He spun, looked at his dead leader, then looked back towards Dan as the colour drained from his face. Boots scrabbled on the loose grit of the road's degraded surface from out of sight on his left, telling him before he could phrase the words that the third man was running for his life.

Directly into the path of a Scottish soldier with as much of a penchant for violence as Dan possessed.

A crack of metal on flesh and bone echoed along the bridge as Dan emerged from cover to advance on the confused man.

"Get on the fucking floor!" Dan bawled, unconsciously adding words he hadn't used in years as though some hidden memory had been unearthed. "Armed police; get fucking down!"

The man in Dan's sights dropped his weapon and put his hands up before processing what he'd been told to do and dropped flat to his front and pushed himself away from his abandoned weapon like it was contagious.

"I wouldn't, pal," Mitch's stern warning came from Dan's left, forcing him to glance up to see his friend pointing his big rifle at a man sat on his backside holding a nose pouring with blood from the rifle butt clothesline he'd run straight into.

Dan returned his attention to the man he'd forced to the ground through sheer terror and the ridiculous fear of being arrested at gunpoint, dropping the carbine on the sling and drawing the pistol from his chest to drop a knee painfully into his back and search his pockets.

"Roll on your back," he ordered as he stood and stepped back, keeping the pistol aimed at his head. "Keep your hands above your head." His actions and his words were fast, clear and forceful; all deliberate to keep his subject subdued and in fear.

The man complied perfectly to reveal the front of his body which Dan checked for weapons, finding none and ordering him back onto his front where he whipped out a prepared set of black cable ties looped loosely together. He slipped one over each hand and yanked them tight, hearing the man hiss in pain as the plastic ratcheted onto his skin. He added another around his boots and snapped his fingers for Ash's attention. He pointed to the man's face and told Ash almost sweetly to watch him.

Ash, enjoying his role as much as Neil did, stalked slowly forwards to treat the detained prisoner to a full display of large teeth by peeling back his lips to issue a low, lazy snarl.

Neil had steered the boat to the bank by the bridge and tied it off. Climbing out amid a string of muttered curses, he clambered up the muddy slope to the bridge and walked to the unmoving man who had caught Dan's bullets.

Glancing left to where Mitch was trussing up his prize and right to where a man cried softly under the caring and watchful gaze of Ash, he stood overlooking the river and cleared his throat, wearing a grin which Dan recognised as the one when he'd already found the joke he was about to make hilarious.

"Yooooou," he intoned loudly, "shall not paaaass!"

ENHANCED INTERROGATION

"Alright, big man?" Neil asked in a conversational tone to the bound and gagged prisoner whose nose had now stopped bleeding. The man glared back at him with murderous intent, which made Neil chuckle.

"You say Big Mac?" Mitch asked him as he walked past.

"What? No! I said big *man*."

"Oh, my mistake," Mitch snickered.

"Okay," Dan said as he hauled a bucket of river water to the roadway and looked down at their two detainees. "Normally I'd take my time and work up some kind of rapport before we chat. You know, establish a baseline and build trust before I start asking questions, but honestly, I ain't got the fucking time. So, who wants to go first?"

Broken Nose glared at Blubbering Man, his eyes promising violence if he talked. Blubbering Man started to blubber louder, making Broken Nose turn his death stare on Dan.

"Ladies and gents," Neil said flamboyantly, "we have a volunteer…"

He grabbed Broken Nose's ankles and pulled, making him buck and twist against the force he was powerless to resist. Dan took a blanket from their hovel and dropped it on his face where Mitch and Neil both put a boot on either side.

"Hold your breath," Mitch muttered to him. "It makes this easier for us."

Dan lifted the bucket and began to pour, spilling some over the sides before he'd achieved a steady flow onto the covered face.

It was cruel, he knew that, and it was inhumane. He also knew that torturing innocent people by nailing them to crosses and setting them alight to burn to death in agony and terror was wrong, so he quickly made peace with his own actions.

On balance, with all things considered, Dan decided he was okay with waterboarding this piece of shit.

He said nothing, simply put down the empty bucket and picked up the second one before repeating the process. He liked to follow a pattern when it came to questioning bad people in a hurry, and that pattern was to establish in their minds from the outset that it wasn't going to stop; the fear and pain was going to continue without reprieves where questions were asked and resisted or ignored.

He carried the two empty buckets back to the water to fill them, passing Jimmy on the way who was intentionally staying apart from what was happening on the bridge. Dan didn't judge him, and he didn't blame him either. This wasn't his thing at all.

Broken Nose was still gasping and spluttering when Dan returned and started to pour a third bucket without saying a word. He added the fourth before Blubbering Man broke.

"I'll tell you anything," he wailed. "Please don't…"

"What's he to you?" Dan asked calmly, indicating the man writhing on the roadway covered in cold river water.

"What? Nothing. I don't care about him, just…just don't do that to me!"

Dan looked at Mitch who wore an expression that was as shocked and amused as his own was.

"What a fucking fanny," Neil muttered disappointedly. "Come on then, twatbadger. Tell us everything."

"Wh…what do you want to know?"

"Start with your name?"

"People…people call me Woz."

"Alright, *Woz*," Dan said. "Let's start with the location of Shergar, the real identity of Jack the Ripper and who *actually* shot Kennedy. And none of your conspiracy theory bullshit."

Woz looked confused, making Dan feel annoyed.

"How many of you are there, what are your orders, who's in charge…everything. Tell me *absolutely* everything or I'll dangle you upside down in the river so your neck's only just out of the water and leave you there."

Even Mitch recoiled slightly at that threat but said nothing. Dan kept his face a stony mask in case he betrayed that he'd actually upset himself with that one.

"*Nasty* pasty," Neil whispered, making Dan fight the urge to laugh. Letting out a chuckle after threatening a horrible death might paint him in a less controlled light than he'd like, plus he knew that both him and Neil laughed under stress.

"There's four of us," Woz answered, glancing at their evident spokesperson who was still lying crumpled in the position he'd fallen in.

"I don't mean here," Dan said with feigned patience. "I mean in total."

"Oh, maybe fifty?"

"Okay, who's in charge of your maybe fifty mates?"

"A guy called Mo."

Dan rubbed an annoyed, exhausted palm over his face and let out a sigh.

"You ever heard the term 'pulling teeth'?" he asked.

Woz's eyes flickered over Dan's shoulder and he quailed, trying to wriggle away without any success as he begged.

"No, God please no!"

Dan glanced behind him to see Neil innocently admiring a set of pliers he'd produced from a pocket for no apparent reason.

"Even for you, that's a low blow," Dan said chidingly. Neil looked aghast at the tool in his hands and pulled a face so innocent that even he didn't believe it himself.

Dan turned back and slapped his willing interviewee around the face to focus him.

"I didn't mean literally," he said. "I mean that every answer has to be dragged out of you by the exact question. Get creative!"

Woz looked at him with pleading eyes as though the stress of his current predicament had robbed him of his cognitive ability.

"Tell me what you were doing here," Dan instructed him slowly.

"Guarding the bridge."

"And?"

"And the road."

"Jesus Harold fucking Christ on a bike," Dan spat in frustration, standing to point at the evidently not clever one of the bunch and looking at Ash. "*Watch him!*"

Ash did his thing, obviously having seen too many of Neil's movies and re-enacting that part where the alien didn't kill Ripley.

Unless he was stupid enough to take a swipe at the dog, which all common sense and self-preservation instincts should warn him not to, then he wouldn't be hurt. Dan lit a cigarette with shaking hands as he faced Mitch who was standing guard over the two surviving members of Team Toll Road.

One, Mr Broken Nose who refused to say a word but still spluttered up river water, tried to fix Mitch with his best death stare. Mitch, a man who'd actually earned the thousand-yard stare even back in the world before, found it about as threatening as a vicious attack from a litter of dachshund puppies.

Dan's first contact was still sleeping, which was the kindest way to say that he was still in the recovery position and likely had a concussion if not some damage that was at least semi-permanent from their brief encounter.

Blowing the smoke directly upwards, Dan gathered himself and turned back to tell Ash to leave it. The dog backed away reluctantly, not once taking his eyes off the terrified man.

"Who sent you to guard the road and the river, and what were your instructions?"

"You say one more fucking word, Woz, and I'll—*oompf*—*eeeeeeeuurgh...*"

From the ensuing noises Dan didn't need to look behind him to know that Mitch had discouraged further comment by the swift and judicious application of boot to ballbag. The interruption also served to focus Woz's attention a little better.

"Mo," he said. "Mo sent us and Goran told him to. We have to watch the road and the river and take whatever anyone has if they came through."

"Like what? What were you supposed to take?"

"Guns, food." Woz shrugged.

"How long have you been here?"

"Two days? No, three. Three days. It was two nights so I got confu—"

"Did you attack the settlement upriver?" The coldness in Dan's voice silenced him, draining what little colour had returned from his face back out again.

"No, that wasn't me. I...I..."

"You don't do things like that?" Neil asked, risking the wrath of his friend who hated being interrupted during an interview.

"That's right," Woz answered, smiling to try and appear less threatening. "I'm not like that. Some of the others came through from that direction; they must've done it."

"Done what?" Dan asked, seeing if he'd trip himself up easily or whether he'd make it a challenge as so few adversaries did under interrogation.

"Uh, attack anyone?" he answered, unsure if he was giving the right answer. Dan didn't believe his innocence just yet; or to be more specific he didn't quite believe that he was too dumb to be trusted with any kind of important information or complex instructions. There was something behind the guy's eyes that he didn't like, but he couldn't put his finger on it just yet.

"So you're one of the good ones, right?"

"That's right! I'm not like them. They're the ones who've hurt people, not us. We just guarded the road."

"And the river," Neil put in.

"And the river," Woz echoed, as though he was happy they understood his place in the world.

"Where's this Mo, Goran and the others now?" Dan asked him. His voice had softened, sounding almost conversational.

"They went that way." He nodded in the direction the road snaked away to the east.

"Walking? Driving? When? How many with him?" Dan listed the questions, feeling his annoyance creeping back to the surface again.

"Not walking…Goran was in a car, and there were a few other cars, well, trucks actually, but some were walking." He looked upwards to his left as if trying to remember the other questions. "Yesterday? No, really early this morning." He smiled as though pleased with himself for getting the answers right.

"And how many?"

"Oh, err, don't know." The smile stayed on, fading slowly as he realised Dan wasn't impressed with him. "Three cars – trucks – I didn't look inside all of them."

"Big trucks or normal trucks?" Neil asked.

"Yeah," Woz answered, sounding as though his IQ was leaking the longer the conversation when on.

"Is this idiot diabetic or something?" Neil asked Dan. "Does he need a mars bar to talk any bloody sense? I say throw this one back."

Dan made a non-committal noise. As hard work as it was, he'd gleaned at least some intelligence from the idiot, even if it wasn't all that actionable just yet.

He'd learned, combined with what he already knew from others, that Goran, whoever the fuck he was, had entered the territory with a mobile force of armed men and had caused at least two settlements to seal up tight for protection. He knew he had at least one lieutenant, this Mo character, who he trusted to pass on his orders.

Steve was aware of it, according to Dave at The Wash, and the last known sighting of Goran was with a mobile force of between fifteen and fifty others, estimating with a massive margin for error given that they were in trucks and not cars, and his direction of travel was north east of where Steve's town was.

Dan walked away from where Neil watched over the idiot and his dead friend to where Broken Nose glowered at him through red eyes beside his friend, who was unconscious but still alive.

"He'll kill you, you know," he said, struggling over the words courtesy of the pain he was still evidently experiencing.

"Who?" Dan asked, knowing the name he'd hear but recognising another way to gather intel.

"Goran. He'll cut you to pieces."

"You think I'm bothered about a little boy like you?" he goaded, hoping for the response he wanted and not being disappointed.

"Little boy?" Broken Nose laughed in spite of his mangled face and bruised balls. "He's bigger than you are, you old prick. He'll set you loose in the dark and find you."

Dan was more concerned about the unprovoked dig at his age than the threat of a painful and terrifying death at the hands of the mythological demon they followed. He fixed Broken Nose with a look and treated him to a fake shudder before snapping his fingers to call Ash into play. The dog glided to his heel and sat, big eyes fixed on the bound man who tried to retain a look of resilient hostility in spite of being so blatantly frightened.

"What's to say I won't find him first?" Dan asked conversationally as he rolled his cigarette between finger and thumb to regard it carefully. "What's to say I don't find him in the dark and have Ash here rip his throat out? Or maybe I'll tie the fucker to a cross and set him on fire, how does that sound?"

Broken Nose sneered at him as best he could past his injuries. His lack of reaction at hearing about the barbecuing of innocent people was enough to tip Dan over the edge but he kept his cool.

"Please," sobbed Woz who had only just woken up to the fact that he was likely to be executed. "Please just let us go. We'll go home, we promise, we won't come back here again, just...please..."

Dan glanced at Mitch, their unspoken words conveyed through facial gestures and body language. Mitch shrugged, as if the proposed plan made no difference to him. That was what passed for support when it came to Mitch; he was happy to follow Dan and rarely objected, so acquiescence was the status quo which made anything he disagreed with worth listening to.

He walked a short distance away after nodding his head for Neil to join him and the two muttered a brief conversation before Dan walked back to Woz.

"Which way is home for you?" he asked.

"That way," he answered, nodding in the direction of the setting sun.

"How far?"

"Three days?" he answered, daring to hope that he'd survive the encounter.

"Good. Take your mates and fuck off, but know that if we see you again – *ever* – we won't waste time talking. You understand me?"

Woz nodded manically, desperate to please and appease the man with the dog who terrified him.

Neil cut him loose, and he stepped back rubbing his sore wrists where the flesh had swollen around the cold plastic. Broken Nose was cut free too, and between them they picked up the third living member of their group uncertainly.

"I'd suggest you stop soon and cut two long branches," Dan told them. "Put your jacket sleeves on the poles and make a stretcher."

Woz nodded gratefully at the advice but Broken Nose sneered.

"Let me get my stuff at least?" he asked. In answer Dan looked behind his left shoulder as a sign for Neil to step up. His friend tossed a single pack at the released prisoners.

"Food and water," he told them. Broken Nose eyed him suspiciously, switching his gaze back to Dan as he slipped his hand inside the top pouch of the pack. His fingers grasped nothing and the look of thunder in his eyes radiated hatred for the stolen weapon he hoped would be there.

"I tossed it in the river. Now go," Dan told them, feeling sorry for Woz as his low intellect had been exploited by bad people but feeling nothing for Broken Nose who he knew would kill him if he had the opportunity. "And don't come back this way."

They watched them leave, as Dan felt the sudden sensation of unease because he'd just released an enemy on faith. He had a sinking feeling he was going to see at least one of them again, and he knew he wouldn't feel quite so merciful the next time.

RING OF STEEL

Steve

He'd spent three weeks ranging out from their town to hunt down any hostile elements in the area. They'd found small settlements which had received the same kind of treatment they had, with people taken and burning crucifixions left as warning, and they had found others totally unaware of any threat.

Those unaffected had been urged to pack up everything and move to the town, and while some of the young and the old were sent under escort most people opted to stay behind and protect their livelihoods. He knew they would, despite the risks, because to give up tending your own crops and caring for your own livestock was to elect for a life of receiving charity from others. Every single one of them had rebuilt their lives from scratch, and understandably none of them wanted to do it again.

"Ready to go, boss," George said to him, leaning his head through the driver's window of the four-by-four Steve sat in and startling him out of his thoughts.

"Okay, send one of our crews back home with them as escort. It'll be dark soon and I want to make sure they get there in one piece."

"We're staying out?" the young man asked him, an air of hopeful excitement in his words at the prospect of extended action. Steve swallowed down the retort forming on his lips because he knew George was a mature and capable soldier for such a young man.

"Us and one other," Steve told him. "We can make it to at least one more settlement tonight and send them back first thing tomorrow." George nodded and ducked back out to get it done, leaving Steve hunched over the map spread out uncomfortably on the dash. Having a map marked with the locations where people lived went against the logic of his former life and extensive training, because a marked map was a treasure trove of actionable intelligence for an enemy.

They had spent so long without having any enemies that such things had grown lax and dropped off from being daily routine. Sure enough they had experienced plenty of problems and minor conflicts, but most of those had been either bad blood or territorial disputes and were ended rapidly without the need for anything resembling warfare.

They had evolved into a peacekeeping force more than a defence militia, but Steve's insistence that they train and recruit in order to be ready to face a threat if one emerged was likely the reason they were all still alive and free.

He jumped again as a hand slapped the metal side of his vehicle, thumping it twice in that way that men do when they think it makes them seem manly. It was probably depicted on screen once back in the dim and distant past, and it had caught on all over the world for all manner of transports. George yelled something back to one of their men and climbed in behind the wheel, shooting Steve an expectant look as he waited for instructions.

"They all set?" he asked.

"Good to go. They'll set off as soon as the village people are loaded up."

Steve chuckled at the young man's words.

"What?"

"Nothing," Steve said. "Village People?"

"Yeah, the people from the village…?"

"Do me a favour," Steve said, "and just say 'people from the village' instead, okay?"

"Okaaay," George answered in a tone that made it obvious he was humouring Steve who was clearly insane.

"Go west," Steve told him, chuckling again as accidental musical nostalgia seemed to be the in thing. The rear doors opened and another two militia soldiers climbed aboard. "Then be ready to turn south when I say." George nodded, started up the clattering engine and nursed it off the mark in first gear.

Steve sat back as George drove, fighting the urge to reminisce too much as it drew his focus away from the need to remain alert. George had been about Leah's age when he found himself orphaned, and after they had overthrown Richards in the far-from-bloodless coup years before, the skinny boy who had survived so long by making himself useful to the guards was in need of employment.

His natural guile, which Steve recognised and instantly liked about him, had been shaped and moulded to make him the capable young man he was now. It struck Steve as a little biased that the boy had been given every opportunity above others, but at no point in his life was he given anything for free that he hadn't earned in effort and achievement. It was merit, not nepotism he assured himself.

"Left left at the next junction," Steve told him, echoing Dan's habit of repeating directions twice for clarity. His finger followed their progress on the map laid out in front of him as he correlated the long, sweeping curve in the road with the bending line on the paper which was starting to become difficult to decipher in the weakening light. "Another few miles and there's a settlement beside the river," he told his driver as he tried to fold the map away neatly and failed so that it sat on the bench seat between them twice the size it had started out at.

They reached the settlement, so obviously occupied by people as the trees and hedgerows were cut back neatly to reveal a cluster of houses and barns. No indication of people was visible, but neither was there any sign of anything going down there to cause them concern.

Steve slipped out of the passenger side and limped softly towards the building with his gun in the low ready position, holding up a hand for the other vehicle following them to stay back until they called them forwards.

"Spread out," he told the other three. "George, go round the back." The sound of boots on old tarmac answered his orders as he stalked forwards scanning the area. He'd only been there once before and recalled that three melded families lived in the cluster of buildings, living off the produce from what was effectively a very large vegetable patch and the products from a handful of farm animals they kept.

He also recalled that they were greeted with a friendly wave and the sight of two shotguns, so the absence of anyone greeting them raised his hackles. His eyes instinctively went high and low, looking for threats at every angle, and came to rest on the open door of one of the houses. His thumb moved slowly, clicking the safety catch on his weapon down one as his index finger stayed horizontal along the trigger guard. He approached the door slowly, eyes darting left and right as his senses screamed at him for the noise the man behind him was making by simply walking over cobblestones.

He reached the door, poking his head and the barrel of his carbine inside before pulling back to assess what his eyes had seen.

Dishes on the table.

A pot on the coal-fired range cooker.

A half-empty glass of water.

He glanced behind him to see that the militia man with him, squinting through glasses repaired with tape over the bridge of his nose, also looked at the abandoned objects with confusion.

"Like a bleedin' ghost tow—" he started to say, before the sharp report of a rifle cracked a split second after the man's body spun, thrown down violently out of control.

Steve's body moved before his mind could decide what to tell it to do. He threw himself through the partly open door and onto the cold, hard quarry tiles of the farmhouse kitchen floor. His cheek registered the chill held in the stones, feeling the smoothness of it in the instant his face rested for a second until he forced himself to his feet to turn and aim his weapon out of the door from a sitting position.

Blood pooled on the doorstep, running down in a thick line as the worn stone offered an escape through gravity. The blood spread out from the wound on the side of the man's head where the bullet had drilled a neat hole above his ear, pumping out in pulses as his dying heart slowed to a stop. Steve's eyes scanned desperately for where the shot had come from, but sticking his head outside to search for the source of danger would be a foolish, and likely terminal move.

He glanced up in panic as he remembered the windows which could offer a vantage point to a shooter outside and expose him to danger, seeing nothing from his position on the floor. He scrambled to his feet, kicking the door shut and rolling to the side in anticipation of more bullets coming through the wood, but the door crunched on something and bounced back towards him. He kicked it again, hearing the same noise as the wood impacted on whatever was obstructing it. Dropping to his knees to lean around the door, his fingers grasped the twisted frame of his man's glasses. He pulled them free as he slammed the door with his body, dropping the broken, bent metal frames and wiping the blood on his fingers against his thigh.

"George!" he yelled, turning his weapon to face the interior of the house and moving low to make sure he hadn't been trapped inside with another enemy. "George!"

"Here," the young man yelled from a room away. He crashed through an interior doorway, another soldier behind him, with wide eyes and weapon raised. "What the hell?"

"They shot…" Steve said, realising he didn't know or couldn't remember the name of the dead militia man he'd been in the truck with for an entire day. He was saved from having to finish his sentence by more gunfire from outside as shotgun and automatic rifle chattered back and forth with one another. The door rocked from a loud impact forcing Steve to raise his gun and flick the safety catch down one more notch ready to drill through and kill whoever was trying to break in from the other side.

"That's Iain," the other soldier said. "Don't shoot!"

The door rattled twice more and Steve held his breath expecting more shots to sound and for the body of his friend to thump against the wood and drop beside the first victim of the hidden shooter. Just when his nerve was about to break, the door swung inwards and Iain spilled to the floor in the same spot where Steve had dropped, kicking his feet desperately behind him as two sharp cracks and their answering ricochets filled the small courtyard outside.

Steve kicked the door shut and ducked low, beckoning for the others to follow him back into the house as the windows began shattering to cascade their glass into the kitchen.

"Come on!" he bawled, crouched so low that his legs burned and he thought it would be easier to lie down and crawl if he could move fast enough.

"What the fuck?" Iain asked in a voice much higher than he usually spoke in. "What the fucking *fuck*?"

The four of them huddled low in the hallway. Polished floorboards bearing a thin layer of dust as though they were the first people to be there in the last week.

Then the smell hit Steve's nostrils. He turned to face the others, seeing George's nose wrinkling but a look of incomprehension on his face. The other man with George, a quiet man named Andy, looked so pale and aghast at what was happening that the stench probably hadn't penetrated to his thoughts yet, but a glance at Iain's face told Steve that he wasn't imagining it; there was a dead body in the house.

Long bursts of gunfire punctuated by the heavy reports of shotgun blasts sounded from outside, over laced with the tinny tell-tale sounds of bullet tearing into thin metal panels; a car was being shot up with extreme prejudice outside.

"My lot," Iain said sadly before he kicked out and slammed a boot heel into the skirting board opposite him. "Fuck sake! I told them to stay back until we came out."

"Would you have?" George asked quietly, not backing down when Iain fixed him with a savage look.

"Irrelevant," Steve said. "We're on our own and that leaves one question: how the hell are we getting out of this?"

NEGOTIATIONS

Steve hadn't seen a white flag used in as long as he could remember. It started with loud cries of, "Cease fire! Cease fiiiiire," coming from outside until the occasional sporadic gunshots died away to nothing. Steve risked a peek out of the kitchen window, or at least the gaping hole of jagged glass where one of the windows had been a minute before, and saw a man in camouflage fatigues waving a piece of white cloth about the size of pillow case lazily over his head as though he was trying to bring an aircraft down on his position.

"Stay inside," Steve told the others. "Cover me if you can but keep back from the windows."

"Steve, you can't go ou—"

Steve rounded on the young man who presumed his history with their leader permitted him to make demands of the former pilot.

"*Don't,*" Steve snapped, swapping hands holding the weapon to jab his right index finger into the meaty slab of George's chest above the top of his vest, "tell me what I will and won't do," he said firmly. He softened, smiling at the young man who he knew was only trying to look out for him.

"You have your orders," he said, spinning away and stopping by the back door to take two full, chest-inflating breaths.

"I'm coming out," he yelled loudly, pausing with his hand on the door handle and silently praying he wouldn't be peppered with a hail of incoming fire as he put his faith and his life in the honour of dishonourable people. He twisted the handle and pulled, feeling the fresh air hit his face at the same time as the tangy smell of gunfire and fresh blood assaulted his senses. He glanced at the man who had followed him from their vehicle, still unable to recall his name which he put down to the stress of the situation, and tried to force away the look in his dull eyes as he stared up lifelessly.

Steve fought down the feelings that came so naturally and made him want to blame himself for the loss of life, but he made the logical version of himself elbow its way to the front of the mental queue and remind him that he didn't start this fight.

He cast his eyes up away from the body, being sure to keep his hands away from the grip of the carbine hanging from the sling and regarded the man he was about to enter the ring with.

The man didn't move other than to ball up the cloth now that it had served its purpose and wipe his hands on it with evident distain before tossing it aside. It was done so in a way that Steve could only take to mean he wouldn't be offering the opportunity to parlay again, and was a blatant power move to open proceedings before they'd even said a word to one another.

Steve carried on walking towards him, seeing his features come into focus as he neared and hating the man even more with each step.

Somehow, years after the apocalypse, this man shaved his head all the way to the dome and had done so that day by the look of him. His pale brown skin glistened with a shine that spoke of a daily moisturising regime which fitted with his sculpted beard of thin, jet black lines of short hair. His eyebrows were shaped, his body lean and his appearance meticulously cared for, and the smirk on his face told Steve that this bastard was a cruel as they came.

"Who the fuck are you?" Steve asked, looking him up and down and deciding to come in a level which would hopefully speed things up. His opponent smiled and picked an imaginary speck of dirt from his pressed military uniform before rubbing his fingers together almost daintily to rid himself of the imperfection.

"My name is Mohammed," he said in home counties accented English with a hint of his first language in there somewhere. "But my people call me Mo."

"Right then, Mo," Steve said. "You've got five minutes to clear off out of here. I've got fifteen more armed men and women out and they'll be heading this way soon enough."

Mo smiled. It wasn't a nice smile, but the sneering, sardonic smirk of a man who knew his opponent was lying and couldn't contain himself.

"You've got three more inside and three dead in a car back there." Mo gestured with a nod of his head back towards the road without taking his eyes off Steve. Steve resisted the urge to look in that direction and kept his own gaze fixed on the man. "And with one dead by the house that leaves you with four out of eight and no way to reach your one working vehicle." Steve sucked in a breath to cut him off but a flash of anger seared across Mo's features and he spoke louder.

"Add to that the third vehicle you sent north from a camp and that leaves you with exactly what you have here; nothing more. I have twelve men posted all around this place, and we have supplies and ammunition to last us days."

Steve said nothing. He tried to keep the features of his own face blank and neutral as though he'd bet it all on a pair of twos, but something must have registered because Mo smiled again and let out a light laugh.

"Nothing to say?" he sneered. "You can surrender now and I'll let two of your people leave with their lives. If you don't…" He gave a theatrical shrug combining it with sticking out his lower lip as if to say, 'Who knows what could happen'.

Steve sucked in a long breath through his nose as he thought. His injured leg, the one he had broken horribly at the violent end of his last flight ever, twitched and spasmed like it wanted to take matters into its own metaphorical hands and kick the living shit out of him there and then.

"I'll tell you what," Steve said as he took a step closer to a man he'd happily kill. "You send your twelve boys in and see what happens. Better still," he said louder with a pointed finger in his neatly groomed face, "why don't you lead the charge yourself and, you know…" Steve mirrored the same theatrical shrug to goad Mo.

It didn't work. The cruel bastard just stepped back and smiled.

"Better get back to your people," he said. "I'm about to call off the truce, and I won't give you another opportunity to discuss this. Remember that when your people are dying."

"Fine by me," Steve said, turning on his heel and walking back towards the house. He wouldn't let himself run, wouldn't allow his enemies to see him showing any fear, but he did stoop to snatch up the shotgun and a belt of cartridges from his dead comrade as he passed.

Bursting through the kitchen door he headed straight for the large wooden table and tipped it onto its side.

"Help me block the door," he said. George was there in a heartbeat, helping him shove the makeshift barricade into place.

"What's happening?" he asked.

"Block the other entrances," he told the others, "and get ready to defend this house."

"What's happening?" George asked again.

"We're under siege," Steve told him, "and I'm going to kill that bastard," he added with a nod of his head to the rear yard.

ENCLAVE

Dan

The gunfire told them which way to head long before the sun reached its peak in the sky. It was sporadic and distant, but it was definitely gunfire.

They walked in the direction of Steve's town, with the unintended risk of that also being the direction the enemy convoy had gone in, when two booms in the distance were answered by a sharp rattle of bangs.

They, in turn, were echoed by a heavier clatter of rapid fire in a slower tempo before the bass of a shotgun added its noise once again.

"A mile? Two?" Dan asked Mitch.

"Two," he said, brow knitted as he gazed over the low, flat landscape towards to source of the distant sounds.

"Sounds static though," Mitch said. "Like two sides in cover exchanging words."

Dan made a *hmm* noise that was frustrating for others as it was totally uncommitted.

"No prizes for guessing who?" Neil put in.

Dan glanced at him, seeing how his friend had developed a slight limp on their march and was red-faced and sweating. If Dan felt out of shape and past his prime, then Neil was outwardly suffering from the effects of the comfortable lifestyle he'd enjoyed back in Sanctuary.

As if the thought of their warm town on the southern coast of France made the country of his birth angry, cold rain began to fall on them from the overcast sky. No dark, brooding clouds had warned of the impending downfall and Dan inwardly cursed the British weather. Mitch, not even bothering to adjust his collar against the rain, seemed unaffected by it at all.

"Bloody rain," muttered Jimmy from behind them.

"This isnae rain, laddie," Mitch told him with more emphasis on his accent than usual. "This is a fine mist at worst. It's positively summer!"

"Here we go," panted Neil, "cue the list of reasons why Scotland gets rain four hundred and six days a year…"

"And twenty-five hours a day," Dan added.

"Soft, the lot of you, southern Nancys," Mitch muttered, ending the conversation.

They walked in silence for another ten minutes, going fast without running and actually feeling grateful for the rain after a while as it kept their temperature down under the effort of moving fast. At the approach of buildings partly overgrown by a line of trees meeting the road at a right angle, the rusted and faded shapes of speed limit signs emerged from the tall hedgerows ahead, warning them to slow down as they approached the residential area.

Gunfire sounded again; a single shotgun blast received the answer of two bullets before the vacant countryside again lulled into silence.

"That's not this village," Dan told the others. "Next one maybe?" They agreed. Dan led them forwards towards the abandoned houses built at a junction of two small, overgrown roads leaving just a strip of pitted tarmac down the middle of each. No sign that anyone had lived there since it happened existed, and Dan led Ash forwards to do a cursory search for sign that anyone was or had been there.

No sign, which made Dan feel both uneasy and encouraged. If he was involved in a stand-off fight nearby, he'd send one of his people back to watch this approach as it was likely, given the way the countryside was, that there were few other approaches where reinforcements of other dangers could come from. He shook his head to focus, knowing that there could be a thousand reasons why he *wouldn't* send someone back there. He called the others to him and set off at the fast walking pace again towards the direction of the small conflict.

"Wait here," he told them at a bend in the road. He slipped his heavy pack off, unzipping the smaller front section which came away as a day pack containing his emergency kit. Mitch automatically slipped off his own Bergen and used it as a firing platform to lay over and defend their rear.

"You're not going on your own, are you?" Jimmy asked concerned.

"Relax," Neil told him. "He's only going for a look. He wouldn't do anything rash." Neil looked up to meet Dan's eye and clearly convey his strenuous objections against him doing anything stupid.

"Relax," Dan told them. "I'm not going to get myself killed and leave you to tell Marie; that wouldn't be fair to you."

Neil scoffed at his weak attempt to make light of the situation, primarily as that was his forte and he firmly believed Dan should leave the comedy to others.

Dan adjusted the straps of his smaller pack and cinched them tight before rolling both shoulders to make sure he still had full range of movement. Fixing Ash with a look he snapped the fingers of his left hand and tapped his thigh once, making the dog leap up as fast as his knees and hips allowed and glued his large snout to Dan's leg ready to play.

He jogged, body bent over slightly, exerting more effort by the crouch, and both hands on his weapon. His gloved left hand slipped on the angled foregrip of his carbine which had never let him down since the day he took it as a replacement for his last weapon after it had saved his life by absorbing an axe blow straight in the ejection port. He adjusted his hold on the gun and pressed on, hearing more sporadic exchanges of fire from ahead. He stopped, seeing the back end of a vehicle on the road ahead and instantly knowing something was very wrong. The angle it sat at, the way the nose of the truck was dipped just off the road, made it look as though it had crashed at a very low speed. Sure enough, when he and his dog crept towards it, he saw a door open and items strewn about the roadway around the vehicle like it had been ransacked. When he got closer still, sticking to the shadows under the overhanging branches of the most out of control privet hedge he'd ever laid eyes on, he saw the pooling blood dripping from the partly open rear passenger door on the driver's side.

More gunfire from ahead, this time accompanied by a shout of pain which rose in volume and intensity until it became a shrieking, hysterical wailing noise until a louder shout silenced it.

"Where are you hit?" a male voice asked angrily, as though it was the gunshot victim's fault for not dodging the bullet. He didn't hear the response, but the same voice that asked the question cursed loudly as the screaming started up again. Before it could reach the rising crescendo a second time, another gunshot rang out and the screaming stopped so abruptly there could only have been one result of what had happened out of his sight.

"Burn it down," a voice snarled.

"How?" another voice demanded.

"With fire, you pathetic little moron," the man who had shot his own soldier spat back.

"I meant how do we get close enough?"

Silence answered the query before the obvious leader spoke up again after having thought about the problem they faced.

"Get a fire ready, something that'll burn fast, and when you're ready everyone shoots at the windows and doors at the same time."

Dan had heard enough, and paused as he fought an internal battle with himself as to whether he should act now, alone, or go back for reinforcements. Age and experience won through, and he melted away towards the road to run back for the others.

WELL AND TRULY SCREWED

Steve

They'd made a few uncoordinated attempts to storm the farmhouse, and he was sure the odds were beginning to lean in their favour after the defenders had definitely hit one. The man, not much more than a boy really, lay face down on the front lawn in an unnatural position with his weapon and hands trapped under his body. He was clearly dead where he fell, but something about the position he lay in was so odd it drew Steve's attention a second too long and kept him at the upstairs window for enough time that he attracted a blast of shotgun fire from outside.

Glass burst inwards from the single-glazed panels and forced him back onto the landing which was the position he'd taken up to cover all sides of the building. He relied on the shouts of his men on the ground floor when they saw movement, and ran to the appropriate bedroom on that side of the house to add a height advantage to their defence. He knew he was exposing himself to too much fire that way, but with his back to a wall in a shitty situation there was little in the way of options.

"Last magazine," called Andy from the hallway below him.

"Shotgun and belt in the kitchen behind you," Steve yelled back. He heard no answer as the sound of Iain's rifle banged away out of the kitchen window as three men rushed the back door hoping that their attention was on the front. Had they been seconds earlier it might've worked but their coordination was off yet again. Steve stepped into the doorframe of the bedroom over the kitchen, seeing the last of the attackers going out of his field of view. He held position, hoping and expecting that they'd be repelled so he could pick off anyone retreating without showing himself at the large sash windows.

Movement out in the yard caught his eye as a man leaned around the edge of a brick outbuilding and lingered for a second to watch. Steve could tell from the angle of his head that he was watching the back door and not looking up, and he brought his weapon up to fill the target optic with the man's body. He ducked out of sight before Steve could focus on taking the shot, and he didn't want to snap-fire and give away his position without a guaranteed hit.

The man popped back out, lingered half a second and ducked back into cover behind the building. Steve held his weapon trained on precisely the spot where the man had appeared, wondering if he was going to be dumb enough to pop out again in exactly the same position.

He was, and Steve squeezed off two rounds with the reward of seeing the man double over and fall back. His feet danced like he was being electrocuted until the body was dragged fully into cover.

"One more down," Steve added, as the shrieks of shock and agony reached him through the shot-out windows. He felt no joy for the pain he inflicted on another person, but he did allow himself a small flicker of hope that he was balancing the fairness of the situation.

The screaming started again, this time ending abruptly with another gunshot. Steve ducked, expecting the gunshot to be aimed their way until it dawned on him what had happened.

"They just put down their own man," Steve called down the stairs. Nobody answered, because the concept was so abhorrent and alien to their whole ethos. These men weren't like them, not one bit.

"Anyone see anything?" George shouted from his position at the sliding patio doors that the attackers had yet to try breaching.

"No," came Andy's response from the front hall.

"Nothing," Iain said from the kitchen.

"Stay sharp," Steve warned from upstairs as he thumbed replacement rounds into a spent magazine.

Tense seconds ticked by with no sign of any further attack and no more shots aimed at them, until a shout of alarm from downstairs made Steve yell for an explanation.

"They're going to torch us!" Iain cried out. Steve looked out into the yard to see a man holding a fence post, fire dripping from the burning clothing wrapped around one end.

"Oh no they're fucking not," he muttered to himself as he took aim and stepped into the bedroom to squeeze the trigger and put him down.

The house erupted with noise and glass as the whole outside world seemed to have opened up on the little farmhouse with everything they had. Steve dropped to the deck, unable to see as the glass of the window burst in on him. He felt the sting of glass cuts to his hands and face and the warmth of his blood as he lay on the creaking floorboards with his eyes screwed shut trying not to scream out loud.

By the time the shooting had stopped he heard a new noise to strike fear into him: Iain yelling in fright from downstairs.

"What's happening?" he yelled as he swivelled and crawled over the shattered glass shards for the door back to the landing. He repeated himself twice more until he was heard over Iain's yells.

"Kitchen's on fire," George yelled, coughing as the acrid fumes of whatever accelerant they'd used burned toxically inside the house.

"Shoot the sink," Andy yelled.

"What?" George yelled back, still coughing as he dragged Iain into the hallway under protest.

"Mains water inlet," Andy shouted over the crackling sound of flames. George understood a second later, dropping a spluttering Iain on his back and unslinging his rifle to tuck it hard into his shoulder and take aim. He emptied the magazine in three long bursts, filling the inside of the house with another chemical burning smell to add to the fire and leave them all with a ringing temporary deafness.

It worked. The mains water pipe under the sink offered no resistance to the bullets that hit it and the kitchen was filled with a hissing noise as the water spilled out into the kitchen and began to fight the fire as naturally as predators hunted prey. He didn't know, mainly because he'd never considered mains water pressure before as he was child when it mattered, but their fire-saving rescue only came through the ingenuity of the people who had lived there and had installed a rainwater collection relying on gravity to provide the pressure.

"Everyone okay?" Steve shouted when he sensed that the risk of death by smoke inhalation had been averted. The hissing noise of escaping water being turned into steam was loud, but any answer was drowned out by the renewed gunfire from outside.

"Here they come again," George yelled from downstairs, filling Steve with a feeling that they had two hopes of getting out of there alive: no hope and Bob Hope.

ATTACK REAR

Dan

Ash loped at his side, looking up at his master as he easily matched the human's pace, turning his body sideways in that curious energy-saving mode he preferred. Reaching the others, he dropped into their position at the side of the road and hissed a rapid report.

"Some kind of ambush up ahead," Dan told them. "From what I heard I'm pretty sure the bad guys are the ambushers." He swallowed, hoping that he wouldn't be questioned further about that opinion as he had been known to use fire as a weapon before.

Mitch stood, shedding unneeded weight from his body as he prepared to go forward with Dan.

"You good?" Dan asked him, holding a hand out to Jimmy as he stood. In answer Mitch simply slid open the breech of the under-slung grenade launcher to show Dan a destructive projectile loaded and ready.

"Stay here with the kit," Dan said to Jimmy. There was no time to be nice about it, he was dismissing one of his oldest friends because he wasn't equipped for the fight he expected them to get into. Neil shrugged out of his pack and loosened the Velcro straps over the magazine pouches on his vest which was already straining at the furthest reaches it could be loosened to. Jimmy hesitated for half a second, torn between wanting to protest that he should come and knowing that if Dan feared the situation enough to order him to remain behind then he should probably just do as he was told. He nodded, turning to take up Mitch's position with his shotgun pointed towards the road they had travelled.

"Covering advance?" Mitch asked.

"No time," Dan answered, "they were planning something bad when I pulled back." As if to demonstrate his point, the world ahead of them erupted in gunfire as whatever had been planned was evidently going down. A thin pillar of black smoke rose from over the rooftops ahead which forced Dan to move faster until the vehicle came into sight. Dull green paint and recognisable straight lines of a Defender felt oddly familiar to them all.

"That was one of ours," Mitch said without a hint of disbelief in his words. The fact that he could recall enough detail to identify a vehicle from the better part of a decade prior, especially given everything that had transpired since, would be a miraculous thing to people who weren't like Dan and Neil.

"You're sure?" Dan asked, wanting to eliminate the tiny shred of doubt.

"Last three," Mitch said, meaning the characters of the registration plate, "GYZ."

Neil allowed a minute snicker of smutty humour as he recalled what they called the Land Rover to identify it.

"I remember jizz," Neil said. "Looks like it's seen better days though."

"There's at least one dead inside," Dan told him, "so yeah, bad day out." The silence hung for a second, each of them scanning over the sights of their weapons as they considered the possibility of recognising one of the victims as people they had known. That it could be Steve or any number of those left behind when Dan and his followers split off to chase the wild goose so long ago gave them a collective cold feeling of dread.

Gunfire from ahead started up again, although with far less intensity than the previous onslaught. Dan moved forwards again, going low and slow with the dog all but belly crawling beside him, until he stopped them with a subtle hand gesture which was passed back from Neil to Mitch. They all froze where they were, being disciplined enough not to drop to the ground or make any other sudden move to make themselves more comfortable.

"What do you mean it didn't work?" snapped the same voice Dan had heard earlier. He didn't catch the reply because it was given softly, as though the man he heard was known for punishing people who angered him.

"Well try again," the same voice snarled.

Dan gestured behind him for the others to bunch up, turning to whisper his instructions when they were huddled as close to him as they could get.

"No time to be clever about it," he said. "We go in hard but stay out of sight of the building if possible; don't want whoever they've got cornered to take any shots at us."

He checked the chamber on his carbine out of obsessive habit like it was his personal nervous tick, gestured for Ash to stay and reinforced the order with a wide-eyed stare to tell the dog he really meant it, then stood and moved.

Two men went down to his rapid trigger pulls on semi-automatic as he twitched his barrel from left to right. Three others dove for cover as Mitch stepped out to Dan's left and engaged another group on the corner of the opposite outbuilding. Neil appeared close to Dan's right shoulder and squeezed off a short burst at the corner where he'd seen two of them go to ground. He wasn't trying to hit anyone but discourage them from reappearing and taking a shot at them in the open.

They moved forwards, stepping over two still bodies to occupy the position their enemy had felt safe in only seconds before. Mitch kept his rifle trained on the place where he'd engaged the last threat.

"Two down," Dan said.

"One down," Mitch answered.

"Two in cover my side," Neil added, gasping for breath at the exertion and the adrenaline, no doubt forcing his blood pressure up a little higher than was safe for a man of his age and size.

"Mitch, hold," Dan ordered. "Neil on me." He moved without waiting for acknowledgment, rounding the corner low and fast with his weapon already up and bullets spitting from the barrel. His head followed, ducking back out of sight and relying on the mental snapshot his mind took to tell him that the two who went that way at least had the good sense to keep moving. Dan rose, stalking along the building line to be rewarded with a head poking around the edge ahead of him. He knew what would come next, and stepped wide to his right to open up the angle and take both him and Neil out of the firing line he guessed his adversary would choose.

He was right again, and was greeted with the awkward sight of someone trying to blind-fire a bullpup rifle around the corner without presenting their body as a target. Dan's chosen angle gave him a sight of the man's left shoulder as he twisted his wrists awkwardly to reach the trigger grip and drilled him with three shots to drop him, screaming. By the time he reached the corner he looked down to see the last spurts of blood gushing from a small wound in the man's neck where it met the collar of his sweatshirt. His eyes were wide and his fingers fluttered like he was trying to type out his last words.

A flash of movement ahead showed another figure fleeing around the corner, but he didn't follow in case the pursuit took him in sight of the house, where he guessed desperate people were trapped and defending themselves.

A bullet fired accidentally killed just as effectively as a well-aimed one, and he wasn't quite ready to die.

Gunfire erupted again in disciplined bursts, telling Dan that Mitch was engaging someone back where they had joined the fight. He turned to see Neil already lumbering back around the corner ahead of him.

"Another one down," Mitch reported after a rapid glance to make sure it was his friends approaching and not the enemy.

"Same around the back," Dan answered, stopping his next words as a new sound echoed around the yard. An engine started, revving loudly before the gearbox crunched as first gear was selected and tyres bit into gravel. A vehicle shot into sight, passing by them to show a wide-eyed man with a shiny, shaved head driving recklessly towards the blocked road where the shot-up Land Rover sat obstructing his escape. The vehicle went out of sight again behind bushes as the sounds changed and the gears crunched again as reverse was selected.

It shot past them again, this time going backwards with a mechanical whine as the speed cried out for another gear before it slewed a weak attempt at a J-turn. Dan raised his weapon to take aim at the driver as he scrabbled desperately for a forward gear just as dust and a spray of stone chips erupted from the wall of the building above his head. Ducking down instinctively, he switched his aim to three men who were running for the vehicle, one of them firing on automatic from the hip as he sidestepped.

The two with him threw themselves inside but the one covering their escape hung on a few seconds to fully expend his magazine before turning to flee, but by then it was too late. The vehicle took off, making him run a few desperate and awkward steps as he tried to keep pace with it until he gave up and was left standing in the open with nowhere to hide.

He turned, raising the weapon again at Dan but in his panic, he must have forgotten that he'd just emptied it to little effect. The trigger clicked onto nothing and he froze, unsure if he should run or try to reload. He chose the first option, sprinting out of sight in the direction of the blocked road.

Where Ash waited.

"Go!" Dan roared. "Get him!"

Growling and barking erupted behind the hedgerow obscuring their view just as the fleeing man managed to reverse his course and run screaming back into sight again, this time holding nothing as he must have abandoned the rifle to allow him the use of his hands to achieve the best possible speed. He pumped his limbs like his life depended on it, managing a fast run which would outpace any human pursuit. He wasn't being chased by a human, however, and when Ash came into sight the conclusion was obvious to everyone watching except the man who still thought he could outrun the dog.

Ash dug deep, back paws reaching far past his front ones as he stretched his body for the best speed he could manage, much as his target did. He appeared to hinge in the middle as he ran hard, not reaching his full speed and still under hard acceleration as he checked his footing and leapt through the air the last few paces to take the man just below his right elbow.

The dog's body weight dragged the running man down with a shriek of fear and agony. He snarled and tugged, barking without unclamping his massive, powerful jaws until Dan arrived to pull his dog back and shout for him to leave it.

The man clutched at the limb, blood showing at his fingers but the sleeves of his clothing hiding the real damage Ash had done. He howled in a high-pitched wail and rocked back and forth on his back as he fought to control his body under the intense fear and pain he experienced. Dan's boot landed on his chest and he froze, looking up along the short barrel of the black carbine, past the attachments on the rail and into the scarred face of the man at the controlling end of it.

"Don't!" a voice yelled from the house. "We need him alive!"

The man who had shouted emerged from the back door and put his head down to run towards them, favouring one leg as though he carried an injury he was well accustomed to. Dan removed his boot and lowered his carbine on its sling as he turned away, muttering to Ash for the dog to watch the prisoner. The man running towards him slowed ten paces away, standing up tall and coming to a stop before his feet compelled him forwards again. The two men walked towards each other, gathering pace until they almost ran before they met in a clash of armoured torsos in an embrace so heartfelt that the emotion radiated out from them.

"Still alive, you old fucker," Dan muttered, fighting the lump in his throat.

"I am," Steve answered, "thanks to you. Again."

SITREP

The seven men swept the settlement to make sure they were alone and safe. The tall, fit and good-looking young man who stayed suspiciously close to Steve's side and eyed Dan warily reported that another vehicle load of the enemy had fled from the side of the building he was covering shortly before Steve cried out to stop the prisoner being dispatched.

Mitch went back with Neil to fetch Jimmy and their gear as Steve made the introductions.

"This is George," he said, indicating the young man who would've been a good fit for Leah had she not already made herself spoken for. Dan checked him out, deciding that his French son-in-law would run rings around him. "Iain," Steve went on. Dan nodded a greeting to a short man who had a look of easy efficiency about him. "And Andy." The last man sat smoking with shaking hands and didn't look up to acknowledge him, no doubt suffering massively from his first real fight.

"This is Dan," Steve finished, seeing both Iain and George open their eyes wide as though they'd been presented to a living god.

"Wait, *the* Dan?" George muttered to Steve. "As in, *Dan* Dan?"

"As in Dan and Ash, Dan," Dan told him with a smile, snapping his fingers for the German shepherd to step up. His tail wagged, thumping out a steady rhythm against Dan's leg as he put his head down and let out a series of small whimpers on recognising a man he hadn't seen for most of his life. He approached Steve, his body language almost apologetic as the older man knelt down for the dog to come to him. Ash slumped into him, trying to climb onto his lap despite being bigger than the puppy he acted like, knocking him down onto his backside where he whimpered louder and licked Steve's face as he climbed on top of him to drive all the air out of the man's lungs.

"Okay, boy," Steve said, "okay, enough now!" They laughed to see how the dog, still with blood marking his grey fur, acted like a baby when it came to the reunion. Steve managed to extricate himself and stand, making the dog issue a playful growl and jump up to take hold of Steve's hand in his mouth gently.

"Got a few more grey hairs around your chops," Steve said as he played along.

"Shh," Dan told him. "He hasn't realised he's getting old yet, so don't tell him."

"I was talking to you," Steve shot back with a smirk.

"Says you," Neil cut in with a chuckle as he returned under the burden of two packs. "What are you now, sixty-five?"

"I'm two years older than you," Steve answered, "and there's a saying about people in glass houses coming to mind…"

"Yep," Neil answered, rubbing his belly thoughtfully after he'd unzipped the tactical vest to relieve the pressure. "They shouldn't have showers."

Mitch and Jimmy arrived with Neil, both being introduced by Steve and greeting the three new men, one of whom would only have been a boy when they'd left the country.

Dan nodded his head for Steve to walk away from the group with him as Neil began to entertain them with a story about their leader they likely hadn't heard before.

"What the hell's going on?" Dan asked him. "You said you'd had an attack, then we get nothing? No other transmissions!"

"I'm really glad you came," Steve said, meaning every word. "This has all come from nowhere, and we're not exactly prepared for it, you know?" The former pilot filled the former policeman in on current events, working backwards to the time he'd first come across the man behind the attacks.

"He was a kid back then, but he was a savage little bastard I should've put against a wall and shot when I had the chance," Steve spat.

"That's not your way," Dan said, softening the guilt he felt by reminding him that he had a code. Dan had one too, but his was a little more hazy around the edges when it came to the categories of 'us' and 'them'. His earlier decision about letting two of them go immediately haunted him.

"Still," Steve said, "people are dying now because I didn't deal with a threat when I had the chance." He seemed to deflate a little, as though the stress of it all was a burden he'd never asked for.

"Hindsight bias is a bitch," Dan said as he reached for the Velcro pouch holding his cigarettes out of habit. Steve said nothing, letting the silence hang as he watched the familiar gestures of a man he hadn't seen in the better part of a decade act in just the way he remembered. The way he struck the flint of the disposable lighter with his right thumb, the way his scarred left hand cupped around the end of the cigarette to shield it from the light breeze that still carried a fine spray of rain with it. He watched as Dan leaned his head back to blow the smoke upwards as he always did around others – a small courtesy and one that was probably as automatic as lighting the smoke – and sighed.

"Zero mileage in blaming yourself for this," he told the older man. "You aren't to blame for someone else's actions; you only have a responsibility for your own now."

Steve nodded, not fulfilled or reassured by the words of his friend, but satisfied that the logic was shared.

"So what do you know about him?" Dan asked.

"Goran? Not much. Cruel bastard who favours a knife, and from what we can gather he's come back into the region with a force of about fifty. Scratch off six from here—"

"—and one back up the road with three others disarmed and sent packing west," Dan cut in. Steve's gaze lingered on him, as though he wanted to offer an opinion on Dan letting hostile people leave with their lives.

"Leaves him still with over forty. I've got that many, minus a few now," he added with an angry, forlorn glance at the shot-up Land Rover, "but we're spread out over a big area trying to warn all the smaller settlements. Lots have gone to the town but a few stayed behind. We...we also found a few after *they* did."

Dan sat on a low wall as he listened to Steve's monotone report on what they'd found. He wasn't surprised, as it was much the same as he'd found not long after leaving The Wash, but it still sickened him to know it was a widespread tactic.

"Any demands made?" Dan asked. "Any indication of what he wants? What it'll take to make him go away?"

Steve didn't answer at first, simply looked at his friend who suddenly seemed so much older than he remembered him to be. He recognised what it was then; in that moment he saw Dan for who he was and not who he'd had to be when they knew each other. It was the weariness of long years in conflict that had aged Dan, but the years spent at peace in comfort and safety which had made him change.

"The Dan I knew," Steve said carefully, "would be more interested in how to kill the bastard and every single one of his followers."

"Trust me. The Dan you knew is still there; he just learned a few new ways to deal with things."

"Like killing everyone who threatened your home?" Steve asked with a hint of ice in his words. Dan ground out the cigarette with the toe of his boot on the ground and raised his head to look up at Steve. He knew what he was getting at, because they'd discussed the events of the previous summer and what Dan had done when pirates showed up off their coast.

"No," he said in a measured tone, "that one's still very much in the playbook. I was going more along the lines of figuring out what he wants first."

"Ah, the whole 'understand your enemy' thing?"

"If you know your enemy and know yourself…" Dan started, stopping not because he didn't want to sound like a know-it-all but because he'd genuinely forgotten the rest of the quote. *The Art of War* wasn't exactly light reading, and finding a French language copy of the book had kept him going for over a year during the rare times he could sit down for long enough to read.

"Whatever," Steve said. "No. He hasn't made any demands, hasn't said what he wants, he just keeps killing people. I rather suspect he wants my seat and the infrastructure we've built, which would make him a damn sight worse than Richards was."

"So we resort to plan A," Dan said as he stood with a groan and a crack of a knee joint. "We kill the bastard and every one of his followers we can lay our hands on."

TOO LATE

The damaged Land Rover was still serviceable, but cleaning out the interior was a messy job none of them wanted to perform. Dan, not knowing any of the deceased occupants, offered to do it to take away the emotional stress Steve's people would feel. Mitch helped him, and the bodies were forced inside their sleeping bags with difficulty to be returned to town for a proper burial.

Neil, thinking ahead as he often did when he wasn't cracking jokes or consuming something, brought a small stack of towels from the house to put inside the truck and save their clothes from absorbing the sticky blood left behind.

"One more place to hit," Steve said to Dan as he spread a map out on the drop-down tailgate of his vehicle. "I just hope we get there before them."

Dan looked at his watch, titling his left wrist outwards to show the face before he looked up at the sky. "You happy moving in the dark?" he asked.

Steve wasn't, going by the look on his face, but that look also managed to convey the total lack of choice they had in the matter.

"How far is this next place?"

"An hour, tops."

"Maybe hunker down there for the night if we can?" Dan asked him, leaving a lot of things unsaid.

Steve nodded, no doubt running a lot of those same things through his mind.

"Agreed," he finally said. "If it's safe, otherwise I don't see an alternative."

Dan held his hands wide and gave a small smile to concede. "Hey, it's your patch, mate."

Dan settled himself behind the wheel of the Defender, sliding his unclipped carbine onto the dash but forgetting to remove the shotgun protruding from over his right shoulder. He swore gently, not quite under his breath, and groaned as he stepped back down to ground level and reached up to remove the brute of a gun.

"Still carrying that thing?" Steve asked him, earning a confused look from George, the tall young man who followed him around as though he'd absorb some precious snippet of knowledge if he stayed close enough.

"Yeah," Dan said as he looked at the shotgun fondly. It meant more to him than just being a backup weapon in a way that few people could comprehend.

"He likes to keep it handy, for close encounters," Neil quipped in an American voice.

"Aliens!" George said, beaming an innocent smile at them. "That's what the man in the movie said when…" He trailed off, realising that all of the older men were looking at him like he'd missed the joke. Steve patted him sympathetically on the arm as he walked around to the passenger's side and climbed in. Their prisoner, a large dressing which had once been white wrapped tightly around one arm, was helped into the back of the lead truck where he was eager to show how compliant he was. As though he was a good guy after all and was just following orders.

Dan followed, keeping a decent interval between their truck and Steve's in front out of a habit that seemed more sensible now than all the other times he'd done it. As he drove his mind replayed the details Steve had given him about the man leading the small detachment whose name he'd already heard earlier that day.

The two men exchanged all they knew, and from the intelligence they had it was pretty clear that if Goran was their ace of spades then this Mo was at least the king of spades, or maybe even the ace of clubs. Either way, they'd identified a lieutenant who needed to be dealt with, and having met the man Steve was at the head of the line of volunteers to kill him.

Brakes lights ahead of him flashed three times as though the driver was pumping the pedal gently to signal them behind instead of attempting to slow their vehicle. Dan responded with a single, momentary flash of headlights. He slowed, stopping when the car in front did and maintaining an interval slightly shorter than he had when moving.

"Mitch on me, Jimmy, Neil, give me a rear guard."

"Aye," Neil responded, sliding his conspicuous girth out of the rear seat before reaching back inside for his rifle. A short, low whistle brought Ash scrambling over the rear seats and out through the still-open driver's door to run a tight circle with his snout pressed to the road before watering the front tyre.

Dan jogged forwards to where Steve was looking through his weapon optic to zoom in on something he'd seen in the distance. Dan saw it even without the magnification; the thin skein of black smoke rose vertically another mile ahead and to their left.

"Guessing that's your people," Dan asked.

"Yep," Steve answered, lowering the weapon and letting out a sigh of exhaustion and exasperation. "And I'm guessing we're too late."

They were.

No evidence of a gunfight existed probably because there wasn't any resistance when the bastards had rolled up on an undefended farm. Even in the dying light Dan could make out two patches on the patio of the main house that were darker than the surrounding stones, and the glistening wetness told him the rest of the story. A further search showed that the two patches of blood likely belonged to the two shrivelled and scorched bodies that were unidentifiable even for gender. The sharp stink of chemical accelerants burned Dan's nose when he neared which only served to heighten his revulsion for the men who could do this to innocent people.

"Non-combatants," he said aloud.

"What's that?" a voice asked from behind him. He turned to see George, no shame in the tears which had fallen down his cheeks at the sight. Dan turned to face him, seeing past the redness and the tears into eyes that showed empathy but also hid a resolve he admired.

"I said they were non-combatants," he told the young man. "They were innocents. They weren't players in our game, so there was no need to harm them at all, let alone kill them and do this." He gestured with a hand at the shouldering corpses lashed crudely to the makeshift crosses with coils of wire.

"I think they're sending a message," George said. His mouth stayed open as though he was about to add more but he shut it after a short hesitation.

"Go on," Dan said.

"It's a weapon in itself," George told him, frowning as though he was thinking out loud. "It's horror. Guerrilla tactics. They want to beat us without fighting us, so they make themselves into monsters we're afraid of before we even face them."

Dan nodded thoughtfully. The kid was right, undoubtedly, but he wondered if he'd come to the conclusion himself or whether it was a regurgitated opinion.

"Is that what Steve said?"

"I...I haven't told him that yet..."

"Well," Dan said quietly, "for what it's worth I think you're right." He was saved any further conversation by Steve's voice cutting over them loudly.

"We're moving," he yelled. "We'll make it back by dark if we move fast."

Dan had an opinion on whether they should be driving in the dark, not for giving away their main position but for the risk of being ambushed on the way. With a last forlorn look back up at the two bodies he turned to leave.

"I'll make sure someone comes back to bury them," George told him. Dan nodded, saying nothing and unable to explain why it mattered so much to him that these unknown innocents deserved a proper burial.

TOWN

Dan was partly grateful for the high speed of their drive back to the place Steve called home. The concentration on the road ahead as he chased the red lights on the back of the truck in front kept him awake after a day spent moving hard with more adrenaline than was normal. Couple the hard day with the time spent at sea before they landed at The Wash, and he was on the verge of exhaustion.

Being back in England made him recall so many of the feelings he had before they'd left, only his mind and his body had changed so much in the seven years they'd been away. Although he felt like he'd slipped back into being the man he was back then, he knew there was no way he could stay awake for days at a time surviving on only a few hours of snatched sleep here and there.

He wound down the window to stick his right arm out and leaned forwards to open one of the dash vents before lighting a cigarette.

"Shut your face," he said over his left shoulder as soon as Ash started grumbling.

"How are we playing this?" Neil asked from the back, leaning forward and raising his voice over the noise of the engine and the rush of air coming through the open window.

"How do you mean?" Dan asked.

"I mean, what's our role here? What are we doing?"

"We're here to visit Steve. Also, seeing as we're here, we could help with his pest control problem," Dan told him.

"Simple as that?" Neil asked.

"Speak your mind, mate," Dan said, eyes facing forward but his mind partially diverted.

"I mean, it looks like we're dealing with a vicious bastard or two here. Like, *Mon-sewer Chasseur*, kind of vicious."

Dan said nothing, waiting for Neil to continue and make his point.

"So I guess what I'm saying is, are we enough to make a difference? Should we be thinking that discretion might be the better part of valour here?" Neil asked, offering Dan an avenue for retreat.

"Let me ask you this," Dan said, keeping his gaze fixed on the road and his voice low and calm. "If our own people at The Orchards or the farms or in Andorra were being attacked like this, what would you do?"

"This isn't a, 'what would Dan do' thing," Neil said hurriedly before Dan cut him off.

"What would *you* do?"

Neil hesitated for a few seconds before letting out a breath as if giving up. "I'd probably do something ill-advised, like mount a machine gun in the back of a truck and go looking for trouble."

"Exactly," Dan shot back. "These people are Steve's people, and a lot of them used to be our people so that makes *all* of them our people." Dan didn't see it but Neil gave a shrug.

"In for a penny, I suppose," he answered. "Just do me a favour and take me home if I snuff it, okay?"

His dark attempt at comedy left their car in breezy silence for a few miles until lights showed ahead. The road seemed more travelled there, as though they were nearing the focal point of a region which Dan guessed the largest population centre in the area would be.

Walls came into view next – a combination of old stone buildings, newly built brick walls and large metal shipping containers craned into place between the more permanent barriers. Lights glinted in reflection off metal to their right, and Dan recognised the coils of razor wire sitting in neat loops above a heavy chain-link fence. Their perimeter was a mixture of obstacles which seemed more substantial closer to the road entrance. Either side of the rutted approach worn down by countless vehicles over time stretched fields of crops larger than any they had seen either at their old prison in the countryside or on the slopes of the French hills that grew the fruit on vines which provided Neil with the raw materials for his booming wine industry.

The lead vehicle slowed as large search lights lit up to bathe the gates in a harsh, bright, artificial glow. The world outside of the reach of those lights wasn't yet fully dark, but when they were switched on those areas outside were obliterated into relative darkness. Dan cringed inside at the use of the lights, and had it been Sanctuary instead of a wet, rainy makeshift town back in England Dan would be out of the driver's seat already, tearing people new holes in a mixture of bad French and bad language.

He needn't have worried that Steve had lost sight of his tactical awareness in the dark, nor that he hadn't chosen his senior people carefully, as the man he'd been introduced to as Iain spilled from the lead vehicle and began yelling at people until the bright lights were shut off.

Left sitting behind the wheel of the second vehicle, Dan was blinded by the removal of the lights leaving him only a small section of the entrance he could see illuminated by weaker bulbs.

"…ow many bloody times have I told you?" Iain's voice drifted back to them through Dan's open window. "Use the red lights at night if you have to. You afraid of the dark or something?" Dan didn't hear a reply, but the words and the tone of the bollocking Iain was dishing out felt familiar. A glance to Mitch beside him was rewarded with a flash of white teeth as the soldier recognised another of his breed.

"Sorry about that," Iain said as he approached the open window. "There's only so much stupid you can beat out of some people."

"Tell me about it," Dan said conversationally as he watched armed men and women come forwards to search in and under the lead vehicle. "Who were you with?" he asked the man to pass the time as they were searched in, and to confirm their suspicions about his background.

"RLC," the man answered flatly, using the acronym as such men did to test one another and speak their own language.

"Driver, huh?" Dan answered. "Nice. I was RMP," he said before jerking a thumb at first Mitch then Neil. "Infantry and REME."

Iain nodded appreciatively, no doubt biting back a choice jab directed to at least one of their former professions.

"Good to have you," Iain said genuinely as the search team approached their vehicle nervously. Dan wasn't sure if the nerves were because these kids didn't know their faces or whether they were embarrassed about making a mistake in front of the bosses. Iain slapped a hand lightly onto the door as he backed away. "I'll leave you to get cleared," he said. "See you inside."

"Everyone keep their hands visible while we search," came the slightly wavering and uncertain voice of the armed young man leading the guards. "Is there anything in your vehicle that could cause us harm?"

Dan paused long enough to give Mitch an open-mouthed look which asked the question, 'This kid fucking serious?' before turning back to answer.

"About a dozen weapons and hundreds of rounds of ammunition along with some explosives," he said back, answering the question with as much accuracy as he could while maintaining a straight face.

The young man's face dropped and his mouth stayed open to frame an 'o' like his balls had just shrivelled up with a 'nope', until someone else cleared their throat.

"Just check it out and let them through," a female voice said. "You heard what Steve told you." Mister Shrivel snapped out of his funk and readjusted the grip on his weapon – an MP5 likely much older than he was – before stepping up to make a show of shining a torch beam through their windows. Dan said nothing as he reached into the back for the rear door handle, waiting until the handle had clicked before muttering a single word to Ash.

"*Speak!*"

As the door opened and Ash shot up to bark loudly, the man scrambled backwards from the door with a yelp of fear and surprise before Dan admonished the dog weakly.

"Leave it, boy," he chided gently. "Good dog."

With as much self-respect as he had left, the young man dusted himself off and waved the two vehicles through.

"That wasn't funny," he complained. "I could've been bitten."

"That *would* be a shame," Dan said, feigning concern as he rolled the vehicle forward, "because I'd have to get my dog a tetanus shot if he did that."

"Was that *strictly* necessary, old boy?" Neil asked Dan in his preferred style of a privileged officer.

"Funny though," Jimmy added, breaking his brooding silence brought on by a fear of open conflict.

"Not necessary," Dan agreed, "but I think you'll find we have reputations to uphold."

THE BURDEN OF COMMAND

They did indeed have reputations, although when word spread of who they were the looks on the faces of people gathering around where the vehicles parked seemed more disappointed than awestruck.

Certainly the weaponry they carried drew some admiring glances, without exception from the male portions of the crowd, but Dan was left with the overwhelming sense that tales of his exploits had made people expect some kind of Action Man slash superhero instead of the fairly average-sized man who creaked from behind the wheel to stretch his lower back and groan.

Even Ash was the subject of some confusion, as though the stories of the dog's escapades had made people expect a hybrid dire wolf instead of the big, and often daft, German shepherd. Neil seemed to recognise and interpret the curious looks the same way and sidled close to Dan.

"Looks like they were expecting you to have two heads or something," he muttered.

"Ha!" Dan laughed. "Or maybe just not be so old and knackered? We can't all be Arnie in our sixties…"

Before Neil's internal rolodex could settle on the appropriate movie-plus-character-plus-reference to make from the vast store of quotes locked away in his mind and start his selected impression, Steve jumped two steps ahead of them and turned to address the people.

"Everyone," he called loudly, waving his hands up and down gently as if calling them to hush. "We've been joined by friends who used to live with me and some others before…before we all came here. They've come from France and yes, these are the men you'll have probably heard of."

"Speak," Dan muttered again to Ash as he tried not to move his lips. The dog let out a single, loud bark and looked up at Dan whose feet he sat obediently beside.

"I stand corrected," Steve called out, "these are the men and the *dog* you've probably heard of." A ripple of laughter went around the crowd which quickly subsided, telling Dan that whatever fun these people could have was constantly overshadowed by the events happening outside their walls. Questions were shouted to Steve as he turned away, making him turn back unable to disguise his anxiety.

"Did you get them?" a woman shouted.

"Has my brother been found yet?" another voice pleaded.

"When are you going to attack them?" demanded a man well past the age of being any use in a fight. Dan's gaze lingered on him, trying to see his eyes in the gloom to figure out if the man had ever fought for anything.

He saw no fire reflected. No burning resolve as though he wished he was twenty years younger and could do it himself and Dan recognised in his behaviour one of the greatest difficulties in leadership: giving people what they needed and not what they wanted.

"Please," Steve said. "We've had a long day and yes, we tangled with them earlier today. We lost people. They did too but it's *our* people I'm worried about." He turned away to climb the stairs to a grand building as more shouts broke out behind him. Dan caught up with him as he reached the doors, seeing him reach up to place a hand on George's shoulder.

"I know you must be exhausted," he told the young man, "but can you please see that the gates are sealed and everyone is appropriately switched on?"

George, who didn't even seem mildly dishevelled by the day's events in spite of his smoke-blackened features, nodded and turned to jog away to see it done.

Dan's eyes lingered on him for a few seconds, suddenly so jealous for the ability to break into a jog when tired without warming up and stretching thoroughly.

"I know what you're thinking," Steve said as he clapped a hand against Dan's upper arm and nodded for them to follow him inside. "He makes me feel ancient too. Always runs everywhere like there's a fire; frightens the crap out of me most of the time."

"Yeah," Dan answered with quiet jealousy. "Little bastard."

Steve led the way inside, handing off his primary weapon to a boy waiting to clean it as two others, slightly younger and just shy of service age, hovered bearing slips of paper no doubt containing pieces of information submitted from various sources. Iain reached past Steve to take the papers and wave the boys away as Steve spoke.

"That last settlement was the only one we know of left," he said. "All the others have either been warned to lock down or have sent some or most of their people here or to The Wash. We've got plenty of accommodation space so that isn't an issue, but our supplies will take a hit. We can make that up next year easily enough, assuming we make it through fine."

He turned a sharp right into a large office and walked with a limp he was accustomed to but still seemed curious to Dan, stepping around to the back of a wide, dark wood desk and groaning as he sat down. He picked up a pair of reading glasses which he perched on the end of his nose to read the messages left for him. He looked up to Iain, wordlessly asking if the messages he'd been given bore anything needing his urgent attention but the man shook his head and pocketed the paper.

"Are there other settlements?" Neil asked, his eyes roving around the well-appointed office.

"Not within our realistic sphere of influence," Steve said. "There were maybe twenty when we first...*took over*, but most of those have moved to the larger settlements or otherwise amalgamated over the last few years. Those left out in small numbers were more of the off-grid types, but we still traded with them and sent supplies to keep the relationship good."

"And how many have you lost?" Mitch asked quietly. Steve looked at Iain before the shorter man spoke for the home team.

"Six," Iain said. "thirty people dead or missing."

The room fell silent for a while until Jimmy cleared his throat.

"This stuff is a bit beyond my paygrade I think," he said hopefully. "Any chance I could go and see Kev?"

"Of course, mate," Steve said. "Sorry." He leaned to one side on his chair and called out, "Sophie?"

A tall young woman with a tumble of curly black hair poked her head around the door frame to treat Steve to a smile of uncharacteristically perfect post-apocalyptic white teeth.

"Kettle or bottle?" she asked. Steve glanced at his audience for a second before answering that a bottle would be more appropriate.

"Any runners still there?" he added. In response she ducked out of sight and returned to the doorway with both hands on the shoulders of a boy who must've been fifteen and had flushed cheeks at being touched by the attractive young woman.

"Ah, Ryan," Steve said kindly as he beckoned the boy to step inside. "This is Dan, Mitch, Neil and Jimmy." The boy set his face and gave his manliest nods to the men he was introduced to as he enjoyed a rare opportunity to practice his best handshakes. Ash stood and loped towards him, making him recoil and pull his hands up to his chest as if he feared losing them.

"Sit," Dan said absently, making the dog stop and drop to his haunches to cock his head and regard the boy. "Don't mind him," he reassured Ryan, "he's just trying his luck to see if you'll feed him."

"Ryan, could you take Jimmy to see Maggie please?" Steve asked. The boy nodded emphatically, still with one eye on the dog the likes of which he hadn't seen before given his evident fear.

"Thanks," Jimmy said, hefting his bag and looking at the shotgun in his hand uncertainly as he hesitated halfway to the door. Neil held out a hand for it and Jimmy handed it over freely, dropping the bag again to pass him the belt of cartridges that accompanied the weapon.

"No problem, buddy," Neil said. "Go say hello to the big man for us? Maggie and Cedric too?"

Jimmy nodded, smiling again at Steve in thanks as he ducked out of the room to follow his guide.

"Don't think he's got the heart for a fight," Dan said quietly after they'd left.

"Don't know as he ever did," Steve answered, "not this kind of fight anyway."

"Knock, knock," Sophie announced as she walked through the open door bearing a tray filled with a bottle and half a dozen glasses. Steve's lips tightened as he fought back the retort every time she did that, knowing that she did it intentionally to goad him. Steve thanked her, cracking open the bottle and regarding it before turning it to show Dan the label. Dan made an appreciative face and gave a small bow in magnanimous mockery before Steve poured a healthy measure for all of them and one extra.

"Good health, gentlemen," he said formally as he stood with a grimace to raise his glass to the men he hadn't seen in seven years. They mumbled the toast back to him and took a drink, letting the fiery liquid warm them all the way down. Dan's empty stomach voiced its anger and replied with a wave of acid.

Bootsteps sounded in the corridor outside and all eyes turned in time to see George stride confidently inside. Steve leaned forwards from his chair that he'd settled back into and nudged another glass towards him. George, showing a lot of the mannerisms Dan recognised in Steve, turned to raise his own glass to the visitors.

"Thank you for today," he said seriously. "We were in a pretty shitty situation until you rocked up."

Dan nodded back, lifting his own glass again in acknowledgement.

Steve stood, groaning and limping towards the large map pinned to one wall and adorned with pins and notes. He pulled the cap off a red marker pen and crossed off two settlements before circling a third. He restored the cap and tapped the pen thoughtfully on the area which was only missing a 'you are here' sticker.

"Starting tomorrow," he said with evident tiredness, "we button this place up tight. We consolidate, we harden ourselves as a target and seal up any weaknesses. We have a safe, stable position to defend with a supply of food and running water, whereas *they* only have what they've stolen and what they brought with them. Let the fuckers lay siege here," he said angrily, "and when they weaken, we can rip them apart."

"But first thing tomorrow," George added, "we have our people to lay to rest."

Steve sighed sadly.

"We do. And on that note, I have some families to give bad news to." He turned to Iain wearing a look that he knew he was imposing yet again on a man who was well overdue a rest.

"Could you show our guests to some quarters?" he asked. "I'm sure they need to sleep as much as we do."

A NIGHT SPENT SAFELY

They spent the night in what had been a small terraced house not far from the large building which was obviously Steve's centre of operations. Iain had gone with them, showing them where to drop their kit and waiting for them to lighten their loads before answering the second most prevalent question on their minds.

"Toilet block," he said, pointing at a wooden building set back from the road as they walked. "The plumbing works in your house, but it can be temperamental sometimes. My advice is that if you want a hot shower, get up earlier than the masses, if you know what I mean."

They did. A look at the toilet block reminded Dan of the kind of thing you saw at campsites all over the UK, and for some unknown reason that thought made him smile a little, as though Steve's people had clawed back a little normality from the ashes.

"The main event," Iain said, ending their brief tour at what was evidently the mess hall. "I'll leave you here," he told them. "Shit loads to do, you know how it is?" Again they did, and they thanked the man for pointing them in the right direction, assuring him that they could find their way back to their allocated billets before he shook their hands again and walked away.

"Let's see what's on the menu then," Dan said, turning to see both Neil and Mitch already fast-walking towards the doors of the single-storey building where the smell of food was coming from as if in a walking race. Abandoning his master for pretty much the only reason he could never resist, Ash followed the others leaving Dan stood alone talking to himself.

The menu consisted of a rice dish with chunks of vegetables and a salty substance in random hunks described on the chalk board as 'meat'. If Dan had to guess from the taste, he'd say it was a pork related product, but somehow the fact that this meal had been cooked hours ago and kept warm made it taste much more appetising that it looked. The wholesome stodginess of each spoonful promised to fill them up and none of them really thought much about the ingredients as they ate until Neil asked a question.

"They grow their own rice?"

"The night-time temperatures in the UK drop far too low to grow rice outside of a controlled environment, and seeing as the cost of building and maintaining a place like that was always much higher than the import costs there was never any point in growing it here," Mitch said, not looking up from his plate as he paused shovelling his dinner into his mouth before the previous spoonful had been chewed. Dan and Neil looked at each other, both men uncharacteristically speechless for a moment before Neil swallowed with evident difficulty to speak.

"Fuck me, mate," he croaked, sensing the danger of a cough threatening to rob him of the ability to crack a joke. He cleared his throat quickly before carrying on. "*Ahemm*!" He dug around theatrically in his plate of sticky rice as if searching for something. "Dan, did you get an encyclopaedia in yours?"

"Nope," Dan said, playing along. "Mister Chinese economy expert must've got it."

"That's tea," Mitch said flatly, still not looking up. "Most of the world's rice got exported from India." He said nothing else, shocking both friends as he possessed the high ground from which to mount a successful piss-taking operation.

"Learn something new every day," Neil said, scraping his plate and shifting the bench he occupied awkwardly to ease his girth out for a second helping.

"Every day's a school day," Dan chimed in, feeling full and not wanting to force the feeling into being uncomfortable. He preferred to stay a little hungry when the chance of having to jump into action was a likelihood, which was probably why he was suffering from a very minor case of over-comfort like Neil had gone down with. He slid the leftovers on his plate to one side with the spoon and dropped it onto the plate beside him where the long tongue of his best friend had already polished the china to a high sheen until all traces of taste had been obliterated.

The dog didn't wait patiently for the serving to be completed before he nodded his thanks and ate politely, instead he turned his big head sideways and began chomping noisily at the falling globs of rice, meat and vegetables as it dropped onto the plate, scattering some in the process which would only serve as a hidden bonus level when he eventually got down to search for it.

"Bets on Jimmy?" Neil asked when he returned with a second plate heaped up as high as the first one had been.

"I think he's probably being hugged half to death by Kev at the moment, and Maggie's likely trying to force more food down his neck than even *you* could manage," Dan said, jabbing his spoon in Neil's direction and laughing at the feigned wound his portly friend pretended to have received directly in the chest.

"What are you trying to say?" he asked, still sounding hurt.

"He's trying to say you've got fat," Mitch put in nonchalantly. "Obviously not an opinion I share, and I think to point out anything about a person's personal appearance as negative is both cruel and unnecessary." He fixed first Neil then Dan with a deadpan look before their faces creased up and they laughed.

"Fine, keep it coming," Neil said through a mouthful of rice before a small voice interrupted them.

"Excuse me."

Dan, wiping a tear from his eyes as he turned towards the source of the interruption wearing a beaming smile of amusement, felt his heart drop out through his guts as he took in the sight before him.

A woman, maybe mid-twenties and clear skinned despite the lack of makeup most women wore, stood nervously running a small, off-white handkerchief through her bony hands. Her face was swollen, and her red, puffy eyes glistened with fresh tears Dan guessed were only temporarily under control.

"My name's Andrea," she said quietly. "My...my husband was killed today by..." She broke down, making Dan rise from his seat and take a pace towards her to offer comfort. She retreated a step and flapped her hands as if to ward off both his sympathy and more tears, like any kindness he could show would break her down and prevent her from saying the words she came to say.

"My husband was killed by those bastards that *you* killed," she said, betraying how fast word spread in the town. "So I just wanted to thank you for...for making it possible to bury him in...in one piece." She held his gaze for a moment longer then fled, sobbing as she half ran out of the room and into the arms of an older woman.

Dan turned back to the others, seeing even Ash giving him a look that made him feel guilty for having fun when others had just lost everything. As if to show how much he was affected, Neil slid the last half of his second helping of food over to Ash who paused long enough to glance judgingly up at Dan again before attacking it.

"I need some air," Dan said. "I'll see you outside when you're finished."

He stepped out into the cool night air, feeling the light film of moisture land on his skin as if the sky was too lazy to rain properly. He dug out his cigarettes and lighter, turning his body to shield the delicate flame from the breeze before blowing out that first long, blissful lungful up into the air. He felt like a callous bastard for having fun where others could see them; felt like he was some kind of alien on his home soil because he'd long ago learned how to compartmentalise and lock away everything he didn't want to remember deep inside where it could just eat away at him like normal people.

The door opened and the others filed out, having put their clean plates into the tubs of cold water and soap suds ready for someone to clean. Dan's gaze lingered on the man who shuffled out from behind the counter of what had been an old café before being appropriated for its current use, and he considered how each cog in the machine had to turn so that the thing as a whole worked. The thing in this case was a society, and just as that society wouldn't function if nobody cleaned their plates and served their food, he knew it couldn't function if nobody stepped up to be more violent than the threats facing it.

That was his role. That was *their* role, just as it always had been in some form or another for his entire adult life. He was the rough man standing ready, as he liked to describe it, reimagined from his former life and born again to do it every day without the reward of money or a pension, and the people who were threatening this society would find out the hard way that he was not a man to fuck with.

CUTTING THROUGH THE BULLSHIT

Dan, despite being dead on his feet after the food had hit his belly to accompany the single malt, struggled to find sleep.

Neil, Mitch and, unsurprisingly, Ash had all dropped off within minutes of closing their eyes, and an added obstacle to Dan seeking slumber was the rhythmic snoring of his dog who had adopted his preferred position on his back with his legs splayed out as though he'd been hit by a truck.

"Rock out with your cock out," Dan muttered softly to him as he sat on the windowsill and smoked. He could hear both men snoring from their own rooms – a luxury none of them expected – and although they all needed it, none of them had the energy for a shower.

The terraced house was decked out like any holiday let in the country, with neutral décor and easy clean surfaces everywhere, making Dan suspect that they were in one of a few places reserved for visitors given its close proximity to the mess hall and the important building where Steve did business.

Dan was up with the dawn having dozed intermittently through the darkness. He slipped out of the room to run a sink of hot water and wash himself before taking the first spin of the day on the porcelain throne and returning to his room to find Ash occupying the bed shamelessly.

He threw on a fresh set of underwear, paying close attention to the condition of his feet which hadn't seen this much action in a very long time. Adding a clean T-shirt, he dressed in the familiar cargo trousers and boots before adding a black windcheater to go under his vest and equipment. He'd run a cleaning cloth over his rifle in the night when his mind needed to occupy his hands with a worthwhile task, working from the small, red-lensed torch in his kit, so was satisfied it was in working order when he clipped it to his body armour.

"Up you get," Dan told the dog, seeing such a careful stillness in the animal that it had to be faked.

"Come on," he tried, still seeing no response.

"Where's the…*catssssssss*!" Dan hissed, feeling the air pressure in the room change as the dog came alive – ears first – and leapt off the bed to fly for the door. Dan set him loose, muttering encouragement for the dog to search the house and hearing a string of curses from Neil who had failed to secure the door to his own room sufficiently to keep Ash out.

"*FAKKARFF*!" Neil shrieked in falsetto, prompting a chuckle from Mitch who was emerging from the bathroom wearing just what he called his shreddies with a towel draped over one shoulder. He'd had the same idea as Dan, treating himself to a strip wash in the sink, and was parading the fact that he was still in pretty much the same condition as he had been when they had first met.

Ash emerged from Neil's bedroom, closely followed by the man himself in the same state of undress as Mitch. His pink and blue striped boxer shorts elicited a giggle from the others, but Neil stuck by his choice and flaunted them proudly.

"You're just jealous of my fashion sense," he told them.

"Very true," Dan said. "I was just wondering if they came as a set with the matching sports bra?"

Neil's bombastic nature fled under yet another joke about what he'd started referring to as his 'off-season' body before they'd even had morning coffee, and he huffed his way to the bathroom before closing the door so firmly it could almost be confused with a slam.

Dan went downstairs, finding a key on a hook and unlocking the back door to let Ash roam out onto the back patio which constituted the entire small rear yard of the guest house. He found the kettle, filled it from the tap which took a long time due to the weak water pressure, and smiled as the little LED light sparkled to denote it was working from mains electricity. Feeling something suddenly off, he put his hand against the side of the kettle to find it still held some residual warmth and began to dismiss it with the assumption that one of the others had already been down for a drink, but knowing that neither man wouldn't have made three cups and brought them upstairs.

"Still goes back to the first spot to lay cable, I see," Steve's voice said from the doorway to the small lounge, making Dan jump out of his skin so much that he didn't even instinctively reach for a weapon.

"Fuck *me*!" Dan said, one hand on his chest as he forced himself to calm down.

Steve smiled, sipped from the mug he held in his right hand, and switched his gaze back to Ash who, sure enough, had returned to the first place he had sniffed to strike the awkward pose and deposit something resembling kebab meat prior to slicing.

"You'll give me a heart attack sneaking up like that," Dan chided him.

"Sorry. Old habits of getting up early and all that...I'd have guessed you three would be exhausted from travelling and..."

"Yeah," Dan said. "More the *other* thing than the travel if I'm honest."

"When it gets easy is when you should worry," he said, telling Dan that it was okay to feel a little messed up about the loss of life only hours before. Dan said nothing, only moving from his spot when the kettle clicked to wake him from the daze he'd been in. He threw freeze-dried coffee into a mug and sloshed hot water in on top of it in the haphazard way of a man simply needing caffeine and being unable to take it intravenously. Dragging out a chair from the table where Steve now sat he winced at the noise it made scraping over the tiled floor. He sat, blowing on the hot liquid in his cup and regarded the man opposite him.

Steve, despite the years and the traumas, still looked very much the same. Dan was aware from his own reflection that he'd gained a little weight, especially in the face, and was sporting a lot more white in his hair and beard than before. He'd gone from salt and pepper to lightly frosted in a few years.

Steve regarded him right back as he sipped his own drink which had cooled enough to slurp thoughtfully.

"Fancy taking a walk?" he asked with heavy inference. Dan stood, slid open the rear door to let Ash back in, and nodded his assent to Steve.

The two men strolled casually, walking it seemed without much purpose as though the entire point of the walk was a roving privacy in place of any real destination in mind. People greeted Steve with smiles and words which he returned politely. Some recognised Dan, insisting on approaching him to shake his hand and nervously offer a greeting to the legendary Ash. Each time Steve was careful to greet the person with their name as if he knew Dan wouldn't be able to recall them even if he did recognise their faces.

"What do you make of George?" Steve asked casually. The way he asked, almost *too* off-hand, betrayed that there was more behind the question than face value indicated.

"Seems...*deep*," Dan said. "I'm assuming he's proficient?"

"In everything," Steve answered. "People like him and listen to him, even if he's only twenty-three."

Dan huffed a small laugh as if to say that he'd give anything to be that young again and go back to a time before life decided to kick him in the balls repeatedly.

"He's a thinker, isn't he?" Dan asked, half turning to Steve to see him nod. "He understood why these bastards brutalised the bodies, and that takes maturity to break through the anger and fear. I thought you'd given him the insight, but it seems I was wrong."

"What insight?"

"That they're sending a message, trying to win the battle through fear before we actually fight them; real guerrilla warfare."

Steve made a *hmm* noise that implied he was thinking, leaving the two men walking in silence for a while.

"I'm rather hoping he can take over my job soon," Steve admitted, making Dan feel a little smug that he'd guessed it was going that way. "I'd like to retire soon, you know?"

"Here's trouble," a woman's voice said from behind them, ending their conversation and making both men turn. Lizzie stood there, hands on hips as though acting like she was here to scold them. Dan noticed a thin young woman beside Lizzie with her head slightly bowed as if she hid behind her hair which fell in glossy waves down past her shoulders. "Need any stitches yet?" Lizzie asked him, stepping close to plant a kiss on his cheek between beard and eye.

"Not yet," Dan admitted, "but it's only Tuesday."

"It's Thursday, dear," she said in mild correction as she patted his armoured chest.

"It's good to see you," a smaller voice said making Dan lean around Lizzie who stepped aside to kiss Steve in a very different way than she had Dan. The speaker lifted her head then, revealing a young woman in her mid-twenties wearing a smile of genuine warmth.

"Alice?" Dan asked, recognising the teenager he'd saved from death and likely a lot more before that. Saving her had meant him taking the first life since the world changed, and he never thought back on that with any kind of remorse because it was the right thing to do.

She closed the gap and hugged him, making him freeze because he didn't expect it. He gathered himself and hugged her back, feeling the warmth of her and breathing in the smell of her hair.

They'd never been that close before, but somehow the symbology of what each meant to the other seemed to hit them both hard in that moment. Both of them represented their rebirth into the new world, and both had been irrevocably changed that day.

"*Doctor* Alice now," Lizzie said with evident pride. Dan disengaged and looked at her with a mix of shock and amazement.

"Really?"

Alice shrugged depreciatively, as if studying medicine from all available sources over the last nearly eight years wasn't an achievement.

"It's not *technically* right," she corrected Lizzie as she looked up at Dan and swept her hair behind her ears. "It's not formal like it used to be or anything, it's just that people call me that now…"

"She's being modest," Steve interjected. "She's studied hard and learned everything there is to know. She started diagnosing this year so people started calling her Doc." He shrugged as if to say that if something happened then it just happened. Taking away how precious people had become over titles in the old world made her elevation an important one, at least in Dan's eyes.

"I'm…" Dan said as he rubbed her upper arms with his hands a little awkwardly. "I'm really proud of you."

She smiled shyly at his words and changed the subject. "I know my dad would love to see you," she told him, "if you get the time, that is…"

Dan assured her that he would try his best to catch up with everyone and share their experiences in France. Steve made their excuses as a small crowd had gathered and tugged Dan's sleeve surreptitiously to draw his guest along with him.

"If you don't keep moving they'll all come out of the woodwork and you won't make it ten yards," Steve muttered to him, prompting another huff of laughter from Dan. They reached the area of the gate, past what was unmistakably a pig pen going by the wafting odour, and Steve saw the wrinkle in Dan's nose.

"We keep the young pigs near the kitchens," he explained. "Most effective waste recycling system in the world."

"They are that," Dan mused, thinking back to a few occasions he'd used the pigs on their old farm to 'recycle' animals that had perished through different means.

To Dan's surprise he saw the lean, fit form of George at the main gate giving orders and inspecting the position. He didn't have the look of a man who had only recently woken up, so Dan calculated he'd probably grabbed only a few hours of sleep.

And, much to his disgust, the little shit looked fresh as a goddamned daisy.

He let his jealousy fade as he watched the man go about his business. He offered an encouragement here, a piece of advice there and a mild warning to another guard who had apparently been known to fall asleep on duty.

"You wouldn't do that again," Steve called out in a loud voice to startle most people on guard at the gate who hadn't seen their approach, "would you, Nick?"

Nick, red-faced at being singled out, shook his jowly head emphatically. Steve smiled, giving some subtle signal to George who stepped away with some parting order thrown over his shoulder. True to form, he jogged the ten paces which could've easily been walked without delaying anyone, and greeted the pair briefly before getting back to business.

"Ready to start the interview?" he asked, looking more at Dan than Steve. Dan turned to his former number two and raised his eyebrows. Steve spoke while maintaining a false smile for anyone who cared to be watching them.

"You think you're here for your good looks and your jokes?" he asked. "Time to go to work."

ADVOCATE

"You…*what*?" Dan asked, cigarette paused halfway to his mouth as they stood outside a small building which had once, ironically, been a very small police station.

"We've assigned him an advocate," Steve answered simply. "No special treatment, just the next one on the list."

"Back up a minute," Dan said. "You have an on-call list of advocates? *Why?*"

"I don't know how you do things," Steve said, speaking quickly in the hopes of avoiding sounding like he was criticising, "but here when we have assaults and thefts and the like, we assign the accused an advocate and I appoint a prosecutor. Both meet to discuss the evidence and if they can't meet in the middle then we have a kind of trial."

Dan's head shook for a second as if electrocuted while the information forcibly downloaded itself into his brain. The fact that they had established a judicial practice was astonishing and his silence led to a question from George.

"Don't you have something similar?" he asked.

"No," Dan told him. "Honestly, the only *crimes* we've ever had have been some public order issues and a few fights. We had a theft once but by the time it became common knowledge, well…let's just say the culprit had already been tried and sentenced."

"You let your people execute someone for theft?" George asked, stopping short of issuing a theatrical gasp.

"What? No! I mean he'd clearly had a slap and the property got returned."

"So, hang on," Steve cut in, "you're saying you haven't had any real issues like that?"

"No," Dan told him with an incredulous shake of his head. "People get unhappy in phases and move between the farms or other settlements like Andorra, but we don't really have any crime inside our own community. That said, we've had raiders who raped and murdered their way across the area but they...err..." Dan finished with a shrug as if to say that he didn't need to explain their end.

"Anyway," Steve said, shaking his own head to try and reset the conversation. "There are rules for how we detain people and care for them, and we have rules for how we establish their guilt."

"What, so someone found the police rulebook and you've decided that applies here? This isn't someone caught stealing chickens, mate, this is a fucking war criminal. He's a murderer, and the only reason he should still be alive is so he can tell us everything we want to know before he gets one to the back of the dome." He tapped angrily with the tip of his forefinger into the side of his head, hoping nobody noticed he said and pointed to different parts of his skull as if it mattered.

"There's this little thing called evidence," George told him gently but with a resolve behind his words that told Dan the inexperienced young man wouldn't budge on the matter. "Did any of us *see* him kill anyone? Did he pull the trigger on our people yesterday? All we have against him is an attempted assault on us in the house. Look, for what it's worth I agree with you – *completely* – but we have to maintain order and, like I said, we need a little thing called *evidence*."

"There's also this little thing called Common Purpose," Dan snapped back as he threw away the end of his cigarette angrily, taking his shock out on George undeservingly. "This prick was there, acting with others in joint purpose so he's just as liable for the actual act as the others. Further to that, given what his little group of pals has perpetrated elsewhere, he's also on the hook for the murder, crucifixion and burning of bodies."

"What if they'd captured one of us? Would they be justified in executing one of us for being the flip-side of the coin?"

Dan didn't answer, but both men seemed to swell as though their disagreement was heading for a physical conclusion.

Steve leaned towards George who stood his ground and returned the angry stare back at Dan.

"You remember what I told you he used to do for a living?" Steve muttered.

"I do," George answered, "so forgive me if I'm a little surprised that someone who swore to protect people is so quick to start executing others. You're forcing me to play devil's advocate now."

"Executing these fuckers *is* protecting other people," Dan told him flatly. "And the devil's advocate is literally in that bloody building."

"We can't have one rule for him and different rules for others…"

"We – *you* – can. If it helps, consider this the Hague and not your local magistrates'."

George looked to Steve who shook his head to say 'not now' for the explanation.

Dan saw it and explained anyway. "This isn't your regular *drunk and disorderly* shoplifter," he told the man. "This bastard is guilty of war crimes, and only when we find out everything he knows does he have a chance of living through this. He's a POW, and you want to protect him?"

George's nostrils flared and he looked for a second like he wanted to take a swing for Dan. Dan recognised it and smiled, shifting his stance slightly in case the boy lost control and threw a haymaker out of temper. Ash, probably smelling the dump of hormones, sprang up and paid attention as if he knew shit was about to get real.

"I'm. Not. Protecting. Him," George snarled through clenched teeth as his hands balled so tightly the skin shone white.

"I get it," Dan said mockingly. "You're protecting democracy and blah blah bullshit, three bags full." He stuck his tongue out of the corner of his mouth and offered a salute that would be deemed offensive to lots of people. George's anger flashed again only this time Steve physically interjected by stepping in between the two men.

"Regardless," Steve said, "of what happens afterwards, he has intelligence we need. Dan, I'd like you to speak to him for us."

"With pleasure."

"Leave all your weapons outside," Steve added, appeasing George slightly as he held up both hands to ward off the coming protest. Dan didn't reply, instead he began stripping off his vest and weapons and dumping them roughly in George's upturned hands.

"We both know I don't need weapons for this," he shot back over his shoulder.

"Ash included," Steve added, receiving a muttered response that didn't fill him with confidence the man would go in alone. Before he went in, Steve grabbed his sleeve gently and leaned in to whisper in his ear. "You know we can't get away with being the ones to do this, right?"

Dan leaned away, searching his friend's eyes for the truth of why he was being called in and seeing that Steve needed him to break the rules because he was an outsider.

"Loud and clear, mate," Dan told him. "Loud and clear."

Dan entered the room alone and unarmed. He sat Ash down using hand signals and the dog waited patiently out of sight of the doorway until such time as he was called for. Dan rapped his knuckles on the door twice before bursting into the room.

It was small, with a single window he noted had been secured with some welded bars on the outside, and it contained a simple table and three chairs. Taken aback for a second as he was expecting a cell, he recovered and beamed a ridiculously false smile at the occupants.

One, the man with the heavily bandaged right arm, looked terrified and began to scramble backwards out of his seat.

"It's okay," Dan said calmingly, "I'm only here to talk, okay? Look," he said as he spun a slow circle, "I'm not armed and I'm on my own."

As the frightened prisoner sat back down he shot a pleading look at a woman who rose stiffly with a groan.

Dan saw it, and marked it out as fake immediately.

"Hello, young man," she said in a voice like low-gradient sandpaper.

"Mornin'," Dan answered. "And you are?"

"Mrs Beecham," she responded, forcing a stunned blink from Dan who hadn't heard anyone refer to themselves by title and surname in as long as he could recall. Even the often irascible Penny never took such a lofty position, and now that he thought about her he realised he wasn't sure if he'd ever even learned her last name.

"I'm young Daniel's advocate," she went on, making the blinking of his eyes start up again.

"Well, okay," he said. "I'm Dan and—"

"Oh!" she exclaimed as she extended a pudgy hand on a short arm from under the folds of her large, knitted cardigan. "Two Daniels in one room! Two Dan's don't make a right!"

Dan tried his hardest to keep his eyes from rolling back into his head and the effort made the muscle in his right cheek twitch. "Hehe. Anyway, I'd quite like a chat with the lad, so if you don't mind…" He opened the door and smiled, waiting for her to get the point. She didn't move, so Dan added a jerk of his head with a smile that was subtitled, 'Off you fuck, then'.

"I'd quite like to get some disclosure from you first," she said as she crossed the small room in a fashion he could only describe as 'bustling'. She stopped in the doorway and craned her neck up at him, demonstrating the foot and a half difference in height as though it gave *her* the advantage.

"Disclosure?" Dan asked.

"Yes, the part where you tell me what evidence there is against the young man?"

"Evidence…you get what's happening here, right?" he asked her, hoping it was all a show for the prisoner. He made to pull the door closed but her foot stomped down with a clap as she intentionally blocked it from moving any further.

"Yes," she said, taking off her glasses and dropping them to dangle on a hideous chain much the same as Dan did with his carbine. Her expression changed from one of politely confrontational to direct and overt hostility aimed towards him. She lifted a gnarled finger and pointed it at him when she spoke. "This young man has been kidnapped and assaulted – *seriously* assaulted – by someone setting a vicious wild animal on him. I can see no justification for his treatment, nor the use of force against him, and I'd like to discuss compensation for his injuries."

Dan fixed her with a look for a second, fighting his rising urge to do something unworthy, and settled on deflating with a sigh.

"I understand entirely," he said, gesturing out of the room with an open hand. He seemed defeated, quieter, as if her bombast had pierced his entire case like the world she lived in had swallowed his reality. "If you'd like to sit down and discuss it?"

She nodded once, triumphantly, then stepped into the doorway before staggering forwards as the door hit her hard in the ample posterior.

Dan saw no lock on the inside, understandably, so he snatched up the nearest chair to wedge it under the handle. The prisoner started shouting, yelling for help from anyone outside the room as though the behaviour and attitude of the do-gooder had given him the wrong impression about what was going to happen. He flapped his one free hand at Dan who was shoving the chair with his boot to make sure it was secure and spun on the man who jumped back at the sight of his face.

Dan slapped him once, pulling a page from the Mitch school of questioning, to establish fear and shock. He followed it up with a second slap, connecting his slightly cupped right hand to the man's cheek in a savage clap that sent him backwards where he unintentionally landed his backside down in a chair. Dan leaned in, grabbed the clothes at the front of his chest and pressed their foreheads together.

"Forget everything that woman told you," he snarled. "You're going to give me every piece of information I want or you won't walk out of here alive, is that clear?"

Over the angry shouts and the banging on the door, Dan heard the weak whimper of total agreement come from him as his head nodded so rapidly it looked like he was plugged into the mains electricity.

"Good," he said as he released him and pulled up the other chair to begin his questioning.

FALLOUT

"There won't be too much shit coming your way over this I hope?" Dan asked as he sat in Steve's office. The pilot waved a hand dismissively, as if to say that there would but it wasn't his biggest concern right then.

"I've been hoping someone would try to overthrow me for years," he said, wincing internally at how callous his words sounded. "I've been offering a kind of general election every year on the anniversary of…of this place entering the age of democracy."

"Let me guess," Dan asked with a smirk. "No takers?"

"There was one, about five years ago…" Steve answered wistfully as he leaned back in his chair and smiled.

"Going to share or what?"

"Oh, yeah, he was…erm…he was very *individual*, shall we say?"

"A fucking loon then?" Dan guessed. Steve's smile and slow nod told him the nail had been struck on the head.

"Yeah. He jumped up and down on the steps handing out fresh produce like he was Oprah."

Dan snorted halfway through a sip of coffee. "Seriously?" he asked, wiping his nose on his sleeve.

"Seriously," Steve said with a solemn nod. "You get a carrot, and *you* get a carrot…that was basically the entire length and scope of his manifesto; to give everyone more food when nobody was going without as it was."

Dan's head shook slowly from side to side as if he couldn't imagine the scene playing out.

"Sad really," Steve went on as he reached for his own drink and took a pensive sip. "From what we'd heard he wasn't the full ticket when we got here, but it looks like the freedom got to his head and tipped him over."

"How so?"

"All rumour you understand?" Steve said to make sure Dan knew he wasn't giving grade-A intel. "But a couple of people said he had the bodies of his family wrapped up when Richards' people found him…kicked off a bit at leaving them behind."

"Ah," Dan said, suddenly not finding the Oprah scene he'd imagined quite so funny when it was at the expense of another man's mental health.

"Anyway," Steve said, "that woman will raise an absolute stink no doubt, but I doubt she'll find much in the way of public support if you get me."

"The 'Wouldn't Hurt a Fly' brigade?" Dan asked, touching on a conversation the two men had shared years before. Those who believed themselves pacifists, who publicly decried the violent arms of the former governments, who campaigned for the rights of the accused while dismissing the damage done to the victims and their families.

"That's them," Steve agreed. "Plenty of them here, too, some are even quite vocal until a wolf knocks at the gates."

Dan huffed a derisive noise to show what he felt about those people, always thinking himself the kind of person they decried in peacetime and screamed for when shit went down. The sheepdog for the sheep.

He knew that was an over-simplified and probably arrogant way to think about life and people, but those who wouldn't hurt a fly screamed first and they screamed the loudest when they needed someone to fight for them and their liberty and their safety.

"Speaking of the wolves," he said as he leaned to one side in the chair to pull out the pencil and notepad from his back pocket; the only items he'd taken into the room where he'd been told everything he wanted to know for the bargain price of two slaps and a death threat. "Goran," he said, starting at the top. "Early twenties, built like a brick shithouse by this guy's account, and likes to cut people who upset him."

"Can confirm," Steve said, his face devoid of all traces of humour and enjoyment. "Jan got up close and personal with him years back."

"Where is he?"

"Jan? He travelled around a bit after the changes here – too many painful reminders of things he had to do – and settled down with a woman from another settlement to be their medic."

"He's safe?"

Steve nodded, giving his guest the impression he should drop the line of questioning.

Dan pursed his lips and looked back at his notes, avoiding the big 'I bloody well told you so' that Steve should've treated the younger Goran to a shallow grave when they'd first met. As if reading his thoughts, Steve offered an explanation by way of an apology.

"In my defence, I'm not in the habit of killing kids in case they turn into evil bastards when they grow up."

Dan held up a hand as if to ward off the defensiveness. "Me neither, but hindsight's twenty-twenty."

"Tell me about it. Next?"

"The only other organ-grinder from what this kid knows - your mate Mo. Reckons him to be the right-hand man or something, even though he's got to be twice Goran's age."

"He's probably your age," Steve agreed, "so yeah. Dibs." Calling his preference to be the one who took the serpentine bastard out amused Dan.

"He's given me twenty names, some details on vehicles and where they'd previously camped but other than that he doesn't know the plan of attack and doesn't know where they've been hiding out."

"No idea?"

"We went down that route," Dan said as he ran a finger down the map to trace a road. "Ten or twenty minutes in a car to get to where we found you."

Steve stood, pausing halfway up as if waiting for one of his joints to catch up, and limped to the map on the wall of his office. It took him half a minute to locate the farm where they'd been besieged, tutting to himself when he found it and muttering something about wood and trees.

"On road or off road?"

"Both, apparently," Dan answered.

"Twenty minutes, averaging thirty-five miles an hour," he said, being intentionally generous on both speed and time to ensure they didn't limit their search to too small an area. "That's what? eleven? Twelve miles?"

"About that," Dan agreed having done the mental arithmetic as Steve thought out loud. He watched as Steve cut a piece of red wool from a small ball and measured it carefully against the scale bar on the bottom of the map. Cutting it off at the right length he pinned one end on the farm and wrapped the end around the shaft of a marker pen before drawing a rough circle. He restored the cap on the pen and banged his fist gently onto the wall.

"Fuckers are in there somewhere," he told Dan.

"Easy as that," his friend answered. "All we need now is an aircraft to…" He trailed off, realising how insensitive his words were.

Steve waved another dismissive hand at him as he returned to his seat. "Don't worry about that," he said with a smirk as if pleased he'd get to show his former boss a trick he had up his sleeve.

A knock at the door interrupted their conversation and it opened without an invitation. It wasn't a lack of manners, but more of an earned understanding between Steve and one of his senior men as Iain walked in with Mitch and Neil hot on his heels.

"Been busy?" Neil quizzed Dan as soon as he walked in and made his way to the tray bearing a flask and empty cups before helping himself.

"What have you heard?" Steve asked, his eyes searching Iain's face for any news of concern.

"Only that the visiting savages beat up a prisoner," Neil answered with an amused look. "Given that Mitch was with me, I'm pretty sure that's your doing."

"Anything else?" Dan asked.

"Maybe something about you setting your dog on his lawyer…"

"That's bollocks," Dan said, sniffing as if his pride had suffered a wound. He took a sip of coffee before muttering, "I only told him to watch her. Ash didn't even nip the silly cow."

"Like I didn't have enough problems with her already," Steve muttered darkly, earning a questioning expression from Dan. "She'd formally challenged what she called a 'shoot to kill' policy when it came to our perimeter guarding protocols."

Neil, cup to his lips and slurping, spluttered coffee into the air as he laughed.

"She ever shot a gun?" Dan asked.

"Leave the politics to me," Steve said to end the conversation. "In the meantime be ready to go out in an hour." He stood and drained the last of his drink before adding, "I need to find someone."

THE WOLF

Goran didn't know that a new adversary had been imported especially for him, but if he did it would only have served to inflate his ego.

As two of the groups he'd sent out slithered back after dark and waited to see him, he spoke to his lieutenant in private.

"Remind me, Mo," he said. "You take how many mans with you this morning?"

"Eight."

"And how many trucks did you take?"

"Two."

"So tell me how you came back with less men and one trucks."

The demand was given quietly, almost gently, but then anyone who knew Goran knew that he didn't need to shout to be intimidating. He made sure all the men and women serving under him had seen how he dispensed justice. Mo swallowed before speaking, clearing his throat to make sure his voice was confident and strong.

"We were attacked by another group," he began. "We had some of them surrounded and trapped and were about to kill or capture them when these unexpected men showed u—"

"Why are they *unexpected*?" Goran interrupted him.

"Well, they showed up from nowhere an—"

"So they are appearing out of the thin airs?"

"No, they—"

"So how were they this, *unexpected*?"

272

Mo said nothing, not wanting to trap himself in an excuse. He stood tall and accepted responsibility before it was forced on him.

"I didn't set guards on the road," he admitted. "I didn't have enough men an—"

"So it was the faults of your men?"

"No. It was my fault for not s—"

"Yes. This is most definitely your faults. Tell me, these others people who attacked you, did they have a dog?"

"A what?"

"A dog. You know, wagging tail and going *bark, bark*?"

Mo racked his brain but couldn't recall any dog. He'd driven out of sight only seconds before the man he'd abandoned was brought down so he hadn't seen it.

"No. Why?"

In answer Goran simply waved for one of the guards posted on the double doors of the room he'd adopted as his grand hall. It had been a school, and it amused him to make grown men sit on small chairs as he spoke to them. The doors were pushed open and two men were ushered forcefully inside. Neither were armed and both had the look of exhausted men who'd walked a long way.

"You, tell me agains about the dog," Goran demanded. The man he'd spoken to hung his mouth open a little as he looked at everyone in the room for more specific instructions.

"It's grey," Woz said helpfully. "And really big."

"Wow," Goran said as he stood from his chair and lazily stretched his arms wide to demonstrate the size of his shoulders and arms. "You should write a book, man. Anyone ever tell you how good you are with the words?"

Woz smiled, lacking the intelligence to know when he was being mocked and mistaking the words for a genuine compliment.

"And what about the man with the dog?"

"Men," the other one brought in interrupted in a voice thick with the nasal twang of a man with a recently broken nose. He held his nerve when Goran fixed him with a murderous stare for speaking out of turn, stepping close and looming over him so that he seemed to suck the oxygen out of his space.

"Tell me," he ordered.

"Four of them. Only two were in the boat when we were told they were all there. Two had got out somewhere and came at the bridge from the banks. There was a skinny one who didn't get involved, a fat one who kept cracking bad jokes and two hard bastards. One of those had the dog. Alfie got his head bashed against a wall and Rick got shot."

"And you two got away?"

The brave speaker glanced at Woz, hoping that his companion would possess enough of a survival sense to keep his mouth shut.

"They let us go," he said. Goran froze in his pacing and slowly turned to face them.

"Why," he growled gently, "would these mans who already killed one of my boys let you two pieces of shit just walk away?"

Woz and his unfriendly friend exchanged another glance before the one who'd unintentionally betrayed their leader spoke.

"I told 'im," Woz said. "I told him that you had a 'undred soldiers in cars and went the other way to what you went."

Goran fixed him with a look, stepping close to intimidate him as he straightened the man's collar.

"You...*talked*?"

"O...o...only stuff what weren't real," Woz stammered. "I didn't tell them nothin' else."

Goran's gaze switched between the two men over and over as he let the tense silence build, expecting one of them to crack and spill something they hadn't already said.

"The two, how you said, *hard bastards*. Tell me."

"One of them was Scottish," he said, gesturing at his swollen and bruised face. "Bastard did this with the butt of his rifle."

"What is his gun?" Goran enquired gently, already thinking about trophies that he liked to take from anyone who defied him.

"American-looking thing," the man said with a shrug. "Long barrel and a grenade launcher underneath."

Goran's eyes lit up at the news, encouraging the frightened man to say more.

"The other one had a shorter version," he said as he mimed the barrel length reducing with both hands. "But he had a couple of pistols and a short shotgun and his guns had silencers."

Goran's face slowly split into a grin and Woz knew he'd pleased his leader which he hoped would go some way to redeeming him for losing his weapons and being driven from his position. Or at the very least would save his life.

"Still, I need someone to make pay for the losses we have suffer-inged from today," Goran said.

Mo cleared his throat and stepped forwards to speak. "Sir, if I may...we have the prisoners from the last place we found..."

Goran kept smiling as he thought, returning to his chair and sitting down to draw a long knife with such an over-sharpened edge that its feathered edge glinted in the light.

"I will have both," he said. "Assemble the men for the games."

UNFAIR FIGHT

Two men, both beaten and bloody with injuries needing medical attention, stood bare-chested with their hands tied behind their back. Fires had been lit around the fenced yard that had once been a place where children ran and played and shrieked in the few breaks they got from their stuffy classrooms.

There were no words, no grand speeches, because they had all seen it before and they all knew what was about to happen. Goran, like nearly all game hunters, liked to have the upper hand over his quarry even if he made it look fair. He stepped forwards and unzipped the military issue vest he wore to let it drop to the ground with a thud. He peeled off his long-sleeved top and let the firelight show the two bound men the size of his muscles as though he enjoyed their fear at seeing his physique.

He recalled being a thin boy, overlooked and dismissed by so many, but his hobbies of human cruelty and weightlifting had made him into everything he admired. He was at his peak, and he loved every minute of it.

He reached down to his vest and drew two small hunting knives to turn them over in his hands and feel their weight before throwing one suddenly into the ground at one of the prisoner's feet. The man leapt back fearing that it had been aimed to hit him but the second knife clattered to the concrete beside the other man.

"Pick them up," Goran ordered as he slowly drew a long, curious blade. "You have one minutes," he told them as he admired the edge of his weapon in the flickering orange light, "and after that I am comings for you. Kill me or escape and you are free." He jerked his head towards the unguarded section of the yard, enjoying their momentary hesitation before both men stumbled to retrieve the knives and run awkwardly into the dark.

"One, two, three," Goran yelled out behind them as his followers picked up the count. Goran walked around the three sides of the square his men formed as he psyched himself up, tensing his muscles and growling like an animal. At sixty he turned and ran low to the ground in the direction the men had fled.

Goran had only once ended a hunt without his victim's blood on his hands, and that was so long ago that none of his people present still lived. One he had killed himself for insubordination but the other had succumbed to an illness and was left behind years before to die alone.

He listened to the snapping of branches ahead of him as both men seemed to be running together and smiled to himself at how simple this hunt would be. He followed, staying low and letting the noises of the two men lead him directly to them. He made some sound himself, but being the follower in the pitch dark made his movement much easier because he wasn't running for his life in panic.

"Shh," he heard from ahead, "let the bastard come to us and we stick him."

Goran smiled, sinking lower to the damp ground and edging to his left carefully. His right pocket was filled with small stones – a favourite trick of his – and he tossed one over to his right to refocus their attention as he made ground. Twice more he did that, stretching their nerves thinner each time until he'd worked around to their left flank.

He preferred it when they just ran so he could demonstrate his superior strength and stamina, but he admitted to himself that he also found it enjoyable to show how a man of his size could move silently.

"Where the hell is he?" one of them whispered.

"Shut the fuck up, Dave," the other replied, "I think he's trying to go arou—*ghccch…*"

"Keith?" the first man whispered, only his friend would never answer him because the sharp point of Goran's knife had reached forwards in the dark to poke a wide hole straight into the side of his neck as effortlessly as a hand would break the surface of a bowl of warm water. He flopped down, his feet thrashing as he choked on his own blood, and the other man responded just as Goran wished he would.

He ran.

The bigger man was up on his feet and following, not trying to close the distance between them but enjoying the panic emanating from the runner. He stopped when his prey stopped, dropping to the ground to listen before his nerve broke again and he scrambled to his feet to run in another direction blindly attempting to find freedom.

Goran smiled wickedly. He liked it when they tried to outsmart him, which was even more fun than the few who had turned and tried to fight him. He looped in a wide run, paralleling the angle his quarry ran in so that the clever attempt to outsmart their pursuer was for nothing. He stopped, holding his breath in spite of his chest screaming at him to suck in air, opening his mouth slightly to accentuate his hearing. Branches snapped and leaves rustled far closer to his position than he expected.

If he could hear them then experience and logic told him that they would have heard his pursuit.

The sound of rasping, panicked breathing drifted through the darkness towards him as he edged towards the cooler breeze where the trees thinned out and gave way to open grassland. That empty field was bathed in a low glow of the residual light of the moon and stars which were so much more vivid than anything he had seen as a child.

The breathing picked up in speed and intensity as the sounds of the terrified man setting off at a run for safety filled the night. Goran had anticipated this and was positioned close enough to cut off the desperate bid for freedom.

The knife flashed in the gloomy night, crossing the man's throat as he stood tall to run hard across the open field and away from the nightmare that his life had so suddenly become. He felt the cold of the steel for only a fraction of a second before the hot sensation overrode it. His brain registered that the sudden heat was his blood spilling from the left side of his neck which had been opened up so far that he registered the faint scrape of sharpened metal on bone.

He staggered, remaining on his feet as both hands came up to grip his throat as if sheer pressure could keep everything inside. Blood pulsed against his clenched fingers, forcing its way out through the small gaps between the digits as a sudden light-headedness overcame him. He dropped to his knees and looked up as a lumbering shadow blocked out the light of the stars ahead of him. The shadow bent down, revealing not the sight of the man but the smell and feel of his closeness.

Without speaking a word, the shadow grunted. Pain exploded in the man's chest as his breastbone crunched, losing the battle of resisting the point of the long bayonet being driven slowly into his heart.

Cheers greeted Goran's return as he stepped into the bathing fire-light. His torso was sheeted in blood – blood which he had wiped on his bare skin for effect – and the sight of it made his men cheer louder.

He knew not all of them felt the same way about their enemies as he did, and that was evident in their expressions even though they cheered for him.

Fuck them, he thought. They don't know what it's like to be overlooked, to be rejected and cast out.

Someone brought him a bottle, thrusting it out to him with a roar of approval. Goran took it, drank a long pull as the bubbles gurgled upwards, and lowered it to gasp and burp as the drink ran down his bearded chin.

Holding the bottle aloft he returned the animalistic roar of triumph, prompting his men to shout louder, before he walked away and let them dismiss themselves. Mo sidled towards him, his unnaturally straight-backed gait annoying Goran as soon as he recognised him but knowing that he needed the man; none of the others in his group of followers had the brains to lead people but by god they were brutal when he unleashed them.

He saw himself as a raider. A Viking roving anywhere he pleased and taking whatever he wanted. Those violent, charismatic leaders he idolised from ancient history were only strong so long as men followed them, and men only followed them if they were rich, drunk and rewarded with spoils.

"An impressive display, Goran," Mo said sycophantically with an annoyingly genteel bow that gave the impression he was secretly mocking him. Goran grunted in response as he took another drink from the bottle and eyed the precise man suspiciously. He had changed into clean clothes which had clearly been packed neatly after pressing because the creases all seemed sharp and fresh.

Goran hated how neat he was, but he was shrewd enough to know that the man's neat appearance mirrored his neat mind. He would've been happy if that was combined with courage to match, but sadly his resident thinker was only capable of true bravery through others.

"What would *you* do next?" Goran asked, changing the subject and phrasing the question as though he already knew what his plan was and he wanted to see if Mo was going to agree or was daring him to be wrong. The thin man cleared his throat in a way that annoyed his muscular leader and paused before speaking as if there would be minutes taken of their conversation which he would have to refer to later.

"I wouldn't have visible fires for one thing," he said, seeing Goran's expression darken as his words had bordered on disrespectful. "I mean, our safety is dependent on them not knowing where we are, so…"

"Relax," Goran told him with a friendly punch to his shoulder that was at least twenty percent too hard to actually *be* friendly. "How can these assholes finding us? They are scared to run back home behind their little walls, no? I asked what you *would* be doing, not what you tell me I should *not* do."

"I would concentrate on their main base," Mo said. "Pick off anyone coming or going and stay out of sight."

"And how long can we be doing this for? Until the cold weathers arrive? Through the winters? How long will food last? Tell me this."

"You would prefer a more direct route?"

"Yes," Goran said. "I want to be sleeping in their beds and eating their food before the first frost." He gripped the neck of the bottle in his hand and extended the index finger to poke Mo in the chest, who seemed to resist the urge to smooth down his clothing after it had been touched.

"Tomorrow, you take men and find me ways in, and Mo?"

"Yes?"

"You fuck this up again and it will be *you* running through the darks from me."

AERIAL SURVEILLANCE

Steve led his entourage of guests and senior advisors into his office which, as grandly appointed and spacious as it was, quickly filled up with six of them and a dog in there.

Neil took a seat, groaning as he lowered himself to the cherry-red leather and let out a comedic sigh as he rested against the chair back. Iain, deferring to a guest with the manners of a generation close to extinction, offered Dan the other vacant chair but he declined because it would mean holding his carbine awkwardly or removing it which was just a minor hassle he could do without.

Iain didn't insist, simply sat down beside Neil before gasping when Ash's large muzzle appeared worryingly close to his balls to conduct a cursory sniff check.

"Fuckin'ell," Iain muttered as he carefully pushed the dog's muzzle away, "buy me a drink first, mutt…"

Dan snapped his fingers to bring Ash back to him where he pointed an admonishing finger at his dog. "Oi, dickhead. What have we said about consent?"

"Naughty, naughty," Neil chided the dog in a Russian accent for no apparent reason.

Steve called them to order. "George?" he asked politely. "Get the door, please?"

George crossed the room in two easy strides to swing the heavy wood for the gilded handle to click into place and seal them inside.

"We all know where we are with everything," Steve said, "and you've had a chance to catch up on what we learned from the prisoner. Iain, any fallout from that yet?"

"You can expect what I imagine will be a strongly worded letter by the end of the day," he said keeping a straight face. "It appears that Mrs Beachball has been rallying support for some kind of socialist uprising against the tyranny of the state and some such bollocks."

"Delightful," Steve said. He felt more upset by the words, as being seen as a head of state ruling without the consent of the people was one of his biggest fears. "What kind of support has she got?"

"Somewhere between two and four."

"Two and four what?"

"People."

"So...three then?" Dan asked, unable to resist.

"Does this cause us concern?" Steve asked, also ignoring Dan's Neil-level comedy.

"I'd be careful what you put in the laundry as someone might throw a red sock in with your whites to teach you a lesson, but no. Hot air is all."

"Good. No rebellion looming on the horizon while we look outwards towards the real danger then." Steve stood and walked stiffly towards the large map again to tap a fingernail on the rough circle he'd drawn in pen. "Our intel might already be out of date, because if I was them I'd have moved by now unless they don't know we've taken one of them prisoner. So if we want to have any chance of making sure we know where they are we need to act fast."

Dan cleared his throat intentionally and shifted his feet on the thin carpet. "I'd probably caution against rolling up on them without a thorough recce."

Steve stared at him and shook his head softly in disappointment.

"After all this time, you must think I've gone soft in the head," he said mockingly. Dan stared back, unsure how to take back his careful words that had caused upset. A knock at the door saved him from stumbling out an apology. All eyes turned to see the door open and the beautiful, beaming face of Steve's assistant Sophie.

"Steve, I have Reuben here? You sent for him?"

"I did, thanks. Send him in please."

Dan and George, the two standing closest to the door, backed away to give the room the space it needed to admit another person. To his surprise, a tall man entered wearing a leather jacket lined with fleece looking like a World War II pilot. He smiled at Steve, the brilliant, arrow-straight lines of his white teeth like a beacon against his darker skin tone which Dan couldn't place, but that smile wavered a little as he took in the room of armed men. Passing off the fear with comedy, he meekly raised his hands like he was being arrested and spoke.

"I swear," he said in a melodic accent that made Dan guess on Turkey or Greece being the man's original home. "It was only a little bit for personal use!"

"Your personal life isn't my concern right now, Reuben," Steve said with a light laugh. "Unless you really have been smoking something and you aren't fit to fly?"

"Wait, what?" Dan said, cursing himself inwardly for Leah's words spilling out of his mouth. "I mean...*fly*?"

"Unless you know another way to cover a lot of ground quickly?" Steve asked.

"Fly what?" Mitch asked suspiciously.

"A Piper," Reuben answered proudly.

"He means a rickety old thing with two ceiling fans on the wings and seats that smell worryingly like cabbage," Iain told the soldier.

"I'm out," Mitch said, standing up and retrieving his rifle from where he'd propped it against the wall.

"Good," Iain said as he followed suit, "you can help me with the defences, if that's alright with you?" He looked at Steve who looked at Dan. Both men nodded agreement.

"You'll not get me in the air in a poxy wee tin can…" Mitch grumbled to Iain as the two men left the office.

"Well," Neil said in his BBC presenter voice as he struggled to his feet and rubbed his hands together. "I for one am *frightfully* excited to get up in the air."

Reuben made a slight noise of hesitation before shooting a pleading look at Steve. Neil saw it and his smile lowered along with his eyebrows.

"Got something to say, pretty boy?" he growled in a voice that he probably hoped was menacing but just served to force a snort of laughter to escape Dan's lips as he turned away to watch something suddenly interesting out of the window.

"No, no," Reuben tried weakly, "is just that the plane…well, iss not built for…" He waved his hands vaguely at Neil as if to encompass all of him.

"Oh! Oh, I see!" Neil stammered.

"Foxtrot Alpha Tango," muttered Dan in his best air traffic control imitation, one hand cupped over his mouth to emulate a radio transmission, "you are not cleared for take-off due to excess weight, over."

"Fuck you too," Neil added, giving him the finger before crossing his arms stubbornly.

Steve's voice was a little higher than usual when he cut over them. "Look, I'm sure it'll be fine, Reuben. We've taken up four people before, haven't we?"

"Yeah…" Reuben allowed, still uncomfortable with how quickly the conversation had turned sour.

"I don't know what you're laughing at," Neil told Dan. "I seem to remember you were a bit of a pussy when it came to heights."

Dan's smirk faded as the facts dawned on him. He was indeed not a fan of heights, although it wasn't so much the height as opposed to the inescapable combination of gravity and the ground that would kill him, and the laughs at Neil's expense were only a momentary distraction.

"Let's get it over with," he said.

It took them almost an hour to reach the place they were headed for. Two trucks operated much the same as they had on their return journey the previous day only with a reduced speed. He realised that Steve must've taken his own standard operating procedures and passed them down to his new people which had, in turn, been written into their manual at some point. Dan felt both proud and weird at the same time to know that shit he'd made up on the spot because it seemed logical years before was now set in stone for these people and they didn't even know why.

The lead vehicle stopped at a tired chain-link fence and the front passenger got out to scan a quick three-sixty before jogging over to use a key in a padlock and unloop a rusty chain from the gates before pulling them over the tufts of grass which had sprouted up through the cracked concrete. The gate was more of an emergency access as opposed to anything that would be guarded, so it made perfect sense to Dan that they were using the side door to get on and off the base.

He knew it was a base when he'd seen the faded signs warning them of entering ministry of defence property. Another sign told of the dangers of RAF police patrolling with dogs, prompting a proud glance at his faithful sidekick on the rear seat beside him.

Ash, true to form, had one leg up in the air and was slowly, almost sensually, licking his family jewels. Dan tutted, earning a nasal huff of irritation from the dog who glared at him for a second before sneezing and returning to the task in hand.

The trucks bumped over the pitted track towards the half-buried hangars covered in thick turf and overgrown weeds before turning a hard left on the first runway they hit. Their tyres made a raucous noise on the rough tarmac, which didn't fill Dan with confidence. He leaned around the front seat to ask Neil if he was sure he wanted to go up.

"Listen, you can stay nice and safe on the ground if you want but I'm sure as shit not missing the chance to go flying."

Dan sat back and waited as the trucks slowed before the huge doors of one of the hangars and stopped, leaving the exit clear. Dan slid from the rear door and lifted his weapon to scan the deserted airfield.

"Find it," he hissed at Ash who rocketed off in the direction he'd pointed his left hand to run a long loop around the grassy half-dome. Doing that served two purposes. One, the dog would make sure nothing and nobody was there who shouldn't be and two, he'd probably find somewhere to lay some cable out of sight and smell of the others. Sure enough, before the doors had been wound open with the manual handles in the hidden building's exterior, Ash bounded back into sight from the opposite side of the building with a renewed vigour in his step like he'd just lost a significant amount of weight.

As the doors opened and Dan laid eyes on the dusty, faded paint of the small plane he began instantly to regret his decision to come. He stepped inside and reached out a hand for the wing which flexed unnervingly and wobbled the entire plane on its small wheels.

"Iss no problem," Reuben told him gleefully. "She looks much worse than she is. Underneath?" He patted the thin fuselage reassuringly with quite the opposite effect. "Underneath she is beautiful."

"I suppose she's got a good personality too?" Neil asked. "Maybe she's *bubbly*?"

Reuben ignored him and opened the tiny door to climb inside where he began to flip switches in the cockpit. He turned a key to make the engine issue a tortured electrical whine like the starter motor was a teenager and the pilot had just thrown open the curtains because it was almost midday and their room was a pigsty. The tortured noise continued as Reuben smiled until the whine became interspersed with the occasional cough and splutter. Reuben began waving frantically at Dan as he stepped closer until Neil recognised the danger and pulled him back a few seconds before the propeller began to turn when the engine barked and farted its way into being fully awake.

Dan jumped as a hand landed on his back and he turned to see Steve smiling widely at him.

"Last chance to bow out," he shouted over the sound of the engine. Dan looked for Ash, seeing the dog had retreated to the wide doorway after the loud noises had simultaneously upset and offended him.

"He'll be okay if you tell him to wait," Steve yelled. "George is staying down here with the others anyway."

"Maybe I should..." Dan started, hoping that Steve would ask him to remain on the ground for their security.

"Don't worry about it! It'll be fine!"

As the plane picked up speed and the wheels inched off the ground, Dan was absolutely certain that 'fine' wasn't the word he'd use to describe the sensation of his own balls heading north for the winter and settling down somewhere above his intestines.

REQUESTING FLY-BY

"Tower," Dan murmured into the boom mic on the headset he wore like the other three men inside the plane as he out-did Neil on the impressions for once, "this is *Toast*rider requesting fly-by."

Neil slapped him in his left arm in annoyance as he stared out of the left side window, but it seemed even Steve was getting in on the joke.

"Negative, Toastrider," he intoned back, playing the part of air traffic control, "the pattern is full."

"Very bloody funny," Neil added tiredly. His quota for being annoyed at other people was fully expended soon after take-off when Reuben had intentionally listed the aircraft to the left and blamed Neil for their aerodynamics being ruined.

Dan was still tense, only relaxing slightly after they'd levelled out from their steep climb. The small plane vibrated worryingly and bounced about in the air like he was driving off-road without a seat belt on. He was securely strapped in, but seeing as how the thing he was strapped in to was what he feared most, he wasn't entirely comfortable. Neil's idle conversation over their headsets served to distract him.

"Were you in the forces, Reuben? Is that where you learned to fly?"

"No." He laughed. "I was a dentist."

"A dentist?" Neil answered, unable to hide his shock.

"Yeah, cosmetic stuff. All implants and whitening, you know?"

"Celebrity smiles," Dan commented idly as he looked out over a swath of green below interrupted only by patches of mist in places.

"Did a few of those," Reuben answered with a hint of mischief in his words as if he expected the following questions to be gossip about which stars he'd treated. The silence that hung when neither guest asked seemed to deflate his ego. "The money was good, so I had expensive hobbies."

"Like getting a pilot's licence?" Neil asked.

"Yeah," Reuben told him. "I used to race cars too."

Dan lapsed deeper into his pensive silence. People like Reuben, as nice as he was, invoked a troubling undercurrent of jealousy within him. He'd worked hard all his life, doing dangerous things with little or no thanks and he recognised in himself that he felt jaded because of it.

He would have loved to have weekends off to do something exciting like racing a car or a motorbike around a track, but that kind of extra-curricular activity required an expendable budget almost as big as his salary had been.

Still, even if he'd had the money, he doubted he would've taken to flying at three thousand feet in something less sturdy than a cat's litter box with two lawnmower engines powering oversized desk fans.

"Confirm heading," Steve muttered into the mic. Reuben checked his instruments, which to Dan looked like they were manufactured some time prior to the moon landing, and answered. He leaned around as far as the straps would allow him to watch the two men at work as they spoke in succinct language he didn't follow. He gathered that they were making sure they were heading in the right direction, calculating speed and time to know when they were over the right area before Steve asked their pilot to climb.

The engine note increased and the shuddering of the fuselage made Dan's boys pop back up into his chest cavity. That shuddering continued as Reuben called out their altitude in thousands before Dan realised he was closing his eyes and holding his breath.

"Level out at seven thousand," Steve instructed. "Slow to just above stall speed."

Reuben responded by pushing the controls forwards to level out the nose of the plane with the horizon, giving Dan another uncomfortable half second of weightlessness.

"Flaps down, slowing to sixty-five knots."

"Prepare to bank left," Steve said.

"Bank left...?" Dan asked, clamping his mouth shut to stop a string of offensive words tumbling out when the aircraft lurched over to dangle him towards Neil who, in turn, was pressed up against the cold glass of the window.

"Binoculars, gentlemen," Steve said in a cool manner that suggested being thousands of feet in the air on his side was just Tuesday for him. Dan fumbled for the set of powerful optics he'd been handed, wishing that they were going up in a glass-bottomed boat so they didn't have to fly at an angle perpendicular to the ground.

He struggled to make out any detail at first until he controlled his breathing, and just when he got the hang of it he felt the overwhelming urge to lose the small breakfast he'd eaten. Reuben flipped the aircraft back down unsympathetically before looping around to explain for the benefit of his back-seat passengers that they'd passed over the target area and were going for another pass.

"Prepare to bank right," Steve announced, giving Dan little time to prepare before his window rushed up to meet his face and he was forced to hold the binoculars with one had as the other braced him away from the cold glass to give him space to use them.

"Not…" he gasped, "not the easiest way to do this…"

"We could go lower and be heard by them," Steve answered. "We're running the risk of being seen as it is but if we drop down much more someone will hear us, guaranteed."

Dan said nothing, just concentrated on searching through the lenses to find them and get the ordeal over with. On their fourth pass, Dan's second turn being the one tipped towards the ground, Steve called out with a triumphant noise that startled him.

"A-*HA*! River, fifty-degree bend with exposed trees, got it?"

Dan took almost ten seconds to locate it after taking the binoculars away from his eyes to first find the water course.

"Got it."

"Follow it to your left. Small cluster of buildings…"

"I see it," Dan said with relish. "What is that? A school?"

"Something like that. Okay, Reuben, take us back. I think we've pushed our luck enough as it is."

The plane returned to a comfortable attitude as their internal organs all settled back into the correct position, and the engine noise grew again as their speed picked up to reduce the buffeting they were receiving. Dan closed his eyes and bent his head forward as if the ordeal was over, only to let out a noise of annoyance and fear as they hit the air equivalent of a pothole and got thrown around a little.

"I seriously don't know how you did this for a living," Dan said to Steve.

"I didn't do *this* though," Steve explained. "A helicopter is very different, and has a lot more shit to go wrong," he added darkly.

Reuben flew them back, looping a low, wide circuit of the neglected airfield to go through the procedure for taking something from a hundred and sixty miles per hour at a few thousand feet in the air to seventy miles per hour fifty feet from the tarmac. A buzzer started blaring with an obnoxious noise that filled the cramped cabin, and before Dan could panic he heard Neil's voice through the headset.

"What the hell's that?"

"Is just the stall warning," Reuben answered as if the terms 'stall warning' and 'just' ever belonged in the same sentence. Before either passenger experiencing the landing for the first time could begin to pray the small wheels bumped down with more force then Dan expected, only to bounce back up twice. The engine note ramped up to be painfully loud before it cut to an idle and the plane, which was as awkward moving on land as a penguin, rolled towards the waiting vehicles.

Dan unclipped his harness with hands that he hadn't realised were shaking, finding it difficult to manipulate the clasp as his hands had cramped up from unconsciously gripping so tightly. He ducked awkwardly to escape the small interior and stepped down where his first instinct was to light a cigarette and say a silent prayer that he was still alive, adding a promise that as he wasn't born with wings, he wouldn't do that again.

DIRECT ACTION

"We have a water source and power generation inside our perimeter," Steve explained. "They're on the outside without in-depth knowledge of the area and without permanent shelter or established supply routes."

"Don't underestimate them," Dan warned. "Yes, you have a perimeter but how many defenders are on it around the clock? Where are there any vulnerabilities?"

Steve looked at George for an answer, not out of ignorance but because he'd learned the one thing Dan had always struggled with when it came to leadership.

He'd delegated.

"Only the vehicle and pedestrian access points are guarded twenty-four-seven," George said. "The rest of the perimeter is patrolled."

"How many and how often?" Mitch asked.

"Two groups working in opposing directions. Two or three per group depending."

"Not enough," Dan said, earning a noise of agreement from Mitch. He leaned over the crude sketch map of the town and made marks with the stub of pencil he carried with his battered notebook. "Cut up the perimeter into sections," he explained. "Have two or three people patrolling *only* that section back and forth. And make sure you rotate them around; it's easy to get complacent doing the same small thing over and over."

George nodded, not arguing against what he saw as a logical approach.

"How long can we maintain that?" Steve asked.

George, seeking approval of saying something potentially unpopular, looked to Iain for support as he spoke. "Not long. A week maybe before we run out of people who've slept enough to be paying attention?"

"A bit longer," Iain added in agreement, "but not much."

"What are they expecting *us* to do?" Dan asked the room.

"They're expecting us to retreat behind our walls and wait them out," Steve answered.

"So," Dan said, drawing the word out as if thinking as he spoke when it was clear to the men who knew him that he was in fact leading others to the correct conclusion, "in their position what would *you* do?"

George looked at him quizzically before he spoke. "I'd look for a way inside," he answered carefully. "Small team, maybe even just one or two, and I'd do some damage from the inside."

"Or storm the main gate with everything they have,' Iain added with a shrug. "All depends on how clever and arrogant they are."

Dan snapped his fingers and pointed at both men briefly. "Exactly," he said enthusiastically. "Either way, depending on how stupid or confident or competent they are, they'll have to come to *us*. Right?"

"Right," Neil answered. "But *they* don't know that *we* know where they are."

"Potentially," Dan allowed, erring on the side of caution that some keen-eyed raider might've been stargazing in the daytime and seen the little off-white aircraft scooting through the skies far above

297

them. "So the logical course of action is to take the fight to them when they won't be expecting it."

"While leaving enough people here to defend a perimeter too large to guard with static defenders," Mitch added.

"Which would mean a very small force going out," Steve said with a knowing smile. "Any ideas who?"

"I was thinking just a couple of people," Dan said mildly with a glance at Mitch who gave a curt nod.

"I was thinking three people," George said with as much casual maturity as he could manage.

Steve glanced at Dan, raising one eyebrow in question which annoyed Dan because he wasn't able to arch a brow like that and he'd always wanted to. He looked at Mitch, who shrugged, and he turned his gaze back to Steve and copied the gesture before giving George a nod. The young man looked relieved, like he was expecting a rejection.

"Options?" Steve asked the room, doing just what he'd encouraged Leah to do so long ago and use Dan's lines before he had the chance just because he knew it annoyed him. Dan ignored the attempt, giving no indication that he'd even noticed.

"Access by vehicle, cross over land under cover of darkness and recce their position."

"That's all?" Neil asked knowingly.

Dan shrugged like a kid caught put in a lie. "Can't promise there won't be an opportunity to covertly undermine the confidence and security of the enemy as well as degrading their combat effectiveness whilst gaining valuable, actionable intelligence," he said sounding very official.

"Meaning?" George asked, irked that he didn't speak the same level of bullshit as the old men.

"Meaning," Iain told him, "that he'll take a couple of them out and maybe ask some questions first if he gets the chance."

George huffed. "Why not just say that then?"

"Because, treacle," Neil said as he laid a reassuringly patronising hand on the young man's shoulder, "when you're planning on killing someone or three, it sits easier with the bosses when you call it" – he turned slightly to cast a hand across the imaginary title emblazoned across the wall of Steve's office and spoke in an over-the-top American movie voiceover growl – "'strategic undermining of the enemy's combat capability through covert night operations executed with extreme prejudice' instead of" – he went slightly cross eyed and stuck his tongue out one corner of his mouth as he spoke – "hehe, run round in dark go stabby-stabby!"

"Point taken," George said slowly, giving Neil an odd look as though he was fairly certain there was something wrong with the man but was too polite or worried to mention it.

"Anyway," Steve said, bringing them back to the point. "When would you two like to conduct your covert night operations to undermine the blah blah?"

Dan turned his left wrist up and outwards to display the face of his watch before he spoke. "Allowing for error, three hours."

"What error?" George asked out of curiosity as if he soaked up everything the man had to say.

Dan lifted the fingers of his left hand to tick off the points as he spoke.

"Allowing to go slow on the road, allowing time to stop and check out any potential ambush sites before driving through them, allowing for the unpredictable stuff like a tree down in the road or a flat tyre, allowing time before dark to find somewhere to hide the vehicle and establish a forward base…" Dan lowered his hand. "Lots of variables, plus being on time is being late."

George nodded sagely as if assimilating the imparted wisdom into his own.

"You'll need a vehicle," Steve said as he glanced at Iain to silently issue the instructions to have one ready. "And I assume you brought enough gear of your own?"

"Depends," Dan asked. "You still got those night optics I gave you?"

FIXER UPPER

Dan drove with Ash's head protruding from the back seat to waft the hot, rank breath of the dog onto his left cheek. Every time he glanced left to look at Mitch in the back or to check the side mirror, Ash mistook the gesture as intended for him and slashed out a hot, wet tongue to mark a point for canines over humans.

"*Pppfffft!*" Dan said, wiping his stuck-out tongue on his sleeve after the dog had managed to lick inside his open mouth before he could speak. "Pfft! Dirty bastard…"

Mitch, instead of answering the question that was never asked, laughed as he leaned away and turned sideways so that his back was against the side window. It wasn't for comfort but in readiness should they need to lay down fire. His own rifle, too long and cumbersome to use inside the cab of the old Toyota they had been loaned, lay on the dash beside Dan's shotgun and in its place he cradled Dan's unslung carbine with the barrel facing upwards towards the open sunroof exposing them to the elements as a compromise towards their ability to defend themselves.

"You were going to say?" George asked from the seat beside Dan over the noise of wind through his open window sprouting the barrel of his L85, fighting the urge to laugh at Dan who was fruitlessly trying to pick a troublesome dog hair from his lips.

"I was going to ask how far off from this village."

Mitch didn't need to consult the map on the seat between George and Dan as he'd studied it enough to retain the basics in his mind.

Leaving the village of South Runcton, which in his opinion was a ridiculous name unlike the Scottish villages of Queenziburn and Lumloch where he'd spent his childhood, he knew they were approaching ten miles north of the place identified as the enemy camp.

Dan drove more cautiously now, twice stopping for Mitch to get out and check around blind bends to make sure there were no surprises lying in wait for them, and their last few miles were travelled at a comparative crawl.

"This looks good," Dan said, pointing ahead to where an old pitched roof sagged under the weight of old tiles. The corner of the building had subsided marginally, which had led to a small cascade of the tiles dropping to form a broken pile which had been reclaimed by a climbing weed intent on bringing the rest of the old brick-built barn down no matter how long it took.

"Stop short," Mitch said unnecessarily as Dan was already easing the truck to a halt as gently and quietly as possible. One of the reasons Iain had given them the Toyota over other vehicles was that he assured them the brakes wouldn't let out a shriek to betray their presence, but Dan was cautious anyway.

The three men slid from the truck leaving their doors open, both front seat occupants holding their own weapons once again as Dan carefully slipped the shotgun back into the custom elasticated pouch on the back of his vest. Dan turned to George, his weapon stock in his shoulder and a look of confidence on his face, and told him with hand signals to stay at the vehicle and guard their rear. If he was annoyed at the instruction then his face hid it well, and Dan was glad because he didn't have the time to explain that the boy was untried and untested by him so he wasn't going in with an unknown quantity by his side.

Ash poured from the open door like furry water as he glued himself to Dan's left leg and sniffed the air. They moved as one with Mitch remaining static on the side of the road away from his own door to cover them. Ash's patented warning system stayed silent in spite of Dan's growing knot of bad feeling he seemed to have swallowed at some point. If the dog had an instrument panel Dan would've tapped it with his finger to make sure it was working because he was *sure* there was something fishy there.

He took a knee, not having to instruct his sidekick who flattened himself to the wet road beside his master, and heard the faint scrapes of Mitch's boots approaching. He kept his gaze forward, scanning either side and concentrating on his other senses as a half-second warning could mean the difference between life and death for all of them.

Mitch stopped, sinking to his right knee with his heavy, bulbous barrel attachment scanning slowly left and right. Dan rose with his dog mirroring his movements, both of them making that transition from 'down' to 'up' a little slower than they used to, and moved forwards where he began sidestepping to open up the view through the gap in the overgrown hedge where the gateway was.

The gate, or at least the rusted remnants of it, lay on the old stones rotting slowly away. As the rest of the yard inched into view Dan moved towards the gap to kneel down again as he continued scanning. He heard and sensed Mitch move up behind him before he felt the gentle tap of the soldier's hand on his back to tell him he was stacked up and in position.

Dan stood again, his left knee issuing a crack as loud as any breaking branch he could've stepped on, and the two men moved into the open to surge into the yard taking a side each. Reaching the reliable cover of a solid brick wall they dropped again and Dan unleashed their organic search drone.

"*Find it!*" he hissed at Ash who tore away low to the ground as he followed his nose into the rest of the yard. Dan continued to scan and asses, his sense of bad feeling dissipating as he saw no sign at all of anything bigger than a dog having been there. No sign of vehicle tracks or worn ground led to and from the broken-down house which seemed as abandoned as anything he'd laid eyes on over the years. Vines crept through broken windows and ivy covered the lintel over the door he could see, making him feel more reassured by the second that there was nothing there.

Ash was out of sight and sound, and if he found anyone or anything, he'd either return to warn Dan or sound off. He readied himself before rising and vaulting the low wall to land on slippery flagstones on the other side. Realising he'd jumped into an old pig pen he ducked to look inside the covered area and saw a few bones under what looked like a thin piece of dark leather to tell him that nothing had lived here for years. Climbing out of the other side where the wall was lower, he saw his dog snake back into view following his nose which was planted to the deck. He looked up, saw Dan and bounded to him for praise.

"Clear," Dan announced, giving the verbal report to translate Ash's 'I'm a good boy' face. He was a good boy, Dan knew. The best. If he said there was nothing there, then there was nothing there.

"I'll go back for the truck and the kid," Mitch said as he pointed to a larger building off to one side. "Get that open if you can and I'll back it in there."

Dan followed the direction of the outstretched hand with his eyes to take in a mostly wooden barn constructed at least a generation or two after the rest of the farm. He let Ash explore as he flicked on the safety to his weapon and rested it on the sling to dig both hands into the gap between the doors. To his surprise it swung open with only a slight resistance but the noise of the seized hinges screeched like the side of the Titanic scraping along an iceberg. He stopped, his face frozen in a rictus which subtitled as 'shit' until logic re-established itself and he swung the door fast to make as little noise as possible over a short duration. Inside the barn it was damp and musty, but mostly weatherproof and secure with the open door being just wide enough to accommodate their vehicle. Weapon up, more for the bright LED beam on the side rail than for its capability as a weapon, he looked over the interior as a cruel idea began forming in his mind.

The noise of an engine at low revs grew louder as Mitch turned to crunch the Toyota into reverse and inched it back towards the narrow opening of the door Dan had pulled wide.

Dan moved a few things aside to allow Mitch room, tipping over a mower as the metal handle all but folded in his grip. He kicked the rest of it aside to clear the interior until the truck was fully under cover.

Mitch slid out to ground level again, leaning back in to retrieve his weapon, before surveying their surroundings and sucking in a long breath through his nose and holding it in his lungs.

"Talk about your fixer-upper," George joked.

"Lovely," he said after letting it out and switching into rough French for Dan's benefit. "*Ça sent comme la vomie de blaireau qui a mangé la merde de moufette.*"

"Nice," Dan chuckled. "Sure, it's big enough but look at the location."

Mitch laughed back, earning an annoyed look from George who was staring at the two men coldly for being intentionally left out.

"*Le gamin n'a pas l'air de pouvoir parler français,*" Dan said to Mitch, keeping his eyes on George.

"*¿Deberíamos intentar hablar español?*" Mitch asked in another language he was more comfortable with thanks to his Spanish wife.

"*Sabes que mi español es peor que mi francés,*" Dan said.

"You've made your point," George cut in. "Care to fill me in on the joke?"

"Sorry," Dan said. "You've got to understand that where we live English isn't the most common language. It's a mix of French and Spanish too, but with a dialect that's strange for both languages."

"Fascinating," George remarked drily.

"Mitch is of the opinion that the barn smells like" – he turned to look at his friend – "a badger ate skunk shit and puked it up?"

"Aye." Mitch nodded.

"And I sa—"

"Yeah, don't care," George cut him off. "In English from now on, please?"

The way he said it made the please an irrelevance, as though the two far more senior and infinitely more experienced men were somehow there on his sufferance or, even worse, with his permission.

"If you've got something to say," Dan said being careful to keep the inherent threat from his voice, "I'd suggest you get it off your chest right now." He took a step towards George not to be threatening but to plant himself in front of the boy in case he wasn't confident enough to speak his mind. Dan needn't have any such worries as the younger man took his movement to be threatening and responded in kind.

He stepped close, moving fast and closing the gap between them to demonstrate the three inch height advantage he had over Dan. Age and height stood for nothing unless both opponents were bound by rules, and if he made a move Dan didn't like then he'd likely find his ability to reproduce be at risk.

But Dan didn't see it as a threat. In fact, he'd stake everything he owned on the man – fresh out of boyhood – not laying a finger on him in a month of Sundays.

"Listen," George snarled. "I grew up hearing about what a legend you were and now...even with all your fancy gear...now I see you're just an old man taking his dog for a walk."

Mitch, not seeing the look in his eyes as Dan did, took a step forwards out of loyalty. Dan stopped him by holding out his right hand just as his left held up a flat palm to his other side.

"An old man," Dan repeated mildly, "just taking his dog for a walk...you know what? I like that. Mitch? Can I get a bumper sticker with that on?"

George scoffed and retreated half a pace, using Dan's de-escalation as an appropriate time to withdraw without losing face.

"Yeah, kid," Dan said, seeing the flash of anger in George's eyes as he was talked down to again. "I may be almost twice your age, and I may be slower and a bit busted up, but what I *do* have is a set of skills. Skills I acquired over a very long career, an—"

George threw his hands up in the air and turned away with an exasperated groan.

"Really?" he asked. "You're going to quote movies at me?"

"Relax," Dan said, pausing to take his time lighting a cigarette to try and impart a lesson in patience. "The truth is," he said as he blew a stream of smoke up in the air, "you're only here out of respect for Steve because he sees something in you that he likes. I can see it too in all honesty, I really can, but you need to calm it down. Master your emotions. If you can't, then the first Mo or Goran or Bronson you come across you'll do something stupid because your nerve broke."

"Wow," George said sarcastically. "Thanks, Dad."

"You're welcome," Dan answered, then he spoke over his shoulder to Mitch. "Rest and go in an hour?"

"Hour and a half," Mitch answered, reaching inside the cab for the map to study in finer detail, "make sure it's getting dark."

"You can come if you want," Dan said to George, "but if you can't keep up or you make too much noise then you come back and you stay here, is that clear?"

"You just worry about yourself," George said. "I can look after myself just fine."

"Sure," Dan said as he turned away. "Whatever you say."

George glared at his back for a few seconds, hating the man for appearing to not take anything seriously, before he spun on his heel and let out a yelp of fear.

Ash, responding out of a loyalty much deeper than Mitch's, had slunk close to George before Dan stopped him with a flat hand. He held his ground just in case, and now treated the stringy-looking human to a head-cocked, dazzling display of big white teeth parting just enough to show the sharp tips only a foot away from a very vulnerable part of the young man.

"Heel," Dan said without turning, making Ash close his mouth and slope past George looking, if a dog could be accused of such a thing, like a smug arsehole.

HUNTING THE HUNTERS

To his credit, and to the surprise of both Dan and Mitch, George knew how to move in the dark. It took years to perfect from a military perspective, but it was the kind of skill some people are born with and it usually, in Dan's experience, steered them naturally towards a life on the wrong side of the law.

He moved carefully, precisely, but with an economy of movement that Dan recognised he could keep up for hours. He wasn't pulling the kid's leg when he said he could see what Steve saw in him. He was always going to come from a different world because of his age, but George was like Leah in the way that he'd grown up in this new, violent world with a much older head on his shoulders. It was sad in many ways, because just like Leah he'd been robbed of a childhood that should only recently have ended.

It took them an hour of crossing fields before the reward of loud music attracted their attention. They were carefully crossing through hedges to leave as little sign as possible and sticking to the outside of the fields so as not to leave a straight line of crushed grass to lead their enemy straight back to their temporary hiding spot. It made for slower progress, but ultimately not getting killed was a strong dictator of tactics.

The music annoyed Dan. It annoyed all of them apart from Ash, but as none of them were so ill-disciplined as to say it out loud he was left only with his own disappointment that their enemy was so unprofessional.

Then, when logic slapped him upside the back of the head, he realised that an enemy without discipline should be an easier one to defeat.

They continued onwards towards the noise, using the thudding bass of whatever track tore the night air as an easy guide to bring them towards their target as well as allowing them to move in greater safety as any sentry posted would be robbed of their peripheral senses by it.

Dan held, waving them to group up behind the shelter of the low stone wall he took cover behind, and slipped off the small escape and evasion pack he wore to retrieve a wrapped bundle from the top.

Cursing himself for not bringing his own set, he was grateful to have the ones he'd given to Steve a lifetime ago. As he settled them over his skull and tightened the straps, he reached up to flip the switch and activate the tiny mosquito whine of the optics to bathe the ground ahead of him in an eerie green glow. He scanned for minutes uninterrupted by any of his companions before he flicked off the goggles and removed them.

"No sentries this side," he whispered. "Lights showing on the other side of the nearest building but no sign of patrols." They could see the dull glow from their position without the optics but he told them anyway as confirmation.

"Suggest we wait another twenty at least," Mitch murmured in a low, quiet voice as he reached a hand out for the goggles and gently took them out of Dan's grasp. Dan allowed it, settling down to keep his weapon trained towards the buildings ahead and placed his left hand on Ash's back to soothe both the dog and himself.

"Did you see any of them?" George asked Dan quietly.

Dan didn't turn his head towards him but answered softly. "No, but I'll be taking a closer look soon enough."

"You're not actually going to walk in there, are you?" George asked in a whisper.

"Why not?"

"Because…because they'll kill you if they catch you!"

"So I won't let them catch me," Dan told him simply, resisting the urge to say that he'd been doing this since before George was born. He hadn't, because *this* wasn't exactly a thing normal people ever did. He wasn't special forces, wasn't an assassin or anything like that, he was just a man with transferrable skills and a flexible attitude towards right and wrong when his own people's lives were at risk. Steve's people, by extended definition *his* people, were most definitely at risk from this group. That made the cause and effect simple enough to understand, which justified a kind of 'by any means necessary' approach in Dan's mind.

Sure, he'd done more than a few things which didn't sit too well with him, but the greater good was a comforting concept when the time came to compartmentalise his life experiences.

He made a mental note to talk to George about how to cope with doing the things that needed to be done, but a shout from the gloomy darkness ahead snapped his full attention back to the moment.

"Two in sight," Mitch reported. Dan fought the urge to demand the goggles back and forced himself to wait for information.

"Standby…one's taking a piss."

Beside him, Dan felt George shift position and bring his weapon tighter into his shoulder.

"You keep your fucking snot-picker off that bang switch, sunshine," he growled low at him.

311

George gave the slightest huff of derision as he relaxed, fighting the urge to snap back that he wasn't dumb enough to fire an unsuppressed weapon.

"Heading off," Mitch reported. "Back the way they came. Not a patrol."

"I'm definitely going for a closer look then," Dan muttered as he stripped off the small pack and readied himself for action.

"I'm coming with you," George said firmly.

"You're bloody not," Dan hissed back. "You ever done anything like this before?"

"All the time," George insisted in an intense whisper that earned a small shushing noise from Mitch. "I spent years sneaking around at night and never once got caught. I used to run messages between people for the resistance before Steve took control."

Dan's eyes had adjusted enough to the darkness to see the wide-eyed look the young man was bearing down on him with. He heard Steve's words in his mind, wishing he had longer to take the kid under his wing for a little more training.

Still, he mused internally, trust was something he was learning when it came to the capabilities of people much younger than he was.

"Fine," he murmured, "but leave the rifle here."

"What if—"

"Here," Dan said, peeling a patch of Velcro carefully back to draw the sidearm holstered on his vest. "Two-stage trigger safety, so keep your finger on the outside of the guard," he instructed. "Fifteen in the magazine and one in the pipe ready."

George took the handgun uncertainly. Even with their policy or an armed militia where the general population were permitted to own guns up until the point they did anything stupid with them, the presence of handguns was still a rarity as there were so few in the UK back when it all began. The most common would be those issued to the firearms-trained police officers, and they were all of the same design give or take only a couple of variations. George's hesitation lasted long enough for Dan to reach out and put his hand on the gun as if he would take it back.

"Can you handle it?" he asked, meaning the weapon specifically but the answer he got told him it was taken at a deeper level of meaning.

"I'm good," George answered. "What about you? Won't you need a backup weapon?"

"If thirty rounds aren't enough then we're well and truly buggered anyway," he answered, sounding a little too fatalistic for George's liking.

"You got me, brother?" Dan muttered without turning his head.

"Aye," Mitch said, "I've got you."

"Ash, *stay*! Good boy."

Dan slipped over their low cover and moved fast for a dozen paces before stopping. To George's credit, he didn't actually hear him following until he settled down a few paces behind him, knowing enough not to bunch up like school kids in a game of hide and seek.

Dan listened, hearing nothing to alarm him, then carried on towards the building and the low, rhythmic sound of the thudding music.

FOLLOWING IN THE FOOTSTEPS

For George, what he was doing right then was both the most frightening and the most awesome, coolest, exciting thing he'd ever experienced in his life.

He'd spent years hearing stories from Steve and some of the others about Dan and his exploits. He'd applied the theories he'd learned to those stories and shaped his tactical decision-making skills around the tenacity and bravery of a man who knew how to get shit done.

Meeting the man and finding him to be smaller than he expected, shorter and slower and with an easy air of indifference angered him because he'd built up the legend of Dan in his mind so much that the actual article was nothing but an underwhelming disappointment.

He'd expected a hulking, fit commando to bathe him in the glory of his knowledge instead of making derisive comments about his age and experience. Steve trusted George, with good reason, and he was upset that the man he'd idolised in theory didn't show him any respect.

If he'd been asked a week before if he'd ever front up to Dan then his answer would've been a resounding no with a side of, 'Are you fucking *insane*?' and a 'hell no' for dessert along with a bottle of sincere apology for even thinking about it. Now that he'd met the man, he realised he was just…just a *man*.

The Dan he'd heard about was a myth whose deeds were probably highly inflated. He was just a man who'd been hurt plenty of times but hadn't died out of stubbornness or dumb luck, and George found himself a little lost as to what he should think about him.

The final straw was when they'd left him out of their conversation and his temper had snapped.

Now, he was using every bit of strength he had and every trick he knew for moving silently in the dark and still found himself struggling to keep up with the man in the lead. He carried only a sidearm whereas Dan was weighted down with a full plate-carrying vest and loadout for his short-barrelled rifle and enough spare ammunition to kick off a minor conflict.

The darker shadow in front of him froze, sinking slowly to the ground and not panicking to drop flat on his face and produce sound to go with the rapid movement. He crab-crawled slowly to the right and George followed suit without knowing why but having the discipline to do it regardless.

"I told you," a voice said, "we'll be in their camp before the snow."

"Not if we keep pissing around raiding little farms here and there we won't," came the reply. "He's on a bloody vendetta again, isn't he?"

"You better shut your cock bin unless you want him to cut your tongue out," snarled the first voice angrily.

"Hey, *heeeey*, relax! I was only joking," the other man answered, backtracking like it was an Olympic sport and he was going for consecutive golds. "It's a *little* like last time though, right?"

"Maybe, but I wouldn't go saying that shit around anyone else," admitted the first voice as he walked, the doppler effect making his words sound strange.

George stayed flat on his belly, straining to hear anything else. Dan crept to his side and placed his lips so close to George's ear that the coarse hairs of his greying beard tickled his skin.

"Stay close now," he breathed. "And keep your finger off the trigger."

George gave the slightest nod of his head to indicate that he had heard and understood but the contact was broken and Dan was moving again like a shadow. George climbed to his feet slowly to keep the noise of his movements down but fast enough so that he didn't lose sight of the man he'd insisted on following.

A stab of panic hit him as he lost that darker patch of night ahead and for a second he thought Dan would intentionally leave him behind to teach him a lesson or just to be an arsehole. He stopped, gathered his bearings and glanced back across the small stretch of open ground back to where he knew Mitch would be watching them. Just as he was weighing up whether to break and return to safety a hand tapped him on the shoulder. He spun to find Dan close to him again, but the words whispered in his ear this time made him feel like a child.

"I'll go slower," he murmured, "stay on me and tap me if there's a problem."

George risked answering in a low whisper and felt foolish because the man he'd just mentally accused of risking his life to make a point had come back for him and acted with no ego at all.

If he was detected, then Dan would be risking his own life so logic told George to get his head out of his arse because it wasn't a hat.

He crept along within reach of Dan, freezing when he felt the muscles of his back tense. More voices, louder this time but on the other side of the low building. He opened his mouth to hear better and held his breath again.

"—bring back a prisoner to tell us where to get in," a voice bragged. "Goran made him personally responsible so he'll either do as he's ordered or he won't come back."

The answer was distorted by the sharp sound of a glass bottle bursting elsewhere in the complex of buildings but George made out the words, "or his family will," and connected the dots in his own mind.

"I wish he'd taken us with him," the first voice whined.

"And miss a barbecue?" the answer came, louder as the sounds of careless footsteps came towards them. George stayed frozen because Dan didn't move. Rustling came from the foliage beside them before the loud patter of a stream of liquid hitting the ground preceded a relaxing sigh.

"Aren't you bored?" asked the whiny voice again.

"Look," the man taking the piss answered, pausing to grunt as he squeezed out a fart to accompany the other actions, "I'm just happy I get to eat and sleep, and if I don't get chosen to go off and scratch around in the dark getting shot at then that's just fine by me."

The stream stopped, started again with another grunt before fizzling out into a lazy shake.

"Let Mo go and play if he wants, but I ain't volunteering for nothin'."

George's eyes grew wide in the dark as the meaning of the words dawned on him. His right hand instinctively gripped the weapon tighter as his body prepared to fight by dumping the all-natural go-juice into his bloodstream to make his heart beat fast and his chest heave to oxygenate his muscles.

"Hey, what's that?" one asked suspiciously.

George didn't get the chance to do anything before another grunt sounded and the man landed heavily on the ground beside him.

"The fuck?" was all he managed before George used his adrenaline-powered frustration to club him on the head with the butt of the handgun and release a loud crack when the metal connected with thinly covered bone.

A choking, gargling sound came from ahead of him and he spun to raise the weapon before Dan's voice cut the air.

"Not a sound, you understand me? Not a sound or I'll cut your fucking head off."

A weak whimper was the only answer he received, as George's brain re-processed the sounds he'd heard and he understood that Dan had a knife to the other man's throat instead of killing him.

"Kid, you got the other one?"

"Yeah, knocked him out."

"Fuck," he cursed, leaving a few seconds of silence. "Search him, what's he carrying?"

George rummaged through his pockets before coming back with some small items of no importance.

"No weapon?"

"Just a knife."

"Search this one," he whispered, yanking up the terrified prisoner.

"Same."

The silence stretched out again as Dan thought, and each second made George want to turn and run away. He knew it was his body responding to adrenaline because that was what he'd read. It was

318

what he'd been taught. But it had never been backed up with any real experience, and only now did he fully understand how debilitating that chemical cocktail truly was to rational thought.

That silence ended abruptly when Dan grunted with the effort of driving his knife into the ribcage of the man he held, clamping a hand over his mouth as the thrust the blade in a third time. The man slumped and twitched as he was lowered to the ground where George knelt in open-mouthed shock.

Dan drew the now dead man's blade and forced it into his hand before dragging the body to the unconscious man he'd been talking to only seconds before. Staging the crime scene as best he could in the dark, he made it look as though both men had taken themselves off into the dark to settle a difference with their blades.

Pausing long enough to check their pockets again, Dan led them back away from the buildings without needing to check his bearings.

"You alright?" Mitch murmured as they dropped down into cover again.

"Yeah, you saw?"

"I saw," Mitch said, "thought the bastard was going to take a piss on your head."

"Nearly did," Dan answered, "what does it look like from here?"

"Looks like two wankers stabbed each other," Mitch told him reassuringly. The scene he'd staged would never pass close scrutiny from anyone with any kind of knowledge base, but it should give them enough time by confusing some people at least.

"Good," Dan said as he took back his unfired sidearm and gave a reassuring pat to George's arm. "They were talking about sending a mission to attack the town. We need to get word to Steve."

THE IMPORTANCE OF GOOD INTELLIGENCE

Neil, after a hearty meal of stew with a second and third helping of potatoes in the rich, thick gravy, rubbed his hands with glee when Iain brought him to a house and a familiar face produced a large bottle of home-brewed beer.

"I knew you wouldn't let me down, Cedric," he crowed gleefully as the top of the bottle was eased off with a gassy hiss that filled the air with a strong, yeasty scent. Neil drank in the heady aroma through his nose as it was poured into a glass. Cedric smiled, waiting patiently to see what his old friend thought of his creation which had been sat gathering dust for over a year until he found an occasion worthy of opening the small batch.

Neil carefully poured the liquid with the glass canted at a perfect angle to ensure none of the thick sediment found its way into the drink he was relishing the taste of already. Maggie returned to the front room, tutting as she tripped on the corner of a rug to make Neil think she did it three times a day and still never got around to moving the offending item. She carried a tray with her and another smell cut through the rich aroma of the alcohol to make Neil's mouth water even more than it already was.

Fresh bread, sliced as thick as was possible without each piece seeming obscene, was placed in front of him beside the fire he was hogging.

"Oh...oh I've missed you," Neil said, feigning tears of emotion as his eyes switched between the fresh bread and the crisp beer as if trying to decide which one to taste first.

The beer won, and after a long, sensual pull of it that left white suds frosting his top lip Neil sat back with his eyes closed and let out a satisfied, "*Aaaah*," of pure bliss.

"Good *God*, man," he breathed. "That hits the spot."

"Glad you approve," Cedric answered with a beaming smile. "We don't have your exotic Mediterranean weather to brew up those fancy wines you've got, but we make do. Maggie here found a book on home brewing, must've been from the bleedin' seventies judging by the pictures, but the recipes work alright."

Neil, already sinking a quarter of the beer with his next long gulps, swallowed before tearing a massive hunk of bread which had been smeared with a thick slice of fatty butter.

"Really good to see you," he said with his mouth full, his eyes flickering to the stairs that creaked as two men walked down them. One was truly massive, and had grown even bigger than Neil remembered him to be, and the other was far more familiar. Jimmy walked ahead of Kev, smiling almost with embarrassment as he caught Neil's eye but something peaceful was conveyed through them. Neil knew Dan was right, and wouldn't take a bet against Jimmy staying behind this time. He'd come out of loyalty to Dan, and given that the willing burden of Kev's care had been taken up by Maggie and Cedric he felt safe enough to explore the world a little. Learning that those they had left behind had endured tragedy and loss made his return home feel long overdue, and seeing how pleased he was to be back with Kev gave Neil his own feelings of loss and happiness.

"There he is," Neil said, "how are you doing, big fella?"

321

Kev smiled and cast his eyes to the floor as he fidgeted and giggled to himself at being directly addressed. Neil knew that he would remember him, because for all Kev's perceived failings he knew the man had a stunning memory in the long term; it was the immediate concerns that rendered him in perpetual need of assistance.

"You're good, aren't you Kev?" Jimmy said, earning an enthusiastic nod from his adopted big little brother. Kev kept his eyes down and giggled as he lumbered forwards to reach out for a slice of the bread before pausing and glancing at Maggie wordlessly.

"Of course you can, sweetheart,' she said kindly. "Grab one for Jimmy too." He picked up two, weighing them and shamelessly handing the smaller one to his friend before he went out and Jimmy followed him.

"He seems happy," Neil said as he held up the glass to assess the clarity and colour of the beer like he was a connoisseur.

"He is," Maggie agreed. "Gets up at dawn every day to work with us."

"I think he meant Jimmy," Cedric added conspiratorially.

"That obvious?" Neil answered with a smile.

"Just a bit," the old man answered. "It'll be good to have another healthy lad about the place to help out. My back isn't what it used to be…"

"Oh, here we go again," Maggie moaned theatrically as she switched into the character from Monty Python, "my legs are old and bent, my ears are gristled…"

"Well, they are!"

Neil smiled at the couple who couldn't even bicker convincingly, so lovingly intertwined with one another's lives that they were two halves of a whole.

"I wish I'd brought a bottle for you now," he told them changing the subject. "Probably would've drunk it on the boat, but…" He reached into a pocket and withdrew a pewter flask to offer it to them. "My own recipe," he said. "It's multi-purpose. Equally good for sterilising equipment, cleaning a rifle or destroying braincells."

"Really selling it," Cedric muttered as he risked sniffing the spout and recoiling to blink before taking the plunge and swigging some to lower it with a chesty cough.

"That's…" he started, his voice croaky and hoarse, "that's good stuff." He offered the flask to Maggie who gave him a mildly withering glance before he retracted his hand and gave it back to Neil.

Before their guest could respond the front door to the house burst open and Iain stood panting in the doorway wearing a look of angry horror. Neil, all thoughts of fresh bread and crisp, beautiful beer forgotten, struggled to his feet from the comfortable chair and snatched up the rifle from where he'd rested it by the front door. Neither man exchanged a word as they left, Iain slamming the door closed behind them unintentionally as Maggie and Cedric sat in silence for a moment.

With a groan, Cedric leaned forwards to lift Neil's beer and raise the glass to his lips, pausing to glance at Maggie before he drank. "No sense in wasting it," he muttered, standing to place the glass down and reach above the fireplace for the two shotguns hanging there with a thin layer of dust adorning them. Calling Kev and Jimmy back in, they began preparing to act as a militia just in case whatever had caused the panic affected them.

"One section…of fence patrol went quiet," Iain explained breathlessly as the two men jogged towards the perimeter. "Sent a relief patrol…and they…haven't checked in."

Neil said nothing, mostly due to the fact that his heart was beating out of his ears now that he asked his body which was still very full of food to conduct physical exercise. He followed the tough, short man through the streets in a direction he wasn't familiar with and guessed they were heading directly for the affected section. Just when he thought he would have to stop and clutch at his ample side until he could breathe and talk again, Steve appeared ahead giving orders.

"I want all sections reporting in on constant rotation," he instructed a woman who was fussing over a radio set, "assume comms are compromised so nothing vital to be relayed. Shut anyone down who gives anything away." He looked up, seeing Neil's red face beside Iain.

"We lost contact with a fence patrol a few minutes ago," he explained, repeating the information Iain had already given him. "Relief force sent to investigate aren't responding."

"Have you got an alarm?" Neil asked. "Air raid siren or something?"

Before anyone could answer the bell of the small church in town began ringing intensely as a pre-arranged signal for the population to arm itself.

"Anyone not vouched for gets shot," Iain told Neil, "so stay close to one of us and don't get separated in case they don't recognise you." Neil nodded, serious about not getting shot by a nervous civilian for being in the wrong place at the wrong time.

"Is this section one of the identified weak spots?" Neil asked them.

324

"One of three," Steve said. "I'll take this one, can you two take another?"

Iain answered for them, saying that they would.

"Dan said they'd come," Steve muttered as he tweaked his kit which had obviously been thrown on in a hurry. "But not this quickly."

TWO CAN PLAY THAT GAME

Mo had no idea what was happening back at his own camp, but when he'd left the previous night with only a few men he trusted he had no idea that someone would have the balls to try exactly what he was doing.

Goran had demanded results and Mo fully intended to deliver those results, but that didn't mean he couldn't enjoy himself in the process.

One of the two men chosen to accompany him was a hardened career criminal who had been a violent enforcer involved in drug trafficking, and what made Mo believe that was that the man didn't make the claim loudly; he waited to be asked a direct question and only admitted what he had been before when it served him to do so. Mo rather suspected that it had been the chance to cause pain to other people and see the fear in their eyes that had attracted him to the life.

His own existence had been vastly different; a high achiever in school and a first-class honours degree in computer science, closely followed by a doctorate in that field had led him to get into the world of network security where the competition was as high as the salary. He'd enjoyed every moment of beating other candidates to jobs, to contracts, to promotions, until as a freelance project manager at the top of his game he'd travelled all over the world to bully teams of programmers with near total impunity.

His methods were widely known, but the results he achieved outweighed the fact that many didn't want to work with him because of his attitude towards the lesser humans.

He knew – he'd known for many years – that he was different. That he *had* to win at whatever he did, and that trait transferred itself into every facet of his life until he was alone because nobody wanted to be around him. He told himself that he preferred it that way, because so many other people were a disappointment to him who couldn't handle having their flaws pointed out to them.

When the bottom fell out of the world and his area of expertise was rendered irrelevant in an instant, he was lost. He snapped out of it, taking over a small warehouse and organising all of the food stocks to spend hours at a time doing the calculations to determine how long he would survive given the calorific content of his available stores. He roamed outside of the city suburb he'd lived in, always avoiding interaction with others out of a mixture of instinct and a lack of interest in the struggles of people he didn't want to be responsible for.

He survived like that for over a year until he'd all but forgotten how to speak to anyone but himself. He'd let his appearance slip, growing out his thinning hair and sporting a beard so wild that he would have appeared frightening to behold if he ever interacted with another person.

When the pressure of loneliness forced him to do things that weren't in his character, he'd shaved his head and his beard, dressed in one of his best suits, taken the shotgun he'd acquired and prepared to place the barrel in his mouth, when shouts from outside grabbed his attention. He'd tried to ignore them, but the insistent, pleading tone tugged at him like the distressed struggling of a fish in water would attract a predator.

He found himself attracted to the sound like it called to him, and he realised that his rapid breathing and beating heart was renewed by the sounds, as if the terror of another human being had revitalised him.

Abandoning the plan to end his own life he threw open the doors of his hideout and instead used the gun on a man holding a knife out towards two others. He didn't hit him in the chest to shred his body, instead he intentionally fired low to debilitate and wound him as the calf muscle of his left leg was blown away in bloody gore to drop him to the ground.

He kicked the knife away from the screaming man, shoving it towards the younger one of his intended victims who clutched at a bag as though his life depended on it.

"Kill him," he ordered, pointing the shotgun barrel at the knife. The boy hesitated. "You think he wouldn't have killed you? Do it."

"Please," groaned the bleeding man at his feet, "I'm just trying to feed m—"

Mo kicked him hard to stop him from speaking. He kicked him again, and again, finding that it made him feel so much better about himself. Oh, how he'd wished he'd been able to do this to all the people who'd failed him. Those who had ignored his instructions or not followed them to the letter, those he'd had to satisfy himself with having fired from their positions instead of doing what he was doing now. He kicked again, timing his blows to avoid the desperate defensive actions of the crying man to land one savage toe of his boot into the man's throat. He choked, clutching at his neck as Mo ordered the boy to kill him once more, reinforcing the instruction with the threat of his gun.

A gun. It made him powerful. It was fire to a caveman. It was a light in the dark and it made him the ruler of everything. He learned a lot about himself – his *true* self – that day.

Since then he'd never lost sight of who he was deep down, and when he embraced it, when he accepted that he was a person who fed off the pain and misery of others like a vampire, he was more at peace with who he was than he'd ever been in his life.

He walked into the camp where frightened people huddled together and he was appalled by what he saw. They were barely surviving, clinging on to life without a plan and with no leadership or direction. He decided there and then that he would provide it, and finding far more people than he would ever have anticipated who shared his enjoyment of exercising power over others proved to be no hardship at all.

Their numbers grew along with their strength, until one day a young man arrived seeking refuge from a nomadic existence. He brought with him a dozen fighters, all equipped as though they were military, and Mo believed he'd found the fighting force to ensure his seat on the throne was secure.

It took only a few months for Goran to take over total control of the group until Mo faced the impossible choice of leaving to start all over again or fall in line, because challenging him for leadership was never an option.

Mo stood over the bodies of three people, all killed silently as they wandered along an empty section of fence chatting amiably as though they didn't have a care in the world. Mo had killed the last one personally, holding a hand over a woman's mouth as she struggled violently to free herself. Her eyes, like beacons in the low light, begged for her life which just made his killing stroke with the knife even sweeter. He kept his hand in place, pressing his own nose into her as he watched her eyes glisten then go dull as if her power supply was running out.

He knew others of their group would want to take her alive, to do more than kill her, but his low opinion of those base animals was a well-known fact that led to whispers about his personal tastes.

Invigorated by the killing, Mo dragged her body back to reconvene with the others and take all of the valuable equipment they had.

"Do we burn them?" one asked.

"Why?" Mo snapped at him.

"Because Goran…"

"Goran isn't here, so you do what I tell you to do. Bring them with us, let these fools spend hours looking for bodies that aren't here."

"And then what?" his once criminal assistant asked.

"Then we come back and get in."

"Here?"

"No, they'll be expecting it here. We attack the other side next time."

BATTLE LINES

Dan didn't want to waste time waiting for daylight. Instead, as soon as they got back to their temporary hideout he gave orders for them to leave immediately.

"Hang on," George said, only without the hostility he'd had the last time they spoke in the barn. "Shouldn't we wait?"

"We need to get back," Dan answered. "Steve knows to expect an attack but I didn't think it would come as quickly as tomorrow. If *I* didn't think that, then I doubt anyone else will."

"He's right on that," Mitch said. "He's always been a right glass half empty man, but I think this time I have to disagree."

Dan turned to look at him, realising after a second that Mitch wouldn't have been able to see the look on his face so he translated it for him.

"Come again?"

"No harm in waiting a couple hours for first light," Mitch argued reasonably. "Be safer all round that way, what with us being so close to where they are and all."

Dan threw his arms up in exasperation at the mutiny, returning to the door of the barn and fumbling in the dark for his cigarettes having gone a few hours without one to remain tactical.

He heard it long before he saw the lights, and discarded the unlit cigarette with a single, desperate warning hissed to the others.

"Down!"

He grabbed a dusty, vermin-chewed plastic tarpaulin and threw it over the front of their truck to disguise it as so obviously out of place before he paused at the back and ordered Ash to jump in and get down. Mitch had already disappeared, dragging George with him to adopt a defensive position as vehicle headlights swung into the yard to lance a slice of bright illumination through their hiding place.

"Stay here," Dan whispered over the rattling sound of the approaching vehicle, "don't go loud unless you have to." With that he slipped out of a gap in the back of the barn where a couple of wooden boards had been chewed away by an animal before the water had got in and rotted the rest away to make the hole wide enough for a person.

He put in a hard sprint for a few seconds to get himself clear of the barn before jumping a low brick wall and landing heavily on the uneven stones on the other side. He stayed still, forcing his breathing not to rasp in his throat as he listened.

Three car doors banged but only one engine idled loudly as a backdrop. A voice sounded but it was too low to make out and the other sounds distorted it to make it useless other than to identify the speaker as most probably male before the engine shut off to leave them all in a suddenly renewed silence.

"There's fuck all here, Daz," a voice moaned.

"Don't fucking call me that," came the reply in a growl that sounded slightly nasal as though the speaker had a blocked nose. "Look around anyway; you heard the orders."

A dawning feeling of recognition began to tickle Dan's mind before a more immediate concern filled his world. One of the three people – he assumed three because of the three doors closing – walked in his direction as he clicked on a bright LED beam and slashed it across the empty farmyard to obliterate his vision for the split second before he could clamp his eyes shut to protect them. He sank to the ground just hoping that he hadn't been seen and trusting the fact that he was wearing dark clothing which was probably pretty dirty by that point in the long day he'd had.

He held his breath, waiting for the shout of alarm to signify that he should rise and unload his weapon at the helpful light source telling him exactly where his closest enemy was, but nothing happened. He'd stayed undetected somehow and thanked the unprofessionalism of these idiots for making the job of killing them that much easier.

"I've got left," another voice grumbled, "you go right."

"Try not to step in fox shit this time, dickhead."

"Yeah, fuck you too," muttered the first man under his breath as he stomped off in a direction that would lead him out of sight of the others past Dan.

"I'll check the barn," the one with the blocked nose announced without the first clue about night operations.

Dan listened, his body acting on instinct as he began to stalk the one with the flashlight from about ten paces behind him.

The flashlight's beam cut the sky as Dan heard a, "*Zzzzzzhuh, zhuh.*" He figured the sound was being made by the man's mouth ahead of him and paused, wondering what he was doing.

"*Zzzzzzzzuh-zhuh-zhuh…*"

Is he… Dan thought to himself incredulously, *is he playing fucking lightsabres?*

In the few seconds it took to lean around his cover and lift the weapon to his shoulder he actually paused as he felt sorry for the man. It was a brief, fleeting feeling before a double-tap to the back of his head and neck dropped him like a stuffed sack but in that moment Dan experienced a brief stab of remorse for having to take someone out who, maybe, wasn't a complete piece of shit.

He froze, waiting and listening for any response to his suppressed shots which he knew would've been audible to anyone paying close attention.

He waited. Ten seconds. Fifteen. Nothing happened.

He turned away, leaving the dead man lying beside his dropped lightsabre and comforting himself with the fact that he would've likely known and felt nothing on his end as the bright beam illuminated the silhouette of his skull which was where Dan knew the first bullet had gone.

His next target had gone around the other side of the buildings in the direction where he and Mitch had gone when they first got there hours before. He was angry at their amateurish behaviour, and that made him angry because he knew these untrained men could still kill him just as easily as trained troops could.

He stalked him, ignoring the sensation of enjoyment and pushing it down into the box where he kept pride in his profession instead of labelling it as anything that would warrant far more concern. He reminded himself that he would always choose a peaceful existence over this, but part of him, the part that nobody ever really saw, was so good at this shit that it frightened him.

He saw his next target, saw that he was more cautious than the last one but reasoned that it wasn't difficult as the last one was pretending to be a Jedi.

I just hope after I struck him down that he doesn't come back more powe—CONCENTRATE! He barked inside his own head, fighting away the tiredness that twisted his thoughts into the random and obscure at the worst possible time.

He tracked the man's progress, moving slowly and carefully as the person just ahead of him was creeping and stopping to listen.

He made a critical error, pausing in the open to silhouette himself, and Dan took the opportunity and fired. The dull thump of his rounds being absorbed by the ballistic body armour the man wore was a sound he'd heard a few times in his life, and he wished for the first time that he'd opted for the heavier version of his weapon that fired ammunition capable of penetrating whatever plate the man wore.

As it was, the half-dozen bullets Dan had fired were enough to break the man's ribs with the force of the projectiles being absorbed by the vest and he dropped to the ground with a strangled cry of pain to accompany the thud. Dan ran, closing the distance before he regained enough sense to shout out or fire a weapon, and stamped his left boot onto the outstretched forearm with fingers fluttering for the dropped rifle. Dan fired one more shot, imagining for a fraction of a second what his victim would've experienced as a dark shape appeared above him to blink out his life.

Before Dan could take cover and listen for any response to his actions, the world erupted in a flash of orange and white light with a booming report loud enough to deafen him and make him throw himself to the muddy ground. His brain registered the *shuck-shuck* of another cartridge being pumped into a chamber which told him that another huge spray of lead would be heading his way in under a second.

He rolled desperately as he tried to make himself as small as possible, but instead of the boom of another shotgun blast he heard the sickening crunch and an anguished yelp of pain before sobbing and the sound of a person hitting the deck.

Dan rolled to his feet, his breath coming fast and almost out of control as he gave a low double whistle to bring Ash to his side. He didn't know why he did that, but the close proximity of the big dog settled him within a few seconds of Ash finding him.

"Stay down, ya wee prick," he heard Mitch growl as he moved towards them.

"George, check their truck," Dan yelled.

"Clear," he heard the young man's voice call back almost immediately. He didn't know if Mitch had told him to do that or if he'd done it himself but Dan was happy that all of the threats were nullified.

"You…fucking…*bastard*!" exploded the floored man in a muffled voice full of tearful anger. "You broke my fucking nose. Again!"

"What?" Mitch muttered, clicking on a torch as Dan instinctively closed one eye to protect his night vision. He needn't have bothered because Mitch had activated his red-lensed beam that didn't destroy their vision like white light did in the dark.

"This arsehole again?" Dan said in disbelief, encouraging Ash to 'watch' the man. "I thought I told you not to come back this way or I'd kill you?"

"You broke my fucking nose!"

Dan looked at Mitch who simply offered an unapologetic shrug as if this was now his new thing.

"You'd prefer my dog to rip your balls off?" Dan growled.

Broken Nose then made possibly the worst decision of his life, and spat a mouthful of blood in Dan's direction.

He blamed himself in a way. He'd never, not once in all of his life, had someone hit him full face with a spit. He'd prefer to get stabbed than spat on, because the rage it unleashed in him was a frightening thing to behold. So angry was he with the disgusting,

336

cowardly move that he laid into the man so hard that Ash took it upon himself to get in on the action before there was nothing left. For all his failings, that dog was the ultimate wing man and had he been born a man he would've been right there beside Dan in the dock when they inevitably landed themselves in deep trouble.

Finally deciding that enough was definitely enough, Mitch interjected and dragged Dan away before he beat him to death.

"Can't answer any questions if you've kicked all his teeth out," Mitch warned him. Dan said nothing, just wiped the hot blood from his face and wheeled away to blast past George on his way to find a bottle of water to clean the blood from his face and hands.

His hands shook and his breath came in gasps like a toddler at the closing stages of a tantrum when the fight had all but left them. He ached all over; the exhaustion of not only the actions of the night but the adrenaline which threatened to curl him up in a ball made him wish he'd stayed in the south of France.

THE STRESS OF CONCENTRATION

Neil's face was slack by the time the sun was fully up, and a night spent in the cold and dark on a full stomach had done him no favours. All he craved was twenty minutes in total peace to take a relaxing dump before his head hit a soft pillow with his face for anything up to, but not limited to, perhaps twelve hours.

They'd found no trace of their missing patrol, nor the two men of the relief force sent to investigate their disappearance, so when the dawn began to break all eyes were on the perimeter waiting for the flames of burning bodies to flare into visibility as a cruel message to the defenders.

None came. It was guerrilla warfare 101 he knew; undermine the confidence of your enemy and hit them from the dark in small numbers before melting away. Facing an enemy you couldn't see and couldn't fight was soul-destroying, but it was becoming increasingly likely. The prospect of all-out war was unlikely to happen again in human history for hundreds of years because the population was now so small that any war of attrition would have two losers, so they now faced round-the-clock patrols with a population on high alert after the rumours of what had happened in the night festered like an infected wound.

Still deadly serious about not wanting to get shot by a nervous, exhausted member of the town militia as an armed stranger Neil had

338

made damn sure he stuck to Iain like glue. Twice he'd been challenged and twice the man had vouched for him, and one time he gave his name a look of dawning realisation crept onto the challenger's face as though he'd just threatened a legend. Under different circumstances Neil would have capitalised on this and made a show, but given the occurrences of the night he was so far removed from making a joke that he didn't even seem like himself.

"Come on," Iain said with a slap to his arm, "let's go check in with Steve."

Neil followed him wordlessly as they traipsed through the early morning dew back to the command post. Steve appeared outwardly as tired as Neil felt but his words and actions seemed electrified by comparison.

"I'm leading a patrol out past the perimeter," he informed them without uttering a greeting first. "You're welcome to join me." Neither man hesitated in spite of their exhaustion.

"We're just waiting for a couple of dogs," Steve went on after curtly nodding his gratitude.

"Trained?" Neil asked, intrigued.

"Partly," Steve admitted with a look that made him mindful of detecting an unpleasant odour. "They'll never be Ash, but they'll follow their noses towards people at least."

Neil shrugged as if to convey that he was fine with that. Before the dogs could arrive and before they could set out, the same woman Neil had seen using the radio base station ran up to Steve cradling what looked like a mobile telephone from the eighties.

"Send, over," Steve said in the clipped tones of a man accustomed to professional radio use as he held down a large transmit button and waited half a beat before speaking.

"Steve, it's George, over,"

339

"No names," Steve said, "comms are compromised. Repeat, comms are compromised, over."

An empty second of transmission came from the other end as though George was going to answer but couldn't think of what to say without giving their enemy vital intelligence. Switching to another channel was irrelevant because they had no pre-determined sequence to follow, and informing the others to change to a certain frequency would serve zero purpose.

Instead, Dan's voice came back with a single word. "Understood," he said, his tone heavy and foreboding.

Steve returned the radio to the woman with a nod of thanks and hefted his carbine again.

"This changes nothing," he said, "patrol still goes out."

There were two dogs joining in: a heavy-set black Labrador, who seemed a little overwhelmed by the amount of people milling about, and a cross breed with so many semi-recognisable traits that Dan would've described it as a purebred street pedigree. They did their best, but after an hour of careful searching all the patrol found was a patch of flattened grass where a light rain had washed away most of the traces of what they were sure was blood.

Steve, determined not to see any more of his people treated like fiery scarecrows, pushed out their patrol a clear mile from the fence line until a quiet word from Iain made him call the retreat. Taking so many of their fighters away from the town was ill-advised he knew, but as a leader he was torn between the priorities of his duties.

By the time they had retraced their steps to the safety of being inside the wire a report of a vehicle returning was spreading by word of mouth as their antiquated and unsecured radio system had been temporarily abandoned.

Neil followed Steve through the unfamiliar streets, seeing nervous expressions on faces all around him as though everyone expected something bad to happen at any moment.

He thought back to the time they had been under threat in their home, only with the high, ancient stone walls of their small fortress and sheer cliffs facing the sea they were in a naturally defended bowl instead of being settled in a place dictated by the production of power and the supply of fresh water. In that moment he felt conflicted about wanting to be back at home and wanting to scoop up everyone to transport them there where they could feel safe.

Walls were hard to climb and even harder to bring down, but a heavy chain-link fence could be defeated by a child with small bolt cutters.

"Steve," George's voice sounded loud and young.

"What happened?" Steve asked, looking past George to Dan who still had dried blood encrusted on parts of his face.

"Got close enough for a recce of their camp," Dan told him, his voice croaking slightly. "They're coming here to probe an attack. We had to kill two there and some came out searching. Killed another two and took this one prisoner," he said as he turned towards the muffled sounds of protest where Mitch was dragging a man with a severely bruised and bent nose. Dark rings of pooled blood gave him the look of a panda but only the look of murderous intent he gave them stopped his appearance from being amusing.

"You're so fucking dead," he grumbled thickly, his speech marred by his most recent injury. His words were ignored as Steve jerked his head for Dan to step away with him. Automatically, George, Iain and Neil followed.

"They attacked last night," Steve said in a low, hollow voice. "We've lost five for their five, so nobody gains an advantage there."

"Dead?" Dan asked. "They didn't..."

"No," Steve told him, "missing...*presumed.*"

"Shit," Dan hissed, drawing out the word as he fidgeted on the spot. "We – you – can't keep trading actions like this. You need to do something decisive."

"Agreed," Steve said. "But we all need sleep and food otherwise anything we do will be half-cocked." He turned to George knowing that the youngest of his command group would be the most alert.

"Can you make sure we have constant guard rotation and some switched-on people running the show for this morning?" he asked, making his orders sound like a polite request without wasting time. Dan smiled to himself at the way the officer breeds must have been taken aside during training to be taught how to do that.

Some took to it naturally whereas others believed the obedience of the lower ranks to be their birth right. Men and women like that weren't followed out of respect, which is why their armed forces had non-commissioned officers so that the wheel never fell off, and if it did at least they'd be prepared to get dirty hands putting it back on.

George promised that he'd see to it and walked away, pausing to exchange a nod with Dan who returned the gesture as confirmation of their continued truce after the previous night.

"Do you need to talk with him beforehand?" Steve asked, jutting his chin out towards the man slumped against the truck with his hands bound.

"Oh, he's already been as helpful as he's going to be," Dan said. He'd personally questioned Broken Nose again with the assistance of Ash and he remained as stubborn, dishonest and resolute as he had been during their first conversation. "He comes with us when we go, though," he added nastily. "Returning lost animals is the right thing to do."

THUNDERBIRD TWO

"Oh," Neil exclaimed as though he'd just been shown a picture of the most adorable baby wearing a caterpillar costume. "Oh, hello, be-*yoo*tiful."

"Thought you'd appreciate it," Steve said after he'd unlocked a half-dozen padlocks securing a roll down shutter door to reveal Neil's oldest and best creation.

The old Land Rover had a few more dents than he remembered, and the rubber mounts had weathered a little to the point where they might need replacing soon, but the shape of the machine gun standing proudly with its long barrel pointing outwards was unmistakable. With a strained grunt of effort, Neil hauled himself up into the flat truck bed amid the protests of suspension springs that groaned and creaked as much as he did, and planted his feet wide, grasping the weapon's controls with both hands.

"Say *hhhello* to my little friend," he crowed in a *Godfather* impression that would've had even the German judge awarding a solid nine-point-six.

"You win," Dan said to Mitch as he offered a reluctant fist to be bumped by the soldier beside him.

"What?" Neil asked, annoyed at them for having a joke he wasn't in on.

"I had money on you saying something from *Blood Diamond*. Didn't even cross my mind that you'd go old-school."

"Anyway," Steve said, seeming to punish himself for enjoying the company of friends even for just a moment. He rummaged in a cabinet inside the lockup and came out with a metal rod that seemed totally innocuous to the casual eye. He passed it up to Neil who regarded it quizzically for a moment before he tucked it under one arm and fiddled with the weapon to slide the entire butt section upwards and off. Slipping the rod into the gun he rebuilt it with the key component added and pulled back on the charging handle to fill the small space with the reassuringly heavy clack of the working parts.

"When Richards…" Steve cleared his throat to remove the sudden lump that had formed and tried again. "*Hmm…*when Richards took the prison and carted us all off, apparently he left half his men there to pick through everything we had stored. It took them a couple of weeks to clear us out, and Thunderbird Two here has been mothballed ever since."

"Apparently?" Neil asked before his brain caught up with his mouth.

"I was in a bit of a state at the time," Steve answered. "One shattered leg and a concussion to rival Dan's worst day out courtesy of the most appalling landing of my career. And I'd been in two helicopter crashes *before* that one."

"How much seven-six-two have you got?" Dan asked, switching the conversation back to the machine gun and away from potentially uncomfortable memories.

"Three belts," Steve told him. Dan looked at Neil, wishing again he could arch an eyebrow for no particular reason.

"Six hundred rounds are enough, depending on what the job is."

"And what is the job?" Steve asked lightly. The atmosphere inside the dusty garage thickened as the ball was placed firmly in his guest's court.

Dan sucked in a thoughtful breath and turned to lean against the grille of the truck. He retrieved his tin, selecting one of his remaining cigarettes and lighting it. Everyone there knew he was stalling for time before he answered, and despite the cool demeanour his exterior radiated they all knew his brain was spinning at critical velocity as he thought.

He epitomised the concept of the duck on water; he may look like he's effortlessly gliding along but underneath the surface his feet were going like fuck.

Exhaling the stream of smoke upwards without even realising they were all waiting for him to do just that, he spoke slowly as though he was figuring it out as he said the words.

"We know where they are," he said, "or at least where they were last night. It's doubtful they'll be expecting a foray so soon after being attacked—"

"A *foray*?" Neil asked mockingly. "Doth mine liege wanteth a charge of the realm's knights?"

"—fuck off—" Dan continued conversationally, "so we need to move fast if we want to catch them out."

"And do what?" Steve asked, wanting to keep the genius flowing.

"Draw them out and ambush them."

"And home for tea and medals," Mitch added drily.

"How?" Steve asked.

In response Dan craned his neck to look at Mitch's rifle. "Start dropping bombs on them, block one route and use the Thunderbird on the other. Go in and mop up what's left."

The room was silent as they considered the simple approach to clearing out yet another infestation.

"Is that really the best way?" a voice asked from the open door. Heads turned to face the intrusion, revealing George standing tall and unashamed to have spoken.

"Got a better idea?" Dan asked him.

George folded, shrinking in stature as he slumped a little.

"No, come one," Dan prompted him almost kindly, "I'm always open to suggestions. I don't own the monopoly on good ideas."

"I…" he began, stopping to look at the ground. "I like the ambush idea, but it would better to lure them out instead of force them out…" He looked up, swallowing nervously as he saw all eyes on him. "Is it too much of an assumption to think they'll be listening to our radios?"

Dan glanced at Steve to see him wearing the same interested look on his face as the one on his own.

"No, but I doubt we can formulate a plan based on an assumption without a solid plan B," Dan said, pushing himself off the Land Rover and getting animated as an idea hit him. "But I like the idea of misinformation. How else can we feed them some bullshit?"

George faltered, his face screwing up as he thought until he beamed when an idea came to him. That idea had already grown in Dan's mind and had two children of its own, but he wanted to let George follow the logic.

"We've got two of their people," he said excitedly. "Couldn't we, I dunno, get them to escape and…"

"Too risky," Steve cut in, "but we could release them and make it believable."

"How?" Dan asked with a snap of his fingers to keep their collective creativity flowing.

Steve smiled before he answered. "I happen to have a petition on my desk to release them as being unlawfully interned without charges."

"You, heh, you *what*?" Dan laughed.

"Seriously," Steve said with a smile. "Seems the advocates council, which is apparently a thing, got their heads together and reviewed the evidence to find no proof that the two people we captured are guilty. They're making noises about them being released unless there's fresh evidence."

"Okay," Dan said, holding up both hands as if he could slow down the spin of the earth for his brain to catch up with the weapons-grade horseshit he'd just had forced into his ears without consent. "These people know why they're safe at night, right? They know who's kept the wolves from their doors for years?"

"It's irrelevant," Steve said. "The fact that they're actively fighting for democratic human rights means they feel...*safe*. Try and see it as a good thing."

Dan shook his head, lost for words at how ungrateful the sheep in Steve's flock were. He justified their actions after reading the look on Dan's face.

"Honestly, I do see it as a good thing. Without strong socialist, libertarian opposition it'd be far too easy to slip into being a military dictatorship. I'm not saying I agree with it, but the fact that they can have their opinions in safety means that it's working here. I'm not beyond having my actions questioned."

"It was working until the nut job who likes to set fire to innocent people rocked up with some like-minded friends," Dan reminded him darkly.

"Yeah," Neil said. "So get thinking about how to make this prisoner release seem legit."

SOCIALIST AGENDA

The key to a successful rouse, Dan knew, was having willing participants who had no idea they were playing the game. Steve appeared to bow to the pressure of the petition and sent for the first three names on the signature list to meet with him, tiredly asking what it is that they wanted for the whole mess to simply go away and leave him to concentrate on more important matters.

Mrs Beecham, who according to the petition apparently did have a first name of Lisa, bustled herself up to her full, if not meagre, height, and berated him for dismissing the human rights of people unlawfully detained in a democracy.

"And might I add," she sneered, "that if this situation persists, we may have to seek a formal indictment of you as the person ultimately allowing this miscarriage of justice to continue."

Steve listened, making out like he was concerned about the rumblings of disgruntled people – he was, just not these people on this particular issue – and called out for Sophie.

"Send runners for George and Dan, please," he asked, making his three hostile guests wait in uncomfortable silence. The silence was uncomfortable for them, but for him it was blissful. He made a show of reading reports and making notes on the scattered papers littering his desk until a polite, professional knock at the door made him look up.

"The men you asked for, sir," Sophie said, calling him 'sir' for added effect as though she was disappointed at not being given a more pivotal role in the charade.

"Thank you," Steve said, standing as the two confused men walked in. "I'll keep it brief. Can either of you offer any irrefutable evidence or eyewitness accounts to prove that the two men currently detained are guilty of serious crimes?"

"*Beyond* reasonable doubt," added the woman brimming with self-importance.

"Hang on a minute," Dan exploded, "you're not seriously giving in to these tree-hugging fuckwits, are you? Come *on*, Steve, you know as well as I do that they're all guilty."

"That's hardly the point," snapped Mrs Beecham as she rocketed to her feet far faster than her ample frame would've indicated was possible.

"Do yourself a favour," Dan said nastily, "just stay in the car and bark at strangers, will you?"

"That's enough, guys," Steve shouted. "Seriously, act your ages!"

One of the other advocate activists cleared his throat and spoke in a tone of voice to indicate it was probably the first time he'd stood up for himself.

"Erm, can we not use gender-specific language like that, please? I find it personally oppressive...?"

Steve looked at him, blinked, looked at Dan to see the same '*What the fuck?*' expression screaming back at him and shook his head as if that would clear the last words his brain had been forced to hear.

"George?" Steve asked. George just shook his head.

"Fine," Steve said, "take them far away from here and kick them out—"

"They must be provided with adequate supplies and means to return home," the third advocate, a woman with such a pronounced chin that she reminded Steve of a cartoon character. "Need I remind you that you have a duty of care?"

Dan threw his arms up and let out a noise a stroppy teenager would be proud of. "Oh, give me fucking strength," he moaned, making Steve hold up a hand to shut him up like he just wanted this whole meeting over already.

"Supplies, yes. No to any transport; they can walk."

The advocates looked at one another in search of any other demands they could make and found only one.

"I insist that a representative of the advocacy program be present to ensure no ill-treatment occurs," Lisa Beecham said formally.

"Fine," Dan said. "Get your coat and be ready to leave in ten minutes."

Her face fell and coloured up simultaneously as her mouth dropped open to pop like a fish.

"I…I didn't mean to imply I would *personally*—"

"Why not?" Steve cut in happily. "That seems like a perfect compromise all round to me. Thank you, everyone, for your time. George, can you make sure this happens immediately please?"

George nodded seriously as if accepting the grave responsibility of what he'd been asked to do, gesturing politely for the shocked Mrs Beecham to file out of the office before him.

~

Dan drove intentionally harshly, snatching the wheel and going fifty percent too fast for the comfort of his passengers. He drove like he was showing off but pretended he didn't possess the smooth skills behind the wheel that had been so thoroughly trained into him that they were hard to forget, even when he didn't drive for months on end.

He enjoyed himself – not for the thrill of driving fast but for the alarm and discomfort he was inflicting on the terrified, wide-eyed woman and the two battered prisoners who still suspected a trap.

She'd taken great delight in informing them that democracy had fought for their rights and that they were to be freed, and when the gratitude she so desperately craved wasn't forthcoming she fell back on a default setting Dan would describe as 'haughty bitch'.

"*Please* will you slow down!" she shrieked from the rear seat as Dan attacked a sweeping bend so aggressively that her sizeable cheeks were lifted off the seat with the angle of the lean.

"Sorry," Dan answered as he deliberately came out of the bend and straightened up too sharply to wobble them around. "It's tactical to drive fast so anyone following us is obvious to counter-surveillance. We have to take certain precautions, you know?"

It was complete bullshit, and vaguely echoed something he'd seen in a movie of Neil's choosing once, but seeing as it was only him who would know otherwise he delivered it with confidence.

His next trick was to slam on the brakes without warning – something he'd only informed George that he was going to do and told him what was required of him to play his part – to wrench on the handbrake and throw himself from the vehicle and set an immediate ambush on their trail.

He kept them there on high alert for almost ten minutes, ignoring the shrieking complaints of the woman nestled between her two ungrateful friends, until he returned to the driving seat and began driving like a dick again.

None of that was necessary, he knew that, but if he couldn't take any enjoyment out of the everyday things then was life even worth living?

Choosing a spot seemingly at random, but knowing that one route would lead them directly back to their own people, Dan stopped the truck and climbed out to draw a knife. He ignored the shouts, turning the first man around to slice the plasticuffs binding his wrists to stop the shouts. Opening the rear section he dragged out two old mountain bikes to drop them on the road beside the bags of food and water after the hardship of them having to walk potentially undermined the plan.

He stood in the road and pointed in one direction.

"Fuck off that way and don't come back." He shot a dangerous look at Mr Twice Broken Nose to remind him that he'd already been offered this deal and hadn't taken it.

Carefully, casually as if to not realise what he was doing with his hands as he spoke, he jabbed a thumb over his shoulder in the other direction.

"If you two go back to your mates then you'll be getting a nasty surprise at dawn, so make sure you aren't there if you want to live." With that he wrenched open the driver's door and climbed inside before he did anything to infringe on their rights. He crunched the gears into first, dropped the clutch out and accelerated hard away from the junction heading home.

"You did the right thing," came the condescending words from behind him.

"Oh, I know we did," Dan agreed smugly.

"Perhaps you can see this as the start?" she carried on, evidently loving the sound of her own voice. "Maybe you could consider your use of force next? If you absolutely have to use a weapon, for example, you could consider shooting someone in the leg if talking to them doesn't yield results?"

"In...in the *leg*?" Dan asked, genuinely intrigued.

"Yes, where they won't die fr—"

"You ever seen anyone bleed out from a severed femoral artery?" he asked, knowing she wouldn't have an answer. "I have. It's fast and brutal, and the person with the hole in their leg knows they're going to die every second it takes them to go. Trust me, there's never been a 'shoot to kill' policy; there's only a 'shoot to hit before you get killed first' policy, but getting shot tends to lead to being a bit...*dead*."

"I'm trying to say that you should at least *consider* peaceful solutions instea—"

"Peaceful?" interrupted George, earning an attempted eyebrow raise from Dan.

"Yes," the haughty advocate answered in a lecturing tone as if explaining a vegetarian diet to a caveman, "we're peaceful people by choice, an—"

"You're not peaceful," George told her flatly, "you're...you're *harmless*. Literally. Not in a good way."

"How dare you," she blurted out. "I consider myself a peaceful person—"

"What he's trying to tell you," Dan cut in, "is that you can't be peaceful if you aren't capable of being violent." He let the words hang in the car as if her mind fought with them and confused her enough to stop her from talking, if only for a short while. "Being peaceful is a choice you make. If it isn't, then you're just not capable of fighting back. Who enforces all the rules you live by? Other people, ones capable of violence, because without the fear of punishment there is no order."

Her mouth opened to speak but no sound came out. A glance in the rear-view mirror showed her slowly shutting it.

He slowed down, smoothing out his driving to work the gears properly and remove all jerkiness from their journey. He caressed the truck along at a speed that seemed effortless and the woman behind him made a hesitant noise as if it was just dawning on her that he had been acting the entire time.

"You've just manipulated me, haven't you?" she asked.

"Us? No. You got what you wanted; the poor murdering bastards have been released in case paying for their crimes hurt their entitled feelings and forced the privileged pricks to take responsibility for their actions."

"That's not—"

"Shut up," Dan told her. "I'm all for protecting the rights of people – I did it for years and put my life on the line to do so and I still do now. I protect *innocent* people, and those shits aren't innocent."

"You can't prove that," she argued weakly.

"I don't have to," Dan answered smugly, "that's the beauty of this new world."

THE SEED

"They…*let you go*?" Goran demanded of the two men forced to their knees after returning to them wet and exhausted on bikes.

"Yes, and they're—"

"*Why* did they let you go?"

"Because their rules, their laws, say they couldn't prove we did anything."

Goran straightened, looking at Mo with a quizzical expression. He misunderstood and tried to explain the meaning like he hadn't comprehended the English.

"He means that they have rules like the poli—"

"I hear what he said," Goran interrupted, "I just do not understands *why*."

"Look, that's not important," one of them blurted out, "you nee—" He stopped talking as Goran lashed out a boot to hit him in the chest and fling him backwards to sprawl out on the dusty wooden floor.

"You, don't fucking tell me what I do."

"Please," the one with the badly broken nose said, "they're coming here to attack at dawn. We came back to warn you."

"You," Goran sneered, "two times now this man let you go. Why is this? What did you do for him?"

"N–nothing! I didn't do anything. I didn't *say* anything either."

"So how do you know they come to kill us in the dawn?"

355

"Because they let us go miles away, told us not to come back," Broken Nose explained.

"And he bragged about coming to attack here," the other one said. At a dismissive gesture from Goran the two men were hauled to their feet and dragged away, leaving him standing beside his thin, precise lieutenant.

"We have to assume they're right," Mo said quietly to the muscled killer. "Regardless of what else they know or what they told them."

"And you are sure you find good place to attack them?"

"Yes," Mo assured him. "We watched them swarming like flies over the section we attacked but no extra patrols were sent to reinforce the section we identified for the real attack."

Goran said nothing, furrowing his brow into deep lines as he thought. Mo knew he would never make a poker player of him because he was incapable of hiding his thoughts or indeed his true nature. Mo liked to think of himself as Goran's brains instead, winding up the metaphorical key in the brutal young man's back and sending him off in whichever direction he steered him.

Goran, even though Mo was too arrogant and self-absorbed to ever understand, was much more intelligent than he gave him credit for. His intelligence displayed itself as an instinctive ability and flare for cruelty and deviousness, and the thoughts he had then followed the same trend.

"We go tonight," he ordered. "As soon as is darkness."

Mo nodded, keeping his head bowed in a gesture of subservience that turned his stomach, but unlike Goran he knew how to act in order to manipulate people.

AMBUSH

Goran's people made no attempt to leave quietly, such was the style set by their leader. The drivers of each vehicle were instructed on the route they needed to take as well as their final destination, and as the four vehicles moved out in a tightly packed formation, they revved loudly with music coming from the windows of two of the trucks.

They followed the route set by Mo who occupied the front passenger seat of the second vehicle in line with Goran in the back of one of the others with his – *their*, Mo reminded himself – men fawning over him to inflate his ego further.

They drove with few of them paying attention or keeping an eye out for dangers, such was their confidence that none had ever challenged them. They were an army. They were raiders who went where they wanted and took what they desired. There were people left behind at the last camp which some of them considered as home, but Goran and his hardcore followers thought of themselves as dangerous nomads like the invading Northmen of the country's history.

When the route ahead flashed with reflected dull red paint the driver of the lead vehicle braked hard which caused the other trucks to bunch up so close it was a miracle that none of them crashed into one another.

Mo steadied himself on the dashboard before winding down the window to lean out and see what the problem was. He had no military training, but his precise nature had taught him to pay close attention to things like tactics in movies and books because it pleased him to point out flaws in other people's work and ideas.

The front passenger of the lead truck got out to peer ahead, before Mo yelled at him.

"Get back in!" He leaned around to face the rear of their convoy and shouted more instructions for them to go back and turn around. The section of road was far too narrow to perform the turns, and before he could yell enough orders to make them listen a noise erupted from behind him that tore the night with bright flashes and the loudest gunfire he'd ever heard in his life. It was as though a thunderstorm was happening inside a metal drum filled with fireworks right beside his head, and one thing he learned from real life that the movies didn't teach him was the way their air seemed to compress and pulse under heavy fire. It hurt all of his senses at once, but his discomfort was forgotten as soon as he heard the screams and saw the sparks erupt from the rear vehicle as bullets tore into it to shred the living contents into bloody ruin.

Knowing the way back was blocked he looked desperately to his front for an escape as his world had turned to shit in a heartbeat.

Emerging from the shadow of what he recognised as a tractor blocking the road, a shape levelled a rifle held at his hip towards the lead truck. In a moment of relative quiet when the machine gun stopped firing, Mo heard a faint pop that didn't sound at all like a bullet being fired from a g—

—the lead truck erupted in a fiery explosion so bright and so loud that Mo's senses were utterly overwhelmed. He saw nothing and heard nothing, falling from the open door of his own truck blind and deaf as he choked on the thick smoke and felt the heat of the blaze that had consumed the vehicle in front of his own.

The heavy machine gun fire started up again behind him, flinging sparks up from the metal of the vehicles and the road surface as the sound reached his brain no louder than a woodpecker would sound. Hands grabbed him, dragging him to his feet and he found himself staring into the unreadable eyes of Goran who checked him over, looking for bullet or shrapnel holes, and when he found none, he reached into the cab to grab his weapon and pack and thrust them on him.

Now, Mo thought to himself, *now he learns a poker face.*

"Go," Goran told Mo, slapping his cheek to direct his eyes into his own. He pointed in the direction of the dark fields leading away from the attacks front and rear. Logic tried to tell him that there must be danger waiting there for them, but Goran ducked at the sound of an incoming round from the darkness behind him to tell Mo that he was right, but to do nothing would mean dying in the dark on a road so insignificant that it didn't even warrant white lines being painted on it.

Mo opened and closed his mouth, bashing his ears with his free hand to try and bring his hearing back to no avail as he half ran, half stumbled into the darkness.

They ran for longer than he could count.

His breath burned in his throat as his lungs wanted desperately to cough and retch out the acrid smoke he'd breathed in. He had no idea what horrible chemicals were released when a car caught fire but he knew it wouldn't be anything that was good for his long-term health.

"Here," shouted a voice from a head of him. He stumbled towards it and piled inside a house which had just been kicked open to give them a temporary refuge. It was hours until dawn, not that he could tell anyone what day it was let alone the time, and the house

359

was filled with the muted, underwater sounds of men shouting and arguing with one another.

He wandered through the rooms, some people asking him questions and others ignoring him, until he found Goran watching one of their people wrap a bandage around a cut on someone's leg that leaked blood every time he wiped it clean.

"What happened?" Mo croaked.

Goran turned to regard him coldly. "What happened?" he asked. "What happened was these pieces of shit ambushed us, and you" – he jabbed Mo hard in the chest, hard enough to stagger him back two paces – "*you* didn't see it coming."

HELLO DARKNESS MY OLD FRIEND

Dan wasn't happy to be missing out on the opening event. Neither was Steve, but for the overall plan to work the men most accustomed to warfare had to be the ones to close the trap fully.

Neil, giggling like a kid playing hide and seek, was hunkered down in the cold, open bed of Thunderbird Two somewhere about a mile to their south just down the road from where Mitch was ready to spring the trap. They'd used the biggest and heaviest thing they could to block the road as it had to be something nobody would be tempted to ram out of the way. Even driving a truck, the sight of a tractor tyre almost six feet tall should dissuade anyone from attempting the kinetic route.

Iain was driving for him, the two finding an almost kindred spirit in their similarities and litany of awful Dad jokes, and George was leading a hand-picked group of his own people he trusted not to fail him or get overexcited and mess it up.

The trap was set, and like the brutal amateurs they were Goran's convoy drove straight into it. Any teenager with a month of basic military training under their belts would be able to describe the basic workings of an ambush. A blocking force at the front, a cut-off force at the rear and the majority of their forces in the middle to make a killing ground.

That was the plan, and it worked perfectly.

Only they left an escape route so that they didn't end up in an entrenched battle where the losses to their own side would be notable, and that open side led to the final part of their trap where Steve and Dan had another half-dozen people ready to seal their fate.

That open side of the road ambush led over an empty field of knee-high grass to an abandoned farm similar to so many that littered the abandoned countryside. They guessed that any escaping survivors would seek refuge there, and when they saw the stragglers running in that direction Dan counted them out for the others using the night vision goggles.

"Fifteen," he said. "All in the main house."

"Any sentries?" Steve asked him from their position overlooking the buildings from a small bluff raised up just enough to give a commanding view. That view was useless to him as he was all but blind past a few feet in the darkness.

"None," Dan answered, "looks like a right shit show."

"Let's start playing then," Steve said, unzipping a padded case and lifting out the weapon he was keeping dry until it was needed.

Officially designated as something sounding like a computer code, the British army's sharpshooter rifle was similar to the HK417 Dan had left behind in France; a kind of middle-ground killer and not a true sniper rifle requiring the user to learn a whole lot more science than was easy to teach.

It had a large optic mounted in the usual place but the additional scope on the rail ahead of it looked as expensive as it did total badass. The night optic used the zoom ability of the usual scope and saved having to replace it from night and day and re-zero it, and when Steve clicked it on the buzz it emitted seemed to signify that it was game time.

362

Dan slipped out of their hiding space to move low with Ash at his side. He instinctively stayed out of Steve's direct line of sight as he ran for the corner of the building their enemy had occupied.

He moved carefully, awkwardly as he felt like he had legs suddenly much longer than before he put on the goggles. Wasting no time, loud cracks split the night as the heavy bullets tore through the windows from Steve's rifle and into the unsuspecting bodies of men who were beginning to feel safe after the ambush. The realisation that they had willingly walked into another trap was late in coming as confusion tore through their ranks in panic.

Men blindly fired out of windows making Dan duck down into cover and reach back to drag Ash in behind his body in the certain knowledge that lucky bullets were still dangerous, and raised his weapon to scan the angle of the house he could see.

Even at the oblique angle he found himself at he could still see three windows with shadows moving around behind them. He moved his barrel between the windows once, returning to the first one and squeezing the trigger twice before switching his aim and repeating.

He didn't wait to check for any reaction, not wanting to invite any return fire, and moved to swing around the rear of the building to repeat the process. He was careful to stay out of sight as there were others positioned nearby ready to light up the killing ground and pour noisy fire into them.

Twice more he picked off shapes brave or foolish enough to show themselves, moving again to go back to the last piece of cover he had used to take out another. The fire coming from the house was sporadic by then, and even though it seemed as though the whole thing was moving fast, he knew the adrenaline was warping his sense of time.

Satisfied that their trap was closing in tightly around their enemy, Dan felt confident that no matter how brutal these men were, a well-executed plan would always win.

~

Steve, methodically playing a whole new version of whack-a-mole, roved the rifle's aim over the green-lit house to take snap shots at anything moving behind the windows.

A fire broke out through some combination of gunfire and the contents of a house left untouched for years, and as flames grew quickly an orange glow bathed the area to mess with their night optics in places.

Steve emptied the first magazine having fired all twenty rounds, sliding in a replacement and feeling the cold metal of the charging handle as he drew it smoothly back to make the weapon ready to fire. He paused at one window, seeing an odd reflection as something peeked hesitantly around it.

Something about the reflection made his breath catch in his throat until an eye, wide and desperate, scanned the open space outside their unsafe haven. The shine of the skull tugged at the memory of the cruel man smiling at him, threatening to kill him, and he found himself returning the smile.

"Remember *this* when your people are dying," he muttered, pulling the trigger and seeing the head snatch back out of sight.

A volley of gunfire sounded in the distance, revealing that the final part of their trap had been successful, and those escaping the house via the only route left open to them were being led directly into the path of the last of their people.

He scanned with the rifle, seeing Dan emerge from cover fast with his weapon up. Steve tracked from left to right in the direction his friend's weapon was pointing, catching the fleeing shape of a person falling down and half crawling before regaining their feet and running again. He tightened his grip on the weapon, preparing to squeeze off a round and make the shot on a running target that was infinitely harder to hit, when the left of his scope twitched with movement. His right index finger immediately released the pressure as the movement streaked low to the ground twice as fast as the running figure.

He watched in silent appreciation as Ash, bending in the middle at full sprint, sank lower and leapt off the ground with a powerful push from his back legs. The dog launched like a missile, front paws outstretched and mouth opening wide as Steve watched in what seemed like slow-motion as the mouth clamped down on the closest part of the body he could reach.

He watched as the runner arched their back, locking out like they were being tasered, to fall hard into the dirt where Ash's large head whipped back and forth with the force of ripping into the flesh on the back of the thigh he'd clamped onto. Steve took his finger away from the trigger to rest it on the outside of the guard to watch as Dan caught up with them and slowed, lowering his own weapon as he let the dog continue for longer than would've been legal under the laws of the old world.

Dan turned and walked away, confusing Steve for a second before he guessed that the man must have been done for, otherwise he'd never leave him alive. Mo, it seemed, wanted to display one last act of defiance because he pulled a pistol and held it like a drunk, aiming it into the darkness where Dan walked.

Steve, feeling no real pleasure for the action, centred the cross-hairs on Mo's body and squeezed the trigger.

TRAPPED

Goran roared at his men, pouring out his anger at them and demanding they return fire. They complied out of fear, unloading automatic fire through windows indiscriminately as he yelled Mo's name over and over. Finding him, seeing the terror on his face and in his wide eyes, he slapped him hard.

It was a backhand blow, designed to humiliate and sting more than it was ever intended to cause harm, and that simple act told him that the full weight of blame would rest solely and squarely on his shoulders if they escaped with their lives.

Goran was already planning to make an example of him. A public execution should suffice, he thought, but that would deny him the pleasure of hunting him in the dark and taking the full satisfaction of feeling him bleed out.

More shots rained in, taking a hideous toll on his men who fell back as though they were surrounded by twenty snipers for each of his men. Convinced he was facing impossible odds, he grabbed Mo by the front of his shirt and dragged him close to snarl in his face.

"Get us a way out of here," he ordered, pushing him away roughly as he stomped to the back of the house where his men weren't being cut down by a hail of incoming lead. Mo ran off, ducking low and crawling between the windows so as not to present himself as a target for whoever was outside.

He peered around the window frame seeing nothing – no muzzle flashes or lights and certainly no approaching enemy in superior numbers.

"This way!" roared Goran's voice as he summoned their remaining forces to him. Mo made to move, went to comply but froze. Why should he follow the man who he knew was going to punish him for this? Why should he submit to the orders of a man who would kill him?

He sank back down, moving to look out the windows on the other side of the building as the decision to go his own way turned to stone. He saw nothing, no dangers that threatened the others from the screams he could hear, and he—

The bullet smashed through the edge of the window frame so close to his face that he was peppered with a shower of glass and splinters of wood that made his bare skin feel hot with a wash of fresh blood.

He scrambled along the floor, cutting his hands as he threw himself desperately away from danger. A noise was loud in his ears over the sounds of gunfire and crackling flames consuming dried wood. The noise was high-pitched and came in gasps which were timed with his rapid breaths but still he didn't make the connection between himself and the noise.

He half fell down the stairs, landing in a heap on the ground floor where he threw himself straight out of the nearest open window to climb to his feet and sprint for freedom.

Another noise behind him caught his attention, but before his brain could connect the sound with a solution, he felt the back of his right leg explode with a heat and pain like nothing he'd ever known. His body went rigid as his back spasmed in response to the sudden, unexpected agony that took over and consumed his entire existence.

He hit the ground hard, driving the air from his lungs as he rolled only to be wrenched backwards with a series of violent tugs that jerked him unnaturally. Snarling growls accompanied the jerking movements that sent renewed torment through his already ravaged body.

He cried out, yelping as the animal ripped at him again to let the pressure off before it came back again harder than before. Somewhere deep down inside his mind, where his thoughts still worked instead of simply reacting, he recognised that the dog was simply getting a better grip on his flesh before thrashing its huge head from side to side again.

The dog was called away by a gruff voice speaking words he didn't hear or couldn't understand, and the relief of pressure when the sharp teeth withdrew was equally as painful as the biting.

His hands clamped onto his thigh as hot blood welled between his fingers and he curled up, sobbing into the wet ground.

"Bleed out, you bastard," said the man standing above him, back-lit dramatically by the growing flames in the building. He stood there, looking down on him for a moment longer before he turned away and called the dog with him.

As weak as he felt, as broken and bloodied as his body was, he wouldn't let anyone turn their back on him like that. A life of being dismissed and underestimated by primitives, Mo reached down to his waist to fumble a Glock free from the holster. As his wavering arm struggled to keep the gun straight and his tear-filled eyes washed in and out of focus, he felt his body hit by a force so hard that his last thought was a flashback to a car wreck he'd survived decades earlier.

Then, darkness.

SAFE

Dan and the others stayed for another two weeks, spending the first seven days ranging far and wide from the scene of their final battles to hunt down the few – the very few – survivors from Goran's piratical army of raiders.

Mitch was the one to find their friend with his twice broken nose. His hair and beard were dusted with a light frost which had turned the early morning white until the sun built up enough heat to banish it from the landscape. He seemed peaceful, his eyes closed and his still body curled up as though he'd simply given up halfway through the field he'd been running through to lie down and sleep. Only the three neat holes through his chest and back told the story of his death, as a burst of gunfire had cut him down.

"Should've chosen door number one," he chided the stiffening body, pointlessly reminding him that he was given the opportunity to live more than once.

So much death, so many bodies to recover and dispose of, was an uncommon occurrence for even Dan, so the pale faces of the militia told the story of how much it affected all of them. Many of them had never been in conflict, let alone been part of a complex ambush involving the deaths of over thirty people.

Neil's part of their trap had taken the heaviest toll on their enemy, with over a dozen men cut down by his murderous hail of bullets before the belted ammunition twisted and jammed in the feed tray. By the time he'd opened the top cover and straightened out the

370

feed to slap it back down, most of his targets had fled into the darkness where his limit of exploitation – the big words Dan used to give the parameters of his job – ended.

Mitch's opening shot at the head of the trapped convoy, whilst spectacular, had killed only the driver and passenger leaving the men in the rear to spill out and mill around until directed to flee in the safest direction.

That trail of death and destruction had been followed to the now burned-out farmhouse where numerous remains had been seen, but as the contents of the building were a charred mess with pockets of debris still too hot to get near, the exact number couldn't be determined.

The trail didn't end there. As expected, and as catered for in one of the most successful barely planned operations any of them had ever seen let alone been a part of, a group broke out under fire only to run into the final element of Steve's forces. There the string of bodies ran dry, and with each corpse being brought back to the charred remnants of the farm where more timber was being added for a funeral pyre, Steve and Dan examined them for proof of Goran's demise.

When he wasn't found Dan asked for a second and then a third search of the area, but the finality of each report was that they'd found all of the bodies left by their action.

Forced to assume their enemy had perished in the flames, and feeling fairly satisfied at that ending, they put the matter to rest and began to rebuild after what they'd suffered.

Emissaries, although the grand title was never used, were sent to the other settlements in lockdown and a contingent from The Wash arrived after six days with supplies and most of their medical people in case they were needed.

When life returned to normal, Dan felt a different atmosphere around the town. He even felt comfortable enough to walk around wearing only a sidearm and leaving his vest and carbine in Steve's office should they be called upon to do something, but with each day that passed in safety he felt the familiar warmth of family and friends all around him.

Steve invited a select group of people to a meal with four courses and more red wine than they could possibly drink. Dan did his best, trying and failing to keep pace with Neil which was never going to end well for him, and the rich ingredients of the roast dinner mixed with the wine in his stomach left him with a waking sensation the next day that he didn't enjoy one little bit.

Unsure which end of his body the world was about to fall out of, he staggered to the bathroom groaning as being upright did all kinds of things to his head that were equally as unpleasant. He lost a day after that with the mother of all twin hangovers – food *and* wine – and when he came out of his funk the following morning, he began to think of going home.

Mateo, still safely aboard their boat, had unexpectedly accepted the invitation extended by Steve via the people at The Wash and took evident delight in tasting the culinary delights of the English. He'd given a good account of himself in the red wine stakes, with Dan being the only one of their party to require assistance in getting to his bed.

He walked around the town with Ash at his side, embarrassed by the thanks and praise bestowed on both of them for what they had done. Ash took the praise well whereas Dan mumbled empty words just wishing that these people would never have to experience the horrors he had. He looked down at his dog, sitting down and focussing intently on a scrap of dried meat on offer as though it was his only focus in the world. Dan envied him that ignorance, and not for the first time in the life they had shared. The dog knew only the moment, and as far as friends went, he was the best Dan had ever known.

A nervous cough behind him made him turn to see Jimmy looking resolute but sad. Dan knew what was coming; he'd guessed it before they were even out of the warm currents of the Mediterranean, and he smiled to make it easier on him.

"I know, mate," he said. "I know."

Jimmy relaxed, saying nothing but radiating thanks with his eyes as he stepped closer to clap his hands on Dan's back in a hug that left both men sniffing as though the air was filled with dust.

"Here," he told Dan as he produced something from a pocket. "I want you to have this." Wordlessly he handed over the lighter Dan had admired on their outward journey. He clasped it in his hand tightly, knowing the gesture was more than merely the transferring of a possession from one person to another.

It was such a small token, barely befitting the moniker of a gift, but it was all he had that he could give to show his gratitude.

No words needed to be exchanged. No justification was required for Jimmy to want to stay and Dan wouldn't pressure him to return to a place where he'd never put down any permanent roots. He knew Jimmy's heart hadn't left the island they were on, and he was grateful for the solidarity and the loyalty that made him follow Dan when so many others had turned their backs on him. He hoped that his own expression could convey that to him; could properly transmit his thanks for that loyalty and sacrifice, but if they couldn't then he hoped that heartfelt embrace would.

~

Mitch went back with Mateo as both men had seen enough of Britain to last them, but Dan and Neil wanted another couple of days to see things through.

They made sure they visited everyone they once knew, and Dan was invited to so many meals as the hospitality of families he had yet to meet were extended to him. One of those invitations came personally from Alice, and she was sure to make it clear that her father really wanted Dan to come.

Mike was almost in tears as he spoke, telling Dan what had happened as if he was on his knees in the confessional booth. He told him how he had wanted so much to believe that everything would be better, that there would be no more conflict, that he was blind to the dangers that Lexi had warned him of.

He told him how he'd been so quick to trust the brothers who arrived at their old home, and how he'd encouraged others not to listen to the arguments raised by Lexi because he saw it as bitterness and not what it really was.

He begged for forgiveness, telling Dan that not a day went by when he didn't regret not listening to her concerns and said that the responsibility of what happened was on him.

"No," Dan said gently when he'd finished, "the responsibility is on *Richards* for being an insane piece of shit. We all have our burdens to bear – God knows I have more than my fair share – but this one isn't your fault."

Mike was grateful, even if he didn't fully believe the words. Dan didn't tell him what had happened to Lexi and Paul after they'd fled the attack, choosing only to confirm that they had found their way to him in Sanctuary and that they lived safe and peaceful lives.

To tell him that both had been tortured so badly by another enemy he'd made would only serve to sour their lives so he kept that truth locked inside where it could only poison him with the steady drip of blame and responsibility.

So many people were dead or damaged because of him and his choices and his actions, but he argued with himself that so many people also lived free and happy and safe from violence because of those same choices and actions.

Leadership was his double-edged sword, and it was one that he carried more to save any others from being worn down under the weight of it than any lust for power.

Perhaps, he thought, that was why he, on balance, was good at it.

~

When he woke on his last day there, he found Steve sitting in the kitchen drinking a coffee as he had the first time, only this time he'd made a second cup which was still hot when Dan sat down opposite him.

"You sure I can't convince you to stay?" he asked.

Dan sipped his drink and slowly shook his head.

"It's been too long," he said. "I have a family there now, and they're more closely tied to France than they are here. If it'd been five years ago?" He shrugged as if to convey that the outcome would have been different.

"And if my uncle had boobs, he'd be my auntie," Steve said with a rueful smirk, using the most bizarre way to agree that circumstances change. Dan laughed lightly, sipping his drink and smiling at his old friend. To his credit Steve didn't ask again. Both men enjoyed their companionable silence, each drifting off into his own thoughts at the things they'd experienced together and all the things they'd done on their own that they relived in their long talks.

Steve knew it was time for Dan to go. In truth he didn't recognise the man who left, turning back before he climbed inside the truck headed north to give him a final goodbye wave.

The man who'd left their home at the prison so long ago seemed younger and harder, but the man who left his new home now was softer and more compassionate. Weaker too, in more than one sense, but those weaknesses made him more human so they were easily forgiven.

Dan didn't see himself as weaker unless they were talking strictly in the physical sense, but he recognised that everything they had been through, everything they'd experienced since they last parted ways, had changed them both for better or worse.

"Good man, that," Iain said at Steve's side.

"Yeah," he admitted with a sigh of sadness that he'd probably just laid eyes on the man for the last time in his life. "Sad thing is, I doubt he realises that most days."

GOING HOME

Dan smoked as he looked out of the window of the truck bouncing along the road to take him back to the sea. He'd relaxed so much that he barely kept watch on the passing landscape, feeling the relief that their conflict was over and mentally preparing himself for the long journey home over a choppy sea even if their boat's captain was a master in comparison to their uneducated efforts.

He was so deep into his own thoughts that he didn't flinch for a weapon when the driver hissed a single curse before slamming on the brakes to throw Dan into the seat in front of him.

The front of their truck hit something hard enough to crunch the metal and deploy the airbag to fill the cab with the stink of gunpowder and smack the driver's head back into the seat with enough force to do serious damage.

Dan was deafened and blinded by the airbags, but he regained enough sense to understand there were shouts as the doors were pried open, sending the sound of tortured, twisting metal through his brain before the cold air hit him and he felt the ground rush up to slam into his back.

Dazed, deaf and confused he coughed and tried to speak but heard nothing except a shrill ringing in his ears. Pain exploded in his chest as a boot appeared above him and stamped down. He coughed and retched, fighting to fill his lungs with air and failing as he was dragged to his feet. His body reacted even though his brain was only partly functional, and he set his feet to shove his attacker away hard.

The push was designed to do nothing but provide him with the space to draw a weapon, but as he fumbled with numb fingers against the fastening that secured his pistol to his vest a heavy hit to the back of his head pitched him forwards where he lost his footing. His hands came up, instinctively stopping his face from being the first point of contact with the hard ground. When he was kicked again to roll him onto his back two sets of hands reached down to haul him up, and this time he reached for a weapon that was far easier to use and had only one working part.

The knife flashed out of the sheath on his left shoulder to sweep a wide cut connecting with at least one of them as his brain registered a hiss of pain and a reduction in the force of the grip. Before he could capitalise on that his advantage was removed with pain in his left side as punches were driven into his ribcage which, even through the vest, felt as if he was being kicked by a horse.

He dropped to his knees again as the strength required to stay standing evaporated, and a weak slash of the blade back to his other attacker was easily blocked and the knife was kicked from his hand which offered little resistance. Gasping for breath as he was dragged away, he summoned his last reserves of strength and clamped a hand hard on the hair of the man laying hands on him. He bit down hard, feeling the sickening scrape of a cheekbone on his front teeth but even the revulsion he felt wouldn't stop him from using everything and anything he could to get away.

He clawed and bit like an animal, abandoning all the weapons he carried as this fight was so close and so desperate that he only had his status as a trapped animal left to use.

Another blow to the back of his head broke the grip of his jaw and tore away a bloody chunk of rubbery flesh to drag a scream from his victim loud enough to raise the dead. Knowing he'd inflicted serious pain invigorated him, fuelled him, right up until a solid punch to his cheek rocked his head to bounce his brain around inside his skull and black out his world.

~

Dan woke feeling as though every hangover he'd ever experienced had ganged-up to revisit him all at once. He'd experienced this far too often for it to be good for his long-term health, and he knew he'd be struggling for days of not weeks with the aftereffects of another concussion.

"Sleeping fucking beauty," drawled an accented voice from behind him.

Dan blinked, the shapes in front of him coming into focus, as did the slumped form of Neil with blood sheeting his face and his hands bound behind his back.

Ash's desperate, livid barking came into Dan's consciousness like a thousand drums, and he found his dog tied to a tree, straining against the rope looped too tightly around his neck. Dan let out a strangled cry at seeing his dog and his friend, and another as Ash's bark turned into a pained whine when another rope around his neck was yanked tight by an unseen hand.

"You…" Dan grumbled thickly, "you bastard…"

"Me?" Goran demanded angrily as he stepped into view, displaying a face with a gruesome chunk missing from the flesh under his left eye. "I am the bastard? No! You, *you* come here and are wanting to be the heroes." He stood, leaning back to take in the man only to regard him in a way that implied he was disappointed.

"You know," Goran said as he squatted down and pointed the tip of a British Army issued bayonet in Dan's face. The lazy way he held the weapon only served to make his intentions seem infinitely more lethal. "I wanted to hunt you like I do to my enemies, only I am thinking that this would not frighten you like it does to them, no? I am thinking you would try to kill me and not run away, so instead I am going to make you feel fear another way."

Goran stood, flipping the knife over in his hand as he turned towards Neil and levelled it at him.

"I kills the fat one first, and make you watch," he said. "Then I stab your dog in the gut and make you watch this too. I think this will take a long time."

Dan grunted as if unable to make the words come out of his mouth, tensing his shoulders and feeling a slight give in the bindings around his wrists.

His mind raced as he tried to think of a way to stall, to escape, and when something bulged in his back pocket against his hand he remembered Jimmy's parting gift to him. Teasing it out of the material, he coughed as he clicked the lighter in the vain hope of burning through the rope binding his wrists.

A chuckle – evil and sadistic – sounded behind and beside him and Dan made a move to stand up not to achieve anything but simply to know for sure what other threats were there. Heavy footsteps thumped twice and he felt a blow to the back of one knee as if whoever kicked him had seen it done in a movie and assumed it would work.

Dan went with it, rolling to his side as he wrenched his hands apart with every scrap of effort he could possibly call upon.

Minus a patch of skin scoured from the back of his hand and with a stinging burn to his left wrist, his right hand came free and he launched himself towards the man who was holding his own shotgun. The short barrel levelled at him and he slapped it upwards in time to go deaf again as the blast hammered him with hot waves of pressurised air. Dan lashed out, fighting again with an animalistic rage that knocked the man back. He wrenched the gun aside so hard that the bone in the finger still on the trigger snapped before another shot could be fired. Dan raised the gun to drive the end of the pistol grip into his face. The man screamed, but the swing was too short and the ground was too soft to do any real damage. Dan tried again but the combination of being restricted by clutching hands and the soft, wet earth behind his victim's head again robbed him of the power required to debilitate or kill him. Leaning all of his weight over the end of the gun in spite of the fact that the safety was still off, he screamed as he drove his upper body down until a sickening crunch stopped one of them screaming.

Belatedly realising it was him still screaming, he had just enough time to take two breaths before he spun to face the last threat. His body, damaged and sluggish, couldn't move quickly enough as Goran lifted his arm to throw the blade at Ash. Dan raised the gun but couldn't pull the trigger from his position without peppering his own dog. He fought to gain his feet, but as he fell back down, he knew he wouldn't make it in time.

Neil, hands still bound behind his back, screamed his own challenge as he launched himself upwards to thump his body into Goran's. Both men went down together as Neil recovered enough to do as Dan had done and use the only thing at his disposal. Lifting his head high he slammed it down to crack it loudly into Goran's before rearing up to repeat the process.

Dan, still unable to move fast like he was watching the battle unfold underwater, saw Goran's fingers twirl to reverse the bayonet which he grasped and drove upwards just as Neil's body came back down.

His head connected hard with Goran's again, but Dan couldn't see the knife hand as Neil had slumped over him. Staggering forwards on his knees, Dan shoved Neil off and drove the barrel of the gun hard up under his chin to crack his bloodied teeth together.

"Nobody threatens the dog," he snarled.

Goran's expression was dull, but a smug smile twitched the corners of his mouth before his head exploded upwards like a gruesome imitation of a party popper.

~

Dan slumped backwards, gasping for breath as he fought to stay conscious.

"Neil," he grunted, twitching a boot out towards where his friend lay on his back. "Neil," he tried again, louder this time. He flipped over drunkenly, crawling on hands and knees towards him until he saw the dark pool forming around his left side where the knife had pierced his body.

"No, no, no...*Neil*," he bawled, getting so worked up that Ash began barking and yanking at the rope around his neck again. The dog turned to start snarling and chewing at the restraint, pushing it to his very back teeth to chomp down over and over as Dan's hands scrabbled to pull away the layers of clothing to expose the pale flesh that seemed somehow whiter than it should.

"Fuck sake," Dan growled as he whipped his head around in search of anything he could find to staunch the bleeding. He rose up on his knees, filing his lungs before bellowing over and over for help.

He ripped away Neil's own shirt despite how filthy it was and balled it up to press it hard into the soft flesh and earned a pained groan from the man who seemed to come around with the new lancing pain he felt.

"Hold it," Dan ordered, grabbing his hands and forcing them onto the bloody shirt. He stood unsteadily, picking up the dropped knife to slash at the rope Ash hadn't freed himself from yet before dropping it as he staggered in the direction his brain told him was towards the road where the vehicles must be.

He didn't know if it was a smell or a sound or a memory that told him which way to stagger, bouncing off trees as he struggled to stay on his feet, but he emerged to find their wrecked truck and a dead driver where he tore through their gear until he clutched the emergency kit from his pack. Fighting his way back to Neil he called out to him, finding him unconscious and with the shirt in his hand which had fallen away from the wound to let red blood pump out with each beat of his heart.

Dan yelled at him, hit at his unconscious body to try and keep him awake, but as his own injuries caught up with him, he fell on top of Neil and passed out.

TOO OLD FOR THIS SHIT

Dan woke, like he had done too many times in his life, to blink and stare at an unfamiliar ceiling. He went to sit up, finding that while he was out of it an elephant or similar sized beast had trodden on his spine just below where his neck met his shoulders and had booted him in the head for good measure before completing the trifecta by taking a shit in his mouth.

He forced himself into a sitting position, fighting the urge to vomit and losing to spill viscous bile onto the floor between his feet. Someone opened the door to the room he was in, rushed over to him and tried to force him to lie back down.

Dan was having precisely none of it, and pushed them away weakly as his numb lips tried to make the right shape for him to say, 'fuck off'.

"Neil," he mumbled. "Where's…Neil…?"

"Easy there," Mitch said as he walked in and overpowered Dan so easily it should've embarrassed the man who had already tried and failed to do the same. "Neil's alive, Ash is fine. Just lie down before you hurt yourself again."

Dan lay back down, not because he was told to but because the room suddenly tipped on an axis he couldn't begin to understand and he was forced to close his eyes and lay flat or he'd fall off the bed.

He slept. He didn't want to, but his body stopped responding to his demands and simply ignored him when he told it to get up. He couldn't speak, couldn't move, and when he began to worry that he had been paralysed his senses started to return to him.

He'd been out for a day, which was about right for his track record, and when they allowed him to stand up, he demanded that the first place he went was to see Neil.

His friend was asleep, lying in a similar bed to the one Dan had occupied but propped up on a slight incline with drips snaking their tubes into his arms.

"The stab wound was deep," a voice said behind him. Awkwardly, unable to bend his neck without causing himself pain, Dan turned to regard the speaker. A fit man with heavy shoulders, piercing eyes and an accent he hadn't heard in years stood before him. "I've repaired the damage, but there was a small cut to his intestine. All we can do now is let him heal and hope his body can fight off the infection."

"He's got an infection?" Dan mumbled.

"My friend," Jan said, "he was *always* going to have some kind of infection after being stabbed with a knife covered in mud, but my biggest concern is that he won't be able to avoid getting sepsis and that…" He made a gesture as if to say that some things were beyond human control.

"You've got antibiotics, right?" Dan asked, displaying enough knowledge to be ignorant.

"That's no guarantee of anything," Jan explained kindly. "At this point it's out of our hands. I hate to say this, but there's literally nothing more I can do. It's up to his body to fight it now."

"Hey," croaked Neil in a hoarse whisper from across the room. Dan looked up to see him gesturing, beckoning him over with a weak flutter of his left hand. Dan went to him, using furniture along the way to keep him upright. Reaching him, Dan took his hand and squeezed it as much for comfort as it was for reassurance.

"Mate," Dan said, "you need to rest—"

"Why...why are you holding my hand? You—" He stopped to cough wretchedly before resuming. "You switched sides on me?" His lips pursed together as if he was leaning in for a kiss, making Dan snort out a laugh in spite of the grimness of their situation.

"I heard what he said," Neil interrupted him. He smiled a sad smile at Dan and spoke softly. "What will happen will happen," he muttered with his eyes closed, "but I don't want to die here. Take me home. Bury me by the watchtower overlooking Sanctuary. Promise me..."

His hand faltered as he lapsed back into sleep.

"I promise," Dan whispered. "I promise."

Dan, not a man to waste time or ever let a friend down, gave his instructions and made his requests that they be taken to their boat to leave immediately.

EPILOGUE

"I wouldn't if I were you," Sera sneered at Dan as she breezed past him in the doorway. He said nothing, for once not having the time or the energy to pick a fight with the woman he could still argue with over the colour of the sky even years after they first got to know one another.

He stepped back out of the way, shifting his weight from one foot to the other unable to stand still because of the sounds coming from inside the medical rooms. Leah had screamed at him to get out as soon as he burst through the door with two German shepherds flanking him excitedly. Leah, in a state of undress and clearly in pain, screamed at him to get out using language that shocked even him.

He'd busied himself by shutting the dogs away, taking the time to do it properly and put Leah's dog, Nemesis, into one of the kennels near to the stables. He put Ash with her, after yelling at his own dog for going batshit crazy at one of the big horses that seemed about as concerned with the dog as it was with the loitering flies. Returning to the central part of their home where their adapted hospital wing was, he hovered uncertainly outside the door.

Marie was inside, naturally, as were Kate and Sera and one of the older French women from the town who knew some things about midwifery, which qualified her to the title in their world. Lucien was there, summoned from his position on the main gate where he'd been taking his turn to keep eyes on the approach road to Sanctuary.

If Dan stopped pacing and placed his head against the thick wooden door, he could hear the young man crooning reassuringly to Leah in French. The kid was a cool customer in most situations, probably due to the high level of confidence he'd always had, and Dan was glad that he was there with her.

A scream echoed down the stone corridor, bouncing off the walls and sounding as loud as if the door didn't exist. He paced again, unable to keep any one part of his body still and feeling the caveman urge to hit something as if the release of energy would make him feel better.

The screams came and went, and if he'd been less of a ball of pent-up stress then he might've had the wherewithal to check his watch in between the bouts of foul language and shrieks of agony to reassure himself that things were progressing.

People came and went, leaving gifts and offering reassuring smiles to him, and at some point the sun had gone down without him noticing. He was forced to leave the doorway once when he'd run out of cigarettes, and even then it was only to go far enough to collar one of the children who ran around the fortress like it was their own personal maze and playground and instruct them to find the right person who could bring him a replacement tin so he could continue chain smoking through his stress.

The sound went on well into the night, and when they reached a worrying crescendo Dan was all set to breach the door and go in tactically before other sounds replaced the screams.

Crying. Sobs of anguish made his chest go cold and tight at the same time as the sinking feeling threatened to take his legs out from underneath him. The sobs intensified as more people joined in, and just as Dan's eyes welled up with the grief and tragedy he illogically expected, another sound reached him.

The sharp, high-pitched and utterly helpless cry of a newborn baby.

He slumped to the cold stone floor, his back against the door-frame as the relief washed out of him through his eyes. He cried un-ashamedly, not only for the joy of his Leah becoming a mother or giving him a grandchild but for all he'd been through recently and not yet had the time to process. He wept for the happiness and the pain until the door opened and Marie stepped out.

"Soppy old git," she laughed at him. "Get off your arse and come meet your granddaughter." She still hadn't forgiven him for return-ing as they had but she loved him enough not to let that dilute the importance of the occasion.

He clambered to his feet awkwardly as he tried to cuff the tears from his eyes and the snot leaking from his nose at the same time as staying upright on legs that had gone to sleep from sitting on cold stones.

He couldn't say anything, just tried to straighten his appearance and followed his wife excitedly inside. Leah, her hair clinging to her face wetly, looked pale and exhausted but the tears in her eyes and the smile on her face made everything right.

Tightly wrapped in a bundle of clean towels was a wrinkly, purple alien with a toothless mouth open wide and puffy eyes clamped shut as she cried. Her skin was streaked with what looked like butter and Dan was totally, utterly in love with her the second she opened her eyes.

She clamped them shut again and began to wail until Leah strug-gled to manoeuvre her towards her breast. Dan was torn between looking away and being unable to tear his eyes from the girl, but Leah had no reservations about him seeing her partly naked; some things were just so important that everything else faded far beyond insignificance.

Dan sniffed, his wits returning to him as he looked up to see Lucien also crying freely without shame as he looked down on their creation. He caught Dan's look and smiled, earning a rough hug that stank up the room with testosterone briefly before Sera muttered something half-heartedly about them getting a room.

"Have you decided?" Dan asked, knowing that they had names in mind but were tight-lipped about their shortlist until their child had arrived safely.

"Dan," Leah said formally, "meet Adalene."

When Leah spoke her name the baby opened her eyes, looking up at her young mother with interest.

"It's nice to meet you, Adalene," Dan said quietly. "Welcome to the family."

~

It was two weeks before Leah was strong enough to make the climb up to the high cliff where their watchtower sat firm and proud overlooking their home. Dan didn't want to go without her, and Adalene went nowhere without her mother so their small ceremony had to wait until she was able.

They went slowly, Leah carrying her baby in a wrapped sling and being doubly careful over every footstep in contrast to their numerous journeys up the steep incline over the years. They had both run the path many times, using it as a gruelling exercise to compete and stay strong back when that kind of thing mattered much more than it did now.

Finally, after many stops not just for Leah but for Dan and the others too, and when his son's head crested the rise first courtesy of being carried on his father's shoulders it seemed that the whole world stretched out below them.

Rows of neat graves lay in uniform lines, all trimmed and tended by those standing sentry at the watchtower as one of their solemn duties as protectors. Dan lifted his son from his shoulders with a groan, setting him back on his feet and sending him in the direction of his mother with a gentle kick up the backside as he went. He walked ahead by himself, kneeling by one specific grave and placing a flat hand on the grass as he spoke.

"I wish you could see it," he said softly, speaking only for himself and the other person in the conversation who couldn't hear him. "What we've built here, all that we've created…it's a long way from the survival we scratched at in the beginning." Ash leaned in against his side to shove his big head under Dan's arm and let out a whimper for attention. He responded, sympathising with the dog who he knew was reacting to what he sensed was his master's sadness.

A hand landed on his shoulder gently as another person approached. Joints cracked as they lowered themselves to crouch beside Dan.

"You telling the old man what we've been up to?" Neil asked, breathless from the climb and the exertion as he was still recovering from his injuries.

"Yeah," Dan said, sweeping some moss from the carved wood bearing Jack's name. "Just checking in with him now that we're home."

ABOUT THE AUTHOR

Devon C Ford is from the UK and lives in the Midlands. His career in public services started in his teens and has provided a wealth of experiences, both good and some very bad, which form the basis of the books ideas that cause regular insomnia.

Facebook: @decvoncfordofficial
Twitter: @DevonFordAuthor
Website: www.devoncford.com

9 781839 190346